SOL ANCHOR

BOOK ONE

Benjamin Darr

ASIN: B0CTTF4VHH

ISBN: 9798322007043

Cover art by bookcoverzone.com

CONTENT

ONE: THE BEFORE TIMES 1

TWO: PLATO'S MAN 8

THREE: A LITTLE BOOST 21

FOUR: MIMICRY 30

FIVE: CHOSEN 42

SIX: SHATTERED GLASS 53

SEVEN: SOFTBALL 69

EIGHT: FLAGPOLE 83

NINE: GOLDEN ARMOR 98

TEN: THE DANCE 114

ELEVEN: SHRIMP SCAMPI 124

TWELVE: THREADS OF WOOL 135

THIRTEEN: SUNROT 146

FOURTEEN: BRAISED LAMB 155

FIFTEEN: THE BLADE ITSELF 171

SIXTEEN: IRON RODS 185

SEVENTEEN: GOLDEN WINGS 198

EIGHTEEN: RAINING COPPERS 210

NINETEEN: TEA IN THE WOODS 226

TWENTY: MUSHROOMS 238

TWENTY-ONE: FIFTH WHEEL 254

TWENTY-TWO: THE WAGER 267

TWENTY-THREE: WARBLECOCK 276

TWENTY-FOUR: THE PRICE OF MONEY.............................. 289

TWENTY-FIVE: TSUNDERE.. 304

TWENTY-SIX: CONTACT.. 316

TWENTY-SEVEN: ARACHNOIDITIS 330

TWENTY-EIGHT: CONCERNING CATGIRLS.......................... 343

TWENTY-NINE: THE OTHER GUY 355

THIRTY: THE DIVE... 365

THIRTY-ONE: THE GUARDIAN 378

THIRTY-TWO: REAPER.. 387

THIRTY-THREE: LIGHT 399

THIRTY-FOUR: THE BIG QUESTION.................................. 407

EPILOGUE: REBORN 411

ABOUT THE AUTHOR 414

ENDING STATS... 415

ONE: THE BEFORE TIMES

It was 2 am, and my walk home from work was lit by flickering neon.

The city got rid of streetlamps when my dad was a kid. Sure, most people saw the city however they wanted, but without AR implants, the city appeared to me as it truly was—dark, desolate, and lifeless.

It's not like I didn't try virtual life. Hell, I bought the special glasses and everything. Well, everything short of implants. I wasn't one of those fanatics who labeled every new tech as the mark of the beast, but the prospect of mind-altering surgery made me wary.

People gave me a lot of crap for rolling 'old school,' as my grandpa called it. Was it such a crime I wanted to live in the real world? Don't get me wrong, I got the appeal, but I just… couldn't. I didn't want a virtual girlfriend or a quirky virtual pet following my every step. It all felt hollow. Like a little bit of me couldn't believe it. It was like getting too old for Santa all over again.

I shook my head, trying to knock away the intrusive thoughts. I was usually better about not getting stuck in my head, but it had been a bad day at work.

Who was I kidding? It had been a bad year.

I was exhausted after work, but it wasn't just that. I'd woken up tired this morning, just like the day before and the day before that.

I took a deep breath, counting down. My AI therapist said I was depressed, but that could've just been the algorithm trying to sell me pills again. Crafty bastards had my mom hooked on that shit since I was born.

A scream broke me from my stupor, making the hair on my arms stand up.

It came from the alleyway behind the abandoned Kacey's gas station because, of course, it did. Between the shattered windows and the missing pumps, the place looked like an advertisement for crime and hauntings.

"Fuck." I already knew I couldn't walk away. Even if someone else was close by, this was exactly the type of thing AR filtered out—literally keeping crime out of sight, out of mind.

I pulled my flip phone from its holder on my belt, dialing 911 but not hitting call yet. The relic was something my grandpa had given me when money got tight.

A chill of fear washed down my spine as I ran into the alley. "Hello," I called. "Is everything okay back here?"

I swiveled my head from side to side, my eyes struggling to adjust to the dim light. The neon signs in the road behind me gave me barely any light to see. I turned on my phone flashlight, illuminating a young woman and a pool of blood around her.

"Oh, shit." I hit call on my phone.

I rushed to the woman as the phone rang, placing a finger to her warm neck. Nothing. No pulse. My stomach dropped. I was too late.

"911, what's your emergency?" a flat AI voice answered.

Boots crunched on gravel behind me, just about sending me out of my skin. The assailants were still here. God, I was stupid. Of course, they were.

Out of the shadows, three men fanned out behind me, blocking me from the road. We stared momentarily at each other as the AI operator announced an officer would be dispatched to my location. A perk of automation, every call was investigated.

Anywhere else, the assailants would've fled upon hearing that. The cops were ruthless, shooting first and asking questions later, but it could be twenty minutes before they showed up in this part of town, and we all knew it.

I wanted to run, but my eyes were glued to the slow drip of blood from the knife in the center person's hand. It was so different than VR, knowing the blood was real.

"What's up, guys?" I said, trying to keep my voice casual.

"Phone and wallet, bonbon." The center assailant shuffled forward aggressively. As soon as the slurred words left his mouth, I knew I was dealing with an addict. I was fucked.

I hesitated, trying to avoid fast movements.

"Now!" He stepped into the cone of light my phone was casting, a grotesque smile stretched across his face. The other two hid something behind their backs in the shadows.

It's difficult to explain how unnerving late-stage drug use was in a person. Skeletal features. Wispy hair. Wild eyes. It sucked the humanity right out and left a husk in its place.

After all, I'd watched it kill my mom, and now it was probably going to kill me, just in a different way.

"Uh," I stuttered, fumbling to get my wallet out of my back pocket. "Here you go. Not much there, boss."

The smiling man lunged forward, snatching the wallet and phone from my hands. The trio huddled together, examining their new treasure, strewing maxed-out credit cards on the ground. A moment passed as they unflipped my ancient flip phone.

"You think we're dumb?" one asked. I couldn't tell who, as adrenaline had crept into my vision, blurring it.

"No, of course not, dude." I stepped backward, only for my foot to snag on the body behind me.

The bloody knife glinted under the fluorescent light. The smiling man waved it back and forth, my eyes following it.

"Smartphone, bonbon. Where is your smartphone?" The man drew his knife across his hand, leaving a trail of blood that was not his own. "I bet you have a nice new one. VR link. Hollo display."

"I—I don't—" I stammered, my hands in the air. The situation was getting out of control, but I didn't know what to do.

I was going to have to fight.

Confusion flashed in my assailants' faces as I looked at them with a new expression. If I wasn't going to get out of this alley alive, neither were they.

The smiling man howled like a rabid animal as he charged me. The others produced a crowbar and a hammer from behind their backs.

Time slowed to a crawl as I dashed forward, arms going wide as I clothes-lined one of the assailants, his body making a crunch on the hard gravel.

I felt the sting of weapons hitting me, but I powered through them. I had to weigh more than all three combined.

For a fleeting moment, I thought I could win, throwing wild punches and grabbing clothes. I felt a bone snap under my grasp as I fought for freedom.

I didn't even last five seconds.

Something hit my knee, shattering it and sending me to the ground face-first. I flipped over, fighting even while being stabbed in the chest. I grabbed the smiling man's head, feeling an eye pop under my thumb as I squeezed.

The knife raised again to strike, but blue and red lights bathed the bleeding man, reflecting in blood running from his eye socket.

A police siren blipped. "Put your hands behind your head," a robotic voice demanded.

I coughed up a mouthful of blood, unable to lift my hands. Blood spurted from the holes in my chest with each weakening breath. It was funny how it didn't hurt.

Everything shifted, and I slipped from reality, entering a floating, dreamlike state. The alley stretched beneath me as a scene unfolded.

An android stepped from the police car, placing a single shot in each of the fleeing criminals. It was bizarre how routine the whole thing felt. I bet it wouldn't even make the news.

The real kick in the gut was just how pointless my death felt. After all, I didn't even save the girl.

Guilt washed over me as I remembered the girl. Her horrified scream. Her last moments in a dirty back alley. If I had been faster. If I responded right away. Maybe I could've—

I felt a hand on my shoulder, stopping my train of thought, a brush of lips on my cheek before vanishing.

I let go of what was holding me back, a last tether breaking from the mortal plane.

I couldn't even see the alley as I rose skyward.

Two: Plato's Man

The nothing greeted me.

Up, down, sideways; all midnight black.

Where am I? My thought startled me, breaking the silence of the nothing. It echoed in my mind like a ping-pong ball with nowhere to go.

My thoughts felt foggy as if I hadn't slept and had slept too long at the same time.

With nothing to look at, I examined myself- or lack of self, as it were. I tried to touch my face, but nothing happened. Memories of a body sat at the edge of my consciousness but slipped through the cracks when I tried to think about them. My brain churned as I tried to comprehend where I was.

All-encompassing darkness?

Check.

Incorporeal form?

Check.

Odd sense of calm?

Double check.

Either I'd taken a nasty hallucinogen, or I was dead. Probably dead. People don't just give out hallucinogens. Well, other than the CIA in the 1960's, but I'd eat my boots before I believed they gave some rando acid. Although, that would be very CIA of them, all things considered.

I was getting off track.

I observed the illustrious afterlife in all its nothing. It was a subject of heated debate back home at the dinner table, but it looked like everyone was way overthinking it. Granted, the black void wasn't exactly my choice of preferred afterlife, but I'd take it over some of the more colorful depictions.

I'm looking at you, Dante.

Tired of ruminating about the nature of nothing, I drifted-mentally, at least. With no point of reference for distance, motion became meaningless.

I was the center of my own world.

My mind wandered to my grandparents. Memories of them filled me with warmth, but everyone else was a wash. My father was never around, and my mother was too addicted to pills to remember I existed. All the friends I had moved on after high school, and the people at work were fellow prisoners at best.

I did have some spirited online adventures with NoobSlayer076 on the ol' PS6. Truthfully, thinking about my buddy waiting to see if I'd get back online sparked another wave of grief. We were some of the few still playing the old IRL consoles. Everyone else I knew had all moved over to VR. I'd meant to meet him IRL at some point, but it never worked out.

A lot of things in my life never worked out: college, relationships, and the internship with my uncle's company. Reflecting on my life, I squandered a lot of opportunities, assuming I had plenty of time. Time I didn't have. Hindsight was 20/20 when you're dead.

Self-loathing faded as resolve built within me. If given another shot, I would be sure of myself. I'd be resilient. I wouldn't hesitate to stick to a workout plan for more than one week in January. I'd go to that IRL yoga class despite my fear of farting in front of the hot yoga instructor.

Sure, I could've overcome those fears back then, but that was then, and this was now. Nothing but a vast universe and a bright future from here on out. Gone was my squishy body of comfort; I was a hardened spacefaring adventurer now.

Probably.

I did my best to stay positive, but the sentiment faded as time passed. How much time, I couldn't tell. It could have been seconds. It could have been years. It could have been eons. The only thing I truly had was an overabundance of time.

Enough time to become bitter about being stuck in the void. No wonder ghosts were so pissed off. Another thousand years of this, and I'd be throwing dinner plates and screaming, too.

I played games with myself to pass the time, recreating stories and movies in my mind's eye. Singing my favorite songs. I even started playing mental chess against myself. It was frustrating when I lost.

Eventually, while I worked through the anthology of Pink Floyd re-imagined as a pop-punk tribute, something emerged from the darkness.

No, it wasn't God coming to strike down my terrible music heresy. It was something far more powerful.

Bureaucracy.

Welcome to the Aspirant Automated Processing System!

White letters filled my vision, giving me something to move around. I would have jumped out of my skin if I was physically capable. They just blinked into existence. Bam.

We appreciate your patience as our wait times have been higher than usual!

Please hold…

The answer to my most persistent question had finally been answered. I wanted to leap with joy. I knew where I was!

I was in hell!

That was the only place that would have a call waiting voidscape! Clearly, they took notes from whatever demon started the internet service provider I used back home.

I examined the letters. They were 2D images in a 3D space, looking closely related to Comic Sans, which was infuriating in and of itself. A soft glow emanated off them, pushing the void back ever so slightly.

Eventually, pondering the letters got boring, so I left searching for something better to do. The letters hung there as I drifted around them, humming 2000s pop-punk hits. Circling the message became my new default.

As the songs drifted on, the presence of the letters became an object of frustration. Before, I had no reference for time, but as I circled the letters, I now had a metric, and it counted in the millions.

I had always assumed I would enjoy a life of solitude, but my soul thirsted for contact, for a way out.

I swear by every god, real, dead, or otherwise, I will never return to this hellscape, I thought-yelled into the void, shaking a mental fist at what I assumed was up.

I waited. I circled. I hummed to myself.

I waited. I circled. I yelled into the void.

The artistic process is an enigma.

The sound of a trumpet blasted through space, sending me into a panicked backspin. The letters disappeared, and different ones took form as I sprinted around to read them.

If I had a heart, it would've been thundering.

Thank you for holding! After a manual review of your moral portfolio, you qualify for one free reincarnation!

You have been labeled a free agent. Please enjoy these additional choices.

Choices for what?

Motion caught my eye. Below the text, three dots pulsed, giving an indication of loading.

I camped before the dots, letting their pulse lull me into a trance, waiting for new letters. Luckily, I didn't have to wait long, maybe a thousand pulses or so.

Ascendant, prepare to select a race.

You are queued to load into: World 2X45T.

Patron Goddess: Solara

Please Note: due to certain individuals holding up the queue, we've recently implemented a time limit of two minutes. Sorry for the inconvenience!

Hell yes! I was so ready for this. New world. New race. It was the fresh start I'd hoped for. All those D&D nights my grandpa dragged me to were about to pay off. My favorite builds came to mind as I rubbed my mental hands together in preparation.

My thought process came to a screeching halt as I conceptualized how little two minutes was. I needed at least a few years to get this right!

Wait a minute. *They* left me here for an eon and then wanted me to hurry up? That was some typical upper-management behavior right there.

Despite my complaints, a timer appeared.

120 Seconds Remaining

Please select from the following list:

Words exploded in front of me, expanding for miles downward.

Hobb

Dragoon

Owlbeast

Nym

Uh, show me Nym, I thought, unsure how to interact with the list. I picked the first one that seemed interesting.

The list moved to the side as a window with information appeared.

Race: Nym

Description: Small, winged fae known for their excellent flute playing. Considered a feral race and kept as pets by larger races.

Habitat: Swamps and shallow water

Racial Perks: +60% Cha, - 60% Con

Yeah, no thanks. Not a big fan of being a Tinkerbell.

The list reappeared as the pop-up minimized.

I think I want a race based on strength, I thought, mostly to myself, but to my surprise, the letters changed.

Limiting choices to races focused on strength.

I hadn't expected the letters to respond. The lists blinked and refreshed.

I checked my clock.

97 Seconds Remaining

Fuck, I cursed, looking back at the list.

Bugbear

Wolfkin

Myrdin

Show me Myrdin! I thought, struggling to remain calm through a rising sense of panic.

Race: Myrdin

Description: A water-dwelling humanoid with the lower half of an eel. Tribes of Myrdin follow whale packs, hunting them for meat and blubber. The males of this species rear and birth their young. Gain +5 Con after consuming a willing female post-coitus.

Habitat: Swamps and shallow water

Racial Perks: +30% Dex, - 30% Wis

Yeah, this wasn't getting me anywhere. Pregnant eel merman can go right in the 'no fucking way' pile.

68 Seconds Remaining

I considered picking one at random and hoping for the best. The choices should all be strength-based anyway. I tended to lean toward barbarian or tank builds in D&D, so any of these should work, but the idea of being a freaky pregnant eel man caused new fears to emerge. I didn't want to end up some giant centipede or be trapped in a dungeon as a reincarnated ant or something like that.

Please limit choices to bipedal humanoid races, I thought.

I hoped the letters understood the intent and not just the parameters of a furless upright biped. The anecdote of Diogenes plucking a chicken and declaring, 'Here is Plato's man,' came to mind.

The list refreshed. To my horror, the list was still over a hundred names long. All the strength in the world wouldn't matter if I got one shot by the closest feral cricket as soon as I spawned. I tried to come up with further parameters, but the pressure of the time limit was making me pull a blank.

The timer counted down to 43 as my anxiety rose. No specific punishment was said about not selecting a race on time, but that didn't stop my mind from imagining some.

Limit choices to ones that also contain high amounts of constitution, I thought, shuddering with the idea of dying again and returning to this place.

The list was shortened to around 25. Still too many to look through with under a minute left. I could feel myself locking up under pressure as I read down the list.

30 Seconds Remaining.

Please lock in your choice, or one will be assigned to you.

Give me a second, I snapped at the words.

The timer continued to count down as my panic rose to somewhere between talking to a cop with weed in my pocket and a full-blown panic attack. I felt like I was missing something obvious as I looked over each race's name.

12 Seconds Remaining

If only I could sort this…

Inspiration struck.

Sort choices by strength bonus, starting with the highest! I thought, yelling at the letters.

The list was rearranged, and I picked the top one as I glanced at the timer.

7 Seconds Remaining

Show me Lightning Golem!

Race: Lightning Golem

Description: Gargantuan humanoid with stone skin and

short tempers. Lightning Golems are some of the most solitary and violent of the feral races. No one is sure if they call lightning to strike them or if they just get hit by lightning frequently. Tends to sleep in the form of a boulder until a violent storm appears.

Habitat: Rocky mountainous terrain

Racial Perks: +90% Str, - 90% Int

Minus 90% intelligence! No fricken way I'm picking this one!

3 Seconds Remaining

Pure static engulfed my brain as I watched the timer count down.

Ascendant, you have run out of time. Please wait for a race to be manually assigned to you.

Well, this just fuckin su—, I started to think, but the letters changed almost immediately.

Outstanding choice! Please wait while we process your request.

Please don't be lame or a monster! I don't want to be a pregnant man-fish! Please forgive me, letters!

Please confirm your name: Ashton McGracen

Stone McGracen, please. I never liked my full name.

Please review your race selection while queued for transport. Clothing and basic weaponry will be provided upon arrival.

A blinking light appeared in the corner of my vision, and a screen appeared before my eyes when I focused on it.

Name: Stone McGracen

Race: Halfkin

Path: Pathless

Level: 0

Spells: Inspect

Blessings: Solara's Mercy, Solara's Hand

Woah, it was an honest-to-god status screen. Although, what was a Halfkin? I hadn't seen it on my list earlier. Maybe it was like a half-elf or something. The implication that Halfkin wasn't a strength-based race became confirmed as I looked over my stats.

Stats:

Int: 7

Wis: 6

Cha: 5

Str: 3

Dex: 5

Con: 1.2

Spirit: 11.2

Ugh, high spirit, low constitution. I didn't know what spirit did, but I could guess that constitution was related to health and defense. I might just get one shot by that feral cricket after all.

My concerns got pushed to the back of my mind as I looked over my spell list, which had more than the nothing I was expecting. I focused on the **Inspect** spell, hoping for a description or an instructional video, but instead, nothing. Typical. At least it was on brand with the rest of the experience.

Expecting nothing, I focused on **Solara's Mercy,** and a screen popped up right away.

Solara's Mercy: Ascendants under level ten respawn at their designated origin point upon death. Limit: 100 years

Hell yes! I thought, doing a little incorporeal happy dance. *I got an inspect spell, clothes, and am functionally unkillable until old age. And here I thought I was about to get royally screwed!*

I focused on **Solara's Hand**, riding the wave of excitement.

Solara's Hand:

Uhh, where was the description? The screen came up with the title and nothing else. My thoughts were interrupted by a new message.

Transport Imminent! Ascend!

Light exploded in the nothing.

THREE: A LITTLE BOOST

Light assaulted my consciousness.

Nauseating light whirled around me, overloading my senses with blues and greens. Thankfully, my old friend, the large white letters appeared, partially obfuscating my vision and shielding me from the searing light.

Now loading into: World 2X45T

Local Name: Terra Silva

Planet Size: Large

Population: Imbalanced

Dungeon Spawn: Aggressive

Stand by for respawn point assignment…

The letters disappeared, but their brief visit gave me time to adjust. My excitement grew as colors sharpened into discernable shapes.

A planet expanded below me, its colored horizon

contrasting with the black of space. Even looking at the darkness sent a shiver through my soul. A slightly blue-tinted sun illuminated a spiderweb of mountains. Flashes of lightning sparked in clouds trailing over mountainside lakes and lush forests—a neat line separating day and night curved from pole to pole.

It felt so wrong to descend on a planet that wasn't Earth. My home planet's geography was so ingrained in my brain that hovering over this foreign mountain chain felt wrong, almost like a betrayal. I tried to make sense of this new terrain, but it was solely mountains and lakes as far as I could see on this little slice of the planet.

I tried to pinpoint what felt so alien about what I was seeing. All at once, it dawned on me. I didn't see the familiar scars of advanced civilization—no roads, lights, or superstructures. I was far away from home, indeed.

Assignment complete!

Prepare for descent…

My stomach lurched as I started to fall, gaining speed at an uncomfortable rate.

My smooth descent was interrupted when something hit me hard, launching me at an unnatural angle toward the upper portion of the planet. I didn't know if it was north or not, but it was in the general direction of an icecap. Whatever hit me dissipated, leaving little streaks of black behind. Just as quickly as it happened, it was gone.

I tried to slow my fall, but if I had a body, it was

unresponsive. The ground approached quickly, only increasing in speed. I caught glimpses of a spattering of settlements as I whirred over mountains.

My angle of approach descended, a mountain rising to greet me. I kept telling myself my descent would slow, but it didn't. If anything, being so close to the ground made me realize how fast I was really going.

I couldn't even close my eyes as I counted down to impact, descending on the mountain.

Three.

Two.

One.

I plunged into the rock, my world going dark for a single heart-wrenching instant, letters flashing in the darkness.

Welcome to Terra Silva, Stone McGracen.

Error. Resolving…

New Spawn Point Assigned!

My heart beat.

My heart beat a second time, pushing blood into numb limbs.

My heart beat a third time. I took an involuntary breath.

My eyes snapped open as water rushed into my lungs. Sputtering water, I sat up into open air.

Rolling to my hands and knees, I heaved, clearing an empty stomach and making way for some much-needed air. New smells assaulted my senses—a mixture of body odor, mold, and dirt. Small waves lapped against my forearms as I got my bearings and my breathing slowed.

A light pulsed in the lower corner of my vision. I focused on it, and a screen appeared.

New Quest Assigned: Escape the Dungeon!

Quest Description: Dungeons are a crucible to test the will of aspirants. Cut your teeth or perish!

Quest Reward: Bronze Loot Chest

Despite the pain in my chest, I laughed, closing the system window with a mental flick. This was exactly like those fantasy AR games everyone was obsessed with back home. I did my best to stay away from those things. AR addiction was real and killed more people than anyone wanted to admit. Once you forget it's not real, that's it.

I hated to admit it, but the quest represented something to me—a clear objective with a clear reward. Simple. Clear. Life back on Earth was messy and frustrating. I dared to hope I would fit in better here.

Bioluminescent fish lit the pool, casting a dull red glow. They looked like goldfish with a flat tail like a dolphin—no bigger than the palm of my hand. The little fish darted around the rocky bottom, the glow from their gills growing with intensity as they sped up.

I wondered what they were called as I watched the fish dart

around my arms.

Oh wait, I literally had a spell for that.

Inspect! I mentally commanded, glaring at a particular fish.

I waited, but nothing happened, and my stomach dropped a bit in disappointment. Of course, it wasn't easy.

I mentally scanned my body to see if anything clued into what I was doing wrong. Maybe it only applied to intelligent creatures? Or objects?

"Or maybe my dumb ass just needs to say it out loud," I said, trying out my new voice. The language was foreign, lilting like Korean but guttural like German, a mishmash of familiar and fantastical. I shook off my mental wandering, recognizing I was getting stuck in my head again—a bad habit from an old life.

"**Inspect**." The word shimmered like it was coated in reverb, hanging in the air for a second longer than it should. Excitement ran up my spine as a window popped up in the corner of my vision.

Red Ribbon Koi: A bioluminescent koi variation from the ichthus family. Favors dark places with high insect populations. Often found in dungeons and cave systems.

"Holy shit, it worked." I closed the window with a flick.

The fish twirled away from my submerged hands as I pushed off the rocky bottom. My body felt awkward, my brain not used to the limbs it was moving. I shook out the tremor in my legs as I stood upright, getting a good look around for the first time.

The red ribbon koi appeared to be the only light source in a cave-like room. Abstract patterns and hieroglyphs spun around hanging rock formations on the low ceiling. Even in the low light, it was obvious the place was a wreck. Broken shelves and wooden furniture lay strewn against the wall. It looked like a tornado had come through a storage room. However, the etchings on the walls had me leaning toward the place being an abandoned underground temple.

All this brought me to the main object in the room—a single stone doorway. While the wall carvings worked around natural formations, this looked built with intention. A glassy shimmer hung in place of a door, giving the entry an ethereal presence.

I took a probing step forward, feeling the rocks under my bare feet. My knees wobbled more than I liked, but I made it out of the pool, dripping onto the cave floor. I curled my arm, flexing. When no bulging muscles popped out, I felt a wave of disappointment. I was normal. Sure, I was lean and bordering on athletic, but still. My dreams of looking like Conan the Barbarian would have to wait.

As I looked over my body, I felt like I was missing something. Everything seemed like it was in the right place. Hell, I looked positively human. Two ears, no horns, and the correct number of toes. I even got a little boost in 'that' department.

I realized what was wrong. "Where are those clothes I was promised?" A touch of heat rose to my cheeks. Being stranded in a cave is one thing. Being naked in a cave is an entirely different situation.

I thought *equipment* and a screen appeared.

Soulbound Equipment:

Clothes: Linen Tunic, Linen Pants, Wool Socks, Leather Boots

Armor: N/A

Weapons: Adventurer's Knife

Misc: Adventurer's Belt

Very nice, I thought, looking over the items. "Equip," I said with a touch of confidence.

Nothing.

"Why is this being so difficult?" I wracked my brain for solutions as I dripped on the floor. "Summon gear? No, that's not it. **Equip clothes**?"

I felt a weight sink onto my body as the clothes settled on my skin. I let out a sigh of relief, checking everything over. Wait. Where was the belt and knife?

"Really?" I said, looking up at where I imagined the system was. "You knew what I meant. **Equip all**." I felt the weight of a belt sinch my midsection.

The clothes were nice. A dark green tunic of dyed linen hung down to my midthigh, secured in place by a brown belt with little pouches. A sturdy-looking knife, bordering on the length of a short sword, hung on my left hip in a hard leather sheath. If I had a complaint, it would be the itchy tan pants and the lack of underwear.

All of this was great, but the boots were by far my favorite part. They were well made and laced up above the ankle, adding a few inches to what I assumed was my impressive height. They looked freshly oiled, and my pants were tucked into the top. It might sound dumb, but it made me feel more secure.

"I love it." I stood in awe of my 'pure drip,' as my grandpa would say. "Thanks, Solara or whoever," I commented offhand, but I could've sworn I felt a warm pulse somewhere in my chest in response. I touched the part of my chest where I felt the flash of heat. "If the gods listen that closely here, I really need to watch my mouth."

A distant roar broke me out of my little world. Bouncing off walls and slowly fading, I felt the hair on the back of my neck stand up. All the bravado I'd felt the moment before escaped from me like water from a cup with a hole in the bottom. A primal urge to get away drove me backward. I stepped back into the pool, getting my new boots wet. My foot snagged on something, sending me backward with a splash.

Water soaked my clothes as I scrambled backward on all fours, trying to distance myself from the door as much as possible. The sounds of my continued splashing sounded like bombs going off in the silence of the cavern.

I reached the far side, receding into the darkness, pressing my back against the wall. I could barely see, having to feel for the wall the last few feet. My breathing sounded loud as it caught in my chest. I held it in, slowly letting it out as my heart pounded in my ears.

Silence. A deep silence where nothing moved, nothing made a noise. I felt too uncomfortable to even breathe now. I slumped further back, trying to melt into the wall.

My hand touched something that wasn't a wall.

FOUR: MIMICRY

If my heart could've thrown itself out of my chest, it would have.

I jerked my hand back, cradling it to my chest. What was that? I could barely see in this dumb darkness. I tried to calm down. It was like thinking there was one more stair and stumbling. Cave walls weren't supposed to squish.

I cursed myself for being such a baby.

As long as I could remember, I had hated everything horror. I hated games, simulations, and even those movies Grandpa made me watch. I even hated Halloween as a holiday. The whole thing gave me the creeps. I was more of a brightly lit fantasy adventure kind of guy.

Metallic clinking halted my mental storm, returning me to the reality in my face. My eyes shifted to see its source, too afraid to move my head.

I froze.

The red light of the pool reflected a silver eye, It looked

human, a shadow of a face moving around it. I closed my eyes, hoping my thundering heart wouldn't give me away. The person kept searching. Whatever they were wearing clinked at they moved.

"Hello?" A raspy voice cut through the silence, barely a whisper before trailing off. It sounded like someone waking up from one hell of a hangover. Was this a prisoner? A lich?

If I wanted to know, I had to go for it. "**Inspect**," I whispered so low I could barely hear it.

Blinding light flooded my vision, and my hands leaped to my face, trying to shield my eyes. It was like the sun burst through the wall like the Kool-Aid Man. My shoulder clipped the wall as I reeled back, pieces of rock falling with me onto the cave floor.

A feminine scream rang out, and I was pretty sure it wasn't me. For the sake of my pride, let's say it wasn't.

I cursed, scrambling to my feet, fumbling to get my knife out of its sheath, but it had this button thing to keep it in place and I wasn't ready for this. God save me. I was going to get eaten.

"Stay back!" we yelled in unison, the stranger and I.

I pointed my knife at the source of the noise. My eyes were still adjusting to the dark, so I was only confident of a couple developing details.

First, and most importantly, the figure was bigger than me. At least a foot taller. Not good. Second, and equally important, it wasn't coming closer and was splayed against the wall. Very good.

"Who are you?" the voice spoke again, a snippet of feminine clarity piercing the cobwebs.

"You first." I finally had my knife out of its sheath. So help me, I wouldn't hesitate to use it. This wasn't the time to play stupid white knight hero. That's how you ended up mimic food. Large women in dark caverns, despite being a particular weakness of mine, wouldn't fool me this time.

The thing scoffed at me. *Scoffed.* Like how my teenage cousin scoffed at her parents for asking her to do the dishes.

"Solara, save me," the voice muttered. "A halfkin has been sent to torture me."

Screw this lady. "The only person being tortured here is me." I let some of the coiling tension in my body release. My hand was starting to cramp from gripping the knife so tight. "I nearly shit my pants just now, and these are my new pants." Grandma always said I joked at the worst times, but I firmly believed all the time was the best time.

The woman snorted. Chains rattled as she laughed, and my brain finally understood what I was looking at.

If I was around six feet, she was at least seven, backing up my decision to be cautious. I didn't want to get swatted into a puddle by the WNBA's newest star. Chains held her limbs into a wide 'x.' Actually, more like an upside-down 'y.' It was hard to tell in the dark, but it looked like her right arm was cut off just below the shoulder, leaving a scarred stump. Red light glinted off golden armor, hugging a feminine form, covering little, and had to be more of an aesthetic choice than practical. Hey, no judging. I was just pointing it out as odd.

I processed the information as an awkward silence stretched. A large, hot woman, scantily clad and chained to a dungeon wall. This was the Nigerian prince scam of D&D encounters. Could this be legit? I mean, I guess, but the chances were slim to none. This chick was a mimic. 100% not a doubt in my mind. I bet it camped this spawn point and ate dumb level zeros like me. Wow, that was vile. This mimic should be ashamed of itself.

All this solidified my worst fear, aside from clowns, spiders, heights, and having to pick a partner in class. Mimics were a mainstay of my favorite video games—a monster that disguises itself as treasure chests, doors, and most disturbingly, women in distress. Disgusting.

The mimic finally stopped laughing at me as I tried to figure out what part of her would open up to eat me. My money was on the chest opening up like a Venus fly trap.

"I'm hallucinating. That has to be it. I've dreamt up a halfkin to entertain me." The mimic hit the back of her head against the wall. Hair covered her face, limiting my ability to read her facial expressions. Granted, women's facial expressions usually confused me, so no loss there. Grandma said I was hopeless. Psh, what did she know?

"I'm afraid I'm very real. At least, I think I'm real." My mind grabbed onto the idea and spun up some paranoia about being trapped in an illusion or a virtual hellscape. This mimic was good. "Yes, very real," I tagged at the end.

"Prove it then." The chains groaned as the mimic arched her disgusting, ab-covered stomach out. "Stab my core and kill me. Death would be a release from this drudgery."

"Drudgery?" I repeated. "Nice word," I laughed. "And fat chance, lady. I'm not coming over there so you can eat me."

The mimic must've been shocked I caught onto her game, her mouth hanging open at my cleverness.

"Why… why would I eat you?" Her bafflement almost sounded real.

"That's what I would like to know. I'm not even level one. Seems like a lot of effort if you ask me." This mimic needed to pick better targets.

The woman groaned. "Surely this is some new spell designed to torture me. Not even a hallucination is this stupid."

"Insulting me won't lure me in, mimic."

Another stunned silence. I had this thing right where I wanted it. It was probably reeling from how fast I caught onto its game.

"Why would a mimic take the form of an imprisoned woman?" the mimic asked. "I've only heard of chests and even that is rare."

Wow. It had been caught and was still trying to wiggle out of it. Unbelievable. "The best ones always do. After all, what could be more alluring than simple treasure? Some chick pleading for help in a dungeon, that's what."

"Your logic defies even my most reaching understanding," the mimic said.

I had her on the ropes. "Now's the part where you insist you're not a mimic."

"I'm *not* a mimic." The mimic's voice rose up near a yell. The chains strained, and I braced to defend myself.

Instead, the mimic deflated, her voice dropping to a grumble. "Can you kill me now? I'm beginning to miss the silence."

"Nice try. I'm still not coming over there." Damn, she almost got me with that one.

"I've prayed for so long for someone to help me, and Solara sends you, the dumbest halfkin alive." The venom in the mimic's voice was convincing. She was good. "What great evil could I have possibly committed to deserve this? Everything I did was for others. Has Solara abandoned me?"

"An appeal to my sense of decency. Nice try." I respected the effort. I was sure a lot of upstanding adventurers would fall prey to such a thing. Using their good nature against them was devious.

"I'm *not* trying to convince you!" Her voice rose in frustration.

"Reverse psychology," I said, genuinely impressed. "Very nice. That's a good one."

"I think I hate you."

"Rejection?" I said, a little surprised. "Really fishing for what makes me tick. I'll give you a hint. I don't trust anyone other than me, and even then, it's only sometimes."

I waited for the mimic's retort, but she was silent. It was uncomfortable, even for me, who was usually immune to that type of thing. Water dripped from the ceiling, landing in the pool with the fish, filling the silence. I turned to go, assuming the mimic had given up in defeat.

Then, the mimic started making weird noises, her breathing shifting to sharp gasps, her chest moving up in rhythm. I jumped back, knife out. Was this some kind of odd breathing magic or a mimic call for help? I looked around for movement.

"What are you—" That's when I realized she was crying. I hated to admit it, but the sound pulled on my heartstrings. How did the mimic figure out my weakness? "Stop it."

"Please end it." The mimic's voice cracked. I admired her commitment to the arts. She almost deserved to eat me for the acting alone. "I've been here for so long."

"Don't do this to me, mimic. I'm tired and want to explore the dungeon a little." I waved to the door behind me. "I would die of embarrassment alone if I didn't make it even a step into the dungeon before dying."

The crying intensified. Damn, this thing was good. I was even starting to doubt myself.

I shifted on my feet, waiting for it to end. The crying continued, and the doubt festered.

I let out a sigh. "Alright, how would someone prove they weren't a mimic?"

The mimic didn't answer. I thought about it more than not at all and realized I couldn't trust her answer anyway, so it was probably for the best.

Shit, now I needed to know for sure.

I snapped my fingers, pulling up that blessing again.

Solara's Mercy: Ascendants under level ten respawn at their designated origin point upon death. Limit: 100 years

I read it back over. It sounded like I had all the do-overs I wanted. I could risk it.

Probably.

"Fine, alright. Let's pretend you aren't a mimic hellbent on murdering me, and I wanted to free you. How would I do it?" I leaned forward, trying to get a good look at the mimic's face under that rat's nest of hair.

The woman answered me, her voice raw. "You can't. You're nothing. A level zero can barely fight an imp, let alone break chains. The best you could do is slip that knife into my core and end the suffering."

"Can I take a look, at least? I'm kind of invested now." This sounded like a dungeon puzzle, and I loved puzzles.

"Do whatever you want, I guess," she said. At least she wasn't crying so loudly now.

I moved forward a step at a time, waiting for something to

happen, but before I knew it, I was right in front of her, close enough to see a tear running down her dirty cheek.

Either this was the best mimic ever, or I had misjudged the situation.

I stopped within arm's reach of the maybe-a-mimic. "If I see a hint of movement, I'll shit my pants in defense and ruin your meal out of spite."

The maybe-mimic stopped crying long enough to laugh, sending a bloom of warmth through my chest. Fuck, I was getting attached. That was mistake number one in these situations.

I examined the shackle on her ankle. It was thin and tight against her skin. It looked painful. If she was real, whoever put her here was a dick. Her feet didn't even touch the floor, and all her weight was on the three shackles. I traced around the restraint with my fingertips, looking for gaps or hinges. I tensed, waiting for gaping jaws to close around my head, but nothing happened. Scars like chain lightning wrapped around her leg. Holy shit, what would even cause something like that?

"No seams," I muttered. "That's crazy."

The woman hung limp, an air of hopelessness about her. In contrast, I was tense and waiting to be snatched up by mimic jaws.

I followed the chain to find it was secured to the wall with a large spike driven straight through one of the links, the rest of the chain hanging limp on the other side. The links were as thick as my finger, making the chain heavier than any I'd held before, reminding me of something you'd see on a large ship.

"Damn." I looked her over with crossed arms. "I'm no doctor, but you might be fucked."

The mimic laughed again, and I got that warm feeling. It had to be some strange mimic magic. Yeah, that was it.

"You're wasting your time." The mimic sounded so tired. To be honest, I thought she was overplaying it at this point.

I ignored her. The chains were a puzzle, and I loved puzzles. This place seemed to operate on some video game logic so maybe I had the tools to solve this right now.

"I haven't tried pulling on it super hard," I said, getting a grip on the chain with both hands.

"You're not even listening to me." The not-a-mimic tried to kick out at me but was stopped by the chain.

"Why don't you tell me something while I work on this?" I said, setting a boot against the wall on either side of the spike.

"What? Why?" The maybe-a-mimic looked at me as if I was an idiot. As if. An idiot would've fallen for her trap immediately.

I ignored the mimic's judging for a second. Getting a good handful of chain, I tested how secure it was in the spike. I was hoping to wiggle it loose, but it didn't budge at all. I would have to try brute force. The veins popped out on my arms as I pulled, but I didn't even make a dent. The only thing I managed to do was pull the maybe-a-mimic away from the wall. Damn, this thing was in there.

I dropped the chain, wincing as her back slapped against the wall.

The maybe-a-mimic looked at me in annoyance.

Oh shit, I'd forgotten she'd asked me something.

"If you're a mimic, you'll run out of backstory eventually and eat me out of frustration. If you're not a mimic, I want to know what type of person I'm helping." I looked around for a rock or something to hit this dumb chain with. "Plus, I'm new here and don't know anything about the world outside. Trying to tick a lot of boxes here."

"Why not just ask about me then? Why are you so paranoid?" Her eyes tracked me as I poked through the rubble along the wall.

"Because people are rarely honest about themselves. Because I don't know what to ask. Because I can." I shrugged.

I could tell by her blank look the answer wasn't good enough.

I sighed. "Storytelling reveals a bit of you to the world. Often things you want to keep hidden or didn't know about yourself. Now, I'm not one to leave someone in a bind, but I have to believe they're a good person before I'll help them. So, tell me something. Anything. You have the floor, mimic. Convince me."

"You're either a genius or the dumbest person I've ever met," the mimic said as I examined a head-sized rock.

"Rude, but the idea's not mine, it was my grandpa's," I said with a wave of my hand.

"He sounds unstable," she said.

"Oh, yeah. Absolutely." I couldn't help myself but smile. "But Grandpa's that special type of crazy that's brilliant in hindsight but baffling at the time."

The mimic signed. "Fine, but only because I have nothing else to do." She cleared her throat. "There once was an insufferable halfkin torturing a poor innocent princess," she started.

"Labeling yourself a princess? That tells me a lot right there." I struck the chain with the rock. Sparks flew in the darkness, giving me glimpses of a baffled woman literally looking down on me.

"No interrupting," the mimic snapped. "Halfkins are so rude."

I struck the rock again, the chain completely unfazed. Just what was this shit made out of?

FIVE: CHOSEN

"Perhaps a passage from—. Don't hit the chain so hard. That hurt."

The woman kicked a wave down the chain, almost hitting me with it. The air whirled around the chain, sending a gust against my face. How strong was this chick?

"Sorry." I had failed to consider hitting the chain downward would pull on her leg. "I'm still listening," I said, prompting her to continue talking while I tried to smash the spike loose from the wall.

"Now, this is an account from the Fourth Lectionary of Solara. It's a personal favorite of mine. No interrupting." The woman shot me a glance that could melt stone; the message was loud and clear. Also, what on earth was a lectionary? It sounded religious. Was she a priestess or something? In truth, I was trying to get her to fill the awkward silence because it made me feel weird.

"No talking. Got it," I said, making a zipper motion across my lips.

"You are so strange," the maybe-a-priestess said. Her demeanor changed as she prepared to speak. Her back straightened, and I felt I got a glimpse of someone else as she recited.

"*The Goddess Solara descended from Mount Zenith to be amongst the common people. In these days, such a thing, while not common, was not yet unheard of. The priestly guard begged the Goddess to stay in the Temple, asking Her not to sully Herself by descending among the masses. The Goddess patted the guards' heads like schoolchildren. 'I belong in all places,' She said. The Goddess descended to the lowest and poorest district of Zenith, taking it upon herself to enter the homes of those in need, healing or offering advice.*

"Now, the day had extended long, when an orphan boy broke through the contingent of priestly guards and threw himself at the feet of the Goddess. The Goddess raised her hand, halting the guards from striking the boy with drawn steel, for even touching the Goddess was a grave offense at the time. 'Speak, my little servant. For I see your heart is true,' the Goddess said.

"'It is the orphanage,' he said. 'The caretaker is taking the money for himself and leaving us with nothing to eat but the rats in the street. Please help, none will answer our pleas.'

"*The Goddess, upon hearing this, was wroth. 'Take me there,' the Goddess said. The simple words throbbed with power, a silence deepening upon the street.*

"*It was found that the boy's words were true and the corrupt caretaker was struck dead by the Goddess even as he prostrated in front of her. The Goddess turned to address the crowd that had formed behind her, the news of the activities spreading through the city. 'Hear me now,' She said, Her voice amplified so the whole city could hear. 'Many impure walk to the Gates of Ascension, but heed my warning. Those that harm the children will die by my hand, their souls erased from this plane.' Thus were the words of Solara, and all who heard them heeded them until their final breath."*

The recitation ended, and the woman let the moment linger before speaking. "So, what do you think, halfkin? What does this story tell you about—" She paused, noticing what I was up to. "What are you doing?"

"Nothing," I slurred around a mouthful of chain.

"Are you really chewing on that disgusting chain?" the maybe-a-priestess said, aghast. "You don't know where it's been!"

"I ran out of ideas." I wiped my mouth on my sleeve. Now that she mentioned it, there was a weird slime on that thing. "Also, I hurt my arm swinging the rock." Hurt might have been underplaying it. I felt something tear around my rotator cuff and my arm hung limp at my side.

"Solara, save me," the priestess said. I got the distinct feeling she would be facepalming if she were able. "So, have I passed your little test, halfkin?"

I'd actually forgotten. I had been checking out while she droned on. "Oh yeah, told me all I needed to know."

"… and that was?" The priestess waited expectantly.

"You're probably a good person, if a little uptight," I replied, shrugging.

"I am not uptight," the priestess said firmly.

"Yeah, okay. Not feeling very convinced." I dusted myself off. "I was thinking about maybe checking out the dungeon and trying to level up, or however that works here. I feel about as strong as a bag full of butterflies."

"Why is everything you say nonsense?"

"That reminds me," I said, snapping my fingers. I rechecked my blessings to ensure that what I was going to say was accurate. "I have a question about a religious thing, and you seem knowledgeable. I have this blessing called **Solara's Hand**, but it's blank. What does that mean?"

The priestess froze. “Show me.”

“Uh, and how would one do that?” I asked.

“View the text and will it to be visible to others,” the priestess said quickly. “Now hurry.”

I did as she asked. It was still blank like last time.

Solara’s Hand:

The priestess gasped. "You? Wait. It's really blank? I’ve never even heard of something like this.” She paused, her mouth twisting in concentration, leaning forward as if to get a closer look.

“Okay, so it is super weird.” My suspicions were confirmed. “I figured it was.”

“The Goddess may be purposely obscuring it from you. It could be a test,” the priestess said, leaning back. “Yes, that is it. Maybe you are just a potential Hand. That makes much more sense." She was mainly talking to herself by the end, nodding her head.

"... and what would a Hand be?" I asked.

The priestess sighed. "The definitive representative of a God or Goddess on the mortal plane, Her literal tool to shape the world. It is a grave responsibility, and every second you waste here as a weakling is another innocent dead."

The information settled on my mind with little fanfare. My emotions hadn't caught up to all the new things happening at once. I was so shellshocked I probably wouldn't have responded to the Goddess herself appearing and doing a tap dance.

"That sounds convoluted. Why doesn't the Goddess just show up and do her own bidding? Why use a middleman?" After all, I'd never volunteered to be a stooge for some Goddess. I wasn't going to just snap to attention and wait for orders.

“Crudely put, but a question that has been debated for thousands of years,” the priestess said. Hands appeared after the age of heroes, but now they are a once-a-century event at most. The last of Solara's Hands died over a thousand years ago."

"Great," I muttered. I had just gotten here and already had a shitty middle management job.

"Potential Hand, as long as you are low-leveled, you are in grave danger," the priestess said. The very concept of a nonhuman Hand will send the Church into an uproar. You need to be strong to serve Solara's will."

"Sounds like leveling up will solve a lot of problems," I said, looking at the solitary door at the end of the room. I still wasn't sure about being a deity's errand boy, but I was highly motivated to not die. Plus, I'd rather not spend a hundred years trapped in a dungeon. The path forward was clear—level up to survive.

The door was way bigger than I thought it was, towering over me with its intricate carved frame. Pestering doubts circled my head like a storm as I approached the dungeon entrance.

Those were later problems.

"Well, here goes nothing," I said, taking a step forward.

"May Solara guide you," the priestess called.

A dark light shimmered around me as I crossed the threshold. Reaching back, the shimmering substance in the doorway felt like glass, blocking me from going back to the room with the priestess.

With nowhere else to go, I wandered forward into the dark. I held my knife in front of me awkwardly, gripped in my left hand. My right arm still hung limp from tugging on the chain, the muscles in my shoulder bunching up painfully into a ball.

Holes in my plan rattled into my brain. What if I respawned somewhere else? Or in a different body? Shit, what if I just abandoned the priestess lady to rot?

Something rudely interrupted my worries by dropping on me from the ceiling.

"Fuck!" I flailed, my feet twisting up. Pain bloomed in my back as something stabbed me.

I tried to catch myself, but my injured arm collapsed, and I hit the floor face-first, breaking my nose. The thing crawled on me, tearing a chunk off my shoulder as I rolled, stealing a page from the alligator playbook, but it stuck to me as if glued on.

I panicked, realizing I was probably going to die.

Logic fleeing, I fought like a rabid animal seeking purchase with anything I could: knife, nails, or teeth.

A sticky wetness clung to my back as something gripped onto my arm with thin, finger-like pincers. I tore off one of the limbs with my teeth as we rolled across the cave floor, my knife forgotten as pure instinct kicked in.

More of the things swarmed me, tearing at my chest and wriggling through the opening. I felt something pop as they burrowed inside of me.

You Died!

Solara's Mercy Activated!

Sent to respawn point...

I gasped, sitting up in the pool.

My hands went to where my chest had been torn open. "Holy fucking shit that sucked." I placed a hand over my rapidly beating heart, trying to reinforce I was unharmed.

Light blinked in the corner of my vision, I focused on it, hoping I took at least one of those things with me.

You Died!

Solara's Mercy Activated!

Sent to respawn point...

"Shit, apparently not," I said, trying to wipe the blurry vision from my eyes. My mind felt foggy.

"Halfkin, is that you?" the priestess lady called to me.

"It's me. Still working on it." I stood up, water rolling off my naked body. Reaching the pool's edge, I **equipped** my gear, its weight dropping down on me. I tried to ignore the tremor in my hands.

"Is everything okay?" the priestess asked. She was nice, I had decided. I doubled down on my goal of getting her free. Plus, I could really use a good ally. Political and religious intrigue were not my strong suit.

"Oh yeah, just a little hiccup. No problems here," I shamelessly lied. My nerves were slipping, and I knew it. A piece of me considered cozying up against the wall and delaying going back into the dungeon proper, but I knew I would never leave the cave again if I didn't go right now.

I pulled out my knife. "All right, let's go again."

I passed through the barrier. Like a glassy bubble, it sealed me in. There was no turning back now.

I set my back to the barrier, adjusting my eyes to the lack of light. My heart ramped up as I waited, the faint outlines of a narrow rocky corridor taking shape.

A morbid thought crossed my mind. Would I come across my body? Was the dungeon instanced? So many questions and so few answers.

I moved forward one foot at a time, holding out my knife with both hands. I still couldn't get over how big this gladius-sized knife was. It was ridiculous, but I was thankful for it. After all, I could use all the help I could get.

I heard the things first, promptly retreating back to the dull light of the entrance. This time, I could see what they were and immediately regretted having eyes.

"**Inspect**," I yelled.

Juvenile Cave Centipede (Lvl 4): A member of the insect family, this is a juvenile variation of the cave centipede. This blind monster hunts larger prey in groups and eats them from the inside out.

Fuck me, it was four times my level. Why couldn't it be a goblin or some large ferrets?

I pressed my back against the barrier, knowing I was thoroughly hosed. The centipedes were the size of pool noodles. It was a whimsical comparison but horrifying in reality. Their legs all came to sharp points, rolling like little waves as they ran me down. Their pincers extended at least a foot in front of them, black and curving inward with a wicked hook.

One of them lunged at me, and I slashed at it, the knife bouncing off its hard carapace but successfully deflecting it at the wall. The others swarmed me, sending me to the floor in a pile of centipede.

I threw them off as I slammed my back against the barrier, eliciting a squeal from one of the little buggers that had clung on. The centipede rolled away as I slashed at it. It felt like I was about to turn the tide.

That's when I dropped my knife. I had slashed too wide, hitting my elbow against the rock wall and dislodging my grip. The centipedes hissed as they saw the knife fly, swarming me with renewed vigor.

I clawed at the barrier with my fingertips, hoping to get back through as the centipede burrowed into my back. I saw the priestess watching in horror as I was torn apart, unable to get back into the room.

I couldn't tell as the vision faded and blackness came for me, but I thought she was screaming.

You Died!

Solara's Mercy Activated!

Sent to respawn point...

I swallowed water as I thrashed in the pool, my brain still fighting the centipedes. Gasping for air, I slumped on the pool's edge, spitting up water.

I hoped I took one of those bastards with me, at least. I turned my attention to the light in the corner of my vision.

You Died!

Solara's Mercy Activated!

Sent to respawn point...

"Shit." I threw a rock at the wall, yelling a string of expletives that would've made a Marine blush.

"Halfkin?" the priestess called. "Please do not be disheartened. The Goddess will reveal the way."

"Working on it," I said. My limbs shook as I pushed myself out of the pool, crouching at its edge to catch my breath. The weight of my clothes settling on me did little to comfort me. I knew I had to keep going.

With a roll, I was on my feet and moving towards the entrance.

I passed through the dungeon entrance, steeling myself for what was about to happen. If I wanted control of my life, I needed power—all the power I could get.

I entered the dungeon with hardening resolve. I wouldn't fail.

SIX: SHATTERED GLASS

I failed a lot, losing track of how many times I died in the process.

If there was one thing I gained from my time in the void, it was a high tolerance for repetition. I'd stopped counting at fifty deaths, and that was a while ago.

It wasn't all for nothing. I felt more familiar with my new body with each run, finding my limitations and strengths. I learned the centipedes were tough as nails, and I hit like a bag of feathers. My low constitution was a real problem, and I got torn up by anything that touched me. I was pretty sure a light breeze could bruise my delicate skin.

I'd tried almost every strategy I could think of. I even tried to use magic or make spells, willing myself to do something 'video gamey.' Nothing worked.

The dumb centipedes would not die.

The priestess continued to assure me that my body would be purified through suffering, that it was all part of the Path. Her words were the balm I had against all the failure weighing on me. I probably would've given up a while ago if it wasn't for her. She was nice.

"May Solara guide you," the priestess called.

I waved as I ran through the dungeon entrance. This time would be different. I had a strategy I had been avoiding.

Conventional strategy had failed me. It was time for alternative combat styles. I had tried so hard to be logical, but now I was past trying to make sense of it all.

The main advantage of all my deaths was I now had the twisting cave memorized. The light bordered on non-existent, but I had gathered that the centipedes lived in a crack in the ceiling. My boots sounded like a beating drum as I ran, letting everything in the dungeon know I was coming.

I had decided to weaponize my low constitution.

I knew exactly where the first centipede dropped and let a long pincer impale my left hand, dragging my assailant with me down the corridor. My brain blocked the pain. It was like an old friend at this point. I had this little shit at my mercy, but it didn't know it yet.

This was an exercise in mutually assured destruction.

I used my body like a hammer, setting the hilt of my knife against my chest. Slamming the centipede into the wall, I used my full-body momentum to ram my knife into the soft underbelly of the insect.

The impact knocked the air out of me. The centipede flailed

in response, tearing at my face and chest, but it didn't slow me down. I rammed it into the wall over and over again. Finally, the underbelly broke open letting the warm viscera flow over my hand. Our blood mixed as its brethren leaped on my back.

"Die, you sack of shit!" I tore at the centipede's insides with my hands, searching for something vital.

Something burst inside of it like a glass bubble. A warm light radiated from inside the creature. For a brief second, it felt like walking into the sunlight on a hot summer day.

I smiled.

Unfortunately, the light revealed its brethren in their full glory. Black and yellow with intersecting plates of armor like a little samurai. Wicked, freaky little things. Some top-grade nightmare fuel.

I'd never hated anything more.

A light blinked in the corner of my vision. I opened it as the centipede burrowed into my back. I ignored them, wanting to see the fruits of my victory before I died.

Error! No Path detected! Sol not absorbed!

Calibrate center for Sol uptake.

"What!?" I felt the warm sunlight passing through me, flowing into the centipedes around me.

Blackness took me as I screamed in frustration.

You Died!

Solara's Mercy Activated!

Sent to respawn point...

I sat up in the pool, holding my head in my hands. I stared at nothing. No panic, no cursing, just sitting. My internal chatter was dead silent for once, like the light had been turned off in my brain. A dull ringing ran through my ears as I sat, my eyes tracing over the markings on the walls.

"Halfkin?" the priestess called. Her voice jumpstarted the engine in my mind, creeping to life and building up to a storm. "Can you hear me?" Why was she talking so gently to me?

"I'm here. Just… Just give me a second," I replied.

"Dying so many times without breaks is known to cause mental damage," the priestess said. The concern in her voice made me irritated. I was fine. "You should rest," she continued.

Rest? How could I rest? I had accomplished nothing but demonstrate I was weak, useless, and, worst of all, trapped.

"Let me sort this out, and I'll be right over," I said. It was touching she was concerned for me, but I needed to figure this out before I let myself rest.

"No path detected," I muttered, pulling up my stats. "What does that even mean?"

Name: Stone McGracen

Race: Halfkin

Path: Pathless

Level: 0

Spells: Inspect

Blessings: Solara's Mercy, Solara's Hand

Stats:

Int: 7

Wis: 6

Cha: 5

Str: 3

Dex: 5

Con: 1.2

Spirit: 11.2

Pathless… Sol not absorbed… I don't see anything on here about a center…

I reread the system log. There was no way around it. No center equaled no magic. It was as simple as that.

"Fuck," I yelled. "Fuck. Fuck. Fuck."

I slammed my fists into the water, little red fish reeling in the waves. I kicked anything I could kick. I threw any rocks I could get a hold of. I said every curse word I'd ever heard and some that I hadn't.

My anger turned into wet tears as I slumped against the wall beside the priestess. I could tell I'd broken at least one of my fists. A cold bucket of embarrassment washed over me. How could I have lost control like that? Was I snapping?

I turned my head away so the priestess couldn't see my face. It all felt unfair. Why didn't I have cool powers or spells or something? This was supposed to be a new start, but now I suspected it might be more punishment.

"Please, halfkin, talk to me," the priestess said. I hated that she was concerned for me.

"I got a message that I can't absorb sol," I said flatly.

Silence hung over us.

"That cannot be," the priestess said. "All who follow the Goddess walk one of the Paths. For a Hand to be Pathless is heretical. Did you do something heinous before arriving here?"

I didn't answer. My emotions had cooled into a vast ocean of nothing, sucking me down with it.

"Halfkin? Halfkin, are you okay?" I heard her call to me. It sounded distant.

Everything snapped back with a whoosh, my brain churning again.

"Stone," I corrected.

"Excuse me?"

"My name is Stone," I said, a chipper mask sliding into

place. "Well, technically, it's Ashton, but I hate that name."

"Wait, you have a perfectly reasonable name and go by Stone?"

I shrugged, welcoming the banter. "I've always liked it."

The priestess paused, allowing a beat of silence. "So, what now?"

"I think I'm done," I said.

"Breaks are important," the priestess said, slipping into a lecturing tone. "With no Path, your strategy will have to change, but it can be done. Some infamous Pathless have terrorized even those far on the Path before." Her tone was reassuring, and it made me recede further back. I'd already given up.

"No, I think I'm giving up," I said. "I can't do this."

"You hit a roadblock, and you give up?" There was a tone in her voice I hadn't heard before. It was cutting, an air of disapproval. It stung me more than I cared to admit.

"Fine," I said, my voice flat as I got up. "I'll go try the dungeon again."

"That's not what I meant! You need to take a break," the priestess yelled as I walked back through the dungeon entrance.

I was slipping. I could feel the irrationality building up. I needed a win. Anything really. For something to go right for once. Despair clung to the edges of my psyche, but the pain in my body kept it at bay, grounding me in reality. I thought about letting the centipedes kill me so I could return to respawn with a fresh body. After all, at least a few of my knuckles and maybe my ankle was broken.

I stumbled down the corridor, planning on letting the centipedes take me, but as I watched the revolting things pour out of the ceiling, I decided against it, leaping on the pile and stabbing with renewed fervor.

The priestess was right.

No matter what happened, I wasn't going down without a fight.

Darkness took me as I fought.

You Died!

Solara's Mercy Activated!

Sent to respawn point...

I gasped, sitting up in the pool.

A notification blinked in the corner of my vision, but I knew what it said.

It said I was a failure.

The priestess's voice reached me as I slipped onto the pool's edge.

"Stone?"

"What's up?" I felt a little loopy.

"I want you to talk to me," she said. "You've been here for so long, and I don't know anything about you."

"Not much to tell," I said, swishing my feet in the water.

"Either way, the insight could lead me to be able to help," she said.

The priestess was so helpful. I hated I was disappointing her, but I obliged, rambling about my life back home.

As I talked about my last days on Earth, I fell into a rhythm, pausing frequently to explain things. To my surprise, she seemed genuinely interested in what I had to say, asking about all kinds of mundane things.

At first, she asked about simple things like what a convenience store was, but we hit a real hangup halfway through the story.

"Neon light?" she asked.

"Yeah, like the lights that go outside of a shop. They're usually red or whatever. Anyway, I could barely see—"

"Why would the shops have light outside?" Confusion laced her voice as she interrupted me. Again.

"Because it was dark out," I said. "Anyway, now the screams had been—"

"You were a Nightwalker? That explains your ignorance of the Path," she said as if any of that made sense.

"I have no idea what that means," I said, desperate to get the conversation back on track. "It was a night out.

Anyway—"

"Apologies, one last question," she interrupted again.

I looked at her in irritation, but she smiled at me and I felt a rush of patience return. I did my best not to sigh audibly. "What is it?"

"What do you mean by it was a night out?" she asked. "Is that a turn of phrase? I'm not sure what you mean by it."

"It's when the sun goes down?" It was my turn to sound confused.

The priestess blinked at me. "Where would it go?"

"Okay, so there's this thing called the sun," I said slowly.

"Don't talk down to me," she snapped.

"I didn't mean anything by it. I don't know what you know," I said. "Why don't you tell me what a day is."

"A full revolution of the moon around Terra," she said quickly.

A day tracked by the orbit of the moon? Sounded more like a month to me. Weird.

"Where I come from, the moon takes about twenty-eight days to revolve around the planet."

A pause stretched. "That's so long!" she said.

"All right, so you know how the planet revolves around the sun, right?"

"Solara provides a source of light. This is common knowledge."

"Sure. Anyway. The planet also spins."

"Wouldn't everything fall off?"

Yeah, this wasn't getting us anywhere.

"Let's just skip over this part," I said, trying to get the conversation back on track. "It was the part of the day when it was dark, and the planet was facing away from the sun." I saw her open her mouth. "No, nuh-uh. No more questions until the end, and no pouting this time."

"I do not pout," she said. It was a lie, but I let her tell it.

The priestess let me finish the story, gasping as I detailed how I was killed. I glossed over most of the void shenanigans. She probably already thought I was a little crazy, and I didn't want to go and confirm it. I left it to 'my soul waited in a void to be reborn.' Simple, elegant, technically not a lie. Her comments at the end caught me off guard, though.

"Typical humans. Preying on the weak," the priestess said. "It was good of your man-at-arms to execute them on sight."

Man-at-arms? Was that what the system translated police officer to?

"That's your takeaway? Not 'oh wow, that world sounded cool' or something?" I said.

"Humans are a menace," the priestess said. It was almost a growl.

"Oh, come on, people aren't that bad. Some are, for sure, but most are decent."

"The only race that tolerates humans are other humans," she said. "Spiteful, hateful creatures that use violence against all others. Just because they are blessed with the Path of Light, they claim to be the Goddess's creation perfected, using it as an excuse to abuse others. They even claim the Goddess herself to be an ascended human! Vile heresy of the highest order."

"Damn, that sounds worse than how we were in my world." I felt I had to get a word of defense in there, but humanity sounded like some scum on this planet.

"We?" It was a simple question the priestess asked, but her eyes bored into me, the silver in them taking a new sharpness.

"Uhm." I paused, should I lie? No, it was too late now. "Yeah, I was human before I came here. That's not a big deal right?"

The priestess actually hissed at me. Apparently, it was a big deal.

"That's uncalled for," I said, pointing at her. "I'm not from this world. I've got nothing to do with whatever you're hung up on."

"You're waiting for your chance to walk me through the street like a dog, *ishta*. I know how your kind treats daggers," she practically spat at me.

The gentle priestess was gone. This was a feral cat of a woman ready to kill.

"Yet, I am Solara's Hand," I argued. It hurt she had turned on me, but the logical part knew this wasn't actually about me. "Would She choose someone evil? Would that make her evil by association?"

The anger in the priestess's face turned into confusion as she made a face at my words. I couldn't discern what it was as her hair had fallen entirely into her face during the outburst. She flicked her head to the side, trying to get the strands out of the way.

"All I'm asking for here is a little faith. Think about how I've treated you. Granted, I did accuse you of being a mimic, but you were suspicious as fuck, and I didn’t try to hurt you. Besides, I'm not human anymore, so it doesn't count. I think it's unfair, is all."

The priestess looked at me, staring into my soul, searching for dishonesty. She kept flicking her head to get the hair out of her face, trying to look at me unobstructed. The stump of her arm even moved as if to move the hair with the ghost limb.

"Do you want me to tuck your hair back? It looks like it's bothering you," I said finally. The truth was her constant flicking was getting annoying. "Wait, was this the plan all along? To lure me into coming close to you with an elaborate backstory and befriending me? A clever ruse, mimic, you won't get me this time." I smiled.

The priestess laughed, choking when a bit of hair got stuck in her mouth. "Fine, you may get this mess out of my face," she said, spitting out a wayward strand of hair.

"Sweet, it's been driving me nuts." I stepped forward to do the task but found myself coming up a bit… short.

I had to stand on my toes to reach the priestess's hair. I sent a mental thanks to my boots for that extra inch or two of height. The priestess was so tall it was unfair. She had to be half-giant or something.

I brushed the ratted hair to the side. For the first time, I got a clear look at her face. She was young, or at least appeared to be so. The angles of her face were high and sharp while delicate and feminine. She was beautiful in a dangerous way, like a sword in the hands of a master or a tiger hunting its prey. Those silver eyes bored into me, daring me to say something.

I panicked. "Nice face. It looks good on you."

What the fuck was that? I twirled the hair into a loose twist like I'd seen my cousins do, tucking it over her shoulder in a hurry. A long, pointed ear sprung from under the rat's nest. "Whoa."

All my assumptions cracked as I jumped back.

"Did you really think I was a human?" she said.

"Giant, actually," I said quickly.

"What? " The priestess gave me a baffled look before recovering. "Well, get a nice long look, *ishta*." A small smile curled up on her lips, revealing sharp canines.

"Your ears are super cool," I said. "So pointy." I stuck out my two pointer fingers neck to my head.

"Are you making fun of me?"

"No?" The very thought made me a little mad. "I've never seen anyone like you, priestess lady. I think it's awesome." I had so many questions. Like why were elves so big? She was an elf, right? Was she only half-elf? Which one of her parents was a giant? Oh god, how did that work?

The priestess sighed. "Please, call me Ae."

"That's your name, right?" I asked.

"Yes, it's my name," Ae snapped back.

"That's it? I expected it to be longer," I said.

"At least my name isn't a mundane object," Ae said, rolling her eyes.

"My name is cool," I defended myself.

"I think it's great you think that," Ae said.

I folded my arms. What did she know anyway? Dumb giant elf. An idea struck.

"I realized there is something I haven't tried." I stood up a little straighter, the idea growing. It was so simple, why hadn't I tried before?

"What do you mean?" Ae asked. "Actually, I already regret

asking. Don't answer."

"I used to train with my grandpa back home. Well, before he got sick, anyway." I rubbed my hands together. This was just crazy enough to work. "Sounds like I'll have to do this the old-fashioned way."

Seven: Softball

I dropped chest first onto the cavern floor.

"Stone, are you trying to be funny again?"

"I'm out of ideas, so I'm trying anything I can think of," I said, placing my hands on either side of my shoulders and pushing up to a plank. I felt good so far. No shaking like when I did this in gym class. "If the system won't give me stats, I'm gonna try to scrape them from the ground."

"Ah," Ae said. "That's not how it works."

I lowered myself to the ground, testing out the motion before doing a full pushup. "Just humor me. Let me try."

Ae clicked her tongue at me but didn't say anything else. I touched my nose to the ground before pushing up again. My eyes checked the corner of my vision to see if there was a notification, but there was nothing.

Yeah, it wasn't going to be that easy.

A pleasant burn ran down my arms after twenty or so

repetitions. It felt sloppy, but I was starting to internalize the motion. I pushed up until my elbows were locked and then down until my nose touched the rocky floor.

The first whispers of fatigue filtered up through my arms around a hundred, but I was still going strong and staying consistent. I had to be banging out a pushup every other second. After all, I reminded myself this was more of a marathon than anything else. A proof of concept, if you will. It had nothing to do with all the anime my grandpa made me watch growing up.

I forced myself to breathe in through my nose and out my mouth, trying to maintain a breathing pattern as I pushed up and down. Breathing in as I lowered down. Breathing out as I pushed up. Slow, steady, consistent.

It was blissfully painful. Was this what exercise was supposed to feel like?

The first bits of doubt wormed into my brain as I rounded one hundred and fifty, but I knew if I quit now, I was proving Ae right.

I couldn't have that.

No, I needed to see this through—no more half-measures. It was time for the whole hog.

I lost count somewhere around two hundred. Sweat ran off the tip of my nose onto the ground.

"Still going?" Ae asked, feigning disinterest. "You're certainly stubborn, if nothing else."

Her admission, though critical, revealed to me she was still watching. I grinned as the knowledge spurned me on further.

I lost myself in the counting. Making it to a hundred and then restarting. Everything hurt. I didn't even know pushups could make your back hurt. My arms shook, and my palms felt raw, rubbing against the rough cavern floor. My breath became erratic, losing the neat pattern I had been sticking to.

What if Ae was right and this was all a waste of time? Precious time we could be using to figure out how to get out of here. No, I was going to see this all the way through, not just give up whenever it got complicated. I was going to push the ground until it killed me. I had spent my whole life wishing I could level up, that I could live this life for real, and I wasn't going to be defeated now. Not so close to having it.

My arms gave out after another fifty or so. I slowed, hoping it would make it easier, but it made it worse. I lamented the lack of air movement in the cave as sweat ran down my arms.

"Surely, you can stop now," Ae said. The undercut of worry in her voice was flattering. "This can’t be healthy."

"No, I want magic," I said through gritted teeth.

"Stone, points only come by processing sol. I've already told you this," Ae said. "The goddess Solara has blessed us with her—"

My hand slipped on the sweat, and my face slammed into the ground. The blood leaking from my nose mixed with sweat as I pushed myself back up. I could taste the blood in my mouth as my heavy breathing pulsed in and out of my chest.

"I can't watch." The priestess looked away.

"Yeah, yeah, I'm fine." I stretched like a cat, trying to shake off some of the cramping I felt.

I kept pushing, but now from my knees. It felt like my body was pierced with hot iron rods running from the center of my chest to my shoulders and down my arms. My abs hurt. My legs hurt. Even my toes hurt from holding myself up.

I pushed. My body was begging me to give up, hitting a wall I'd never even known was there. My arms stopped responding, struggling even though I was on my knees.

Should I give up? Maybe Ae was right, and I was taking this too far. No? With **Solara's Mercy** protecting me, there was no reason not to go all the way.

I moved into the pool, the buoyancy helping keep me up at the cost of only being able to breathe in the top position. My vision swam as the red koi twisted and turned around my hands. I was flagging under stress, but all the dungeon runs had given me an edge on pain management.

My will slipped as I indulged, resting on the pool floor. I forced myself to think about why I needed this.

I pushed.

I thought about the monsters tearing me apart. How I felt weak, just like my old life.

I pushed.

I thought about my failure to free Ae.

I pushed.

I thought about the void encroaching on the edges of my vision, threatening to swallow me, mocking me for being weak.

I pushed.

I hit the last of my strength. Everything had come to this. A final action. Defiance against the system, against the creator, against any gods that were watching. I would not be bowed. They could refuse to give me a path. Leave me without a center. Dump me in some shitty dungeon. They could mock me and leave me in the void as long as they wanted, but I would never give up. I would never stop, an eternal wraith pursuing what I felt was mine.

I pushed, screaming into the water as bubbles formed around the sides of my face.

I broke the surface, looking for that blinking notification light.

Nothing.

I collapsed back into the water, unable to push myself out, my will finally breaking.

I tasted blood and water. I tried to get back up, pushing

beyond reason, but my body was breaking down. I was out of gas.

My body settled against the bottom of the pool. As the water stilled, my will finally broke. I stopped struggling, accepting I was a failure. The fish returned near me as the weight of being trapped tightened around me. I had moved from one prison to another, trapped but in different ways. This new life was just as bad as the void. At least the void didn't pretend I could get out.

I stared at the fish inching closer, swirling around me as I lay still. I closed my eyes and waited for death to take me as fish brushed against my cheek. I needed the power to protect those around me. I would do anything not to feel weak.

Solara's Hand activated.

The furnace of my instinct roared to life, commanding me to execute a single action. The sensation was more potent than anything I'd felt before.

The urge to pull.

Like a black hole, I pulled everything towards me, the pool's light dimming as lightning ran through my veins. Something popped in my throat, a twisting sensation—a burning around my Adam's apple.

The burst of energy was enough to let me break free from the bottom of the pool, but no air entered my lungs as I surfaced.

Already air-deprived, I plunged back under, clawing at my

swollen throat. It felt like someone was pressing on my airway with their thumb, blocking me from breathing in.

My face hit the rock at the bottom of the pool, and I felt something break. A light blinked in the corner of my vision as my consciousness fled.

You Died!

Solara's Mercy Activated!

Sent to respawn point...

I gasped, sitting up in the pool.

The room's light was noticeably duller. What smelled so sweet? It was like someone made a candle store out of cinnamon rolls.

A light blinked in the corner of my vision. I opened it with bated breath, hoping to manifest what I wanted it to say.

Congratulations, Ascendant!

Throat Meridian unlocked! +5 Cha.

Center Formed. Location: Throat Meridian.

Path Assigned!

Spell Gained!

"I did it." I looked to Ae. "Ae, I did something! It's not a stat but something else!" My stomach growled. Had I been hungry this whole time?

The look on the silver-eyed woman's face squashed my

jovial attitude. Why was she afraid?

"What have you done?" Ae asked. "What happened to the light?

"I, uh. I unlocked my Path," I said. "We had a whole talk about it. You were like, 'No, you can't,' and I was like, 'Watch me.' You know?"

"A path is something you're born with," Ae said, hesitating. "This isn't possible."

"Clearly it is," I said, opening my character sheet. "**Solara's Hand** even activated. I feel like I'm really getting somewhere."

Name: Stone McGracen

Race: Halfkin

Path: Hunger

Level: 0

Unlocked Meridians: Throat

Spells: Inspect, Feast

Blessings: Solara's Mercy, Solara's Hand

Stats:

Int: 7

Wis: 6

Cha: 9 (+5)

Str: 3

Dex: 5

Con: 1.2

Spirit: 11.2

Hunger? I focused on the Path, hoping a description would come up.

Path of Hunger: +1 Cha, +1 FP per level. A Path for those with indomitable will. Consume what is yours.

"Charisma?" I said, feeling confused. "Oh god, am I a bard? What is this?" My mind tumbled over 'FP' not seeing a stat called that on my sheet. "Oh, it must mean free point."

My hand went to my throat, feeling pressure in it. The sensation was hard to quantify, and it wasn't pleasant. Something had changed. It was like I had an extra muscle stuffed in there.

I pulled up **Solara's Hand**, expecting it to be blank, but it had something new.

Solara's Hand: The mortal representative of the Goddess Solara.

"What does it say?" Ae asked. "Stop standing there and tell me already." The priestess looked at me with intensity. She was practically bouncing.

I closed my stats, realizing I was just looking at my changes and mumbling. "I unlocked the Path of Hunger and got a spell called **Feast**."

Saying the word did something odd. I had an urge to swallow as my hunger increased. Also, what smelled so good? I looked at Ae as a dark desire grew in my subconscious. *Solara, what have you done to me?*

Ae talked, unaware of my internal conflicts. "A deviant path? And one I've never heard of," Ae said, trailing off. I could see she was deep in thought.

"Deviant path?" I asked. The feeling was fading, but I needed Ae to keep talking and distract me.

"I forget how little you know," Ae said, switching to her priestess voice. "Each civilized race makes up a majority of a Path passed down by their people. It's a lot to explain at once, but an example is that elves mostly inherit the Path of Water, which is linked to the Sacral Meridian and increases dexterity at every level."

"Is that your Path?" I asked

Ae's smile faltered. "I am mixed, and my Path is unique."

That made sense. I considered asking what her other half was but thought better of it, seeing the dark expression on her face.

"So, my path pumps charisma," I said. "Does that mean I'm a performer or something?" I tried not to be ungrateful but that was the last stat I wanted a build around. My days playing D&D with Grandpa had instilled a deep-seated hatred of bards. The last thing I needed was to be forced to seduce every dungeon created as my last line of defense.

"Any path can do any profession. It's just that some are

inherently better at it than others," Ae explained. Her stump moved as if she was making a hand gesture. "Charisma is one of the hardest of the seven holy stats to quantify. It has been described as adding weight to your words or increasing how others perceive you. High charisma can be felt like a magnetism—people feel good being around you."

I nodded along. "Sounds complicated."

"You have no idea," Ae said. "People spend their whole lives trying to understand Solara's gift to us. Every detail possesses a depth that only demonstrates the benevolence of the creator."

"So, what now? I don't feel any different." Well, other than the urge to bite my only friend. Luckily, an equally strong instinct told me to keep my mouth shut. Maybe that was the charisma at work?

"It is important to remember stats show potential, not current ability. Someone with high strength who never trains will be weak because their body doesn't know how to activate all their strength. It is the same with all stats. Those that do not train, squander the Goddess's gifts."

"Oh, okay. So, I wasn't far off by exercising but had the wrong goal in mind." The pieces were falling into place in my mind.

"Exactly." Ae smiled at me. I felt myself smiling back, pulled in under the magnetism of the priestess.

My stomach audibly growled.

"Got any food hidden in that armor?"

Ae laughed. "None that I can reach." The priestess wiggled her stump of an arm.

"So, what about casting spells?" I asked, changing the subject.

"You have to bask in the light of Solara to cast magic," Ae said. I could tell she was enjoying this and was a natural teacher. "Since you don't possess a core, you can't store sol for later, so you have to be actively in the presence of sol to cast a spell."

"So how do people cast in a dungeon?"

Ae smiled. It made me feel like I asked the right question. "That requires skill and speed. When a beast or dungeon creature dies, they release a burst of sol. If collected on time, this can be used to power a spell. Sol will only stay in your center for a brief period. A center is like cupping water in your palms, whereas a core is like a jar."

"Holy shit, I have to keep killing, or I will lose access to my spells? That's intense." I believed Ae, but part of this didn't jive with what I had experienced. I seemed to be able to use **Inspect** whenever I wanted, and I felt **Feast** activate earlier despite having no sol.

"The exception is **Inspect**," Ae said as if reading my mind. "Solara wanted all to be curious about the world, and the spell draws on the body's natural energy. The downside is it can only be used a few times a day."

Excitement filled me. It felt like I was getting somewhere. "No time like the present." I bounced on the balls of my feet, throwing punches in the air. "So, how do I practice? Do you have some hidden training or secret techniques for me?"

Ae laughed. "This is the easiest part." A smile pulled at the corners of her mouth. "**Solara's Mercy** is not called so for no reason. There is only one way to learn."

Ae looked pointedly at the dungeon entrance behind me. Shit, this was going to be a trial by fire.

"Dive in. Figure it out, got it," I said, throwing her a smile. "Wish me luck."

"I'm not a barmaid," Ae snapped, but I felt her heart wasn't in it.

I passed through the portal, knife in hand. I could barely contain my excitement, running off down the familiar pathway, but something had changed. A strong scent hung in the air.

Why did it smell like a plate of buttered lobster from my favorite lobster-themed restaurant?

I did my best to ignore the new smell as I copied my strategy from last time, slamming the centipede into the wall and cutting open its soft underbelly as it tore up my hand.

"**Feast**," I said, my hunger ramping up to ten.

My mouth salivated as the creature's viscera leaked out from around it. A weird mixture of extreme hunger and disgust ran through me. The centipede smelled like lobster, filling my nostrils with a heady fragrance.

A pulling sensation filled me, and I tried to pull, but nothing moved. I had my hand in the centipede, but it felt like trying to suck through a clogged straw. I could feel my center pulling, but the pathway between my palm and my center wasn't working.

Something in the centipede burst, sol flashing before fading away over a few seconds. I closed my eyes, trying to ignore being torn apart from behind, searching for instincts for pulling in the light. Ae made it sound natural, but the light passed through me like last time with no difference.

My only instinct was to bite the monsters burrowing into me.

One of the centipedes finally pierced my heart, sending me into the black abyss, confused as ever.

You Died!

Solara's Mercy Activated!

Sent to respawn point...

EIGHT: FLAGPOLE

I gasped, sitting up in the pool.

I took a deep breath. I could've sworn there was a hot plate of cinnamon rolls below my nose. It was suspicious, and I hated it.

"What's wrong now?" Ae asked as I **equipped** my clothes and wandered over to the wall. Was the smell her? My mouth watered a little, looking her over. Disgusted, I squashed that thought process and plopped down beside her leg.

"I think I need a break." I leaned my head back against the wall. "It's getting really old, dying over and over again."

"Did it work? Did you gain a level?" Ae asked. "The barrier between level zero and one is thin." She wanted me to explain everything in detail, so why was I holding back?

"Would I get a notification if I did?"

"Leveling up is not something you can do by accident," Ae said, her smile fading.

"Ah, I don't think I did then."

"I was hoping you would level. There is no sense for both of us to be trapped here."

Did Ae really think I'd leave her here? I mean, I knew we hadn't known each other for more than a couple of weeks, but come on. Friends didn't leave each other behind.

"I'll get you out, you'll see. I'll pour some stats into strength."

"If strength alone were enough to burst out of these chains, I'd have done it long ago," Ae said. "Seeing how it motivated you, I didn't want to say anything, but you should leave as soon as possible."

I hadn't considered that Ae was a lot stronger than me, but it made sense in retrospect. I closed my eyes. "We'll figure it out. Don't worry about it."

"Stone, these aren't normal chains. They're imbued with sol. They're unbreakable as long as the magic lasts."

I looked at the chain next to me, wrapping my hand around one of the links. Confused, I felt a hunger surge and an urge to pull. It sat on the edge of my thoughts, waiting for me to pull the trigger.

I put my hand back in my lap. "Hey, is it normal to feel really hungry once you've unlocked a Path?" I asked.

"I think hunger is a normal part of life," Ae said carefully. "Why do you ask?"

"I just realized there's no food down here. I think it's getting to me." My mind wandered back to the chain. My instinct was still yelling at me to bite it. Could I tell her?

Fuck it. I went for it. "Ae, what if my instincts told me to do something weird? Something that started when I unlocked my Path."

A dark look passed the priestess's face. "Define weird?"

"I have an urge to bite this chain. Like I can smell it." I waited for her judgment.

"That is certainly odd but not dangerous." Ae shrugged. "No harm in trying, I suppose."

"Gotcha," I said, trying not to expose the level of stress this whole thing was causing me. It was like starving to death at a buffet.

I put the chain in my mouth. It was sweet, intensely so, almost bordering on spicy, as I ran my tongue over a link. My mouth salivated as my instincts told me to swallow, but nothing happened when I tried to eat it, and the feeling remained.

"**Feast**," I said around the chain.

Something surged, and I swallowed for real, the new muscle in my neck activating.

A string of fire ran from the tip of my tongue, tracing down my throat, stopping at a swirling storm building in the middle of my neck. The storm crackled with energy, sending an electric power surge through my body.

My muscles immediately locked up like I'd been struck by lightning, clamping my jaw shut and pulling more of the fiery substance into the growing mass in my neck. The stream had turned into a torrent. My breathing became tighter as my throat swelled to painful levels.

"Stone? What's happening?" Ae said, twisting to look at me. "Stone! Let go!"

I tried to. I really did. I mentally struggled against the torrent, my body not responding. Ae kicked, trying to shake me off the chain, but I stayed locked on. The seconds dragged on as I struggled to free myself from the fire continuously rolling down my throat.

Suddenly, the flow of fire stopped, and I reeled onto my back, my hands going to my engorged throat. Icy pain ran through my veins as I writhed, choking on seemingly nothing. My hands felt a bulge the size of a softball in my throat just below my Adam's apple.

"Stone!" Ae yelled. She was becoming frantic, continuously asking me what was going on, struggling against her restraints.

The sound of something breaking tore through the air. Was it me? Did I break? Something collided with my head, sending me to my back. What hit me?

"Solara's grace!" Ae slammed into the wall face first like a flag swinging around a pole. The chain on her right leg snapped, sending her flying, her foot taking me out on the way. The chain-link flew across the room, hitting the opposing wall with a heavy clang.

Darkness encroached on the edge of my vision. What was happening? All I felt was an impulse to dislodge the pressure, but it had nowhere to go.

The feeling reached a crescendo and mercifully released.

You Died!

Solara's Mercy Activated!

Sent to respawn point...

I gagged, sitting up in the pool.

I coughed up water as my hands went to my throat. The lump was gone, but a pressure remained, making my adrenaline pump.

I took deep breaths, trying to assure myself I could breathe. The very edge of tears collected in my eyes as I barely restrained my panic. I let the feeling wash over me, trying to accept the new normal.

As the panic faded, an instinct appeared. Flexing a muscle I didn't know I had, my throat constricted, clamping down on the feeling of fullness.

I just wanted to be alright. To go back to feeling healthy. The pressure built and released. The feeling compressed.

Congratulations! Ascended to Level 1. +1 Cha, +1 Con

The notification washed over me as a wave of warmth ran across my body. Wait? Constitution? I thought I got to choose my free point.

"Stone, is that you? I need some help." There was more strain in Ae's voice than usual, derailing my thoughts.

Ae hung by a single chain, the manacle digging into her wrist. Without the other chain on her leg to keep her splayed, all her weight was on her remaining arm. Her shoulder twisted at a weird angle, her face showing discomfort as her feet hung inches from the floor.

"Coming," I said, **equipping** my clothes and scrambling out of the pool. My problems could wait for a second.

Thinking quickly, I grabbed some of the wooden refuse from along the wall, piling it under her feet. She settled her weight on it, and for the first time, the chains went slack.

"Oh, Stone, you have no idea how good this feels," Ae said, standing up on her tiptoes and lowering back down to stand flat.

"Glad to help," I said with a laugh. "So, what happened to these chains being unbreakable? Maybe you're just weak?" I teased.

Ae shot me a look that could melt steel. "As if," she scoffed. "I could crush your head with my bare hands."

"Good to know." The smell of the remaining chains called to me, and my stomach audibly rumbled.

Ae raised an eyebrow, clearly having heard the sound. "Why don't you tell me what happened?"

I told her everything—well, everything but how her thighs called to me like a ham dinner. My charisma stat told me that was an inside thought, and I should keep my mouth shut.

I started talking about not getting any sol from my kill, the hunger, the throat swelling, the whole thing. She didn't interrupt me, but her brows scrunched further together as I talked.

"Stone, this is bad." Ae looked concerned.

"What? What's wrong?" I asked, instinctively covering my neck.

"I think your center is in your throat meridian," Ae said. "That shouldn't even be possible. Not to mention the urges you're describing. They sound bestial. Your center should be above your navel in the gate meridian. It's what lets the ambient light of Solara into us. I didn't even know anything else was possible. The church is going to kill you if they find out about you."

"But I'm Solara's Hand or whatever. Shouldn't the church be a bit more understanding?" I knew this was a leap, but I hoped the religion here was more tolerant than those I knew back home.

Ae laughed. "The church stopped being about Solara a long time ago. You will be seen as a threat to their power and summarily removed."

"What about Solara?" I asked. "Wouldn't she have something to say about that?"

"Stone, Solara is gone," Ae said. "It's been thousands of years since She was seen, and no one knows what happened.

Only that She abandoned us."

"Shit. One step forward and two steps back." My eyes glanced up at the chain as my stomach rolled again.

"Stone," Ae said. "Stone, look at me. When you look at me, do you feel hungry?"

My charisma told me to lie. To lie my pants off so hard they caught on fire on the way down. I hated it, but I agreed. Admitting to wanting to eat your friends was a real mood killer.

"No, just the chains," I said. "Maybe it's only towards monsters and magical objects. Like, the chains smell like hot cinnamon rolls, and the centipedes smell like buttered lobster. It's very confusing."

"Thank Solara." Ae nodded, clearly relieved. "Tell no one about this. There are superstitions about creatures masquerading as humans, eating the sol of their prey. Any adventurer would kill you on the spot if they even suspected you to be something like that."

"Duly noted. Keep my mouth shut." Another question popped up. "Shouldn't I have gained more than one level? You said the chain was powerful."

"You can't fill the same cup twice if it hasn't been emptied," Ae said. "Some can chain leveling together, but the source would need to be overwhelming and constant. Not to mention the level of concentration and skill necessary to do it right. Such a thing is rarely available in a fight where even a second of distraction can be fatal."

"Is that what that feeling is? Emptying the meridian?" I felt my throat with my hand. I did feel much better after leveling.

"More like compressing," Ae said. She wiggled back and forth, enjoying her new freedom. “Eventually, you'll form a core and be able to store Sol without side effects."

"There was one other thing," I said. "It assigned my free point automatically."

Ae laughed. "That usually happens the first time. What did it go into?"

"Constitution."

"When you leveled up, were you feeling weak or had a strong desire to be more durable? When you level, you're supposed to focus on what stat you want, willing it to manifest as your center compresses."

"So, I can't pick afterward?"

"No, that wouldn't make sense," Ae said, making a face. "Your body has to build structures to accommodate your new growth."

"Shit. Alright." I looked at the chains still holding Ae, dreading what I knew I had to do. "Alright, let's get this over with. I'm sure you're ready to get down."

"You don't have to do this right now," Ae said. She had that patient priestess smile on. "I've waited this long, what's a little longer?"

"Let's get you down, and I can have my mental breakdown later," I said, trying not to show that my hands were shaking.

Ae nodded, lifting the chain and standing on her free leg.

I placed the chain in my mouth, savoring the moment of flavor. "**Feast**."

I bit down the chain as the spell activated. This time, I could feel the swirling in my throat open as the string of pain ran from the tip of my tongue back. I touched my tongue to the metal, trying to limit the flow to a stream, not a tsunami. The energy running along a distinct path and not tearing through everything like last time.

Ae strained against the chain, bracing against the wall and kicking out, the muscles on her leg bulging under tension. The priestess grunted as the chain stretched like a semi-truck was pulling it.

My throat swelled continuously, hindering my breath but still allowing its passage.

Ae groaned, pushing harder against the flexing chain. It just wasn't breaking. I knew I hadn't weakened it enough. Memories of suffocating to death were holding me back from opening the floodgates.

I needed to quit being a bitch and do it.

I swallowed the rest of the power, opening the channel to its maximum. It hit me like a train, boring into me and locking my body up. My teeth cracked as they clamped down, the chain snapping in my jaws.

Ae jerked forward, scattering the wood she was standing on and falling heavily on her remaining chain, her toes barely hanging an inch from the floor. She kicked out with both legs, enjoying her new range of motion, smiling as she swung on the chain.

It almost distracted me from the fact that I was choking to death.

Ae's face shifted as she picked up that something was wrong. Her eyes widened as I collapsed onto the floor. "Cast a spell, you idiot, dump your sol. It's swelling your meridian!"

Yeah, I had no idea how to do that.

"Push it anywhere," she said, picking up that I was clueless. "Your neck looks like it's going to pop."

I only had one channel I knew was open, and it was the one that got me into this mess. I imagined the reverse of what **Feast** was doing, trying to vent the pressure.

The pain traveled back up my throat and down my tongue. I would've screamed if I had been able to. Black flames erupted from my mouth, singeing my lips and filling the room with a purple glow.

Spell Learned: Wyvern's Breath!

The flames moved wildly, connected to my tongue like a firehose. If I thought my pathway hurt before, now it was beyond measure. I writhed on my back as the flames licked the ceiling.

"Too much! You'll destroy your pathways!" Ae yelled, tucking up her legs to get out of the way of the wandering jet of flames.

I squeezed my pathway, limiting the flow to a trickle, pulling the flame down to a few feet. It was nowhere near enough, my meridian still tight. Blackness encroached on my vision as I dumped the sol. It was like swallowing an ocean.

My hand grasped onto Ae's leg, seeking comfort as I suffocated to death.

You Died!

Solara's Mercy Activated!

Sent to respawn point...

I sat up in the pool, retching water, cradling my face in my hands.

"Holy shit. Holy shit," I mumbled. A familiar tightness in my throat tormented me as my deep breaths didn't satiate the feeling.

I clenched down on the pressure on my throat, focusing on a desire to get stronger. It took a lot more pressure than last time, but I felt the discomfort disappear within a few seconds.

Congratulations! Ascended to Level 2. +1 Cha, +1 Str

I sighed, and relief washed over me. It worked precisely like Ae said.

Ae called out. "Help, please, this hurts a lot."

I rolled into action. Ae was hanging upside down, her legs wrapped around the remaining chain on her wrist, her hair and skirt hanging loose downward, giving me a glimpse at some previously unseen golden armor. She flipped back around, landing heavily on her shoulder.

"It… That position took away some of the pressure," Ae stammered. Even in the dull light, I could see her face redden.

I pretended I hadn't noticed as her feet stretched for something to stand on. Her stump flexed as she instinctually tried to grab the chain with her missing arm.

"Just hang on." I winced at the accidental pun, but Ae didn't notice, her face scrunched in pain.

I grabbed bits of wood that didn't look like they were on the edge of dust, piling them under her feet.

"That's so much better." Ae rolled her shoulder. "The first few hours were fine, but it has long since lost its charm."

"What? Really? I assumed I was only gone for a few minutes," I said. "How long does it take me to respawn?

"Hours, days, it's hard to tell, really," Ae said, shrugging. "Sometimes it feels longer."

"Well, shit, I'm sorry." I looked up at the last chain. Panic seized my heart as it beat louder in my ears. I was not looking forward to dying again.

"Stone, help me with this last chain, and I swear I will do everything I can to help you," Ae said calmly, but her eyes were intense.

"Hey, I'm fine. You're the one chained to the wall, after all," I said, shrugging it off. "Ready to pull that other chain off?" I rested my hand on the hilt of my knife as I looked up at her, a dark idea jumping into my mind.

"I am prepared," Ae said, but as I looked up at the chain suspending Ae in the air, I realized there was a problem. I was two feet too short to reach her shackle, let alone the chain.

Ae watched me as I piled refuse beside her, trying to form a mound I could climb, not wanting to scale her like a ladder.

Ae's confusion faded when she put together what problem I was trying to solve.

The priestess laughed at me.

"It's not my fault you're so tall," I said defensively.

Ae laughed harder. "It's nice not being the shortest anymore," she said. The comment was confusing, but my nerves about the chain were starting to get to me.

I scaled the ramp, trying not to use the priestess as a handhold, but I did have to grab her arm to steady myself. "Almost there," I said.

Ae looked at me with a strange expression in her eyes. I opened my mouth to say something, but the feeling I was associating with my charisma screamed at me to shut up. *Fine, then, mysterious voice. Keep your secrets.*

My ramp wasn't tall enough, forcing me to improvise. I grabbed onto the chain, pulling myself up in an awkward pullup. "**Feast**," I prompted the spell to activate.

I bit the chain, taking in the sol in one big gulp. My jaw locked onto the chain as tension flooded my body.

Ae twisted and put her feet on the wall, pulling with everything she had. The chain snapped with a pop, sending us flying backward.

We hit the ground hard. Ae slid a few inches, but I tumbled, landing near the pool. I would've had the breath knocked out of me if it wasn't trapped. I scrambled for my knife even as I rolled to the edge.

"I'm free," Ae said, feeling her face. "I'm free! Stone, I—"

I plunged the knife into my chest, stopping my heart and letting my lifeblood spill into the pool. It was so much faster than suffocation, my vision going black in seconds.

It felt like someone grabbed my hand as I died.

You Died!

Solara's Mercy Activated!

Sent to respawn point...

NINE: GOLDEN ARMOR

I sat up in the pool, greeted by a now-familiar choking sensation.

Ae tackled me before I even got my eyes open. Water splashed everywhere as she wrapped her arm around me, burying her face into my neck. I couldn't help but feel her stump as she pressed it against me in the hug. A smattering of scars made it look like the limb was ripped off, not cut. I withheld a shudder as I wondered what could do that to someone her level.

I compressed the feeling in my throat, noting it was getting harder, taking a handful of seconds to squash the rolling power down. I focused on health and durability. My body felt a flash of heat for a second, and my center compressed.

Congratulations! Ascended to Level 3. +1 Cha, +1 Con

"Stone, you did it. I can't believe it," Ae said. "I owe you a debt I could never repay."

I registered the tantalizing scent of cinnamon rolls was gone. It must have been the chains, after all. Relief that I didn't want to eat my friend washed over me.

"You don't owe me anything. Let's get out of here and call it even," I said, scooting back. I didn't like being touched but didn't want to make the situation awkward.

Now that we were on even footing, it turned out Ae wasn't a whole lot bigger than me. While she was up on the wall, I thought she was a good foot or so taller, but now that we were sitting, I concluded she just had some long legs.

Suddenly, Ae looked up at me, her eyes wide with borderline panic. What did I do? My brain scrambled to figure out what went wrong. It seemed like we were having a nice moment of shared success, and now…

Oh.

My cheeks flushed as I **equipped** my clothes. Wet boots were a small price for dignity.

The ends of Ae's chains dragged behind her as she wrapped a flowing skirt around her ornate and frankly ridiculous armor. The golden metal couldn't have covered a single vital organ.

"Alright, I have to ask," I said, stepping on dry ground in my soggy boots. They squished as I walked.

"Stone, I swear I didn't realize. I'd been waiting for you to respawn and didn't consider that..." Ae trailed off, letting the implication hang in the air.

"Oh yeah, not that." I laughed. "It's the armor. Like, what is it blocking? It's so… small."

Ae covered her chest with her hands, blushing to the tips of her ears. She had her hair in a messy braid, leaving the long, pointed ears exposed. "Enchanted metal is expensive, so it makes sense to use less of it."

"What if I stabbed you here?" I poked her stomach with my finger. She slapped my hand. "Well, I mean, other than getting my ass kicked." I cradled my stinging fingers.

"The armor generates a field of sol." Ae pointed at the cracked gemstone on her cuirass. "Or at least it did. Now, it's useless."

"At least it looks nice," I said. Ae turned a deeper shade of red. "So, what now? We tear through the dungeon and make a run for it?"

"I believe you have some skills to work on," Ae said, pausing. "In the dungeon."

"Why do I get the sense you're kicking me out?" My charisma told me to shut up.

Ae's eyes flicked to the pool briefly before returning to me. "Because I am." She narrowed her eyes when I didn't immediately act. "It has been so long since I've been able to get this armor off, and I didn't know when you would respawn."

Grandma sometimes talked to me in riddles like this, too. She said I needed to read between the lines, whatever that meant.

"I've suddenly remembered I have a dungeon to run," I said, playing along.

"Good, work on those skills," Ae smiled, leading me toward the door. I turned to say something, but she placed a hand on my chest, pushing me through.

The glass-like substance slid over me with ease. Ae gave me a little wave before turning on her heel and walking towards the pool. I was glad she seemed like she was doing better.

Taking a couple of deep breaths, I steadied myself and cleared my mind. I had new tools, but I needed to have a strategy.

My stomach rumbled as I picked up the scent of fresh baked lobster in the air. Images of me laughing maniacally as I shot flames into a nest of centipedes crossed my mind, eliciting a grim smile.

I tore down the path, snatching one of the little shits out of the air. I wasn't sure if it was the new constitution or what, but its pincers were not able to sink into my skin this time.

I tried to draw sol out of the monster but barely got a fraction of a trickle. The centipede thrashed in response, tearing at my arm with renewed purpose.

My few seconds of action were gone, and in a heartbeat, its brethren were on me. They smelled so good. My mouth salivated as the scent of blood mixed with the scent of fresh food.

"**Feast**." My inhibitions cracked, and I bit the centipede, sol rushing down my throat as its leg writhed in my mouth. Pressure built in my meridian as it sucked down the small amount of sol. The centipede stilled as the last drops of the fiery substance ran down my throat. It curled into a ball as I discarded it.

"**Wyvern's Breath**," I mouthed. Luckily, I didn't have to say the spell to cast it, just making the intent seemed to count.

Dark flames erupted from my mouth as light filled the cavern, fully engulfing the centipede on my leg and setting it ablaze.

"Yall are fucked now!" I could tell by the wetness I felt that I was close to bleeding out, so I needed to do this quickly.

I picked up the sizzling centipede and bit into it, filling my center, and spitting flames all over the retreating centipedes. The acid ate holes in their carapaces as if they were covered in sticky flames. Sizzling filled the black soundscape of the otherwise quiet dungeon. I laughed maniacally, eating sol and breathing flames.

Silence. I stood over their corpses, bleeding out all the while. Wet stickiness ran down my arms and legs, telling me my time was short. Darkness encroached on my vision as I grinned, collapsing upon their remains.

You Died!

Solara's Mercy Activated!

Sent to respawn point...

I sat up in the pool, laughing as I spit up water. Memories of fresh lobster crossed my mind, and my stomach grumbled. I could feel a tightness in my throat meridian, but it didn't feel full like the other times. It was a bit uncomfortable, but for the power to cook centipedes to death, I'd take it. I tried to clamp down and get a level, but nothing happened except me looking like I was trying to shit my pants.

Ae sat with legs crossed at the side of the pool. She almost looked like a new person, her hair in an ornate braid that brazenly displayed her ears. Her armor even reflected the light with a new glimmer. She cracked open an eye, a twinge of a grin flicking across her features. "Successful run?"

"I'd say so. It could have gone better, but I took them all with me this time. Little bastards."

"I've been thinking," Ae said.

"A dangerous pastime," I said, unable to hold back the quip.

Ae snorted. "I can't decide if you're clever or annoying." She opened her eyes, and I felt a pressure build in the room. "But quit interrupting me, or you're going to find yourself respawning in the pool."

I laughed, not rising to the bait. I could tell she didn't mean it. Probably.

"We're about to put that willpower of yours to the test," Ae said. "I meant what I said when I said I would repay you. I spent a long time training in the temple as a battle maiden, and now I will train you."

"But I don't want to be a battle maiden," I said.

"Stone." Warning coated Ae's voice. "Don't make me regret

this."

"Yes, ma'am," I said. Ae was reminding me of my grandma more and more. She didn't like my jokes either.

"Now, if you're done saying nonsense, I need you to show me your stats. It's not that I don't trust you. I want to know what I'm working with."

"Gotcha. One stat screen coming up, boss."

Name: Stone McGracen

Race: Halfkin

Path: Hunger

Level: 3

Unlocked Meridians: Throat

Spells: Inspect, Feast, Wyvern's Breath

Blessings: Solara's Mercy, Solara's Hand

Stats:

Int: 7

Wis: 6

Cha: 12 (+3)

Str: 4 (+1)

Dex: 5

Con: 2.4 (+1.2)

Spirit: 11.2

"Well, at least we know where to start," Ae said. "Your strength and constitution are so low it's embarrassing. No wonder you're so weak."

"I take it all back. I should've left you on the wall," I said.

"Look at you, acting like you can even reach the chains," Ae said, pinching my cheek.

I smacked her hand away. "It's not my fault you're so freakishly tall." I put my hands on my hips, standing as tall as I could. Ae was a handful of inches taller than me and she used every single one to look down at me before laughing.

"By the goddess, you don't know, do you?" Ae laughed, almost doubling over.

"What?" I said. "What's so funny?"

"Stone, I'm not even five feet tall. I'm short for an elf," she said, wiping a tear. "I used to get made fun of all the time, people speculating my other half was gnome."

"Wait. So, if you're just five foot..." I trailed off, looking at how big the medium knife was on my hip. "Holy shit, I'm a fucking hobbit."

Ae politely covered a smile with her hand. "The mighty human brought down. There is some poetic irony there."

"Shit," I said under my breath before yelling it again. "Shit!"

Ae placed her hand on top of my arm. "Halfkin are known for being powerful Ascendants. Don't worry about it too much. There are many ways to measure a person other than height."

"I'm going to get fucking stomped to death," I complained.

Ae snorted. "That's probably not what's going to get you killed."

"Uh…"

"So, let's start with intelligence," Ae said, changing the subject.

"Why do I feel like this is a dig," I said.

"It's important to use the stats effectively." Ae conveniently ignored my comment. "When you level up, your subconscious thinks you're the same, and those extra points go to waste. You must train to keep yourself on the edge of your abilities."

The implications of what she said tumbled in my mind. "How the hell do I train something like constitution?"

"That one I'm saving for later. I'd watch the snarky comments if I were you." Ae smiled. "Now, I've got some theories on how to push intelligence. These are all exercises mages use to push against the edge of their limitations."

Ae stopped to make sure I was picking up what she was saying. I nodded.

"Intelligence is linked to spell casting.

Its meridian is located at the crown," Ae said, patting the top of her head. "It's memory. How fast you can think, how many things you can remember, and, most crucially, your defense against magic."

"Oh shit. So, I could get one shot by a fireball?"

Ae moved on as if she didn't hear me, proceeding to ask me some basic math questions. I thought I did pretty well. I was a lot of things in my old life, but bad at math wasn't one of them.

"I'm glad to see you at least have a basic education."

"Yeah, that's pretty standard where I come from."

"The dungeon's challenges have probably pushed you to the edge of your intelligence. So, we're going to skip it and train wisdom. You can blame your education for that one. Sit across from me."

I mimicked her cross-legged position on the ground. I could see a crack of a smile on her lips as she tried to maintain the stoic teacher persona she was currently going for. Ae was a person of many masks, slipping seamlessly from one personality archetype to the next. I wondered if I'd ever seen her true self.

"Wisdom is located in the third eye meridian on the center of your forehead. On the surface, wisdom and intelligence might seem similar, but in truth, they are opposites. Wisdom is all about rituals, intuition, and insight. If someone hits you with divine energy, a high wisdom score will be helpful."

"Sounds difficult to train."

"Less than you think." The elf smiled. "My mentor used to do this to me, and now I get the pleasure of doing it to you."

"Alright, I'm ready."

"Doubtful," Ae said. "Alright, I want you to close your eyes. Let your mind go blank. Listen to your instincts."

I let my mind wander, closing my eyes and attempting to let everything flow over me, but my subconscious must secretly have hated me because I had absolutely no warning when Ae slapped me in the face.

"What the fuck?" I put a hand to my stinging cheek.

"Again," Ae said, all business.

I closed my eyes, looking for anything out of the ordinary. I tensed up my face. Ready for it to come. That's when she kicked me right in the shin.

"Holy shit, Ae, that hurts."

"That's the point. You need to listen to your subconscious."

"I'm trying."

"That's the problem. Stop trying and listen."

"That makes no fucking sense," I complained.

"Stop thinking and concentrate."

"Have I wronged you in some meaningful—"

The elf interrupted my complaint by flicking me in the nose. "Focus, let go. Your mind is a river, drift in it."

"That's what I'm saying," I said, my eyes still closed. "It's not—"

I caught her hand. I opened my eyes in shock. I had snatched her hand out of the air mid-strike. Even she seemed a little annoyed.

"Stone, if you wanted to hold my hand…" Ae grinned, showing off her sharp canines.

I dropped her hand like a hot potato. "Ew, gross."

"Again," Ae said.

It took over five minutes for me to catch Ae's hand again.

My stomach growled as the hours dragged on. This was the longest I'd been alive in one go.

"I'm tired of beating you up. We should move on," Ae said. "Now let's try spirit. It is located here in the gate meridian." She pointed to just above her belly button. "It should be a good morale boost for you."

"I'm not sure my face will ever be the same," I said, feeling my swollen cheeks.

Ae laughed. "Spirit is like wisdom but internal, governing mana channels and growth rate," she instructed. "Now, deep breathing in and deep breathing out. You should feel something deep in your center as you let your mind wander. Like an energy ball. My center is in my stomach, but yours should be in your throat."

I scanned my throat, looking for what she was talking about. I scrunched my eyebrows in focus as I found a tiny pencil point speck of something. "I think I feel something. It's small."

Ae snorted.

"Shut up, you know what I meant."

"You're at level three, so that does make sense," Ae said. Now you're going to take that energy and spin it slowly, feeling the energy rotate throughout your body."

Absolutely nothing happened. I tried to make the speck spin, and all that was happening was that I was getting frustrated. The sensation was uncomfortable, like everything was gummed up.

"Are you sure it's a spinning motion? My center is different, so maybe it's something else."

"It's typically difficult initially, but it should be fairly intuitive. Most people even have a specific direction they like to spin." Ae made a clockwise motion on her stomach. "Try some different patterns. Maybe one of them will do."

I tried every shape I knew about, even doing star patterns. Nothing moved. My frustration grew with each mounting failure, but then I stopped trying to think about what I was attempting to do.

My intuition was trying to link a motion with swallowing, but I was unsure how to accomplish that. So, I turned the spinning sideways as if half the circle was going down my throat. Then, the circle exited, came back up to my face, and circled back around.

"Now that's interesting," Ae said.

"Can you see it?"

"Yeah, it's weird. It's like heat distorts the image in front of your face."

"Yeah, it wants to spin like this," I said, showing her the motion.

"Keep that cycle going," Ae said, "I'll need you to answer these basic math questions to test how you handle multitasking. And don't worry, we'll keep adding things until it becomes strenuous."

"What do you mean become strenuous?" I said, a little sweat collecting on my brow.

The math questions began to flow as I spun my center. The pain was unlike anything I'd experienced so far, like a soreness in my soul.

"It seems you're getting used to this. So, we're going to go further," Ae said. "Now we're going to add some memory conditions. You will nod your head whenever the answer is between zero and ten. You'll shake your head when the answer is ten and up. Now let's start."

"Ae, you're going to kill me."

"You can always ask me to stop." Ae smiled so sweetly that

it almost seemed like a genuine offer, but I knew if I turned this down, she would just come up with something worse. That, and I suspected she was mocking me. She was relentless.

Hours passed as the elf seemed no worse for wear, riddling out math problems and adding additional things for me to do.

"Let's take a break," Ae said after my stomach growled for a fourth time.

"So, what's next? Some sort of charisma training? That's the last of the mental stats, right?"

"Oh no, that one's a lost cause," Ae said, laughing. "Lying, convincing others to do things, and performing music or plays are all ways to push charisma to the max. You can try those on your own time." A predatory grin crept up her face. "Up next is dexterity. Are you familiar with juggling?"

These words would haunt me hours later.

It started with two small stones and some sarcastic clapping from Ae. The rocks were maybe the size of walnuts and barely had any weight to them. I did well whenever I had two, but I dropped it a lot whenever she instructed me to start doing three. It's like she could sense I was feeling accomplished, making me add more stones or change directions, doing things like standing on one leg or walking around. She did this without even opening her eyes, seeming to be able to sense what I was doing. I started to get a genuine appreciation of the powerhouse that was sitting across from me.

"Take away one of the smaller rocks and add one of the big ones," Ae instructed, pointing precisely at the rocks without opening her eyes.

"Wait, I'm not completely switching to the bigger stones?"

"So you can zone out and not have to pay attention?" Ae finished, her tone only slightly mocking.

The different-sized rocks messed with my muscle memory. My brain felt like it was on fire. I had to stop as I dropped them increasingly, my arms too sluggish to move on.

I plopped down next to the elf. "So, when are we going to try the dungeon?"

"Oh, *we* aren't doing anything. I'm not the one with Solara's Mercy. Not until you can almost completely run the dungeon by yourself am I going in there with you."

That made sense to me. It also confirmed Ae was at least level ten, if not much higher. "So, what's next?"

"Oh, my dear Stone," Ae said. "It's time to train constitution. You're going to learn how to fight."

Images of having the shit beat out of me ran through my head. I must've been easy to read because Ae laughed.

"Now go run the dungeon. I can't have you starving to death during our spar." The predatory smile on Ae's face made me think this wouldn't be a gentle experience.

TEN: THE DANCE

I sat up in the pool, the excitement of death becoming mundane.

"Excellent," Ae said, clapping her hands in a single crack. It was like a gong going off. "Do you have any formal training with fighting?"

"I did some wrestling in high school," I said. I left out that it was only two years, and I got my ass kicked the whole time.

"Show me."

I hesitated, my eyes flicking to Ae's missing arm for the briefest of seconds. By the look on her face, I knew I'd messed up.

Ae's eyes narrowed. For the first time, I saw anger flare behind the silver of her eyes. "You're going to pay for that in blood."

Ae was on me before I knew what was happening, striking me in parts of my body I didn't even know existed. A strike just below the rib cage on my side. A finger jab to the shoulder, making me lose all feeling in my hand. I lunged, trying to grab ahold of her. Maybe if I took her to the ground, I wouldn't embarrass myself completely.

Ae twirled out of the way, moving just enough that my fingertips barely grazed her side. She made it look easy. With a single step, she was within my guard, slipping a foot behind my ankle and sending me to the ground with a light tap on the chest.

The whole thing was mortifying.

I rolled with the fall, tucking my feet under me and lunging for Ae's legs. The attempt was valiant, a fruitless endeavor to save the remains of my pride that ended with her foot pressing my face into the ground.

"Why are you so damn fast?" I complained.

"To keep thieves from touching the merchandise." Ae let me up, offering a hand to pull me to my feet. "Did you learn something?"

"Yes," I said, taking the hand. Ae practically jerked my arm off, my boots leaving contact with the ground. "A couple of things."

Ae did the head tilt, ruining her tough fighter persona. "Tell me."

"Well." I paused, putting my thoughts together. "I have no idea how to fight, appearances are deceiving, and I should strike first and think later."

"Good enough," Ae shrugged. "There are many paths to competence. Take whichever one gets you there fastest." Ae squared up, her demeanor taking on an edge. "Again."

To my credit, I didn't hesitate.

The demonstration continued. It was brutal. My face got familiar with the ground as she showed off how little she had to try. Sweat poured down my face as the bored priestess barely paid attention. It felt like we trained for days but it could've been an hour or minutes. With no clock or sun, my sense of time warped.

"Okay, you can stop now," Ae told me mid-lunge.

I came to a stop just inches from grabbing her. "Oh, come on, I was so close."

"It's great that you think that." Ae smiled. "That little demonstration told me everything I needed to know. You're slow, clumsy, and not using your size to your advantage. You did try to corner me, and your footwork was pretty decent, but you fought like you were double your size, no offense. You appeared to know enough to know what I was doing but not enough to stop me."

The walls I had built around my ego crumbled. "Damn. That bad, huh?"

"Yes," Ae said. "Now, let's practice some striking. Legs wide, drop your center of gravity slightly. This stance is your new home."

I dropped down into the stance, mirroring Ae. A piece of me was excited, and another piece of me knew I was in for a rough time. The premonition of bruises I hadn't earned yet ached.

In contrast, Ae looked happy. It was almost like the walls around us had faded, and she was somewhere else. I felt this was taking her back to a different time. My grandpa looked this way when he talked about his friends in the war or the adventures of his youth.

"Now, breathe out, extending one arm out slowly towards me as if you're going to punch me in the mouth," Ae instructed. "Copy what I do."

I extended my arm slowly. Painfully slow as Ae brushed my hand to the side with the back of her hand. It was obviously a well-practiced movement. The remains of her right arm moved. Her body coiled as if throwing a punch with the ghost limb. I followed along with the intent, mimicking deflecting the invisible blow, but Ae froze. Had I done something wrong? Her gaze flicked to her missing arm, her bubbly aura falling apart.

"I forget sometimes," Ae said quietly, dropping the fighting stance. "This may not work."

"Ae, you literally just kicked my ass into next week. I think we can make it work," I said. "We're both overcoming some physical challenges here. Hell, I'm half the size of the body I'm used to. So what if you're missing one of four limbs? I'm confident you can turn it into an advantage."

Ae nodded, taking a deep breath. The mask of a fighter slipped back into place. "Okay, now push my fist to the side and throw a punch. You will be alternating arms. Follow my intent, not my actions."

"Yes, ma'am," I said, dropping back into the stance.

A dance began as we circled each other. I loved every second of it. Ae did everything with one hand, but her aura carried weight. No movement was lost. It dawned on me just how much she was taking it easy on me. A dance of light touch, push and pull. A feeling that had been barren to me in this new life bloomed in my chest.

Joy.

The dance sped up, my body getting used to the motion, but as I watched her, I felt like a flimsy mockery of something beautiful, like a crayon drawing of a famous painting.

Ae talked to me as we moved. "The punch does not come from the arms. It should originate from your legs and spring up into your core. Your core should twist and fling your arm out. If anything, your arm should be a participant, the energy coiling from the ground."

I tried doing what Ae told me. It felt weird, like I was bouncing slightly before I threw a punch. How was this so hard when she made it look so easy?

"And… now you're telegraphing your movements," Ae said, mimicking my motion. "Your feet are telling everyone what you're about to do. Your attack should be sudden and without warning. Solid and smooth. The perfect strike is a mixture of contradictions. This is why control is the deciding factor in a fight. Controlling where you are looking.

Controlling what you're telling your opponent. Lie to them with your body and make them strike where you are not. Your goal is to look not where you're going to hit but where you want them to think you're going to hit."

Ae's eyes flicked to my midsection, and she launched a punch. My hands swept to my stomach, but her fist stopped a hair from my nose.

"This sounds complicated," I said, ignoring the beads of sweat springing from my forehead.

"This is barely the beginning. Now add magic and different combat styles, throw in a weapon or two and more opponents, and you'll begin to understand why the master trains for a lifetime."

"So, what's the point of me learning this if I'm so outclassed?" I asked.

"Because the weak are prey to the strong," Ae said. "You offered me freedom, and now I do the same in return. The only way out from under the sword is to wield it."

Ae launched back into the dance. Sometimes, she shifted her body instead of deflecting a blow, moving just enough to get out of the way. I mimicked her at every turn, moving around the pool. We locked eyes as we moved.

Despite my attention locked on Ae, I never saw the leg kick that took me to the ground.

"You should probably block that next time," Ae laughed as she pulled me up by my collar. "You are maybe halfway to throwing a punch that wouldn't make me go into exile in shame. Punch the wall until you die from exhaustion or are too broken to move on. I need to recover my energy."

"I forgot you can't just die and come back recovered," I said. "How are you surviving without food, anyway?"

"I'm ascended," Ae said, using the word like it should mean something to me.

"And that means what, exactly?"

"My body feeds on my core." Ae pointed to the center of her stomach just above the ribcage. "I could survive for multiple mortal lifetimes without food or water."

"Damn, that's horrifying and awesome at the same time."

"Everything has tradeoffs," Ae explained. "All choices come with consequences."

I felt there was a subtext I was missing, but I decided to move on. "So when will we train magic?"

Ae raised a brow. "Do you have some sol you've been hoarding?"

I immediately felt dumb for asking. "Yeah, I guess that's right. I thought we could do something to help me with the magic part."

"We are," Ae said. "Spells are a part of you, just like your heart or your arm. Meditation, physical training, and cycling your core are the foundation of any developing magic user."

Ae returned to meditating, and I got the air that any further interruptions would be met with violence, so I squared up against a well-lit portion of the wall. I let out a deep breath, bracing for how bad this was going to suck.

"Make sure you squeeze your fist just before you strike, but otherwise, keep everything loose," Ae called.

I knew for a fact she hadn't opened her eyes.

I fell into the stance she showed me earlier, throwing a slow punch, tapping my first two knuckles against the wall, gauging the distance. I felt the energy coming from my legs as I lightly struck the wall, letting the impact flow through my body.

As I slowly built up momentum, the bite of the wall stung my knuckles. The shock ran down through my arms and shook me deep into my shoulders. It felt so much different to hit something than to punch into the air.

I ended up diving into the dungeon with broken knuckles. An experience that taught me to practice kicking with more vigor.

We locked into a routine as days passed. Well, as deaths passed. I counted waking up in the pool my morning and dying in the dungeon my nightfall. We cycled through the exercises, juggling, punching the wall, and meditating. My muscles responded faster, calluses formed on my fists, and my reaction time doubled, at least. It was equal parts pure bliss and utter hell, but to my credit, I did not once ask to stop. We kept up this cycle, training furiously. Every time I felt an ounce of confidence, Ae would snuff it out.

Frankly, the training helped me understand what she meant

about not using my stats to their full potential. I hadn't gained an ounce of sol but felt like a whole new man—or halfkin, as it were. My respect for Ae bloomed into total awe. She was a weapon and nigh untouchable.

I was upset when it ended.

"This will have to do," Ae said, sighing and stopping me. "We are reaching a roadblock, and I can sense we have reached the limit of what you can learn. I think you're ready for a real shot at the dungeon."

"Do you really think I can do it?" I said, glancing at the dungeon entrance.

"Life very often gives us no choice," Ae said.

"When this is over, we should take some time to hang out like normal people," I said. "It would be fun to have a drink or something." I waved around me. "This shit sucks."

Ae looked sad. "I would love nothing more."

"Not to get all soft on you," I said, leaning against the wall next to Ae. "I don't want to lose this when we walk out. Us being friends, I mean."

"I think it's best you try the dungeon now," Ae said in a strained voice. Had I said something wrong?

I made my way towards the dungeon portal. Did Ae have problems up on the surface? Despite all the time we had spent together, I knew so little about the elf.

I walked through the portal standing tall. I felt stronger and leaner, faster. I could even see a little bit better in the darkness of the dungeon, everything looking more like a dull gray than a pitch black.

For the first time, I saw the centipedes coming. Were they always this slow? I snatched the lead one out of the air, biting it as it futilely scratched at my face.

Fire filled my throat, my deep breathing bordering on a wheeze. Purple light bathed the corridor as flames leaped out. My stomach growled as the scent of steamed lobster filled my nose. Blood ran from the scratches on my face as the centipedes tried to kill me.

Chitin cracked as I punched a centipede off my leg, stomping it with the heel of my boot. I scooped it up, inhaling the light as it left the little shit's body. For the first time, I was in control of the fight and not on the edge of exhaustion.

I laughed maniacally. The rest of the dungeon awaited.

ELEVEN: SHRIMP SCAMPI

My evil laugh was rudely interrupted by a cockroach the size of a bulldog barreling into me.

Its pincers opened a gash in my leg as it rutted in the soft flesh. It happened so fast, the pain barely having time to register.

"You little shit!" I wasted no time biting its antenna and sucking out enough sol to close my throat completely.

I held on with both hands at the cockroach rodeo as I acid-broiled the vile insect until it curled into a ball. It was a disgusting creature with sharp edges all over its dumb body. I hated that it smelled like a surf and turf dinner with a side of shrimp scampi. Its deliciousness only fueled my contempt.

"**Inspect**," I croaked out, holding my leg as blood dripped through my fingers.

Caveroach (Lvl 6): Caveroaches are part of the arthropod family. They are hardy, well-built creatures with a weakness to fire. The worst part about them is when you realize they can fly.

"They can *what*?" My pants were soaked in blood as I put pressure on the wound. "Goddam it, I'm supposed to be a fucking wizard," I said, trying to will myself to heal, but no matter how much I tried to send the scraps of sol I had hung onto into the wound, nothing happened.

I had an idea for how to close the wound, but I hated it. It was a terrible idea, but bad ideas are often better than no idea.

I dumped my last bit of sol into **Wyvern's Breath**, my wounds sizzling as the acidic flames melted my pant leg away. My flesh melted into a funky cherry red as the bleeding slowed. The cave smelled like pork as the wound sealed up, hurting like crazy the whole time.

"God damn it, now I know what people smell like." The weight of this cursed knowledge rested on me with a physical weight.

I limped up the thinning path as it climbed to a distant light source. The light ebbed and flowed with a living movement, smoke clinging to the cavernous ceiling. I stopped, a little voice in the back of my head letting me know something was wrong.

A thin, deep buzz was all the warning I got as a weight slammed into my forehead. For once, my wrestling experience came to my rescue as I pinned the cockroach trying to gnaw on my face. It hissed as my teeth cracked its chitin, sol flowing even faster than last time, like dumping water into a bucket. I spit the fire into its face, at least, what

I assumed was its face. I dragged my knife across its soft underbelly as my flames petered out.

The feeling of fullness didn't recede as the sol emptied, letting me know it was finally time to level up. After the chains, I had thought the levels would come quickly. Oh, how wrong I was. Ae laughed at me when I asked about it. Leveling was a slow thing, and my unique situation of having to drink sol instead of being near it wasn't helping.

I dropped into a lotus position, trusting my senses to warn me of an impending attack. Ae warned me that leveling up got more challenging with each level. One's determination was often more limiting than sol exposure. High level was often more of a testament of will than fighting prowess.

I circled my spirit, moving my center into a spiral, tightening down like a screw, each rotation packing the sol a little more condensed. Ae said squeezing only worked the first level or two, if at all.

I focused on willing myself to be faster. Ae's training had revealed that strength, for me, was borderline useless. I needed speed to avoid hits and get close. My short arms gave me no advantage, and a little strength wouldn't fix that. Ae was so blindingly fast. I was jealous of a lot about the elf, but that speed was what I coveted.

Sweat sprung on my brow. My teeth clenched as I pushed the scraps of sol down. I felt something in my throat pop. Relief washed over me as my center compressed down to a pinpoint.

Congratulations! Ascended to Level 4. +1 Cha, +1 Dex

"Thank Solara." I felt slightly more limber, but that was probably confirmation bias.

Moving through basic strikes, I worked the cracks out of my new stats, my body feeling off balance as I pushed myself. I could feel my brain stretching to understand the new speed. It struck me just how unnatural it all felt. The last thing I needed was to trip over myself in a fight. Ae had drilled into me that control, not strength or speed, often decided a fight. I owed the elf a debt of gratitude.

I poked my head to the new cavern. It was huge. How big, I wasn't sure with billowing smoke obscuring the ceiling. Lit candles were scattered around haphazardly, and rolling smoke sprouted from the center of the room. A scent of rotten pumpkin spice clung to the room like slime. It was like a cursed coffee shop.

I skirted around the edges of the cave, stepping over debris like what was in the resurrection chamber below. Nails littered the floor, the wood they held together long ago turning into dust.

I didn't know if I was alone, but if I was, I wanted it to stay that way. This was the furthest I'd gotten into the dungeon, and I didn't want to stop now.

The toe of my boot caught on a bent nail. The sharp end of the nail dragged across the floor, leaving a white line, eliciting a sound that make my teeth hurt. I waved my hand like I was waving off a fly, hoping the noise would break into silence.

The dungeon reacted immediately to my cardinal sin of

making noise. Snarls and growls emanated from the source of the smoke in the middle of the room. A lone figure emerged from the smoking candles.

It was short, so around my height, apparently, humanoid with an insectoid lower half like a freaky centaur. Its crackled green-gray skin wept blood down its naked upper body as it babbled in a foreign tongue, foam dripping from the corners of its mouth. Its only accessories were a suitcase and broken steampunk goggles. It would've been cool if it wasn't so stupid-looking. I didn't know what to make of it. All of this was a large leap from the 'what if bugs were big' theme of the dungeon so far.

But that's not what really stood out to me. What stood out to me was the fucking gun it was holding.

"**Inspect**!" I yelled, diving for cover behind a stalagmite.

Mantagnome (Lvl 7): A dungeonborn homunculus of a praying mantis and a gnome. It might not be as smart as its gnome ancestors, but it's twice as mean!

"That description is useless!" I yelled, breaking into a full sprint.

A blue glow radiated from the base of a potato launcher-style weapon. A low hum built up as something came to a head.

With a yell, the mantagnome fired, throwing its whole body backward. The blue projectile moved slowly enough that I could duck out of the way before it splashed against the cave wall, sending bits of sticky fire onto my leg, searing skin and clothes alike.

The mantagnome tried to reload the gun, pulling something out of its suitcase as I swatted out the flames on my shirt. Letting it reload that gun would be a problem, and I knew it. Death by napalm was a bad way to go, too. I'd rather die by blood loss, so I rushed it, moving across the cave like a child running down an ice cream truck.

It tried to scamper away into the smoke but failed as I grabbed it and pulled it to the ground. It smelled like a vaguely Italian seafood dish. The barrel of the gun sizzled against skin as it landed on top of the mantagnome. The thing was pitiful and mindless, screaming as I bit its arm, drinking in a rush of sol. I vomited flames immediately, sending the monster into a fit of pure panic.

I think it was surprised as me when it landed a blow that sent me flying back. I landed halfway to the wall, rolling over before stopping. Blue energy crackled around the mantagnome as it popped a blue vial into its mouth. Muscles bulged, and skin tightened to the point of almost tearing as its screech turned into a roar.

"Fuck me," I yelled, swiping away its outstretched hand with my knife, drawing a line of blue blood. It circled, ready to charge again as I rolled to my feet.

Ae's training saved me. I didn't even think about it. I felt the move coming from a mile away, rolling to the side as it hit the wall so hard it got stuck in the crevasse it created. If I had gotten hit by that, I would have been a toothpaste splatter on the wall.

I jumped on its back, using my knife to slit its throat. It gagged on the pooling blood as I drank in the golden light before it could disappear.

My meridian immediately swelled like a baseball, leaving me spouting flames like a sideshow act at a circus. My channels burned as I pushed the flames out, licking the ceiling with the purple light. Darkness crept into my vision before I was able to get a painful breath.

"My greed is going to be the death of me," I croaked before venting the rest of the sol onto the floor.

I pulled the now-cool gun onto my lap as I leaned against the wall to take a breather.

I went over the gun's construction, trying to figure out how it worked, but it looked like it was held together with a combination of silly putty and toothpicks. The fact that it even successfully fired at me was an absolute miracle.

"Inspect." Nothing.

"Inspect!" I said again, but nothing happened. "The fuck is this thing?" I muttered, putting the gun back on the ground.

I quickly looked around to see if there were any chests or any rewards. I mean, this was a dungeon, so you know, don't fault me for looking, but alas, nothing. I had a growing suspicion that the gun was the reward.

"I feel like a fucking idiot bringing a knife to an actual gunfight," I said. "I'm lucky that he was so bad at it. All it's going to take is one person with a functioning brain to just completely nuke me. If that bullet had hit me right on, it would've sent me right back to respawn."

The smoke had calmed down while I sat back and relaxed. Adrenaline crash was a real thing, and I almost felt giddy coming down from that last fight. I understood why people got addicted to almost dying. It took a while to shake the limp out of my leg as I explored the cave, finding it covered in slimy moss, trash, and droppings. Disgusting.

A narrow corridor led up from the far end of the cavern. A couple of centipedes thought they could get the drop on me, but they didn't bring near enough to do more than minor damage to me. Their sol satiated some of the growing thirst that was coming for me. My center felt close to leveling up. Leading me to think that mantagnome took something loaded with sol.

Blue light bathed the end of the ascending ramp, bringing me out of my head. I peered around the corner to see a massive cave littered with tree-sized mushrooms that glowed underneath their caps. The blue iridescence of the room gave it an ethereal quality.

I couldn't see it, but a scent of Italian seafood hung in the air, returning my mind to the mantagnome I fought. I knew one was up here, so where was it? I looked for it in the mushroom forest but couldn't see anything, which was way worse. Knowing an enemy was out there but not knowing where? Didn't like that.

I moved through the mushroom forest methodically with an eye over my shoulder. Little creatures like frogs and small rodents scattered as I ducked behind the enormous stalks. Just where was this guy? I could smell him clear as day in this room.

I leaned back against a stalk. My heart beat so hard it was all I could hear. Why was this getting to me so badly? I hated this feeling of being stalked.

The cavern was huge but well-lit. I could see two obvious exits from where I was. A massive pair of iron doors sat opposite of where I came from, a hardened path leading to it. Too obvious. I definitely wouldn't be taking that path if I had a choice.

Luckily, I did. Through the thick mushroom stalks, I could see a round wooden door against the cavern wall. It wasn't far from where I was. I moved from my cover, and a noise pierced the silence.

Pain bloomed in my leg.

An arrow sprouted from the back of my calf, sending me falling forward into a stalk. Now, I didn't weigh much, and it was awfully dramatic of the mushroom to bend as much as it did, its cap almost touching the ground.

Spores exploded from the surrounding mushrooms with enough force to knock me onto my stomach. The situation was getting out of control fast, and I needed to isolate my attacker or get to cover ASAP.

I sprinted towards the round door, resisting the urge to flinch every time I flexed the calf the arrow was in. I felt a tickle in the back of my mind as I threw myself to the side, an arrow barreling through the space I had just occupied.

It was enough. I whipped my head around to see a figure

near the ceiling above the small door, standing on the wall like a spider. The figure was a mantagnome like the last one, but he wore a plague doctor-style mask with a heavy filter on the side. He loaded another bolt into the crossbow as I scrambled for cover.

I made a beeline for the round door. Another bolt shot at me, but it glanced off my arm as I rolled to the side, drawing a long line of blood but not finding purchase. Everything grew hazy as I brushed the spores out of my face. I felt the telltale tingle in my throat like I was drinking sol, and my vision cleared up a bit.

I slammed into the round door, abandoning stealth entirely. Flames leaped against its dark wood as I vented the mystery sol I was collecting, grasping for the handle in the middle of the door. I opened the door enough to slip in, falling against the wall as I closed it behind me.

My eyes adjusted to candlelight. Massive figures lorded over me. I choked on a panicked yell but managed to keep it down as I realized they were statues of men and women encircling a sandy pit. My stomach turned over. Each one had been beheaded.

Glass shattered. I limped behind a statue, seeing a figure in the middle of the pit. It was a man-sized praying mantis, and it had blue liquid dripping from its mandibles. A high-pitched squeal turned into a roar as it tripled in size, muscles bulging under hard green armor, scythe-like blades where hands should've been.

Light glinted off of a large key hanging from an outstretched hand of a statue, distracting me from the mantis charging me.

I considered hiding but decided against it since I was bleeding heavily and dizzy from the spoors. I'd rather die on my feet than sniveling like a rat. My knife reflected the candlelight as I drew it, standing against the towering monster.

"Come and get it, bitch." I leaped toward the monster, stabbing my knife deep into its thorax. Maybe I had more of a shot than I thought.

The whole world turned upside-down as my head separated from my body.

You Died!

Solara's Mercy Activated!

Sent to respawn point...

Twelve: Threads of Wool

I woke up in the respawn pool.

All things considered, beheading was one of the better deaths I'd experienced so far. It was almost refreshing.

I let out a sigh of relief. I could tell by the pressure in my center that I was close to leveling up.

Ae sat by the side of the pool, swishing her feet in the water. "How far did you make it?"

"A lot further than last time," I said, launching into the story. Ae laughed and gasped politely at the right parts, and I only embellished a few details here and there. The dive had been harrowing, but I could barely wait to try again. If it weren't for the elf smiling at me as I told my story, I would already have been back in.

"That's quite the umm… tale, you're telling me." Ae did that thing where she tilted her head to the side. "Did you know you look up and to the left when you're about to lie? You should probably work on that."

"I was just trying to work on my charisma," I shot her a smile.

Ae gave me a deadpan look.

"Fine, most of it was true. Even the part about the guns. What's up with that anyway?"

Ae shrugged. "Dungeons make bastardizations of real things, a mimicry of things above. The dungeon pulls inspiration from all over the place. There are theories that all the dungeons are linked and talk to each other, and if you die in the dungeon, it gets your memories."

"I better not die in the dungeon. My world had some freaky weapons."

"Stone, you literally just died."

"Oh, you mean like at all? Not like a forever death?"

"Stone, who do you think is remaking you?"

"The Goddess?"

"Psh. The Goddess doesn't concern herself with us. It has been so long since she appeared, she's practically a myth."

"I'm more worried about the guns this dungeon is about to be making."

"Guns are for pathless vagabonds," Ae said, waving her hand dismissively. "They are only effective against the lower levels anyway. After that, it takes an ascended weapon to take us down."

"Yeah, well, I'm one of those lower levels, so I'm feeling pretty threatened," I said. I made finger guns, eliciting an eye roll from the elf.

"Give it time. Eventually, you'll just be threatened by worse things."

"Speaking of that, you were right about leveling up getting harder," I said. "I took in a large amount of sol and might be up for the leap to level five."

Ae pulled her legs out of the pool and assumed the lotus position. "Why don't you sit across from me while you try? I'm curious to see how your center is coming along."

"Aren't we in something of a rush?" I said, glancing back at the dungeon entrance. My curiosity was getting the best of me. I'd spent so long thinking about what was out there, and I was so close to seeing it.

"Stone, sit across from me and stop being difficult. It's simply an observation ritual."

"I get the feeling I never really had a choice." I shot Ae my best grin.

Ae motioned to the empty space across from her.

I enjoyed teasing the elf, but our conversation before my dive buzzed in the back of my head, holding me back from going much further.

I sat down across from Ae.

"Closer," Ae said. I scooted forward, but she waved me on

until our knees touched. She closed her eyes and held her hand out for me to grab. I hesitated for a second. I really didn't want to offend her by refusing. I steeled myself, grabbing her hand. We were friends, it was okay.

"Now, level up like normal. If you feel anything out of the ordinary, it's me monitoring your progress."

"Sounds good to me." I did my best to keep the strain out of my voice. The physical contact was all I could think about. I hated it. I felt so uncomfortable.

An icy chill ran up my arm. I jerked back, but Ae held firm.

"Relax, Stone," Ae said. "I'm checking your channels. Any pain is from a lack of use."

I was trying, but forcing yourself to calm down is an exercise in futility.

"You're trying too hard. Just let it go," Ae said, squeezing my hand. "Just let it happen."

Just let it happen, I repeated to myself. Was I trying too hard to control everything? Did I really just need to let go?

So, I let go, falling back to my center and starting a corkscrew spin. Ice water ran up the veins of my arm. No, it wasn't my veins. It was my mana channel.

"That's better. You have good channels, but a lot of impurities are clogging everything up. This should help clear some of that out."

I focused on my free point. I needed more speed. I was

getting real sick of being caught and injured. Pumping constitution was a losing battle with my race modifier. My only real choice was not to get hit.

The ice reached my chest, putting a chill into my breath. My body felt like it had been plunged into a freezing river. My center spun in a descending spiral, pulling in some of that cold, letting it twist with my sol. The ice didn't feel so bad because I knew it was Ae's presence. If anything it was calming, something I wanted to mimic, folding it into my center. My breaths came deep and strained as I concentrated.

Ae squeaked, squeezing my hand harder as I clamped down on my center, compressing it into something the size of the tip of a needle. Ae gripped my hand so hard it hurt, the icy feeling twisting into my center flared with power as my new level snapped into place. A feeling of relief washed over me.

Congratulations! Ascended to Level 5. +1 Cha, +1 Dex

"Awesome," I said. I expected the icy feeling to fade, but it stayed rooted. Ae's face furrowed in concern. I opened my mouth to say something, but something snapped into place.

Core connection formed. Bond accepted by both parties.

Ae jumped as if she sat on a tack. Different emotions flashed in the back of my head, an echo of embarrassment, a flash of confusion. I wasn't embarrassed. Was I? I looked down, thinking about the new spell, and something like a piece of golden wool stretched between me and Ae when I focused on it.

Ae was doing that head tilt thing, looking at me in a way I couldn't discern. She was so funny. She tried so hard to be harsh and distant, but I saw who she was under the cracks.

Ae backing away, covering her mouth with her hand. The feeling of embarrassment abruptly cut off in the back of my mind. What was that about?

I looked Ae in the eyes, and I knew.

I had felt her emotions, and she felt mine.

"What did you do?" I said, jumping up. "You didn't say this would happen."

"What did I do?" Ae yelled back. "What did you do? This isn't normal."

I wasn't sure if she was going to shut down, cry, or kick my ass, so I tried to be ready for all three. She was my friend. We would work this out.

"How dare you," Ae yelled, balling her fists. Option three it was. "I have tried so hard to keep my distance, and you latch onto me like a puppy."

I rolled out of the way of a punch. "I'm allowed to like you," I yelled back. "Is it a crime to be someone's friend?"

"Stop feeling bad for me," Ae yelled, sweeping my legs and pinning my face to the floor with her knee. She jumped up immediately. "How dare you like that!" Her voice rose in pitch.

"Get out of my head!" I yelled back.

"Stop letting me in!" Ae looked frantic, lost at what to do.

I slammed a mental shield around my mind, imagining a bubble keeping everything in.

"Thank Solara," Ae said, slumping to the floor. I started to move towards her. "No, stay back. In the dungeon now."

"Ae, I can—"

"You idiot, I'm going to die!" Ae yelled, slamming a fist into the wall. A crack spread across the swirling inscription. Her voice dropped low. "I will make you hate me if I have to. Get. Out. Now."

"Fine," I said, stepping through the dungeon portal. I slumped against the wall once I was out of sight of the dungeon entrance.

"Fuck," I said. I looked at the connection spell, noting that it still headed back towards Ae through the wall. I could feel the cold dam she was using to block her emotions from me. I wished she would let me in. I didn't know what was going on with her half the time. Did she hate me? Shit, that would suck, feeling someone's dislike for you in real-time. I'm sure there was a way to sever the connection. I'd have to look into that. Besides, what did she mean she was going to die, and why did the way I feel about her matter so much? The logic was confusing. My charisma stepped in, telling me not to think about it too hard.

Besides, right now, there was a dungeon to run.

I mulched through the centipedes like a lawn mower running over a rattlesnake. I was frustrated, irritated, and, most of all, pissed. I legitimately had no idea what had just happened or what I did wrong. Since when was caring about someone bad? I wished Grandma was here to explain.

I used **Wyvern's Breath** to burn a wing off of a caveroach, sending it spiraling to the cave floor. Why should I have to police the emotions in my own head anyway? I bit into the caveroach's leg, drinking its sol before searing it with acidic fire.

The caveroach sizzled in a still mess as I clutched my head. I was going to get myself killed. Why was what Ae said getting to me so bad?

It was because I respected her and wanted to have her back in a fight. I needed her to understand. I didn't want anything but her company. I struggled to make close friends and it hurt to think only one of us thought we were friends.

I let out a deep breath, my boiling emotions slipping away. I put one foot in front of the other, making my way to the smokey room with candles all over the place.

I poked my head up over the ledge into the room with the candles. Just because things seemed like they were staying consistent didn't mean I was going to assume. It would just take one wrong assumption to completely fuck me over. If I was managing a dungeon, that was precisely what I would do—wait for someone to get complacent and then make changes.

Everything seemed like it was in the right place. The candles didn't even look like they had moved. It was suspicious.

I thought about all the strategies I could use to close the distance to the mantagnome, but my best chance was to get the drop immediately. I wanted that gun. I didn't want the mantagnome firing at me. The weapon would be useless to me if it wasted ammo.

"Fuck it," I muttered. I was in a daring mood.

I took off across the room in a full sprint, digging into the ground with the soles of my boots, dropping any pretense of stealth.

I made contact with the mantagnome with my forehead, unable to see it through the thick smoke. The sudden impact made me see stars. I think the smoke was supposed to have some effect on me because I could feel sol being pulled in when I breathed.

Biting anything I could get a hold of, the mantagnome scratched at me as we tumbled, opening up a wound in my arm. I was able to spit **Wyvern's Breath** right back in its face, causing it to give out a gasping scream. It scrambled, trying to bring up its weapon, but luckily, I knocked the gun from its hands as I took it to the ground.

It was over quickly. I saw the flash of sol within the thick smoke as my enemy died. Drenched in blood, I scooped up the suitcase and the gun, rolling out of the smoke and gasping for fresh air.

I slumped against the wall, laying the gun across my lap. The smoke made me dizzy, like I'd been holding my breath for the last minute. I couldn't seem to stop coughing.

I opened the suitcase first since I'd seen the gun before. The suitcase had one broken latch and one functioning one, which I snapped open to reveal a cavity with three foam spaces. Each space held a cloudy glass vial filled with a blue viscous liquid sealed in by a cork. I swirled the vial, noting that the substance flowed like honey or molasses. The vial's diameter exactly matched the gun's bore, meaning this had to be the ammo.

The gun was basically a potato launcher for potions.

I checked to see if there was gunpowder or some type of explosive in the case, lifting the foam and feeling for hidden compartments. The gun was muzzle-loaded, so I assumed I would pack something in first, but there was nothing else. The truth was I still had no idea how the gun fired and had to sum it up as magical nonsense, hand-waving it away.

I took one of the vials and gingerly loaded it into the gun. I wasn't sure if it was supposed to go cork down or cork up, so I went cork down since that made the most sense to me. None of this was aerodynamic or made any particular amount of sense, so I could've been entirely wrong.

The gun had a strap, which I slung across my back, heading deeper into the dungeon. I handled the centipedes in this corridor, careful to keep the fighting away from the fragile weapon. The last thing I wanted to do was accidentally blow myself up.

I marched into the mushroom forest, standing brazenly out in the open. I held the launcher at the ready, scanning around, trying to figure out where that archer was. I remembered him being above the round door, off to the side, but no one was there. I kept an eye on it.

Scanning around, I saw the glint of the bolt's tip as it shot towards me.

Rolling to the side, I squeezed the trigger, which was more like a lever, letting the gun load up. After 20 painful seconds and another dodged bolt, the blue projectile launched into the air with a nasty kick. The potion arced, landing before the archer, splashing blue flames all over, catching the archer and the surrounding mushrooms on fire.

I slipped back into the previous room as the mushrooms spouted their spores. The blue specks hung in the air as they slowly filtered down like toxic snow. It took them almost ten to fifteen minutes to finally settle. Launcher at the ready, I walked gingerly across the cavern, trying not to stir the spores back up.

I charged the gun before entering the room with the headless statues. I watched the launcher with growing tension as the charge slowly built. After it hit halfway, I turned the door handle, bursting into the room and taking aim.

Pop! The blue projectile slammed into the praying mantis before it could drink the glass potion in its claw. I could hear the popping and snapping of fat and skin burning as the blue flame did their job. I crouched down, popping the last vial into the launcher, waiting to see if any other creatures wanted to make a guest appearance.

Thirteen: Sunrot

I moved around the smoking remains of the mantis, snatching the ring of keys from the back of the room.

I couldn't tell if the key ring was comically large or if I was just that small. It was nearly twice the size of my outstretched hand, a large golden skeleton key type thing. I threaded my belt through the open part of the key, letting it hang from my side. The last thing I needed was to have my hands tied up or to lose a critical item.

I made sure all my gear was in order, tossing the suitcase since it was useless now. I poked my head through the round door, looking back into the mushroom forest and searching for motion in the blue snow. When there was none other than the scurrying of small animals, I crept towards the large door.

It took me much longer to reach the door than I thought. A hard path opened itself up, cutting through the mushroom forest. It was dilapidated and covered with moss, but the flat paving stones still shone through in certain sections. At first, I kept to the shadows, but it was apparent no one was in here but me and a thousand of my closest mushroom friends.

The skeletons of buildings gathered around the large door, forming what looked like a small town if each rocky foundation was indeed a building before.

I had assumed the door was a little over ten feet tall, but now that I looked at it, it was at least ten times my height. It was iron with swirling golden mosaics running along the center. A square box with a keyhole conjoined the two doors together in the center at a height well out of my reach.

"Well, isn't that just perfect," I mumbled, looking around for things I could pile up.

It took me nearly half an hour to pile up all the debris I needed to get up to the keyhole, careful not to block both doors. Even with all that stone, I still ended up having to stand on my tip toes to put the key into the lock. The key turned easily, as if well-oiled, resulting in a pop sound as the lock tumbled. The door noiselessly opened on its own, opening about two or three feet before stopping.

"Well, if this doesn't scream boss fight, I don't know what does," I said, looking at the crack in the door. "Do I even want to know what needs a door this big to get in?"

Holding my potion launcher tight to my chest, I poked my head through the crack. A cavernous room spread out before me, but my eyes were immediately drawn to the ceiling. For the first time, I saw daylight. True, for real, daylight. The light shone down into the center of the room from a hole in the high-arched ceiling. The hole was surrounded by a mural of swirling geometric patterns, forming a giant spiral in the domed room.

The light was shining ominously on a single hill in the center of the room.

"No time like the present, I suppose." I swallowed hard. Even with unlimited respawns, this had me straight-up sweating.

I slipped into the room for a smell to slam into my face. There was seafood with hints of lobster, but gamey like wild deer. It left a sharp stinging in my nose, almost like wasabi. I pinched my nose as my eyes watered, the pain spreading through my sinuses.

I took a few steps into the room, and still nothing appeared. My head was on a swivel, constantly checking back and forth, hands gripping the launcher so tight my knuckles were turning white.

It started with a deep rumble, the floor trembling slightly. To my growing horror, a dragon-sized centipede unfurled itself from the mound in the middle of the room, shaking off the dirt like a wet dog. Roaring into the air as it stretched skyward, the monster glowed in the light, drinking in the sol from the ceiling.

"**Inspect**," I said, scrambling backward. My hand had already compressed the lever on the launcher, the wine immediately drawing the creature's attention.

Corrupted Cave Centipede (Lvl 26): A fully grown cave centipede warped by sunrot. Engorged with sol, this cave centipede has doubled in size, becoming crazed to fuel its addiction.

"Fuck!" I hit the wall as my gun finished charging.

Thum! The projectile shot from the launcher barely needed to arc as the centipede charged straight at me.

The thing made no effort to avoid it. The potion slammed into its head, dousing its upper body in blue flame. The fire clung to its hard chitin as it charged me, completely unbothered.

I stumbled backward, trying to get back to the door, but the thing had picked up speed and was faster than I was. The monstrosity scooped me up and pinned me to the wall. Purple fire engulfed me in the thing's mandibles as it repeatedly slammed me against the wall like a rag doll.

You Died!

Solara's Mercy Activated!

Sent to respawn point...

I sat up in the pool, frantically brushing my body as if the flame still clung to it.

A hand grabbed my arm. "Stone. Stone. It's okay. You're safe now," Ae said, pulling me out of the water. I **equipped** my clothes, lying on the cold stone, catching my breath.

"I made it," I said, panting as I calmed down. "I made it to the boss. You can finally be rid of me." I didn't intend the words to hurt, but Ae looked like I'd slapped her in the face. Her face hardened, clearly misunderstanding my intent. I dropped the guard around my mind, letting her see I was trying to be helpful.

Ae's energy collapsed as she got the message. "You're an idiot," she said. "How could anyone say something like that and mean it."

"My grandma always said I was hopeless," I replied. I couldn't control Ae, or how she felt, so I wouldn't even try. "Especially with girls. I would be confused, and they would be mad. It was like there was a list of rules I never got, and no one would tell me what they were." Multiple examples came to mind, but I kept them to myself. High school had been a bad time for me.

"You are baffling," Ae said, sitting seiza-style next to me.

"I can't hate you," Ae said in a way that sounded like she wished she could. "Stone," she said slowly. "What do you think will happen when we leave this dungeon?"

"I guess I really haven't thought about it that hard," I said. It was the truth. I didn't even know enough about the surface to form the beginning of a plan. "All my problems have been right in my face. Honestly, I hadn't even considered the outside world much. I figured we would play it by ear."

"Stone, we can't," Ae said. "If anyone finds out you even talked to me, you'll be killed."

"What did you do? Start a war?" I joked, but Ae stayed dead

serious.

"Yes," she said. "I got a lot of people killed. I thought I could do better, but in the end, I failed everyone."

"Is that why you think you don't deserve to have friends?" My charisma had been screaming at me this whole conversation, but I squashed it down. I needed this to be a real conversation, not the best conversation.

"I won't bring you down with me," Ae said. "My core signature is known. They will know the instant I step out of this dungeon."

I tried not to sigh. "Ae, you know I respect you, right."

"Yes?" Ae said slowly.

"You know I value our friendship?"

"Yes?" Her tone was darker as she knew I was building up to something.

"Stop being dumb," I said. "You warned me, and I decided I don't care. Someone put me here, Ae. This isn't a fluke. I think I'm supposed to save you, even if it's from yourself."

"I envy how simple this seems to you." She did not say it like a compliment.

"It is simple, Ae. You warned me, and I decided I didn't care. How is this hard?"

"You should care," Ae said. "You should care that I'm a monster with blood on my hand. You'll be the next name on a long list of people I've failed."

"You need to stop feeling guilty about everything."

"I *deserve* to feel guilty, Stone," Ae said, her hands balled up into fists in her lap. "I failed everyone. I promised them it would be different and got them killed for believing me."

"I'm not going to abandon you because you think you deserve it," I said. "Now stop telling me what to do. It's making me mad."

"You're so infuriating," Ae said, pacing around the room. "You take these complicated problems and completely sidestep them. I thought you'd hate me. I spent weeks planning on how to tell you, but all you've done is tie yourself to me further. It's like you have no survival instinct. Stone, I'm level forty-six. Do you not understand what type of people we're dealing with? I am wanted *everywhere*."

"I didn't free you so you could walk out of here and die, Ae," I said, still sitting on the floor. I did better not making eye contact in these types of talks. "Look, I would have freed anyone, but I actually like you, and that's why I'm treating you this way. You're smart, you're interesting. You're exactly the kind of person I would want to be friends with entering into a new world. I feel grateful to have been trained by you and won't let you face this alone. I'd rather live a short life where I stood by my friends than a long one abandoning people who needed me."

My charisma wanted to fight me to the death at this point. It urged me to consider her feelings or say something nice. I disagreed. Ae needed to break the cycle of self-hatred, but now she was crying, and I had no idea what to do. My instincts told me to run back into the dungeon.

Truthfully, I had no idea what our friendship even was. I even wondered if it wasn't a form of mutual Stockholm Syndrome. There was a master-apprentice thing going on and a prisoner-rescuer thing as well. It was confusing.

Ae sat back down beside me, looking out over the little pool. I sat awkwardly as she wiped her tears with the back of her hand. I had no idea what was happening.

"You're an idiot," Ae said. "But I respect your choice to be dumb and stand by me, even if I think it's a mistake."

There it was, those signals I needed. How hard was it to communicate this type of thing? My charisma was baffled. It was like I had critical failured into success.

There was a lot going on here, and I was confused by most of it, but she needed me to be some stability. I could do that. This was exactly where I needed to be. I wanted to be this type of person this time around—someone others could trust and lean on. Not the big hero or anything conceded, I just wanted to make a difference to those around me.

"Did you mean what you said earlier?" Ae asked. "You mean that you didn't care and that you would back me up no matter what?"

Maybe it was ridiculous, but I was trusting my gut on this. Granted, I wasn't the best at reading people, but Ae seemed like a good person caught up in some bad circumstances.

"You're my friend. As long as you have my back, I'll have yours. I owe you a great debt for helping me," I said. Was she really asking me this again? How many times did I have to say it?

Ae scoffed. "Me helping you? I feel like I'm trying to dig my way out of your debt, and here you are, piling it back upon me."

"You owe me nothing," I said. "Friends don't keep tabs on debts."

"I'm going to ask something of you before we leave the dungeon. I want you to know I'll forgive you if you say no," Ae said.

"Whatever you need, I got it," I let the moment stretch.

Ae nodded, curling up on the ground. Within a few minutes, I could tell by her breathing she was asleep. What a strange girl.

FOURTEEN: BRAISED LAMB

Ae woke up from a nightmare, yelling and knocking me out of my meditation.

Ae didn't immediately clamp down on her emotions, giving me a glimpse into an alien mind. I could sense a burst of embarrassment, but it was twinged with something else. Contentment? Victory? Shame? I had no idea. I was finding out that even if I could feel Ae's emotions, they were so foreign that I had no idea what they even meant.

I opened my mouth to say something, but Ae put a finger to my lips.

"Not a word," Ae said. "I'm embarrassed enough as it is without your inane commentary." She twisted her hair back into a messy braid, fidgeting with her armor to get it to sit correctly.

I followed suit, getting my gear situated and ensuring my few belongings were in place. Ae walked over to the wall and yanked a chain free. It was the one that was attached to her left ankle, a good three feet of chain coming loose from the spike in the wall. Ae swung it around, the air cracking as she did so.

"Are you ready to face the dungeon?" Ae said, all business, letting the chain hang to her side.

Ae looked back at me, ready to face the dungeon as a team for the first time. The image locked its place into my brain. This was a big moment. We were really doing this.

"Ready as I'll ever be," I said, giving her a double thumbs up.

Ae nodded. "Let's go."

Ae walked through the portal, and for the first time, I watched someone else pass through the dungeon entrance. It wavered like a bubble, snapping closed behind her as she passed.

I looked back at the room behind me, realizing it could be the last time I saw it, as this wasn't just another run. This was it. Now that Ae was in the dungeon proper, she couldn't come back here. It was almost sad. This had been my first home in a different world for the last couple months. It felt surreal to be leaving it behind.

I took the step, allowing the portal to snap close behind me.

"Get lost on the way through?" Ae asked, arching an eyebrow at me. She tapped her foot impatiently, an unusual amount of stress passing over her normally cool demeanor.

"It's gonna be alright," I told her, stepping past her.

I took the lead. I knew Ae was way more powerful than I was, but I wanted her to see that I wasn't going to let her take care of everything while I rode on her coattails.

Visibility dropped to nothing as we moved down the familiar passage. Even though my ability to see had improved, I couldn't see more than a few feet on either side, so I had to rely on the silver rope extending from my chest to let me know where Ae was.

I caught glimpses of Ae watching me in the purple light of **Wyvern's Breath**. Her silver eyes on me were ever-present in the back of my mind as I destroyed the centipedes with renewed vigor. Every scratch, every minor wound I took, just served to cast doubt on my competence.

The smell of lobster and seafood filled the corridor as the light faded from the dying centipedes. To my surprise, instead of the extra sol blooming and fading into nothing, little strands of it flowed towards Ae. I watched in wonder as it swirled around her core, briefly lighting up her eyes.

Ae smiled at me as a scent of mint and braised lamb filled the air.

Horrified by the implication, I busied myself with sealing a wound on my arm, spitting a small amount of flames onto a long gash. It had to have been a fluke or hallucination. Surely, **Feast** only applied to dungeon monsters or enchanted objects.

"You know, I picked up some of the sol from those kills. I could've healed that," Ae said quietly, indicating to my arm. She was so close. Her smell was rich and intoxicating. It took every scrap of my being to resist. My center yearned, pushing me to do something unthinkable.

"Nah, I'm good." I shoved those dark thoughts deep into the recesses of my mind, locked behind an iron will and a greater sense of decency. "You probably need to save your sol for what's coming later. I'll be fine handling all this little stuff." Ae nodded along as I quickly turned to go further down the dungeon.

The next fight with the caveroach went smoothly. It was a welcome distraction, and I felt pretty good about my progress so far.

To my surprise, the other caveroach was already inbound, a low vibrating filling the air. It was early.

I braced for impact, but instead of barreling into me like normal, it flew right over me towards Ae. In the darkness, I didn't get to see what happened. All I heard was a sickening crunch and a flash of sol. The smell of mint became more potent, as if the steaming meal was directly beneath my nose.

Ae grabbed my arm, bouncing giddily, unaware of the turmoil it was causing me. "These low-level monsters are so fun. I almost forgot what it was like."

I leaned in to talk to Ae. My mouth salivated. I needed to get away. "Hey, so if I'm about to do something stupid, do you want to know beforehand, or would you rather be surprised?" I said quickly, sweat showing up on my brow.

"Oh goddess, I'm afraid to even ask," Ae whispered back.

"Surprise, then. Got it," I said, untangling myself from Ae's arm.

"Wait," Ae hissed. "Stone!"

I was already moving through the entrance of the smoke-filled room. The scent of pumpkin spice was already assaulting my senses, pushing away the traces of mint that were tormenting me.

I knew exactly where I was going, barreling into the thick smoke. If the mantagnome heard me coming, it wasn't enough for it to react, its gun still pointed at the floor like last time.

I was within its guard in a heartbeat, tearing at its neck with my teeth and drawing out sol. I satiated my hunger, letting it coat the inside of my center. For once, the restriction inside my throat came as a relief.

The gun clattered to the floor as the mantagnome struggled to grab a blue vial out of the suitcase. I smacked the vial out of its hand, the glass shattering as it burst onto the floor. I grimaced, having wasted a shot already.

The mantagnome basically gave up after that. I snapped its neck, drinking its remaining sol and spitting the excess up into the air, avoiding the globs of flames falling onto the floor.

"Was that really necessary?" Ae asked, her arms folded.

I about jumped out of my skin. I didn't even know she was there. The scent was gone, so she must have done something with the sol she stored. Relief immediately washed through me.

"Why, yes. Yes, it was because, you see"—I paused dramatically, pointing to the gun and briefcase—"I am now ready to face the rest of the dungeon."

"Guns are cheaters' weapons," Ae said. Her tone was flat, but her disapproval was apparent.

"Yeah, and I'm a huge cheater, so…"

Ae clicked her tongue.

I made sure to drink all the sol from the centipedes in the next passage. I could tell from the looks Ae was giving me she knew my fighting style had changed, but she was polite enough not to say anything. I kept the gun slung across my back, careful to keep it from being damaged.

I waved my hand, indicating for Ae to drop down. I dropped to my stomach as we crested the top of the passageway overlooking the mushroom forest.

"It's really beautiful, as deadly as it is," Ae whispered in my ear. A shiver ran down my spine as her breath brushed against me. Was she doing this on purpose?

"Oh yeah, the spores make me feel really dizzy. I almost couldn't fight last time," I whispered back.

"Stone, those are king blue caps. They kill people in seconds," Ae said. "Inspect them if you don't believe me."

"**Inspect**," I said.

King Blue Cap Mushroom (Lvl 12): This large variety of

the fungi family is easily identified by its dark brown stalks, grey and white caps, and blue gills. Easily disturbed, the spores are deadly upon contact, suffocating victims within seconds.

"Holy shit, you're right," I whispered, confused by what I was learning.

"Dear goddess, are there any other secrets you want to tell me about?" Ae's tone was playful, but her face was serious.

"Hey, I'm doing my best over here," I said. "So, you see that round door off to the side? You can see it around the patch of mushrooms right there. There is a key in there we need to grab real quick. It's not a big deal. I was able to take out the enemy in there with one shot last time with this bad boy," I said, patting my hand on the launcher.

"Okay, if that's the case. Why are we hiding here?"

"Yeah, that. There's an archer in here somewhere. He tends to be in a different spot. Last time, I drew him out by walking in, but I wasn't sure if I wanted to do that this time."

"I got it," Ae said. "Just get to the door."

Ae was gone when I looked over to say something back. A gentle movement of air was all the indication I got that she moved.

"Damn, she's scary." I strolled across the mushroom forest, barely taking five steps before I heard a muffled scream and a crunch.

Another few steps and the smell of mint announced Ae's

presence. I whipped around to see she was a few feet behind me.

Ae froze, obviously surprised. "How'd you do that?"

I tapped the side of my nose with my finger. "A magician never reveals his secrets."

“What’s a magician?”

I opened my mouth to respond but I realized the explanation sounded like nonsense. “You know what, just forget I said anything.”

Ae shrugged. The smell of mint faded as her eyes glowed. I wasn't sure exactly what she did, but I noticed the scars tracing along her exposed skin faded slightly, her stump even looked longer. She was healing herself.

We got to the door, and I turned to her. "Just hang out here. I'll be right back."

"All right," Ae said. "Please be quick, though."

Just like last time, the mantis didn't even see me coming. I hated wasting a shot on this thing, but I also remembered how useless the launcher was against the boss.

I stepped over the mantis's smoldering remains, grabbing the key from the statue's outstretched hand. I walked back out the door to meet up with Ae.

"Where did your bag go?"

"Oh yeah, I don't need that anymore. I got the last shot in here,” I said, tapping the side of the launcher.

"Oh wow, you have the boss key already?" Ae said, looking at the key in my other hand.

"Is that what this big dumb thing is called?"

"Yeah, the boss key always looks like that. Or some variation of it anyway."

"The door it goes to is over there," I said, pointing to the large doors on the other side of the cavern.

"I think the dungeon likes you. This seems pretty easy for a tier-three dungeon."

I groaned. "How dare you say that. You just cursed us."

"What do you mean?" Ae said, tilting her head to the side.

"Whenever you say something out loud like 'this is pretty easy' or 'this should be real quick.' It always ends up going wrong."

"Sounds like the work of some vengeful deity. Did you earn their ire or something?" Ae asked.

"It's starting to feel that way."

We took our time walking to the boss's door, idly chatting as we walked. Neither of us was looking forward to what was about to happen, although probably for different reasons. I was dreading the boss fight, and I think she was dreading what was coming after.

We arrived at the door, looking up at it. "Yeah. So last time, I piled up a bunch of—"

Ae snatched the key out of my hand, jumping to the air and hovering for a second as she placed it into the door, turning it swiftly before dropping back down. Both doors opened as she landed, giving us enough space to walk in side by side.

"You're a freaking show-off, you know that?"

"Says the fire-breathing halfkin," Ae said. "So what are we dealing with in here?"

"Corrupted cave centipede," I said, pausing to see what sort of reaction she had. Her relaxed look didn't even change, waiting for me to continue. "It's like a level 26 or something."

"Oh, that's it?" Ae's shoulders relaxed. "You had me worried for a second."

"That's it? Does the word corrupted mean nothing to you? That thing in there is insane. I thought it would be a big deal."

Ae stared at the light in the center of the room. "Oh yeah, with all the sunlight coming down from the roof in there, it's going to be corrupted. That much sunlight isn't good for anything."

"Great, now I find out the sun gives you magic cancer."

"It isn't a problem as long as you level up after filling your center. Things go wrong when you hold it all in," Ae said. "Ready?"

I didn't feel ready but nodded.

Ae was off in a flash, running across the room at a speed I could never match. The light seemed to stick to her as she dashed through it, swirling around her as she landed on the awakening centipede.

Ae's chain swung, cracking as it collided with the centipede, lifting it in the air and sending it tumbling towards the wall.

The elf spread her arm wide, and the room darkened. It was like a black hole open in Ae's stomach as everything distorted. Her eyes glowed like spotlights with all the sol flowing around her.

"**Permafrost Regeneration**!" Ae yelled.

Ice covered her body in a ten-foot-tall twisted cocoon. All of this happened while the centipede was airborne, hitting the wall with a crack, pieces of rock falling from the ceiling.

A second crack filled the air, the ice cocoon exploding into shrapnel, revealing unscarred skin and a regrown arm.

My breath caught. Ae looked every bit of what I imagined a goddess should look like. Light swirled around her, highlighting her perfect skin and gleaming armor. The gem on her cuirass was still cracked but everything else looked remade.

A strong smell hit me like a shockwave, making my nose feel on fire. Ae's smell was magnified a thousand times what it was before. My feet were moving before I even realized what was happening. My tongue rolled out of the side of my mouth as I sprinted towards the source.

I slapped myself in the face, falling clumsily to the ground.

I gritted my teeth, getting my mind back under control.

Ae hit the cave centipede again, a crack forming on the heavy plate chitin. I could smell its wild seafood scent behind the blast of mint. I squeezed the lever on my launcher, aiming at the recovering centipede.

"Stone, get back. I got it," Ae called, but it was too late. My launcher had already fired the potion at the centipede.

Thum! The potion arced through the air. Everything slowed as the centipede roared, the potion disappearing into its mouth.

"Yes!" I cheered. Hopefully, that giant piece of shit would cook from the inside out.

The centipede thrashed as if stung by electricity, making dents in the cave wall as it writhed on the floor, its stomach bulging unnaturally. I kept waiting for it to explode, but its body continued expanding.

"Stone, what did you do?" Ae said, landed next to me. Her very presence had weight.

Ae grabbed the launcher from my hand and flung it against the cave wall, shattering it. I couldn't handle her being so close. Her eyes glowed with power as she looked at me. Her mouth started to move, but I couldn't hear any words coming out, my instincts propelling me forward, mouth open.

The whole world shifted as a hand struck me on the side of the face.

"You had all this time and now you try to kiss me?" Ae sounded far away as she yelled.

A roar filled the cavern, turning my blood to ice. The bass of the roar was so deep it vibrated in my chest. While we were distracted, the centipede had nearly tripled in size, blue liquid dripping from its mouth. I wasn't even sure it could fit through the double doors anymore.

The ground froze around Ae as the temperature in the room dropped. The limp chain in her hand extended outwards, wreathed in a translucent blade of ice. I felt the stone floor flex as Ae pushed off, her sword extended in an arcing swing.

Ae's sword connected with the centipede, but instead of flying across the room, it stayed stock still, barely grunting as she hit it.

With no warning, its mandibles moved in a blur, knocking Ae airborne. The elf hit the wall so hard she made an indent as she crumpled to the floor.

My jaw dropped, knowing I would be a smear if I got hit by an attack like that. A shockwave hit me, carrying the mixed smells of the two fighters.

Ae wiped blood from the corner of her mouth. "Run!" she yelled, sounding far away, almost like she was underwater.

I couldn't move, transfixed on the mass of sol before me. It was all I could smell. It was all I could taste. I needed it. I ran towards the fight, instinct overriding better sense.

Luckily, the centipede didn't take my charge seriously, barely putting any effort into intercepting me as I ran towards it, focusing entirely on Ae as she struggled against its strikes.

Ae erected a shield of bloody ice, huddling behind it, her shoulder braced against it. The centipede's pointed mandibles slammed against the red shield, leaving long gouges in its wake.

I wove around the centipede's halfhearted attempt to knock me back. I was nothing to it. Not even worthy of putting down.

Ae and the centipede circled each other as I followed the beast from the side. It shifted every time I tried to grab on.

Ae screamed, and the centipede stopped for a second. I couldn't see what was happening, but this was my chance.

It was all I needed.

I grabbed onto one of its legs, biting down so hard I felt my teeth crack. I tore a chunk of chitin away, my tongue connecting against a pumping mana channel.

My center bulged under a torrent of sol, immediately getting to the point where I could level up with barely a thought. I swirled my center, pushing down as I drank the sol in like I was packing down an overstuffed suitcase. The sol tasted weird, sour and too spicy.

Ae screamed something incomprehensible as she slammed a bloody fist against the face of the centipede. It weathered the attack, roaring and pushing her against the wall.

I kept drinking the sol unnoticed. Drinking and

compressing. Drinking and compressing. I needed more. I needed it all!

Congratulations! Ascended to Level 6. +1 Cha, +1 Spirit

Congratulations! Ascended to Level 7. +1 Cha, +1 Spirit

Congratulations! Ascended to Level 8. +1 Cha, +1 Spirit

The notifications came in a flurry, each one allowing more sol to pack into my center. Everything about me stretched beyond what I thought was possible.

Ae screamed as pincers descended on her. Her arm had gotten trapped in a crack, leaving her vulnerable. She couldn't defend properly, a pincer piercing into her side.

Anger ran through me. My thoughts felt like molasses in my brain. Ae was mine. She was my meal, and no one else would have her.

I let go of the centipede, hitting the ground hard. My body felt weird, like I had on a sumo suit. Way more than my neck was swollen, with most of my chest and stomach being swollen as well.

The centipede whirled around, sensing a new threat, leaving Ae bleeding in the dirt. Even in my addled state, I was relieved, ready to die for my friend.

Solara's Hand activated!

I barely caught the message in my darkening vision. Pain on a level I didn't know was possible rolled through me, threatening to tear me apart. A voice spoke in my mind alongside my mental screaming. The centipede rushed at me, time becoming a crawl. At first, the voice was quiet but grew to a roar as the words flowed.

'The Goddess Solara, addressing the young priests on the nature of mortal death, told them thusly.'

The centipede reared back like a snake about to strike. My body acted on its own. The sol in my engorged center flowed towards my mouth like a geyser.

'As surely as the sun rises, ***dusk shall fall.****'*

The whole world turned black as a purple beam exploded from my mouth. A tearing sound like a jet engine filled the room as my back hit the wall, the beam driving my head into the stone, my skull flexing under the pressure. The centipede didn't have time to react as it slid apart in two perfectly cut pieces, its sol exploding into a cloud of light tainted with black streaks. Viscera and gore rained down as pieces of cave separated from the ceiling.

Everything went black.

FIFTEEN: THE BLADE ITSELF

For the first time, I felt the sunlight on my face.

I couldn't even move my eyes, and for a long moment, I just breathed, staring at the light coming in the crack in the ceiling. A notification icon blinked in the corner of my vision, but I ignored it, looking at the ruin we had left. The cave was half collapsed, clouds visible through the holes in the ceiling, but the sky looked odd, like a projection. Just where were we?

The feeling in my body came back in a flash. My brain, unable to specify where the pain was coming from, indicated it was from everywhere. A pressure filled my mana channels as my body popped and writhed. Bones snapped into place with sickening thumps, and organs inflated like water balloons.

Ae glowed with power as she pressed her hand into my chest. Her eyes were bloodshot, and she looked like she hadn't slept in a while. "Thank the Goddess, I thought you were gone."

Ae smelled tantalizing, but after the intensity of swallowing all that sol in the fight, it seemed tame in comparison. The temptation flitted at the edge of my will, but it was no longer overwhelming.

"I—" My mouth felt like cotton. "I'm sorry. I really fucked—"

Ae shushed me. "I saw the sunrot take you. The very fact you're conscious is a miracle from the Goddess herself. I've never seen anything like that before."

"But, I—"

"Just check your system log," Ae said, grabbing my hand and pulling me to my feet. The world rocked a bit, but she was there to help steady me.

I acknowledged the blinking light.

Corruption detected! Damage to mana channels imminent!

Solara's Hand Activated!

I stopped reading and pulled up **Solara's Hand**. After all, last time it added more to the description.

Solara's Hand: The mortal representative of Solara, Goddess of sunlight and sacrifice. Hands become closer to their patron by upholding their tenets.

Was that what was happening? When I sacrificed for others Solara lent me her power? I shelved that philosophical twister and kept reading my notifications.

Gate Meridian unlocked! +5 Spirit!

Dungeon Boss Slain!

Quest cleared: Escape the Dungeon!

Reward: Bronze loot box

A bronze box appeared beside me, clattering onto the ground. It was small, like the size of a loaf of bread, and had a simple latch on the front.

I was unimpressed.

"This is it?" I asked, gesturing to it. "All that for this tiny-ass box?"

"Are you going to open it or stare at it?" Ae asked. She was clearly more excited about this than I was.

I scooped up the box, moving slowly to tease the elf.

"Come on, I have to know what you got," she said.

"Fine." The box opened right up with an authoritative snap. The inside was lined in white pillows and had a single item. I pulled the red scroll out for Ae to look at. She was impressed. I had my doubts.

"A spell scroll in a bronze loot box? You are truly blessed by the Goddess," Ae said, a bright smile contrasting with all the dirt on her face.

"Yeah, that's cool and all, but how do I use it?" I turned the scroll over in my hands. It was nice, but I wasn't even sure I could read.

"Just try to read it." Ae was practically vibrating. "You'll see."

I opened the scroll, its bright red velvety page unfurling almost as wide as my arms could stretch. Wild symbols and drawings filled it in tiny print, like the mad scribbles of a genius.

It made no sense to me.

"Just look at it." Ae held the scroll to my face as if smothering me with it would help.

"Fine." I looked again. I stared at the page, willing something to happen. A diagram that looked like a college-level math problem caught my attention. The numbers I understood, but the kanji-like symbols were meaningless to me.

I was about to give up when the writing seemed to move. Why did that drawing kind of make sense now? Suddenly, everything made sense. I leaned forward, trying to absorb the information, but it was too much. Pain ran from the center of my forehead to my throat, expanding the channel as it connected to my center. The spell snapped into place all at once, leaving me feeling like I'd been slapped in the face. "Fuck, that hurts!" I said, rubbing my temples.

Congratulations! New Spell learned!

Ae laughed. "Yeah, it always does. What did you get? Come on, I want to know."

I opened my stats.

Name: Stone McGracen

Race: Halfkin

Path: Hunger

Level: 8

Unlocked Meridians: Throat, Gate

Spells: Inspect, Feast, Wyvern's Breath, Cleanse

Blessings: Solara's Mercy, Solara's Hand

Stats:

Int: 7

Wis: 6

Cha: 17 (+5)

Str: 4

Dex: 7 (+2)

Con: 2.4

Spirit: 22.4 (+11.2)

Holy crap, my spirit had doubled! Was that what this feeling was? It was like I could finally breathe.

My hand drifted to my gate meridian above my belly button. It felt like my center, but not at the same time. It was like a hub or a pump for sol, but all the channels around it were gummed up. In fact, everything felt gummed up.

"Don't keep me waiting." Ae smacked me on the shoulder.

Why tell her when I could show her? I breathed in the sol filtering around me, feeling a pleasant swelling in my center. "**Cleanse**," I said, smiling.

Ae pushed me away as she jumped back. Pure fire ran through my mana channels as I fell. Sludge poured out of my orifices: eyes, ears, nose, all emptying black snot. I gagged on the tarlike substance, wiping it off my face.

Ae laughed. "Don't use that one around polite company, and take your clothes off next time."

I looked down to see black stains on my clothes. "God damn it," I said. "Don't look."

Ae looked around politely as I **unequipped** and **reequipped** my clothes, wiping as much of the substance off my skin as possible. The clothes reappeared clean and stuck against my still dirty skin. I had always hated being dirty under clean clothes, but it would have to do.

Ae clapped a single time. "You should feel a lot better now." The elf crouched down to look at the gunk on the ground, careful not to touch it. "I was working hard to eliminate all that corruption, so I'm glad you got the rest."

I looked around at all the damage we had done to the cavern. It looked like a bomb had gone off, and all things considered, that's kind of what happened. The remains of the centipede lay in two pieces, releasing foul fumes underneath the sunlight. Then again, that smell could have been me. This black tar was putrid to the max.

Ae joined me in looking around, just standing there, looking up at the light filtering through the ceiling. If she had pockets, her hands would've been in them, the very picture of avoidance.

My eyes focused on a door I was sure wasn't there before. It was identical to the one in the resurrection room.

"So, what now? We just leave?" I looked at Ae to see her refusing to make eye contact. Her entire energy was nervous. "You're stalling, aren't you?"

"You know that amount of corruption would have killed anyone else." Ae nodded at the bisected centipede. "By the time I saw you absorbing it, you were too far gone, lost to whatever madness corruption brings."

"I can't help but feel you're avoiding something," I said.

Ae ignored me, staring at the sky through the destroyed ceiling. "For the last few months, I've been asking myself what it would take for me to trust somebody. I used to believe in people, but now… Everything has gone so wrong. Everybody is gone. All the naive parts of me died with them." Ae trailed off.

"Where are you going with this?" Her speech was making me nervous.

"I'm getting there," Ae said. "I've been planning to talk to you about this for a while, but every time I thought about bringing it up, I couldn't. Now, I've run out of time."

The elf tapped her center. "I'm being tracked, and no, there's no way around it. The spell is absolute and binds to the core. As long as I draw breath, I can't leave. As soon as we step out of whatever dimension this dungeon is in, every bounty hunter, adventurer, knight, and peasant will swarm down upon me with a vengeance."

Ae paused, but I waited for her to continue. She took a deep breath.

"My name is Ae'silin, and my titles are meaningless now. My father was a human and my mother was an elven maid in his house. The official story is my mother seduced my father, but I don't believe a word of it." Ae clenched her fist. "I was kept around as a playmate for my half-sister, little more than a slave, treated as another of the servants' children. I got to watch as my mother died a slow death that any healer could've cured. In the end, she was just a servant, something to be replaced when it broke."

Ae stopped. "I'm rambling, aren't I? I'll get right to it."

"No, it's okay," I said. "Ramble away."

"I'll skip to the part that matters," Ae said. "I freed thousands of elves in the capital before they figured out it was me. Servants talk, and we had caught wind of the raid, fleeing a full hundred miles away by the time the paladins hit my father's temple. We fled into the Twilight, where we thought they wouldn't follow. We wanted to be left alone, but they hunted us like dogs. For twenty years, we ran, freeing elves and other non-humans from settlements in the Fringe. We grew in number, becoming strong, but it was for nothing. I sacrificed myself so the last of us could escape, but the commander intervened, stopping the fatal blow. Citing his friendship with my father, he seared a tracker into my core and left me to rot."

The information rolled over me, pieces falling into place. "You hinted at a plan?"

"Before I tell you, I want to ask you one last time. Am I really someone you want to be involved with? If you leave now, I won't blame you."

"I'm in," I said. Ae waited for me to continue, but I said everything I thought was necessary.

"Are you sure?" Ae said, searching my face. "I'm putting a large amount of trust into you. More than anyone should put in anybody. Are you good for it? Are you really the person I've seen down here?"

"I hope I'm always the person you think I am," I said, meeting her stare.

Ae nodded, staring back. “Swear to me one thing," the priestess said. "You’re Solara’s Hand. You might not understand what that means, but you will be a harbinger of great change. Free any nonhumans you find. Do it as bloodless as you can. Do what I couldn’t.”

Ae stared deep into my eyes as she waited for an answer. Could I really live up to this? I gave her the only answer I could. “I will do my best.”

Relief washed over Ae. "Give me your knife."

The request caught me off guard, but I pulled my knife out of my sheath and handed it to her hilt first. I’d trusted her judgement this far, no sense in doubting it now.

Ae flipped the knife around in her hand. "These system-made weapons all have something in common. They can be upgraded. They lack all the impurities of manual crafting. Weak, but perfect." Ae cut the palm of her hand with the knife, letting the blood drip down the blade. "One of my closest confidants told me of this in the hours before I was captured. A method to start over, to hide in plain sight. At the time, I thought he was mad for suggesting it, but now, I understand."

"Ae, let's talk through this," I said. “Rituals involving blood and knives make me nervous.”

"Stand back," Ae said. "It has already started. I placed the weave on the blade as soon as I touched it."

"What has already started?" I said, my panic rising.

"This is my choice," Ae said. "Now stand back."

Ae held the knife up in the sunlight. She said words I didn’t understand, speaking so low and fast it was unintelligible. The knife practically vibrated as sol flexed around it, darkening the room. The power she held was startling, feeling like a weight on my shoulders.

Ae's knees gave out as the light returned to normal. I barely caught her arm, holding her upright. Dark bags formed under her eyes, leaving her looking paler than usual.

Ae grabbed my hand, wrapping it around the hilt. The knife was cold, the sweat on my hand freezing instantly. Ae moved the blade, placing the tip against her bare midsection. She pulled me close, taking my other hand and putting it behind her back.

"Ae, please," I said as she pulled me close, the knife wedged between our bodies. "What is going on?"

"There is more to a person than a core," Ae said, her lips turning a shade of blue. "There are many magics that are better left untouched. This is one of those. The cost is great. The risk is greater. Death is often a preferable fate."

My gut instinct was to pull back, but I held firm. "How does killing you solve any of this?"

"Your knife is a sol anchor now—a device used to trap the spirit of giant beasts. When you stab me, my soul will not go into the abyss, but instead, it will be trapped in this anchor, reset to level zero. My consciousness will fade, but as you raise the level of the blade, I will return." Ae's breaths deepened, her body shook as she held on to me.

The color drained from my face. "Is this really the only way? There is no other option?"

"As long as I exist in this form, I will be hunted. Do this for me, and I'll be the fiercest ally you could ever imagine, bound to you forever. You are Solara's Hand. Let me be your weapon. Let my suffering mean something."

"You can count on me, Ae," I said, our foreheads touching as she leaned on me more and more. "I'll keep my word. I swear."

Ae smiled. "I know."

Even in her weakened state, Ae's strength was

overwhelming, pulling our bodies together in a single motion. She gasped as the knife plunged into her core. I could feel the tears on her cheek as she wrapped her arms around my neck, leaning on me.

For a second that lasted a lifetime, she clung to me before going limp.

"Ae!" I yelled, trying to hold her up. The blade was so cold, but I couldn't let go. Blood flowed from the wound in her stomach, twisting around the blade. Frost ran up my hand, but I held true, cradling Ae as her eyes frosted over.

A light blinked in the corner of my vision.

Congratulations! Weapon upgrade successful!

"Shut up!" I yelled at the system, cradling Ae's body in my arms. Even as I held her, she began to flake, scattering like snow. I cradled her remains as I watched them fade into the stillness of the dungeon.

"Ae, you dick!" I yelled, wiping a hot tear from my face with my sleeve.

I activated our bond. A golden thread ran to the knife, now lying on the floor.

The knife had changed. Gone was the base equipment I had been given upon arrival. In its place was a beautiful dagger. The blade itself was slender, double-sided, and deadly. The hilt was a work of art, silver surrounding diamonds, with white leather wrapped around the grip. It was deadly and beautiful. It was weird to say it looked like her, but it did.

I picked up the knife with both hands. "Ae," I said, whispering to it. "Ae, are you in there?" I needed confirmation it worked. I caught a familiar scent of mint as I held the blade close, listening for a response.

In the silence, my emotional wall broke.

"**Inspect**," I said, holding back tears. What if she could see me? Maybe she couldn't talk yet. I needed to be strong.

Chainbreaker (Lvl 0, Soulbound): This evolving weapon is bound to the soul of Ae'silin DeArdent, the Chainbreaker. This is an evolving weapon and will change with time. Kill beings with sol to upgrade.

I sat there for a while, looking at the words. The dungeon was quiet, and I took my time. The weight of it all settled onto my shoulders. Ae bet everything on me.

Why did it have to turn out like this?

Something caught my eye as I slid Ae into the reformed sheath on my belt—a glint of something on the ground. Ae's armor was nowhere to be found, but something remained.

I brushed aside the dirt to see a silver ring. Confused, I picked it up. I didn't remember Ae wearing a ring. "**Inspect**," I said.

Silver Ring of the Hunt: This enchanted ring glows in the presence of ascended creatures.

"Just what is this," I said, holding it up in the light. I put on the ring, twisting it to see a little gem in the shape of a crescent moon on it. Where had this come from?

My eyes wandered beyond my hand to the doorway against the far wall. I gathered myself, taking a deep breath. There was nothing left but to take the next step.

The portal flexed like a bubble as I walked through, leaving the dungeon behind.

SIXTEEN: IRON RODS

It was dawn.

I rested a hand on Ae's hilt as I admired the red of the rising sun. I missed her already. A golden strand stretched from my center, searching for a hint of life. Even now, the memory of her walking through the dungeon door filled me with a bittersweet warmth. How could she smile at me like that, knowing what she was about to do? She probably made the right call by not telling me.

The weight of what she said to me had started to sink in, but even then, I felt like only time and context would make me truly understand what I had gotten myself into.

I stared at the dawn sun, daring it to move. A piece of me didn't believe what Ae said about the sun staying in place here. It felt so foreign. Unreasonable even. No days or nights, just a permanent state? What about time keeping or sleep schedules? I'd just gotten here and was already confused.

A frigid wind whipped around me, channeled by the valley

below. I was surprised at how little I felt the cold through my clothes. It nipped at my nose, muting the smells wafting from the forest. Hints of smoke clung to it, leading me to look for people.

I found it below me, nestled in the sun between the mountains, a moderate-sized town on the side of a snow-melt stream, smoke rising from myriad chimneys. There had to be a few thousand people living down there.

My gut reaction was to avoid the town at all costs, but instead, I sat on a boulder, observing the town from up on the mountainside before making a decision.

Guards in mismatched armor occupied the stone walls—a jarring contrast to the picturesque brick and clay homes decorating its interior. People walked on the streets clothed in furs, ambling about to their business. I could see the gleam of weapons slung across their backs and children playing in the snowbanks. It was a place of contrast, a mixture of hard and soft, peaceful and violent.

I decided.

I wanted none of it.

Instead, I looked to the wild places. A forest of evergreen filled the space between the mountains, growing taller where the sunlight touched.

I breathed deep, pulling a drizzle of sol out of the air and to my center. The sol was thin, barely enough to power a spell. The energy quieted one type of hunger, but the other rumbled in my stomach. I imagined fresh bread melting on my tongue, almost groaning at the memory. I knew I had time, but food and water were top priorities. The last thing I needed was to finally get out of the dungeon, just to starve.

I marveled at the size of the forest. It reminded me of when my grandpa took me to the redwoods in the United California States, but more, well, everything. All the trees were thirty paces across—evergreens, maples, and ash alike. They were so big, or maybe I was just that small. Ae's comments about my size wormed into the back of my mind. Surely, she was just fucking with me, some joke among giants.

Yeah, screw that town and everyone in it. I'd met enough people to know I generally wasn't a fan. For now, I'd brave the wild, only going to town as a last resort. Besides, I still had Solara's Mercy. I'd rather learn the hard lessons now and not when I could truly die.

A cold that had nothing to do with the temperature ran down my neck. How would I get back out of the dungeon if I died? Would I have to fight the boss on my own? The thought of getting stuck in the dungeon alone sent a shiver of fear through me, taking me back to all the time I spent in the void.

I hopped down from the boulder and landed in the light snow that blanketed everything. I heard the distant roar of a river—a good place to start as any. Many animals frequented places with water, and a good meal would do wonders for my attitude.

My footfalls revealed stone as I walked from the dungeon entrance. The doorway was crumpled on the outside, decayed. I was surprised it was still standing, its entrance barely visible from ten feet away.

I slipped into the woods, listening closely to the background chatter of the woodland creatures. I smelled the air, looking for changes in the wind. The smells out here were muted, lacking the intensity of the dungeon creatures or Ae.

I walked through the woods. It was pleasant and set me on edge. Everything I identified was low-level—level two or three at most. My suspicious nature ramped up with every nonthreat I saw.

A bird with vibrant golden feathers landed on a branch. I stopped, gearing up to identify the creature. I didn't want to assume anything. My low constitution was permanently present in the back of my mind. I was stronger and faster than ever before but I felt like one bad fall would send me to respawn.

A roar followed by a girlish scream cut through the chatter of the woods.

"I fucking knew it," I said, my head whipping towards the sound. "I know how this place works, everything sucks, no exceptions."

I set a hand on Ae. "What do you say? Do we play the hero?"

In lieu of a response, I guessed. "No harm in checking it out."

I caught a heavy scent of chicken in the air, and something was stomping all over some underbrush, making a racket. Another smell mixed in with the first, something foreign I didn't have a name for.

I could tell by the sound I was close. I pulled Ae out of her sheath as I poked my head into the clearing.

"Holy shit, what is that," I whispered to my knife.

A massive bird, easily as big as a legendary dinosaur, stood over a woman, her basket of winter berries emptied on the ground. I did a double take on the girl. The cat ears on the woman's head looked like they belonged at one of the anime conventions my grandpa would drag me to.

Even though I was hidden, the woman locked eyes with me, her mouth opening in shock. I got the impression she was more scared of me than the tyrannosaurus chicken nugget pinning her to the ground with a taloned foot. Its feathers were a mixture of blues and greens, with little black eyes facing forward over a serrated beak.

The beast followed her gaze, and I knew the jig was up.

"Hey, you big piece of shit," I yelled. The creature roared at me as I jumped out of hiding. "**Inspect**!"

Lesser Murderbird (Lvl 16): One of the smallest of the gigantus avian family, this creature is flightless, unlike some of its larger cousins, and an omnivore. These avians are known for their massive size, short tempers, and low intelligence.

"Bad bird," I yelled, throwing a rock at the avian.

The woman scrambled back as the attention of the murderbird shifted to me, grabbing her basket and covering her cat ears with her arm. She disappeared into the woods, not even looking back at me.

"People these days," I said, running, ducking behind a tree, blocking a lunge from the open beak of the murderbird.

It was probably for the best, anyway. Ae did say I needed to keep my abilities to myself.

The bird lunged again, squawking in frustration as I weaved around the trees, moving just out of reach.

Finally, what I was looking for happened. The tree shook violently, almost knocking me down on the other side.

I peeked around to see if my plan worked. The avian issued muffled squawks, its beak buried into the tree, its serrated edges keeping it stuck.

It was all I needed.

I plunged Ae into the creature's leg, letting her drink. The bird struggled but was truly stuck. Almost immediately, I got a weird feeling through my bond with Ae. She was done.

I pulled her out, wiping the blade on my shirt, and set her carefully in the hilt. I got a feeling again through the bond. She was… sleepy?

I lit the lower half of the bird on fire with **Wyvern's Breath**. I wasn't trying to kill the creature but set a precedent not to be messed with. I had no intention of leveling up anytime soon. I needed to be way more powerful before I was ready to take the training wheels off.

The murderbird went wild as its shining feathers smoldered under the sticky acid flames. It flapped its flightless wings, trying to put out its feathers. I would've felt bad if it hadn't been trying to eat me.

I ran off into the woods, leaving the bird to sort itself out.

"Well, that was fucking weird," I said, checking to see how close I was to leveling. To my relief, I was a tenth of the way, if that.

"I wonder if that was a bona fide catgirl or just a weirdo. What do you think?" I asked my knife.

Realizing what Ae would say, I smacked my forehead. "I should've inspected her! Damn."

I **inspected** Ae instead, seeing if anything changed.

Chainbreaker (Lvl 1, Soulbound): This evolving weapon is bound to the soul of Ae'silin DeArdent, the Chainbreaker. This is an evolving weapon and will change with time. Kill beings with sol to upgrade.

"Yes," I said, scaring off a squirrel. Ae had already gone up a level. I searched for the bond, but it felt the same. It was like she had gone to sleep after a big meal.

A few hours later, I found myself on the banks of a massive river. Never had I seen water so clear, like flowing glass, leaving the bottom for all to see. Black and white pebbles decorated the riverbed, almost like an exotic aquarium. Even plants and animals had adapted to this color scheme, taking on a mixture of the two colors.

I crawled onto a log that was half floating on the riverside and half in the water. The log bobbed as I got out to the end, staring into the clear water. Many creatures darted about, but the crocodilian fish were the most abundant. They were basically armored fish like a small gar. I was already salivating at the thought of fish over a fire. I thrust out my hand, trying to grab one of the fish as they leaped into the air.

I almost used **Wyvern's Breath** but felt exposed on the river's edge. Who knew how many eyes were on me right now? After the catgirl's reaction, I didn't want to draw more attention.

I gave up after a few tries. How dare these fish not leap into my awaiting hands. The gall.

I sorted through downed branches on the riverside. Most were huge, more like logs than branches. I looked up at the trees stretching like skyscrapers overhead, feeling a little paranoid about getting taken out by one of these things as they fell. I ended up having to break a piece off of one of the fallen limbs.

I looked at the branch, reaching for my knife to carve it, but stopped as Ae was halfway out of her hilt. Was this okay? I got that stabbing something was fine, but would she be mad if I used her to carve a stick?

My stomach rumbled. "You better say something," I told Ae.

All I got was sleepiness in response.

I shrugged, whittling down the end of the branch with the blade. Ae cut through the wood like soap, leaving satisfying curlings of timber. "Damn," I commented.

A moment later, I had a wooden spear, and after a few good practice thrusts, I felt good about my chances of a hot meal.

I left my boots on the shore and waded into the water. The fish scattered, but I knew they would be back. I let my mind relax, enjoying the quiet moment while I had it, standing stock still.

I thrust with the spear, the point driving through where a fish swam, almost dropping the spear when I felt resistance.

Success! My spear pierced the gills of a particularly large crocofish. It wiggled on the end of my spear as I waved it around in victory, doing a little dance.

I built a little fire on the side of the river, opting to cook the fish directly on the spear it was caught with. Grease dripped down its flat tail as I cooked it over the fire, my eyes never leaving it as the flames licked the skin.

After what felt like an eternity, it was done. I took the first bite of actual food in this new world. It tasted like salmon, but it had the consistency of chicken.

I froze mid-bite, the distinct feeling of being watched rolling down the back of my neck. I gently sat down my meal and stood up, facing the forest.

The forest was too still. Only the gentle roar of the river kept me company. It hadn't been this quiet the whole time, right? I set my hand on Ae's hilt. To my surprise, she responded, a feeling of contentment rolling through the bond.

A warning sparked in my subconscious, pulling me out of my distracted state. I threw myself backward as something flew over just where I had been standing.

I whipped around to get a good look at the newcomer.

The thing was something like a wolf, something like a badger, and stood at eye level with me, even on all fours. Not good at all.

"**Inspect**," I said.

Dirt Wolf (Lvl 6): Dirt wolves belong to the canine family and are distantly related to the land wolves that share their name. Dirt wolves are a hardy race and only leave their underground burrows to hunt in packs.

"Fuck," I said, looking around me. "Where are the rest?" I picked up my short spear, my fish still hanging from the end as I pointed the end at the dirt wolf creeping towards me. Two more emerged from the underbrush, pinning my back to the river.

A moment of tension hung over us as we stared at each other, their eyes looking at the fish hanging off the tip of my spear.

A reasonable person might have offered the fish, but I'd worked hard for it and wasn't feeling particularly reasonable.

"If I can't eat my dinner in peace," I said, flicking the spear up so the fish flew off. The dirt wolf's eyes moved in unison after the fish as it landed in the river behind me. "No one can."

The splash was like a starting gun, the three dirt wolves lunging at me in unison.

I set the spear against the rocks, letting the beast's weight do the job for me. The spear pierced into flesh, sending the first dirt wolf to the ground, blood already staining the black and white pebbles.

The next wolf caught a burst of **Wyvern's Breath**. It was just a puff, but it was enough to catch its snout on fire. The beast pawed at the sticky flames, abandoning me.

By this point, I'd started to feel like the fight was in the bag, but the last dirt wolf gave me no time to prepare, barreling me down and pressing me into the pebbles.

I grabbed the dirt wolf's ears, stopping its snout less than an inch from my face, its fetid breath splashing all over me. If I could reach Ae, this thing would be mincemeat, but both hands were needed to keep its jaws from sending me to respawn.

I sent out a splash of flames, but the wolf ignored it, made of sterner stuff than its brethren. I knew I didn't have long before the other wolves got involved. I pulled as hard as I could, trying to bring the sol through my hands, but it felt like I was trying to drink through a clogged straw, my channels still gunked up.

I breathed in a scrap of sol out of the air. "**Cleanse**."

The sol flowing through my center disappeared instantly,

dirt exploding off me. The wolf sneezed and almost knocked me off my grip. I tried to pull in the sol again, but nothing more than a trickle responded.

"**Cleanse**," I said again, gritting my teeth. Something in my arms was blocking the flow. My center spun like a tornado, sucking up sol as fast as it could. It felt like I was so close.

One of the other dirt wolves slammed into the wolf on top of me, fighting over its conquered meal. Their attention turned to each other, and something smacked me across the face. Realizing it was a tail, I grabbed it with both hands, biting hard enough into it to taste blood, drinking a mouthful of sol.

"**Cleanse**," I yelled, specifically thinking about my arms. It was a risk, but if one of them pinned me again, I needed to be able to pull sol from them.

Pain rained down my arms as something solid slid out of them onto the ground, clinking against the rocks. The hardened corruption almost sounded like iron rods.

The third wolf was on top of me before I could think about it, my hands pressing into his chest as it snapped at me.

I pulled sol through my hands, a rush running through my palms, up my shoulders, across my collarbone, and into my center like a clear highway. It was nowhere near as effective as biting, but I could feel my center filling up.

Flames exploded from my mouth as I used the sol immediately. The dirt wolf howled in pain, its whole front end hissing under acidic flames. I slammed Ae into its neck, blood clinging to her while grip.

"Come and get it, fuckers," I said, pulling out Ae and gearing up to fight the other two. She wasn't content yet and I hoped the other two would bring her up to level two.

Blood dripped down my arm, but I'd done this enough to know I was still fine. I had a lot of blood to lose before I was in danger.

An arrow slammed into the lead dirt wolf's neck, dropping it to the ground in a flurry of choking snarls. The other dirt wolf soon followed it, becoming still on the ground.

"There's always a bigger fish," I muttered, gearing up for what was probably going to be a worse encounter.

I **unequipped** Ae. I regretted it immediately but knew it was for the best. This was probably going to get ugly.

SEVENTEEN: GOLDEN WINGS

Soldiers on horseback poured in from the forest, armor shining in the dawn light.

In a flash, I was surrounded—a ring of spears pushing my back to the river.

Covered in mud and blood, I probably looked like a monster. At least, that's what I hoped was happening—a little misunderstanding. I saw a few of their eyes start glowing as they pulled in sol, the smell of pork reaching my nose and making my mouth salivate slightly.

My gut twisted. Ae's remarks about my height appeared true. Each one of the men were at least two feet taller than me, and their horses were monstrously intimidating from the angle I was standing.

"Hey, Captain, it looks like we found your gremlin," one of the armored men said, patting me down. Another elbowed him in the side.

"I bet if you ask nice, he'd let you kill it. The thing is somehow all the way up to level eight," a second man commented.

I'd already had enough. "First off, I'm right here, and I'd rather you didn't," I snapped back, despite my charisma's warnings to shut up.

"Ah, so it speaks." The Captain rode between the parting soldiers, his silver helmet crested with golden wings like Viking horns. "We have had reports of a gremlin causing unrest in the forest. Surrender or be struck down."

What the actual fuck was going on?

"I assure you, I have been minding my own business." I looked at the scowls all around me.

I barely dodged the butt of a spear lashing out at me.

"You will remain silent unless spoken to," one of the men said.

"The Captain was speaking to me, dipshit," I replied evenly.

Weapons all moved at once, but the Captain stopped them by raising a single clenched fist.

"Until we get confirmation, we will give you the dignity of walking under your own power, so long as you don't resist. Is this fair enough for you, gremlin?" The Captain's gaze bored into me from under the shadow of his helmet. It was phrased as a question, but I understood that there was a threat behind it.

It may have been time to listen to charisma, after all.

I mentally turned to that little voice, listening to what it had to say. My charisma score was one of my highest stats; surely, it would lead me right. It wasn't like I had much of a choice by the looks of things.

I swept into an extravagant bow, sweeping one arm wide and slipping my ring into a pouch with the other, hoping the motion had gone unnoticed.

"Stone McGracen, halfkin merchant and adventurer extraordinaire, at your service." I snapped up from my bow. "Now, if you would be so kind as to escort me to your town so we can clear this up, I would be happy to come with you." The words came out in a torrent, a wide smile plastered on my face.

The Captain burst into laughter. "Never before have I heard such a sharp tongue on a gremlin. Perhaps you were a scholar's assistant or part of a wandering menagerie?" A chuckle ran out among the men. "No, don't tell me. I'd rather find out at the Town Nexus. Come now, gremlin merchant, I am eager to discover the truth."

I honestly wasn't sure if that worked or not. The group did relax, but only because now I seemed like a joke.

The Captain gave out a sharp whistle before riding back into the forest. The soldiers fell into formation, riding behind him in a single-file line.

While I was distracted, a collar snapped around my neck. It was a clunky metal thing with a nasty hinge. Immediately, access to channels below my neck disappeared. I stifled a laugh. Was this for real? I could feel the sol in it, calling me to draw it out. These idiots just unknowingly slapped a battery on me.

A rope tied to the collar pulled me behind one of the men on horseback. I had to run to keep up with their easy trot. It was either that or be dragged on my face behind them.

"So, are you guys town guards or something?" I said to the soldier pulling me along.

"Silence, gremlin." The soldier refused to look at me. "It is only through the Captain's kindness that your tongue is even in your mouth. Speak again, and maybe I'll remove it for you, nonner."

"**Inspect**," I muttered, targeting the guard pulling me along.

Human (lvl 3): An adult male of the hominid variety. One of the seven civilized races, humans have no particular perks or weaknesses, making them unpredictable generalists. Notably dangerous in groups.

Level three? These guys sucked! They wouldn't even make a good meal for Ae. Maybe I should've fought them after all.

I eyed them and the horses they rode on. There were around a dozen of them, and they all were so much bigger than me. I liked my chances one-on-one, but I was hosed in a group like this. I had no choice.

My legs burned as I was pulled along through the snow. The pace was relentless, leaving me unable to catch my breath. Hours stretched as I was dragged through the uninterrupted forest—no semblance of a path anywhere.

If I could have, I would have fallen on my knees and kissed the pavement as we merged onto a cobblestone road.

The road soon turned into a bridge, crossing a small stream near the town gates I'd seen from afar. It looked so small from the dungeon entrance, but the gates had to be twenty feet tall and wide enough for four horses to walk through without touching each other.

The town looked much like I witnessed from above. It was idyllic, like a Thomas Kincaid painting, but it didn't smell like the scented candles I associated with urban mom aesthetic. It smelled like rancid ass and freshly baked bread. It smelled of roasted meat and vomit. Deep channels were dug onto the sides of the road for excrement and other refuse to flow into the nice little ice melt stream we had just crossed. I had to suppress the instinct to cover my nose. How did people live here?

All eyes were on me as we marched into town. Everyone looked disturbingly human, with blonde hair, light skin, and rounded ears. Most were tall, sporting braided beards, like someone you'd see in Scandinavia.

People cleared out of our way as we moved through town, arriving at a stone obelisk. It stood in the middle of a square, twice the height of a man but only a few feet in width. It came to a soft point at the top, a clear jewel pulling in sol at its tip.

My handler pulled me forward. His long strides were challenging for me to keep up with without running. The obelisk towered over us, giving off a sharp smell of bleach. It was pungent and unappetizing.

"Here we are, gremlin," the Captain said, placing his hand against the obelisk. Now that I was standing next to him, I noticed his scent was much stronger than the others. "The Town Nexus will reveal what we need to know."

The Nexus appeared to be smooth stone, but as it lit up, symbols and hieroglyphs appeared along its length. The light reached out, swirling into my center, the foreign energy probing me.

"Hmm," the Captain said, his eyebrows raising in surprise. "It says you are free and hail from no established clan. It's almost as if you appeared out of nowhere." He moved his hands as if making selections on the screen we couldn't see. "Your respawn point is in the middle of nowhere? Hmm."

I waited patiently as the Captain continued to read. "Ah," he continued. "It looks like Ms. Azul's official statement doesn't detail any physical harm. Curious. Did you strike Ms. Azul?"

"Unless Ms. Azul is a level 16 murder bird or a dirt wolf, no I did not," I replied.

The Captain looked at another invisible screen. "The Nexus indicates your words are truth or at least that you believe them."

"So, does that mean I'm good to go?" I said, glad to have been proven right.

"Quite the opposite," the Captain said. "It is illegal by Solendian law for a nonhuman to be without a handler. We might only be a territory, but the law still applies. Your level and intelligence will bring in quite a windfall for the town once we find a buyer."

I had a line, and this was past it. These bastards were about to have a rude awakening if they thought they could sell me to the highest bidder.

"Peace." The Captain pressed a sword into my neck. I hadn't even seen him draw it. "A professional organization will likely pick you up. Most are staffed by high-level nonners."

A pressure settled on my shoulders. I swallowed hard, understanding where I stood on the pecking order.

"A misunderstanding," I said, letting charisma take over. "I am no fighter and am eager to hear of this new opportunity when it arises."

The Captain smiled a thin smile, suspicion clear in his eyes. He knew I was up to something, but he wasn't sure what. "Then it is time to get you settled in."

The Captain handed off his horse and walked me across the town square to a plain building made of stone. People stopped what they were doing to look at me, none of them friendly. I came to the conclusion it was a barracks, judging by the weapons lining the walls. We passed through the barracks and into the back, coming into a room of holding cells. Most of them were empty, but a few humans squeezed their faces between the bars with their hands reaching out, grinning or spitting as we walked past.

The Captain guided me to a large cell at the end, opening the door and gesturing for me to enter.

The Captain stopped me just as I was about to step through the door. "Behave, gremlin," the Captain said. "I know you have tricks up your sleeve. You're too calm, and your level is too high. I have a bounty ready to go if you escape. The amount is high enough that nowhere would ever be safe again."

"Captain, I am just a wandering merchant. This is a misunderstanding." I smiled up at him, and his frown deepened.

The barred door slammed closed behind me.

"I will assign an extra guard." With that, the Captain twirled and walked off, his cape flashing behind him as his boots thumped on the stone floor.

I looked around my temporary home. Some soiled straw had been dumped in the corner with a bucket opposite of it, and judging by the smell—I knew what its purpose was. My gut instinct was to escape immediately, but a piece of me knew it was best to wait and see what happened.

I turned to the wall as if taking a piss, lifting my tunic for effect.

"Equip Chainbreaker," I whispered, Ae appearing on my belt.

She was pissed.

I pulled her sheath off my belt, tucking it under my tunic. I held the angry knife, leaning in to talk to her.

"Shit got squirrely," I whispered, hoping no one was

watching too closely. I'm sure I looked insane. "I had to do it."

The feeling from Ae remained unchanged. I wasn't sure if she could actually understand me or was reacting to base stimuli.

"Quit being a baby. I'll make it up to you later," I said, tucking her in the sheath under my tunic. It was awkward, but having her on me made me feel better.

I finished my 'piss,' letting out a breath. "Well, no time like the present." I got down on the floor into a lotus position.

Immediately, a light smell of cinnamon roll wisped into my nose, and my stomach grumbled loudly. "God dammit, I never got to finish my fish," I realized. In all the excitement, I forgot I was starving.

I tried to meditate, but the smell persisted, breaking my concentration. They smelled close, almost like they were right next to me. I looked over, seeing the bars at the cell, realizing what I was smelling.

I placed a hand on the bars, taking the time to look around. The room looked like it could house 200 prisoners in a pinch, about a dozen wooden stalls on each side of the room. My cell was at the end, facing the entrance on the other side. I was unimpressed.

"Well, I don't mind if I do," I said, leaning my face against the bars and sucking a bit of the enchantment out. I wasn't near strong enough to bend the iron, enchanted or not, but the little bit of sol did help stave off some of my weariness.

"**Cleanse**," I said, ready to feel clean again. I had washed a little in the river but felt disgusting and probably smelled worse.

Dirt only fell off my face and neck, stopping at the collar, my back still sticky with sweat and grime.

The collar was going to be a problem.

I pulled sol from the collar. I was surprised at how readily it came out. It was barely a trickle before going dry.

"**Cleanse**," I said again, dirt flying off my whole body this time. "That's better." It felt like I had just stepped out of the shower. To my dismay, a bit of black ooze ran down my nose, but otherwise, I was fine. Any corruption left in my system would need to be deliberately expunged.

I fiddled with the heavy collar. It came apart immediately. I grabbed it and snapped it back, but without sol, nothing was latching. As luck would have it, a guard was walking down the rows, visually checking the cells.

I placed a hand on the bars, pulling out a trickle of sol and pushing it into the collar. I felt it snap into the place again. The collar barely had a wisp of sol, negating its ability to block my lower channels.

The guard came and went on their rounds, eyeing me with suspicion. For a moment I through there would be trouble but he just clicked his tongue and moved on.

I decided I hated this town.

I decided to run through some basic exercises and take

advantage of the relative peace of the prison cell. Besides, after that bite of sol, I was feeling peppy. Ae's hard sheath was a bit uncomfortable under my tunic, but I shifted her around until it felt acceptable to the picky weapon. I needed to be ready for whatever was coming.

I became aware of a presence in front of me. Sweat clung to my body as I opened my eyes to see a lad standing before me. He was no older than ten, standing a bit over my height, which was annoying in and of itself. Wordlessly, he slid a bowl of loose porridge under the bars before scurrying away like I was some monster hidden behind a cage.

"Oh, come on. I'm not that threatening," I called after him. My charisma said I wasn't helping.

The loose porridge tasted like cardboard someone had once rubbed a boiled chicken. It was like those 'flavored' sparkling waters my grandma would drink, but the porridge did its job, and my stomach felt significantly fuller than it had felt at any point before.

I slid the empty bowl back under the bars, coming to sit in a lotus position. I tried not to wince in pain as I mentally ran through my channels. Even though a lot of corruption had been cleared out, there was still a lot of work to do. The tarlike substance was clogging or restricting just about everything. Had I had always been like this or did my run-in with the corrupted centipede do a number on my mana channels?

Regardless of the reason, I needed my channels cleared sooner rather than later. With my low constitution and my tiny size, I was a sitting duck to anybody and everything that

I wasn't able to suck the magic out of. I needed to be able to pull from any contact. Biting people was a hard thing to pull off.

I smelled people coming before they arrived. The pork smell I was getting used to, but there was a gamey meat I wasn't familiar with. It was strong too.

The cell door opened with a rusty squeal, pulling me from my concentration. A collared figure barreled into me as they were thrown into the cage, causing me to roll against the wall. The person's ram horns clacked loudly against the floor as they fell on their back.

EIGHTEEN: RAINING COPPERS

The goatman rolled to his cloven hooves, charging the guards.

The guard at the gate slammed the door shut just before the goatman could reach them, his horns going through the bars and hooking on the other side.

The goatman let out a panicked bleat, a flow of guttural curses coming out of his mouth as he struggled to get his horns out of the bars.

I stood up, making a show of bracing my hands on my knees, as I rose to my full height of what I was painfully learning was about four feet tall. The goatman had to be about five foot five, if not a little taller. He was built like a sprinter, his limbs long and spindly. He had a short beard and cloven hooves instead of feet. His only clothing was a button-down shirt with a rumpled collar, his lower half completely covered in coarse fur.

"Hey, need some help?" I asked the newcomer. His head whipped around, looking at me, his horns still stuck in the prison bars.

"Silence, filth," the goatman said, spitting at me.

I dodged the projectile, raising an eyebrow at his outburst.

"Now, let's be polite," I said, putting on my best smile. Charisma told me to be diplomatic. "We both find ourselves stuck in a cage. It seems like getting along would be in our best interest."

"Human pet. Talk like them. Waiting on master, nonner?" the goatman said, his demeanor increasing in hostility.

I wasn't sure if that could've backfired any harder.

My smile evaporated. "Fine, be like that," I said, shrugging.

The goatman bleated, and I was pretty sure it was a curse. He continued to struggle, his curled horns getting more stuck into the bars.

I settled back against the wall. "**Inspect**," I said under my breath. The light from the goatman was blinding. I covered my eyes out of reflex.

The goatman laughed. "Fly-mouse should not inspect gilded aurox."

My stomach dropped a little bit. Was this what happened when you inspected something way above your level? I recalled this also happened when I tried to inspect Ae and she was level forty-something.

The goatman continued pushing and pulling against the bars, bending them slightly. I hoped the guards wouldn't notice that, as I imagine the now weakened enchantments were meant to keep this exact kind of thing from happening.

"Hey, Mr. Goatman, how about a truce?" I called. He seemed like he was getting tired.

"No tricks, gremlin," the goatman said.

"An oath, then, to do each other no harm while we are in this cage," I offered.

The goatman struggled against the cage, but I could tell his heart wasn't in it. Finally, with a bleating sigh, he gave up. "Gwap agree. Gremlin help."

I grabbed the horns, trying to twist them to get him out, but he was well and truly stuck. All that sliding and mucking about only made it worse. I had to grab him by the other horn and manhandle him before he was free.

The goatman bleated in joy, doing a little trot around the cell. I returned to the lotus position and practiced sending bits of sol down my channels. I figured I wouldn't accidentally instigate a fight if I ignored him.

I felt a presence settle in front of me. Cracking open an eye, I saw the goatman, mirroring my pose, sitting across from me, his cloven feet tucked neatly beneath his knees.

"Can I help you?" I tried to hide the annoyance out of my voice. I was making some real headway and didn't want the distraction.

"Why here?" the goatman asked.

What was this? Twenty questions? Charisma urged me to be patient. I needed allies other than a half-sentient knife.

"A misunderstanding," I said, laying on the fake smile. "If I may ask, why are you here?"

"Business," he said.

"Well, that definitely sheds light on that," I said. This conversation was ten seconds in and more painful than being stabbed.

"Talk like human. How curious," the goatman said, stroking his beard. "Human raised?"

"You could say that," I said. Charisma could shove it. "Now, if you excuse me, I'm in the middle of something."

"Ah." The goatman looked at me with more intelligence than his eyes than I expected. "Is this why bar enchantment weak?"

"I don't know what you're talking about," I said. "See, I've got the suppression collar on. I couldn't do anything even if I wanted to."

"I do see collar." The goatman waved to the bars behind him. "And yet, enchantment nearly gone."

I shrugged, going back to closing my eyes.

"The guards say halfkin fight like little dragon. This true?" the goatman asked.

This got my full attention. I reevaluated the goatman staring at me. That spark of intelligence I'd seen earlier was now lit into a bonfire. He was openly evaluating me, his back straight and his chin raised up slightly.

"Why would the guards—" Realization dawned on me. "You're not a fellow prisoner, are you?"

A grin spread across the goat's face. "Intelligence higher than one. Very good." The goat made a grating sound between a bleat and a throaty laugh. "Gwap represents Avila Adventurers Guild. A little dragon they hope to buy."

"So, I've been bought then."

"No," the goatman corrected. "Scare human. Fight like little dragon. Gwap sent to check for demon. Are you a demon?"

"No?"

"Then is solved," Gwap said, leaping up, his hooves clacking loudly on the stone as he landed. "Ricolo, let Gwap out!"

The Captain strolled in, eyeing Gwap carefully. Just who was this guy?

"Is he good?" the Captain asked. He eyed me suspiciously.

"Good? Yes. Peculiar? Also, yes." Gwap rested a hand on my shoulder. "Little gremlin breathe fire like a dragon. Talk like a princess. The Giulia family is interested."

"Ah, then I release him into your care." The Captain pulled out a ring of keys and unlocked the cage. "Stone, please follow Mr. Cliffside." The Captain leaned down to eye level with me. "Mr. Cliffside here represents the most powerful family in the Fringe. I'd advise being on your best behavior or the executioner's ax will seem like a blessing."

"I'm always on my best behavior," I said, taking my collar off and handing it to the Captain. He looked at the collar, then at me, unsure what to make of what happened.

Gwap laughed, patting me on the back. "Little dragon has teeth. Good. Very good."

We left the baffled Captain behind as we walked through the barracks and into the square. It felt good to walk out after a few hours.

Gwap whacked me on the back of the head.

"Slouch. Humans no like proud nonners," Gwap whispered into my ear. It dawned on me we were the only nonhumans I'd seen since leaving the dungeon.

I looked around at all the eyes on us. People were afraid, careful to give us a wide berth as we stood in front of the guard barracks.

I let my posture deteriorate, slouching my shoulders and bending my knees slightly. The change in atmosphere was almost immediate. It was like a sigh of relief had been let out of the crowd as I looked defeated.

"Follow," Gwap said. "Fix dragon's mistake."

The goatman darted off, skipping and moving around the square. I never knew exactly where he was going and had to zigzag around him as he picked flowers blooming in snowbanks and handed them to random people. Children clapped as he did a little dance. Twirling, the goatman shot me a grin as I did my best not to die of secondhand embarrassment.

I looked around at the square. People smiled and moved on, barely acknowledging the goatman frolicking about. With a start, I realized what he was doing. The people felt comfortable thinking of him this way, and he played right into it. Once again, I was shocked by the depth of intelligence I got from the goatman.

The goatman finished with a flourish, scattering coppers and flower petals into the air as they rained down amongst the children scrambling to grab them. I stared at the display with an open jaw as he looped his arm through mine, pulling me towards the Nexus.

Something sharp stung me, and a bit of blood welled up on the end of my finger, but before I had any chance to think about what had happened, Gwap pressed it against the Nexus, pressing his hand next to mine. I again felt a weird probing sensation from the Nexus, but it was over in a blink.

"It done, little dragon. Much money paid for your services," Gwap said.

"What services exactly?" I asked. This was all happening so fast. Had I just been bought?

The goatman scoffed. It almost sounded like an offended bleat. "The Giulia family famous. You live under rock?"

"That's not far off, to be honest," I said, shrugging.

The goatman clicked his tongue. "The Giulia family Fringe Adventurers Guild founder. Staff with powerful nonners.

Dangerous work, yes, but much freedom, much reward."

"Nonner. I keep hearing that thrown around. What does that mean?" I asked.

"Nonhuman, little dragon. Maybe too much time in wild turned brain to mush." The goatman produced a bronze amulet from inside his shirt. It was a simple thing: a chain with a small amulet with two crossed swords and a large, stylized 'G' printed over top.

Gwap placed the amulet over my neck. "Never remove. Bounty already put in system. 10,000 gold for your head. Only head, remember." The goatman slid a finger across his neck. "Oh, do not eat enchantment either, little dragon."

"Gotcha. Don't take it off. So, I do quests now? Like, am I more or less free to go?"

"Everyone else? Yes. You? Ah, you get special job. More details later, still evaluating."

"I'm still being tested?"

"Nonners always being tested," the goatman said. "Best realize before too late."

Gwap twirled away before I could reply. His demeanor had gotten serious for a flash before snapping back. I tucked the amulet under my tunic, running after the insane goat.

The town, Avila, was far bigger than I thought. Gwap greeted everyone as we weaved through alleyways. Sauntering and twirling, he always seemed to produce something from one of the pockets lining the inside of his shirt—a bit of glitter or spark of light, a coin, a flower petal.

Twenty minutes later, we arrived at our destination with a trail of debris in our wake. We stood in front of a large wooden building on the edge of town against the wall. It was three stories and looked like it had been thrown together by someone who had only ever heard of a building but had never seen one. The words 'Adventurers Guild' were sprawled across the top of the entrance with two crossed swords with a stylized G replacing the 'G' in guild.

"Come," Gwap said, opening the door with a flourish and a bow as I stepped in.

The sound of many conversations hit me at once as I entered. A combination of body odor, alcohol, and cooked meat filled the air, leaving a smoky haze at the top of the room. The room was huge, holding at least a hundred comfortably, and this was probably far beyond that, with many people standing.

Everyone was human, and most were looking at us—some people in curiosity, some in indifference, some in annoyance. A barmaid carrying multiple mugs of ale stopped in front of us.

"Gwap, you ass. You were supposed to finish the expense reports this morning, and you disappear, leaving me to do them all." The barmaid stamped her foot to emphasize the last word, the mugs on her tray spilling some beer.

Gwap put a hand on the back of his head, looking up at the ceiling. "Gwap, sorry. Pepper best."

Pepper sighed heavily. The motion of her abundant cleavage drew the attention of multiple patrons. Her low-cut top looked like it was about to burst.

"Don't let this old goat fool you, halfkin." Pepper bent down to talk to me, and I could've sworn I felt Ae grow cold under my tunic. I kept my eyes up, sensing danger from multiple angles.

The barmaid continued. "Old Gwap is sharper than an assassin's dagger and three times as deadly. Be on the lookout for his pranks. They're normally vicious and teetering on fatal," Pepper said, pointing at the goatman.

"Gwap would never." The goatman covered his heart, vowing as the barmaid rolled her eyes and walked off. The eyes in the room followed her like a wave, her hips swaying in a practiced fashion. I knew who was running this place, and it wasn't Gwap.

"Come," Gwap said, leading me through the packed tavern room toward some stairs in the back.

The adventurers we passed were all decked out in mismatched armor, improvised weapons, and body paint like they were preparing to film Mad Max. I gave polite nods to everyone who made eye contact, carefully avoiding the sharp weapons sticking out of booths and beneath chairs.

I struggled to keep us as Gwap jumped all over the stairs, walking on the handrail at one point. They were rickety and uneven, a nightmare of a staircase that could've only been built by an insane person. It had to be some defensive decision like the twisting staircases of medieval castles.

I emerged at the top, crawling up the last few stairs to see Gwap standing before a bookshelf. He looked around to see if anyone was watching before tugging on a book. The whole shelf opened to reveal a room.

The entire thing was so ridiculous-looking that there was no way anyone didn't know that's what this was there for. Hell, there were literally wear marks on the floor from the door being opened so many times.

Gwap closed the door behind me. The room we entered was wonderfully furnished, with a giant desk dominating the center and a massive window overlooking the town. It would have been nice if everything didn't have bite marks. The chair had multiple spots where an entire bite had been taken out of the leather, and the cushioning underneath stuck through.

Gwap jumped over the desk, landing on the plush high-backed chair, twirling to face me. "Sit."

There was no chair for me to sit on. So, I plopped myself down on the floor across from the desk, my head maybe reaching halfway up. I felt like a preschooler in the principal's office. Gwap laughed hysterically.

"So is there like a reason I was brought here or…" I trailed off.

The goatman cleared his throat. "Yes. You odd. Human scared. Now explain."

I paused, unsure how much to tell him. I liked Gwap, and that was, to be honest, part of the problem. I could feel myself wanting to tell him, even though Ae warned me to keep my mouth shut.

"Gwap can smell secret. Maybe trade, secret for secret?" The goatman was now dead serious, his aura pressing down on me.

I considered the offer. It was a gamble, but I deemed the risk worth it. "I believe it would be best if you went first as an act of goodwill."

"The little dragon learns. Must be good secret." Gwap tapped his chin. "First secret, center not always located here." The goatman tapped just above his stomach, watching me closely. "This fact. Church not like. Kill all who know."

"I have heard this, yes," I said, not wanting to give anything away.

The goatman nodded, seeming satisfied. "Suppression collar not work. Center must be above neck." He pulled his beard, evaluating me. "Intelligence, Wisdom, or Charisma? Wisdom? No. Intelligence, maybe. Charisma, maybe. Too smart, too smooth."

Sol flared into the goatman. A sharp scent of roasted goat and spiced curry filled the air. My nostrils flared for a fraction of a second, but it was enough for the goatman to catch it. His sol vanished in an instant as he appeared next to me in a flash.

"Sol eater?" The goatman tapped the desk, lost in thought. "But little dragon in control? Dangerous. Powerful," Gwap commented.

"Hey, I didn't ask for –"

"Perfect." The goatman smiled. "The old master much pleased. Quite a bargain Gwap paid for you. Now where little dragon from? Time for secret, yes?"

Wait? That wasn't the secret he wanted? I was completely thrown off at this point. I don't know what to hide. Charisma pushed me to tell the truth like a joke. I agreed.

"I woke up in a dungeon, dragged here from another world," I said.

"Spawn point in dungeon not town? Not good. Not good." The goat man got up and poured himself something from a brown bottle sitting on one of the bookshelves. He swirled the liquid in the little glass before drinking it all, belching, and sitting back down. "Listen, little dragon, tell no one about secret. You threat. Human kill. Monster kill." The old goat's eyes bored into me.

"Yes, sir." I shifted uncomfortably on the floor.

"Listen close. You normal adventurer, hailing from Redfield Grasshold to the east. You taught breathe flame as part of menagerie. Path is shadow. Clear?"

"Redfield Grasshold. Shadow. Got it," I repeated.

"Stone smart, maybe?" The goatman chuckled, his mirth coming back. Bells tolled outside. I didn't count, but it was at least twenty. "Is late. Ask Pepper for room. Meet me alleyway. Seventh bell." Gwap began leafing through papers neatly piled on the desk.

I sensed I was dismissed, rising and walking towards the door. When I turned around to say goodbye to the goat, he was gone. The large window behind his desk opened just a crack.

Yeah, that tracked.

Pepper wasn't hard to find. She was bustling around the tavern, shouting insults and being grumpy. Mugs of ale sloshed as she basically threw them at patrons, but all the guys gave her warm smiles, complimenting her as she moved around. The whole dynamic was weird.

"What do you want?" Pepper snapped at me as I walked up to her.

"Gwap said I should see you about getting a room?" I shifted back and forth as she narrowed her eyes at me.

Pepper placed a hand on her hip. "I don't like it."

"Like what?" I asked.

"You're the size of a child, and your accent is odd. It's weird." Pepper turned to walk away.

"So, am I getting a room?" I followed Pepper through the tavern as she swept up an armful of empty mugs.

"Yes, I'll get you a room," Pepper huffed as she stalked back towards the double doors leading into the kitchen.

I felt eyes on me as I waited, trying not to acknowledge them. Being the only nonhuman in the room felt weird.

Thankfully, Pepper came back quickly, putting a key in my hand. "Follow me."

I followed the woman up the stairs to the second story. She led me down a twisting hallway to a series of rooms.

Pepper stopped me in front of door twenty-three, handing me a key. "Some advice? Don't come down tonight. Keep to yourself. The Red Dawn is still fresh in the memories of this town, and I don't feel like cleaning blood up off the floor."

"Got it. Anywhere I can take a shower?"

"Running water in the rooms." Pepper looked offended. "You think we're hissfolk savages or something?"

I shrugged, and she twirled on her heel to leave. I was glad to see her go, a sense of danger lifting from my mind.

The key turned the lock, opening into a room that would make a college dorm look like a luxury suite. There was barely enough room for a bed, let alone the end table crammed between it and the wall. A small door opened into a shared bathroom. It was cramped, but a large bronze tub sat next to a dirty sink.

It was perfect.

I pulled Ae out. She had been digging into my side the whole time. I got the impression she was mad at me. I sat her on the end table, and the feeling only intensified.

"Okay, okay," I said, picking her back up, heading towards the bathroom.

I tested the water, and it came out warm. "Thank the goddess herself."

I sat in the hot bath, twisting the silver ring around my finger and looking at the knife beside the tub. Ae was irritated, but I was confident water wasn't good for knives, so she had to deal with it.

I felt like a new halfkin as the water drained from the tub, my **reequipped** clothes settling comfortably on my body. Judging by the sloshing I could hear from the street, I knew where the sewer let out.

The bell rang in the distance, four groups of five and then two more.

It was like that dumb military time my grandpa used. It took an embarrassing amount of time to realize twenty-two bells equaled 10 pm.

Was it really ten at night? I opened the dirty curtains to look at the unchanging dawn light outside. My sense of time was all messed up from the lack of a day-night cycle. This place was weird.

I settled in, tucking Ae under my pillow and trying to get comfortable on the bed. I was out before I even realized how tired I was.

NINETEEN: TEA IN THE WOODS

I covered my head with a pillow as I counted six bells.

I groaned, struggling to come upright. I was sore, really sore.

"Holy fuck, is this what working out without dying afterward feels like? It almost seems worth it just to die." I laughed, stopping to massage my lower back.

All the kinks slowly worked out of my muscles as I moved around.

"Why am I naked?" I said, looking over myself. It had not been a restful night. I woke up at least every hour, unable to get comfortable. The soreness started about an hour after I lay down, and it became my companion through the night. I must have unequipped my clothes at some point.

Bringing Ae with me, I splashed my face in the sink water and smoothed my brown curly hair. For the first time, I got a good look at myself.

"Ae, you didn't tell me I looked like a kid," I said, feeling my face. I had been imagining a rugged adventurer type, some scars, maybe a five o'clock shadow, but instead, I looked like I'd just rolled out of the Keebler elf factory. My ears came to soft little points, and I had a happy look about me. It was disgusting. If not for the hollow look in my eyes, I would've looked like the Pomeranian of humanoids.

"Solara damn it all." I rested my hands on the sink, struggling to find the gumption to get dressed. I felt like a lot of people wanted shit from me. I didn't feel up for it. I needed one of those bikini beach filler episodes from the animes my grandpa used to watch.

"My grandpa would have loved this place," I told Ae. I had decided to talk to her whether she could hear me or not. "He's the one that would flourish here, not me."

The smell of bacon wafted up to my nose. "Man, I sure hope that's actually bacon and not just a person again." I was getting sick of people smelling like pork when they used sol.

I grabbed Ae and **equipped** my clothes, fastening her back on my belt. She looked gaudy against my simple outfit, but I wasn't going to say anything. I checked in to see how the ex-elf was doing. She seemed to be… ready? The mix of emotions was weird to me. It was like she was anticipating something.

Climbing to the bottom of the world's most dangerous stairs, it looked like a bomb had gone off in the tavern. Between the turned-over chairs and the mystery liquids on the floor, I was glad I missed whatever had happened down here.

I followed my nose to the kitchen, hoping desperately it was someone cooking.

I opened the door, poking my head in. A heavyset woman hummed to herself as she cooked over a fire, meat sizzling in a cast iron pan. After a glance in my direction, she smiled at me, but then she stopped, her head snapping back to me, her eyes wide.

"Don't scream," I said, raising my hands.

"Back, gremlin, this meat ain't for you," she said.

This was starting to get old.

I dodged a knife. "Did Gwap not tell anybody that I was here? I'm just here to find out if breakfast is included in my stay."

"Show me your Guild amulet," she said, holding another knife.

I pulled the amulet out of my shirt, and she deflated immediately, pushing the wrinkles out of her apron. "Welcome, adventurer. Gwap most certainly did not inform the staff. It has been a while since we've had a nonner here and I was not prepared."

"Gwap did not what?" The goatman climbed through the window from the alley even though there was literally a door not even ten feet down.

"You know I hate it when you do that," the woman said, smacking the goatman on the chest with a spoon.

The goatman gestured to me. “Griselda, meet Stone, newest

halfkin adventurer."

"Never seen a halfkin before," Griselda said, stirring something in a pan that smelled like it was burning a bit. "The others are going to be upset."

"Others not Guild Lead," Gwap said.

"As you keep reminding us," Griselda mumbled, stirring aggressively.

Holy shit, wait a minute. Was Gwap actually the Guild Lead? That wasn't an inside joke or something? I'd half suspected we just broke into the real leader's office.

Griselda cleared the pan, throwing a handful of vegetables and grasses in. The goatman rubbed his hands together, dancing back and forth. I still wasn't convinced I wasn't being pranked.

"Make sure eat lots," the goat man said to me, nudging a meat-laden platter towards me. "Young dragon need meat get strong." Griselda gave him a cross look but didn't stop him. I got the distinct impression I was not the intended recipient of that food.

Griselda saw my hesitation, letting a ghost of a smile flicker across her face. "Take it. You'll need it if you're going to be with him all day."

I settled down at the single table in the kitchen, setting the platter full of meat in front of me. I almost groaned as I bit into the bacon. Almost. I wasn't one of those weirdos who made sounds as they eat, but the moment nearly called for it.

Within a few minutes, Gwap settled across from me, diving face-first into his pile of greens like a starving wildebeest. An errant thought ran across my brain. What if he finished his food first and made us leave? I could see the goatman doing that. I couldn't let that happen, diving into my plate of food and stuffing myself as fast as possible.

Gwap took my increased eating speed as a challenge. To my horror, he started eating even faster, prompting me to eat even faster myself. I wasn't even chewing now, desperate not to be robbed of yet another meal.

"You both are disgusting." Griselda said, tisking at us. "I expect there to be no mess."

The goatman looked at her in irritation, but Griselda's attitude stayed true, a firm grip on the wooden ladle she was smacking threateningly in her hand. Gwap relented. The Guild Lead only had so much power, it seemed.

I stuffed the last of the meat in my mouth, even to the point of being tempted to lick the plate clean. I felt like I was a bottomless pit.

"So, what's on the agenda for today?" I said, pretending there wasn't still food in my mouth.

"Training," the goatman said through a mouthful of greens. I was pretty sure I understood what he meant, but then he winked at me, making me less confident in my assumptions.

I went to bring the platter back to Griselda, but she instead pointed me toward a wash bucket, where I scrubbed it clean and returned it to a rack with similar platters.

I pulled the ring out of my pocket. I had removed it, not wanting to lose it in the murky dishwater. I stared at the ring momentarily, a sense of loss hanging over me for a second.

"You seem troubled," Griselda said, washing off some utensils.

"I'm worried for a friend of mine." I didn't want to trauma dump and kept it vague.

"Worrying won't help them none. Better to trust they'll be fine and be prepared to help them if the need arises." Griselda took the tone of a concerned mother. It made me glad she was getting over my nonhuman status.

"Yeah, it's hard," I said, laying a hand on Ae's hilt.

Griselda smiled sadly. "Always is."

Gwap ruined the moment by kicking me in the shin with his hoof. "Out of Gwap's way. Be sad somewhere else," the goatman said, pushing me to the side and popping his own dish into the wash bucket.

Unfazed, Griselda returned to what she was doing as Gwap scrubbed his platter. I started laughing, which earned me a weird look, but I was just acknowledging the insanity of it all. I ended up at the table, idly spinning the ring on my finger while Gwap took way too long to wash his dish.

"Follow." Gwap was already at the door and had tapped me on the way past. I didn't even realize, lost in thought.

The goatman led me out of the Adventurers Guild through a back door that emptied into a muddy alleyway. People, who I assumed were adventurers from the previous night, leaned up against the town wall, sleeping off the night. Gwap silently jumped over them with an amount of grace I could never dream of emulating.

I had assumed we were heading towards an arena or a dojo or something, but instead, Gwap led us to a single wooden gate with a solitary guard.

The guard leaped up from his stool as Gwap approached, opening the gate and ushering us through. I saw the entrance had the Guild symbol on it, and it closed with a thud behind us. I was shocked to see we were outside the walls. Why were we leaving the city?

Gwap must have seen the question on my face.

"Less eyes," Gwap grunted.

Before I knew it, we were racing through the forest. I could barely keep up with Gwap's casual pace, and then, just like that, he was gone.

I followed his scent, ascending the mountainside. I was having difficulty keeping on it, feeling the amount of sol increasing as we ran higher up the mountain. The trees smelled stronger, and the air smelled thicker, masking the traces of curry I was chasing.

When I arrived in the clearing, I was in a dead sprint, just trying not to lose him. I fell to my knees, heaving. I'd stopped being able to catch my breath a full minute ago.

Gwap was waiting for me, sitting on a stump. "Fight."

That was all the warning I got before Gwap kicked me hard enough to make me go airborne.

I landed hard, clutching my stomach as I rolled over. I hadn't even smelled him using sol, which was terrifying in and of itself.

"Disappointing," he said. "Again."

This time, I was ready for the goat. He flashed, moving so fast I could barely see him run. I rolled out of the way of his punch, my gut instincts taking over as I did my best to divert his strike. I still caught a glancing blow, using the momentum to hook my foot behind his, but he moved at superhuman speed, poking me in any areas I wasn't guarding as I desperately tried to land anything on him.

"Stop," the goatman said. "Gwap seen enough."

I was both offended and relieved. I still hadn't caught my breath from earlier and was trying to push myself through the fight. Not to make excuses, but my muscles felt like they were full of concrete, and were not as responsive as they should have been. I wasn't sure what well-rested felt like, but I knew this wasn't it.

"Okay, cool. Like, give me a second," I said, leaning against a small tree, its leaves turning a sickly shade of brown. "Shit, sorry," I jumped away from the tree, and hadn't even meant to draw sol from it.

The tree's sol felt sticky. It was like the difference between drinking water and drinking tea. They were fundamentally the same thing but also functionally very different.

The goatman watched me, an unreadable expression on his face. "Tell Gwap about dungeon."

"Not much to tell, really. It was dark and full of bugs. I honestly don't like talking about it too much. It was an absolute slog, and I died a lot more times than I want to admit."

"Nothing else?" Gwap asked. He had his hands folded in his lap, his legs tucked in a crossed position. At the moment, he looked every inch the wise old master.

"No." I poured every ounce of my charisma into the answer, but I could tell he didn't buy it, and he knew I could tell he didn't.

"Is ring from dungeon?" Gwap asked, his eyes boring into me. "Interesting symbol. Rising crescent moon."

I felt the tension rise in my neck. Ae had all kinds of enemies, and as much as I wanted to like Gwap, he could be one of them.

Gwap waited for me to elaborate, but I didn't. I just stared at him.

"Interesting," the goatman said, stroking his beard. "Ask Elder Waza about local dungeons. Maybe learn something new." The goatman paused. "Maybe not."

I did my best not to look tense, feeling defensive about the ring. I knew I couldn't beat Gwap in a fight, but he'd have to kill me to take Ae or the ring.

A smile spread across the goatman's face. "Show Gwap

dragon's breath." He clapped his hands, springing to his feet.

I breathed in sol, pulling. The ambient sol barely put pressure on my center. I kept pulling, wanting a good showing. This was some kind of job interview, after all. In truth, I was fine being bought by the Guild so long as I got to stab powerful things with a certain knife.

"Wyvern's Breath," I whispered, trying to get in the practice of not announcing my attacks. I shot a stream of black and purple flames into the air. It reached nearly twenty feet, but it petered out immediately as I dumped my whole center. The sticky flames stuck to the plant life it landed on, eating through whatever it touched.

"Dragon's breath that not," the goatman said. "Acidic like wyvern. Fascinating. Very rare. Very rare."

"I'm glad you liked it," I said.

Gwap stroked his beard, entering a long bout of silence. I stood there, waiting for some kind of verdict. My hand drifted to Ae, wishing she would talk to me. Without someone to vent to, I was buckling under the pressure of everything.

"Very good. Little dragon get job," Gwap said, shaking my hand and patting me on the back.

"You still haven't told me what the job is," I pointed out.

The goat laughed. "Of course, of course. Little dragon is babysitter."

"Excuse me?" I wasn't sure I heard that right.

"Young Master Giulia dreams of being adventurer. Needs one more person on party. Who choose? Who choose? Ah, little dragon will do," Gwap said. I didn't feel particularly honored.

"This isn't a little kid, right?" I said, trying not to show a grimace.

"All children to Gwap, but no, young master be young man. Much see, much learn. Much like little dragon."

"So, what was the point of all this then?" I waved my hand towards everything around me.

"Always test, little dragon, always test," the goatman said. "Little dragon is weak, no threat to young master."

"Weak? Those town guards are like Level 3?" I protested. "How am I weak?"

"But resurrect during battle they will, but little dragon, maybe not. Maybe a few kills away and little dragon fly away forever."

"Wait, so people don't level up on purpose?" This revelation rocked me. I had assumed leveling up was good and hadn't considered that people would avoid it.

"Many choose coward's way, embracing the Mercy," Gwap said. "Dragon need team. Young master need team. Level ten, die alone. Level eleven, die alone. Only team survive." The goatman paused. "Now come, time see Elder Waza."

I could hear the bells chiming 11 am as we walked back to town. The guard at the small gate gave us a nod after Gwap flashed his medallion. The little alleyway was just as dirty, but everyone was gone. Their indents left little puddles to walk around.

We didn't go back to the Guild but into town. Curious now, I identified people as we wandered. I was surprised to find most people were level one or two. It was like they were going out of their way not to level. Every once in a while, I'd see an older person who was like level 4, which was weird. Everyone was either low-level, scrambling to survive, or high enough level to not be scared of anything.

The dynamic it created was peculiar. I had assumed that I wouldn't be perceived as a threat because I was much smaller than everyone else, but the reality was quite the opposite. Between my gear and my level, it boldly proclaimed that I was someone comfortable with violence. I got lost in thought as I followed the goatman.

I turned to Gwap as we exited the main gate on the other side of town. "Where exactly are we going?"

"Elder Waza. You have fur in ears?" Gwap huffed in annoyance. "Little dragon, listen better."

TWENTY: MUSHROOMS

The distant bell chimed thirteen as we approached a quant cabin halfway up the mountainside.

It was built in full view of the sunlight with a well-maintained herb garden on both sides of the path leading to the front door. A hand-painted side was staked out front, boldly declaring 'no visitors' in capital letters.

"Waza," the goatman called, cupping his hands around his mouth.

The sound of thumping and cursing could be heard from inside.

"What do you want, you thrice-blasted goat demon?" A rolling pin flew out of the window, barely missing Gwap as he moved out of the way, colliding instead with my stomach.

The door opened with a thud, and a pair of angry eyes surrounded by wrinkles looked at Gwap before flashing down at me. "Oh joy, another one."

"Elder Waza being extra nice today," Gwap said with a bow. "Elder Waza meet Stone, newest frontliner. Stone needs Steadfast spell. Charge Adventurers Guild."

The Elder was an older woman, pushing the bounds of the one-hundred-year protection of Solara's Mercy. Buttons covered the entirety of her jumper, a smattering of colors and designs. They clinked a little as she frowned at the goatman.

The goatman pulled me up off the ground. "Behave," he whispered in my ear before fleeing into the woods.

"You aren't as much trouble as he is, are you?" Elder Waza asked, snatching the rolling pin off the ground.

"I mean, I try not to be." I shrugged.

Elder Waza narrowed her eyes. I got the sense before she was just passively judging me. Now, she was actively judging me. "That remains to be seen. Come inside."

The interior of the house looked like someone threw a bookstore off a cliff. Scrolls and tomes were everywhere, stacked from floor to ceiling, bursting out of shelves, or stuffed in trunks and drawers. A spear rack was currently being repurposed to hold spools of scrolls with the spear tips poking out of the top.

The Elder sat at a small table, indicating I sit opposite her. A kettle had steam rising from it in the center, and half a cup of tea kept a closed book company off to the side. "Tea?" she asked.

“No, thank you,” I said, placing my hands in my lap. "Not

a tea drinker."

"Shame," the Elder said, sipping her tea, her eyes never leaving me. "I'm assuming you're Gretchen's gremlin."

My brain spun, trying to place a Gretchen. "I'm sorry, I don't know who Gretchen is."

"Ah, so she must have been attacked by some other halfkin in the woods two days ago?" the Elder said. "Caused quite the stir when she ran into town. Dramatic affair, lots of tears." Waza sipped tea from her cup, watching for my reaction.

That sack of shit catgirl not only abandoned the fight but also ratted me out to the guards? I took a deep breath, trying not to get visibly mad. "Yeah, that's not what happened at all," I said, "A lesser murderbird was about to turn her into its dinner when I showed up."

"How peculiar. She claimed you attacked her in the woods and got the guards all stirred up. I wonder why she would lie." The elder sipped her tea in a way that made me think she knew exactly why. My grandma was a pot stirrer and the only way to win was not to play.

"I have no idea." It wasn't a lie. Part of me wanted to press the issue but the charges had been dropped so I wanted to move on at this point.

Elder Waza nodded. "You'll have to excuse the locals. There are many horror stories passed down about halfkin. Nonners as a whole aren't well received, but halfkin were the fiercest of the nonhuman races to subjugate. The Red

Dawn is still fresh in the minds of those here."

"Red Dawn?" I asked. "I am not well versed in the history of this place."

"Odd for a halfkin. Don't your people pride themselves on being scholars and historians?" Elder Waza took another sip of tea.

"I've been separated from them for some time," I said. "You could say I know almost nothing."

"It is a shame to not know your people's history."

"I'd appreciate an explanation. I've been surprised by how cold everyone treats me. I mean, I'm maybe 100lbs and look like I make children's toys for a living."

Elder Waza gave me that 'bless your heart' look. "The Red Dawn isn't something people just forget." The Elder leaned forward, her voice dropping. "At the dawn of Solendia, non-human races fell one by one, but the halfkin were more slippery than a creek eel. They say a monster is most dangerous when it's trapped, and the halfkin army found themselves pinned. No one knows how, but they harnessed the very spirit of the sun. They say the explosion was brighter than Solara herself, a cloud like a mushroom casting daylight deep into the Twilight. Armies gone in an instant. Those that respawned were mad with terror, still feeling burns on their bodies. The Fringe was unlivable for generations."

This sounded familiar. There was no way right? "A nuclear explosion?" I asked, leaning forward. Everyone back home knew about the Pakistan Incident that rendered most of central Asia inhospitable. The images they showed us in school still haunted me.

"I don't know the word, but you seem familiar with what I'm talking about, which is concerning." The Elder looked at me pointedly. "Should I be concerned?"

A weight of spirit settled on my shoulders, sweat immediately sprouting from my brow. "No. Nothing to be concerned about. I have heard of this… magic, but don't know how to do it."

"Good." The pressure disappeared. "Let's talk of something else, tell me about your Path."

"Shadow," I replied, leaving it at that. I didn't know much more than the name anyway. I hoped Gwap was setting me up for success.

"Uncommon for a Halfkin. Although they are rarely allowed to leave their villages, so who knows anymore. Where did you say you were from again?"

"Redfield Grasshold."

"Of course, you are," Elder Waza said. "How conveniently far away that is. It is odd you were found so near the abandoned dungeon. No main paths go that way."

I could feel the Elder fishing for information, so I kept it simple. "Didn't even know it was up there. I just like to wander sometimes. See new things."

"A curious type? You might be interested to know this town

was tasked with protecting an abandoned dungeon up on the mountain. The guards routinely kill the overflow, but the area is dangerous, especially alone."

"Certainly sounds odd to me."

"With your path, I understand the old goats interest. Not many follow charisma Paths aside from Gwap and some hissfolk and even then it's rare they'll admit it."

"Wait, Gwap? That old goat has a high charisma?" I said. "He can barely talk."

"I've suspected he could talk normally for years but likes to mess with everybody," the elder said. The subject of Gwap made her look tired.

"That does mesh with what I've seen from him." I was now reviewing every interaction with him I had.

"Now I believe the old goat wants you as a front liner, weird choice for a halfkin, but that damn goat is rarely wrong. I'll go get that steadfast spell."

The Elder left me staring out the window. I could hear the paper being thrown about as she muttered to herself in the other room.

It felt like the pieces were coming together. These people had a different view of halflings and hobbits than I did. Back home, they were seen as cheerful heroes or steadfast companions, but here, they were walking nuclear bombs. I wasn't just some short guy, but a walking threat, able to take out a whole village.

The Elder returned. "Here it is. It's a bit of an odd one, but that infuriating goat tends to know what he's talking about." The elder returned with a brown scroll under her arm.

"Steadfast, right?"

"Correct. It's also known as the statue spell, making you too heavy to move and hard to hurt, but unable to do anything while the spell is active. Now, come out into the sunlight."

I followed the Elder around the house. She led me to a little stone pavilion nestled amid a flowering garden. A spiraling mosaic of the sun decorated the center.

"Be sure to pull in sol the whole time, or it might stunt your progress. The more thoroughly you understand the spell from the beginning, the less work you'll have to do later to integrate it."

"I thought it was just that you read the spell scroll and understood the spell?"

"Oh, Solara, no. There is much more to it than that. Spells have untold depth. You could spend your whole life working on a single spell and still have unfound applications and nuance. The spell stroll teaches your body how to do the basic mana channeling, nothing more."

"What is the difference between mana and sol anyway? I thought everything was sol."

"You sure ask a lot of questions." The Elder whacked my forehead with the scroll—the speed with which she did so was startling. "Everything in there is mana. Everything out here is sol. It's the same thing, different place. Now hurry up. I don't have all day."

I dropped into a Lotus position, pulling the scroll into my lap. I wasn't entirely sure about the spell, but I wasn't about to look a gift horse in the mouth.

I cracked open an eye to see Elder Waza had wandered off to fiddle with some flowers in the garden. I took a deep breath, drawing the sol into my center, spreading open the spell scroll and looking at its contents.

Just like last time, the scroll was covered in symbols and letters that I didn't directly understand, but my body seemed to know what it was, a heavy weight forming somewhere deep in my abdomen. I felt never used mana channels crackling under the tension as sol pushed through, working up from a point close to the ground and up to about my stomach.

That's when the pain began.

The mana ran to my solar plexus and stopped, searching for somewhere to go. With a flash of panic, I realized the scrolls' originator wouldn't have a center like mine. Unlike the system-made scroll that was meant for me, this spell was designed for someone with a center in their gate meridian.

Immediately, sol started leaking out of my stomach like someone had turned on a flashlight under my clothes. Spots decorated my vision as I found myself on my side.

"Contain it!" Elder Waza yelled. "Your center is leaking!"

I moved all my willpower to close my gate meridian and contain the sol. My vision tried to fade as my body wanted to pass out, but as much as I tried to stuff the sol back in, nothing worked. It was like trying to stop a stream with your bare hands. The flow was too much.

The sol needed an outlet. The spell scroll trying to teach my body needed to be completed, trying to loop the spell through my gate meridian. I needed to connect the spell to my center.

I channeled upwards, trying to push the sol up to my throat meridian. It was so close. The channels in my upper chest and neck were completely free, but it felt like there was a roadblock in the center of my chest, like a golf ball stuck in a water hose. I cast **Cleanse** on my chest, trying to clear whatever the blockage was—nearly passing out from the pain. My heart struggled to beat, becoming slower and weaker as I felt my blood pressure drop. If I weren't already on the ground, I would have passed out.

Elder Waza placed her hands on me, pushing sol into my gate meridian, adding additional pressure to where she thought my center was. "Halfkin, push through, close the leak, or you will die!"

I groaned, casting **Cleanse** again, desperately sucking sol out of the air to power it.

Something in my chest popped like a dislocated joint being reset. I writhed as my blood pressure dropped, darkness coming for me like a wave, black ooze piling on my chest.

"Halfkin, no! Fight, you little bastard." Elder Waza sent another pulse of sol through me like a surge of electricity.

A single booming beat thrummed in my chest, the darkness retreating as my muscles contracted like steel cables. My body stiffened as every muscle contracted, pulling my bones so hard they creaked under the tension. My heart meridian thundered to a crescendo as sol ran through it. It felt like my heart was truly beating for the first time, like a deep drum in my chest.

Heart Meridian unlocked! +5 Strength!

The sol passed through with little resistance, getting to the familiar mana channels of my neck and shoulders as soon as the pathway connected with my center, **Steadfast** activated. My skin turned to grey stone for a brief second before all the sol in my center disappeared. I was surprised by how much the spell used. Far, far more than **Wyvern's Breath**.

Darkness took me as I collapsed into a liquid pool of corruption, the world turning black.

...

I woke in a soft bed, frilly curtains and figurines decorating the walls—clean and covered in a light sheet. A light blinked in the corner of my vision.

Congratulations! New Spell learned!

"You're lucky you're so small. I wouldn't have been able to carry anybody larger than a child." Elder Waza sat in a rocking chair beside the bed, knitting something unrecognizable.

I placed a hand on my aching chest. "What the hell

happened?"

"I hoped you would tell me," the Elder said. "Never in all my years have I seen that happen. It's like there was nothing where your center was supposed to be, and then your heart meridian was unlocked for some reason. Meridian activation is highly dangerous, and you're lucky I was there. You came perilously close to death."

"Maybe it's a halfkin thing. Wasn't the scroll meant for humans?" I said, thinking on my feet.

"That is true. I hadn't considered that." Elder Waza tapped her lips with her forefinger. "I have given spell scrolls to other nonhumans before, but they have been few and far between. You know, I believe it might have been something else. I'm just not sure what."

I sat up. My midsection was sore, but it was fading. "Either way, I appreciate you helping me."

"A favor for a favor, perhaps," the Elder said. "Maybe you can satiate an old woman's curiosity." Sol flashed in her eyes as the smell of mint and pork filled the air, a shimmering bubble covering us. "This spell keeps out unwanted ears."

"About what exactly?" I said, trying not to show I was worried. Charisma urged me to relax. "There's not much to me. I'm quite boring."

The Elder laughed. "Such a blatant lie said so smoothly. A Path of Shadow user, indeed." A cold look crossed her face. "No, I would like to ask you how you got the ring on your finger."

The change took me off guard. "I got it from a friend."

"Gretchen said she saw you near the dungeon entrance, walking down from it, to be precise. Were you in the dungeon?" the Elder pressed.

I raised my hands, trying to de-escalate the conversation. "While I appreciate you helping me, I don't see what that has to do with anything. Am I free to go? I have work to do with Gwap later, and he is expecting me."

The Elder shook her head. "I'm not going to kill you, halfkin, but I need this information. It is personal, and I won't let it slip through my fingers."

We shared an uncomfortable silence. While I appreciated what Elder Waza had done for me, I wasn't about to spill my guts.

Just as I moved to leave, the Elder spoke. "Stay, even if just to listen. I am going to tell you a story."

I sat back down on the bed. "Alright, I'll listen."

The Elder looked into the distance. "My grandmother was there when the Solendian slave revolts broke out around... Solara save me. Was it truly a hundred years ago now? Hmm, she was a seamstress in the capital and madly in love with my grandfather—an accomplished adventurer and her human master. Her elven heritage kept them from being together publicly, but behind closed doors, they were all but married, saving money to move away. Then, the killings started. Slaves disappeared, and human masters were found with their throats slit wide and their ears trimmed down to points. Fear of elves escalated, leading to a man beating my grandmother in the street over a single glance. My grandfather stepped in but went too far, killing the man by accident. That night, they were visited as they packed to flee, a group of elves offering a new place to live deep in the Fringe. They accepted, joining a secret exodus from the capital and gaining the symbol of membership, a silver ring with the rising crescent moon." Elder Waza opened her hand to show me a ring identical to mine.

I looked down at the rings. "You're part elf then?" I said. "I couldn't tell at all."

"Barely." The Elder moved her hair aside to show her ears came to a point so subtle you'd miss it if you weren't looking for it.

"So, what happened? Is there still a place to live out here?"

"If they kept to themselves, maybe there would be, but it crumbled not even a decade after it was established. According to my father, most were content to live their lives, but many sought revenge, raiding deep into human territory, capturing humans, and enslaving them as they had been. The human response was vicious. They killed the leaders, and like a snake with no head, the budding nation died, scattering to the wind."

My brain spun with the new information. Just how long had Ae been in the dungeon? I knew it wasn't hours or minutes, but I had assumed it was months at most, not years.

Elder Waza dropped her voice to barely a whisper. "There were rumors the leader wasn't just some upstart elf but a noble half-blood. After the fall, rumors said someone locked her away somewhere in the Fringe, unable to kill her due to her noble blood. My father spent his life looking for her, leading him here. He traced sightings of the Solendian officers to Avila just after the final battle, convinced she was near here. Around that time, the dungeon became inaccessible, no longer letting anyone in and only expelling monsters. He joined the guards here, waiting for an opportunity, but the dungeon gate never activated. So, Stone the halfkin, was my father right, or did he die a fool?" Her eyes searched me, a lifetime of curiosity boring into me.

"She's dead," I said. Charisma screamed at me not to place my hand on Ae's hilt. "I found the ring on her body."

The Elder's eyes went wide. "He was right?" She let out a sigh. "If only I could go back and tell him."

My hand subconsciously drifted to Ae's hilt, and her eye caught it immediately.

"Did you find that knife as well?" the Elder asked. "May I see it?"

I hated that charisma had been right. I could feel frustration from that part of my mind.

I handed Ae to the Elder.

"Beautiful," she said. "Obviously elven." She traced a finger along the blade, a line of red in its wake.

Excitement emanated from Ae, the blood disappearing into the blade. The Elder stopped, looking at the knife with intensity. "Interesting." She handed me back Ae.

"What do you mean?" I placed Ae back in her sheath right away.

"Secrets on secrets," Elder Waza said. "Why don't you run back to the Adventurers Guild? I get the feeling a little lordling will be tasked to go into the wilds for a while."

I didn't need to be told twice, as I was escorted to the door. "Thank you for the story. I feel I understand more than when I came."

The Elder nodded, closing the door to her home behind her, leaving me alone in her front yard. My brain spun with all the new information. I wished Ae could talk. I felt adrift in a strange sea with no guidance.

I should've been thinking about everything as I ran back to town, but instead, I checked out, going on autopilot. The guards stiffened as I approached, but a quick flash of my medallion was all it took for them to let me through, side-eyeing me the whole time.

People looked uncomfortable as I passed. The streets were packed with people going in and out of shops and visiting food vendors on the side of the road. I smiled at people that made eye contact, but it just made their frowns deeper and looking more uncomfortable.

Fuck it. I would just try what the goat did.

I picked up some stones and started juggling as I made my way across town to the Adventurers Guild. People were unconvinced, but it felt like their eyes were sliding over me instead of sticking. There's like some weird reverse psychology, like in order to not stand out, I needed to stand out. The fucking goat probably got all these people used to this kind of nonsense.

My arms were tired from juggling, a problem I never anticipated having, as I arrived at my destination. The Adventurers Guild was packed, it being somewhere around dinner.

Pepper wandered over to me immediately, looking annoyed that I had bothered to exist anywhere near her establishment.

"It's about time you bothered to show up. Gwap told me you've been assigned to Jackson's party. They're in the corner." Pepper pointed with a head nod, a predatory smile across her face. "Have fun."

I followed her gaze, seeing four adventurers in clean gear sitting in a small booth together. "Why are they all sitting on the same side of the booth?" I asked Pepper.

Pepper grinned. "Oh, just wait. It gets worse. I'm sure you'll figure it out. It's nothing you couldn't handle."

I made my way over to my new adventuring party, placing a hand on Ae as I walked.

Twenty-One: Fifth Wheel

Against the back wall, four adventurers sat on a bench meant for two.

Worse, they looked like they were arguing.

I ignored the weird looks I got as I wove through the tables filling the floor. The party was so wrapped up in their spat that they hadn't seen me yet, so I slipped into the next booth, its high back obscuring me from the party.

"I just don't get why we need a fifth," one said. Her voice was flat, with a bit of a growl in it.

An upbeat voice responded. It was almost valley girl in tone. "Gretchen, you just need to be positive. Your aura is dimming."

Gretchen? I hoped that was a coincidence.

A masculine voice cut Gretchen's response off. "Both of you quiet. Father said we can't mess up this time. I think he might cut us off if we get wiped again."

A shy voice spoke. I could barely hear her over the background noise of the tavern. "Don't worry, he wouldn't do that."

"See, Gretchen, even Rochelle is being positive," the valley girl said.

I caught Pepper shooting me a questioning look, making a motion for me to join the party. I motioned for her to give me a minute, but she moved her hand in a circle, indicating for me to hurry it up.

I'd missed whatever had been said, going back to eavesdropping. The male voice was talking. "—frontliner, so Marie will be getting some help. Hopefully, that will balance us out."

The valley girl spoke. "I don't want to go to respawn again. Wixia is so far from here, and my father said he would make me walk the next time I got wiped. It was only my third time, for Solara's sake! My brother died nearly twenty times by level ten."

"It's okay, Marie," the quiet one, Rochelle, said. "Not all of us can respawn close like Gretchen."

The angry barmaid gave me a pointed glare as she passed by, stopping at the table with the party.

"I heard your fifth is on his way and should be here *very soon*," Pepper said.

Shit, she was forcing my hand. I was going to have to dive right in. "Fuck," I muttered as I slipped back toward the entrance. The party was focused on Pepper as I wove through the tavern, happy to be ignored. After a deep breath, I stood a little straighter, turning to approach the table.

"Oh, look, there he is," Pepper said, pointing to me the instant I turned around.

I locked eyes with a familiar face at the table. It was that backstabbing catgirl, after all. I felt my stomach drop a little, the nervousness converting to dread.

As for the rest, I got to see the disappointment on their faces in real-time. Well, except for Gretchen, who went white as a ghost. Jackson schooled his reaction the best, but the redhead on his arm looked like she wanted to cry.

The walk to the table felt like it took minutes.

"Nice to meet you. I'm Stone," I said, standing next to Pepper. "Gwap had nice things to say about you all."

"*Commandant Cliffside*, you mean," Pepper said. "Junior adventurers need to use the right title."

"Oh, right." I shuffled uncomfortably. This was literally the first time I'd even heard that title.

"Sit, please." Jackson motioned to the empty bench across from him. "Thank you for the introduction, ma'am," he said, nodding to the barmaid.

I slid into the bench, feeling their stares. I felt like a kid at a restaurant, the table about chest height. I hated it, but I needed one of those booster seats.

"We're very excited to have you join our party. I had heard there was a halfkin in town but didn't know they were part of the Guild," Jackson said. "**Invite**."

Jackson was the very image of a young hero, or at least someone cosplaying as one. He lacked the edge of a true warrior, and his gear looked too new. Everything about him looked untested.

Party Invitation Received! Thunderbreak (Junior Level)

Accept?

"**Accept**," I said.

Immediately I became aware of where the members of the party were. Nothing as intimate as my bond with Ae but more like I could close my eyes and point to them in a room type of sense.

"Excellent," Jackson said, reaching out to shake my hand. "Have you been adventuring very long?"

"It's a new thing," I said. I didn't want this conversation to be about me. "Would you mind introducing yourselves? I'm afraid I don't know your names."

"Oh, forgive me. These three lovely ladies are my girlfriends: Rochelle, Marie, and Gretchen," he said, pointing to each.

"You all are an item?" I asked. Holy shit, it was a harem. I wasn't sure if I wanted to congratulate the overeager adventurer or feel bad for him.

"Is that going to be some kind of problem, gremlin?" Gretchen cut in, venom barely hidden behind her voice.

Gretchen stood out among the others, looking more like a country girl than an armor-plated murder machine. She wore a simple black jumper with a white ruffled long-sleeved shirt underneath. A black choker hugged her neck, but my eyes were on the wide black hair band on the top of her head, completely hiding her cat ears.

Gretchen noticed the glance, her expression shifting from irritation to murder. This catgirl had a fucking problem with me, and I wanted no part of it.

"Gretchen—" Jackson started, a warning in his undertone.

"Hey, no problems here," I said. "It's just abnormal where I'm from. As long as you don't include me in it, I'm good." I smiled hoping the joke would land.

Jackson laughed, and some of the tension dissipated. Gretchen laughed along, but it never reached her eyes.

"Halfkin don't take multiple mates?" Marie asked, brushing a strand of red hair out of her face. Her leather armor was form-fitted to her thin frame. My eyes would've slid right over her if the armor hadn't had what was basically a polished metal bikini top built in. It was like a beacon that screamed, 'Hey, I'm a girl under here.'

I laughed. "Oh no, not where I'm from they don't. Most women would kill you for even asking."

Grandma once threw a dinner plate at Grandpa when he asked if she would like it if he brought home another wife.

The memory of her chasing him with a broom while he laughed made me homesick.

"Is halfkin society so brutish? The punishment is death?" Marie asked.

"It's more of an expression. Although, it might not be far from the truth," I said, trying not to look at my warped reflection in her chest. I couldn't help but think the bulge was probably exaggerated.

"To be fair, it is abnormal here in the Fringe as well. Many don't seem to understand," Jackson said.

I looked at the four adventurers crammed into a bench meant for two, smushed together. Yeah, this seemed like it was going to be a pain in the ass.

"As long as you fight well, I don't give a shit," I said.

"Same to you, halfkin. I am eager to see some of this famed prowess." Jackson smiled. I didn't know how much charisma it would take for me to be this smooth but it was a lot more than what I had.

"Awesome," I said. "Can I still get those introductions?"

Jackson nodded. "Of course. The brown-haired beauty on the end is Rochelle, path of light and the best archer under level ten I've ever seen."

The mousey girl smiled, barely bringing her eyes up from the table. Her armor was conservative and practical. A real breath of fresh air compared to Miss reflective tits sitting next to her.

"Nice to meet you. I wouldn't mind some pointers on archery if you have time." I've always been interested but there weren't a lot of archery ranges in the city.

Life came into Rochelle's eyes.

"Here we go," Gretchen muttered.

Rochelle leaned forward, shyness gone. "I would love to! I studied under Master Feurl Wandont and would be interested to see its applications to halfkin physiology. Your draw length would be short, but a variation in grip might compensate for it. Maybe a variation of a horse-riding grip would do? I would need to sit down and sort out a best strategy."

I had clearly opened some kind of Pandora's box. "Sure thing." I lifted up my little hands. "I have a short reach, so I'd like to add a ranged weapon."

"Hmm, don't most halfkin use atlatls?" Rochelle asked, a little confused.

I looked at Rochelle blankly, wondering if the system didn't translate the word.

Unfortunately, Gretchen noticed and took it upon herself to answer my question. "It's a spear thrown by a wooden stick held like a club, *snake bait.* How do you not know a gremlin's main weapon?"

I kept my tone even. "Never was taught." I still had no idea what the fuck an atlatl was.

Jackson cleared his throat. "This is Marie," he said, patting the redhead on the shoulder. She clung to his arm, squishing her freckled cheek into it. "Path of Terra and our current frontliner. She has a full-body armor spell and could defend against an ascended. Nothing can get through her."

"Awww, babe," Marie said, lacing her hand through his. Gross.

I hated every second of this conversation. I wished I was alone in the woods or even maybe back in the dungeon. A piece of me even missed the void.

"It's nice to meet you. I also have a full-body armor spell so we should talk sometime. I recently got it."

"Of course," Marie said, politely.

Charisma informed that was a no.

"And last, we have Gretchen, Path of Light, and the real brains of the operation. Gretchen is our strategist and closest to level ten. She’s even from around here and knows the area well. She specializes in small blades, hand combat, and even some wind magic."

"Nice to meet you." I didn't even grit my teeth. I didn't think Gretchen appropriately appreciated my restraint. We glared at each other, a mutual dislike on the edge of breaking into a fight.

"Babe, you forgot to introduce yourself," Marie said.

Jackson pulled himself up higher. "Jackson Giulia, Path of Light, spellblade," he said proudly. "Like my father, I fight with a two-handed sword and lightning magic."

"Jackson is the best swordsman of his brothers," Marie said, running a hand along his forearm.

"Very impressive," I said, trying to ignore the PDA. All things considered, they sounded like a good group. I wondered why they were struggling so much.

"And what's your Path?" Gretchen asked, smiling at me sweetly. That was all the warning I needed to be careful.

"Path of Shadow," I said. It went over about as well as I thought it would.

"Like a bard?" Marie asked. "I thought halfkin were normally Spirit-focused? You're not a monk?"

"Nope, I fight with what I have. Picked up some weird spells along the way."

"Weapon?" Jackson asked.

I set Ae on the table. "I like to get close."

Jackson frowned. "Forgive my confusion. I thought you were a frontliner and not some kind of rogue."

"Well, I also breathe fire, can turn to stone, and have an ability that makes my bite stronger." I figured explaining my need to bite things would make my life easier.

"Strange and stranger, aren't fire abilities normally Path of Fire? So, what are you, some sort of fire-breathing bard-rogue?" Jackson asked.

"They're keeping the freaks together," Gretchen muttered.

"I can't get wiped again. My father will kill me," Marie said, looking panicked.

Rochelle hmm'd to herself but otherwise kept silent. She was my favorite so far.

"Will you all keep your fucking pants on. I guarantee I've fought way more dangerous shit than any of you and came out on top. In fact, I can think of a specific scenario where I fought a level sixteen lesser murderbird, lighting it on fire and walking away unscathed." I pointedly looked at a paling Gretchen.

I realized I was standing in the booth, leaning over the table. Where the fuck was that angry barmaid? I needed some food or something.

"Peace, halfkin, we meant nothing by it," Jackson said. "If anything, your ferocity reassures me." He had one of those fake politician smiles plastered on, and I could tell he was not convinced.

No, I couldn't blame him. Despite being young, they looked like a real deal adventuring party, and I looked like I was about to try out for the renaissance fair sideshow.

"So, what is the plan?" I asked.

"The Commandant said we would receive our quest in the morning," Jackson said. "He was vague, which is suspicious. Normally, we take quests that are up on the board."

"You should be prepared to stay the night in the wild from here on out," Gretchen said. "Any supplies you bring will be for the better, but make sure you pack light."

"Any idea what kind of pay we're getting from this?" I asked.

"Well, it should be a junior-level quest, so we'll probably take home ten to fifteen coppers each," Marie said.

"That sure doesn't sound like a lot." I wasn't sure how the local economy worked, but it sounded like I was about to almost die for pennies.

"Joining the Guild was never about money." Jackson tapped his gauntleted finger on the table. "Everyone in my family serves ten years or up to ascension. It is tradition. I will cover the costs of anything you need, but if you leave the party, I will need to be reimbursed, or the items returned."

"Sounds fair to me." I pinched the fabric on my shirt. "I don't know if you can tell, but I don't have much."

The conversation died at that point, and an awkward silence grew. Pepper saved the day by bringing mugs of ale to the table. "We're having mutton tonight. You want any?"

"Yes, please," everyone said in one way or another. Pepper didn't even acknowledge it, turning on her heel to leave.

I picked up the alcoholic beverage Pepper had put in front of me. It was strong, chunky in texture, and tasted like it had been filtered through a dirty gym sock, but I was going to need this and a couple more to deal with wherever this conversation was going to take me over the course of the evening.

I felt a bit of sol running to my center. I almost asked one of the party about it, but I stopped myself, figuring I'd sound crazy. There must've been some kind of sol in the drinks.

Before I knew it, I was already flagging down Pepper for a second.

"He on your tab?" Pepper asked Jackson.

"Yes," the spellsword replied, taking a sip of his ale.

Pepper produced another mug of ale and put it down in front of me.

"Careful, it's really strong," Jackson said, his pale complexion already reddening.

"Really? I barely even feel buzzed." I sat the mug down, showing them it was nearly empty.

"It's sol infused," Marie said her face so flushed it almost matched her hair. The mug swung around in her hand as if she was already blitzed. "Makes it extra strong."

"Why else would we drink this swill?" Gretchen said. She was obviously intoxicated too, but no less mean. It must've been her actual personality. Lord bless Jackson for taking in literal strays.

I took another sip of my drink, but as hard as I tried, the sol was sucked right into my center. Was this going to become a problem? Just how much was I gonna have to drink in order to forget this place?

The rest of the party seemed content to forget that I was there, slipping into their own little conversation. I thrummed my fingers on the table, lost in thought.

As I took a bite of my mutton, I couldn't help but feel like a puppet on the end of a string.

TWENTY-TWO: THE WAGER

A sharp smell of pork flooded the tavern, snapping me from idly tracing a finger across Ae's pommel.

Someone was using sol. A lot of it.

The tavern door slammed open, and a mountain of a man filled the frame. "Where is it? Where is the filth that's been let into our Guild?"

The man was freaking huge. He had to duck his head slightly to come in through the door. A door whose knob was right around my collar bone in height. He had a bear pelt wrapped around his shoulders like a cape. A trophy, no doubt. Even though he ducked, the massive broadsword on his back still clunked against the top of the frame.

"Stone, get down," Jackson hissed.

Jackson and company were all shaking their heads, trying to stop me from getting up. Rochelle even motioned for me to get under the table.

Unfortunately for them, my charisma activated, urging me

in a specific course of action. I didn't have a better plan so I went for it.

"Have you checked the door?" I said, jumping onto the table. Silence washed across the room. "You want a piece of this? What will it be? A game of wits? Spirits? I recommend a dick-measuring contest," I said, looking down at his loin cloth. "I suspect I'll win."

The party looked at me like I'd lost my mind. A part of me agreed, but charisma was insistent this was the way not to turn into halfkin burger. If I let people in the Guild think they could walk all over me, I would never see the end of it. It would be more worth it for me to get my ass kicked this once than to sit by and let it happen continuously. Besides, I was still under the Mercy, so even if I died, I would end up back in the dungeon. So, the time to do this was now and not when I was in real mortal peril.

The sound of metal on metal filled the tavern as the man drew a large two-handed broad sword from over his shoulder. "A duel to the death!" he yelled, extending the sword in front of him with a single hand.

A cast iron pan launched out from the kitchen, smashing into the man's sword and knocking it clean out of his hand.

"No duels in the Guild!" Pepper yelled, stepping out of the kitchen. An aura of pure power filled the tavern, making everyone slink down in their chairs. The scent was overpowering and not something I could place, but it made my mouth water. It was definitely spicy. Maybe citrus?

The man sheepishly put the sword away. Like a breath of

fresh air, life returned to the room. Just how powerful was Pepper?

"We are all civilized here. Let us solve this dispute like gentlemen," I said, desperately trying to steer the conflict in a direction that wouldn't be fatal. "I challenge you to a duel of drink. Come now, human. Are you afraid of someone a quarter your size?"

Marie came in clutch, starting a chorus of, "Drink, drink, drink, drink, drink, drink, drink." The chant gathered steam. Fists pounded on tables, and people stood up out of their seats as the chorus grew.

"Thragdor never backs down from a challenge," Thragdor yelled. The tavern roared in approval.

"Stone, I sure hope you know what you're doing," Jackson said. The party was standing beside me, fanned out defensively. What was about to happen would probably reflect on them as well. I hadn't even thought about that.

Tables screeched across the floor as I was pushed forward, leaving a single table with two chairs in the wide room. The fact this was so well practiced meant my gut was right. This was something that happened often.

The kitchen door opened, and Pepper appeared with a cart of drinks. Her expression was bored but I could tell this was her element. The whole room quieted as she approached.

A pair of strong hands sat me down into a chair, pushing down on my shoulders.

"Getting out of the chair, throwing up, or passing out

counts as a forfeit. The loser is responsible for the bar tab for the night." Pepper had a steely gaze in her look. "What is the wager?"

"This gremlin never sets foot in Avila again!" Thragdor declared.

The crowd murmured.

"No," Jackson whispered in my ear. “Get him to wager something else.”

"I got this. You just have to trust me," I replied.

"See, I told ya he was a bard," Marie slurred. "Tell me this isn't some bard crap?"

"The guild will allow it," Pepper looked at me. "Do you have a counter?"

"I want…" I looked Thragdor over. I could see the hilt of the broad sword poking over the edge of Thragdor's back. It was obviously well taken care of and easily as tall as I was. “I want the sword," I said, folding my arms and leaning back.

Thragdor looked like I’d just asked to fuck his wife in front of the whole town. He sputtered, visibly offended.

"What? Not confident you'll win?" I asked, raising my voice so everyone could hear. "If I'm just some nonner, shouldn't this be easy?” I gave Thragdor my best smile.

"Something. Else," Thragdor said between gritted teeth, enunciating each word.

"Hmm, I could use a mount. I have little legs." This got a light laugh from the crowd. "You supply me a mount. It has to be appropriate for my size as judged by an impartial party."

"Agreed," Thragdor said, a smile curling up on the edges of his mouth. Had I made a mistake?

Pepper slammed two mugs on the table. "Begin!"

I pounded back the first mug of gritty ale in one gulp, a trick I learned back in college for shotgunning beers. Deep down, I knew I could potentially be in trouble, but charisma was firm this was the right path.

Thragdor slammed his mug down as Pepper swapped them out, a new pair appearing faster than I could even blink.

Trying to appear dominant, I grabbed it and drank it in one gulp, just like the other. My center continued to swell, making me wheeze. Fuck, I hadn't thought about that.

I lifted the mug to my mouth, "**Steadfast**," I whispered into the mug, fervently focusing on my lower half. Sol ran down my throat, through my heart and gate meridians to my lower half, turning my legs to grey stone. The chair creaked, and Pepper shot me a sideways glance, her brow arching slightly but didn't say anything as she placed a new drink in front of me.

My stomach churned as the alcohol set heavy in my stomach. I laid out a huge burp, feeling better. I expected the oaf across from me to comment, but if anything, he looked impressed.

"Disgusting," someone said from the side. I was pretty sure it was Gretchen. It had that energy.

We were matched head to head for the first ten rounds. Pepper would dish them out, we would slam them back, silently staring at each other, waiting for the other to blink. The chair creaked as I kept casting **Steadfast** to keep my throat clear, but with every drink, more sol swirled through my center like ice water.

The world swam as I slowly drank down my eleventh drink, still trying to go as fast as possible, but now it took me seven or eight gulps to get it down. My opponent was no better, borderline nursing the thing. The fact that we were head to head had to be embarrassing.

"You got it, Thragdor," a voice from the sideline called. "Just because it has the Guild fooled doesn't mean the rest of us are."

I couldn't see who said it but added them to my growing list of enemies.

"Y'all are a bunch of racist fucks," I said, my words slurring a little. "I ain't done nothing to a single one of you, and all you've done is give me shit."

"Your kind are scum," Thragdor said. "There isn't no one who doesn't know about the Red Dawn. We remember what you did to us."

"Yeah, but *I didn't*, you fucking nugget," I said, feeling exasperated. "The only one who even cares about this shit is you."

My stomach turned as I downed drink number twelve.

"Squawk, little bird," Thragdor said, wiping the foam off his mouth. "Just jealous of the Light."

"Psh, I don't give a shit. You can make your butthole glow or whatever. Oooo. Who cares?"

Thragdor's drunken face twisted in confusion, trying to absorb the words I was slurring at him.

"Go, gremlin," Marie called, raising her mug to about chin height and support. Jackson was basically holding her up as she leaned up against him, but I'd take it. It was about as enthusiastic of support as I was going to get.

At fifteen drinks, it felt like I was on the deck of a ship. The crowd's cheering rose to fervor as Thragdor and I yelled insults at each other, each more clever and colorful than the last, before dissolving into middle-school name-calling.

"I bet you shit the bed," I said, just trying to string some words together. It had taken a while, but the alcohol was definitely hitting me now.

"You take it up the bum," Thragdor countered, leaning heavily on the table.

"Nah, that's your mom," I retorted.

"My mum's dead," Thragdor growled, but there was a hint of a smirk. I bet she was alive and well. Liar.

I leaned over, casting **steadfast** too high and almost falling out of my chair as I became top heavy. My fingers gouged into the table.

"No damaging the table," Pepper said, putting number sixteen in front of us and smacking my hand.

"I never even wanted to be in this dumb town, anyway," I said, trying not to lean my forehead on the table and stay upright. "The fucking Captain dragged me in here after some bitch said I attacked her."

I heard a sharp intake from someone in the crowd, but no one else responded to my comment. Everyone in the room was five drinks past gone.

"The Captain's a right prick," Thragdor said. I didn't think his eyes were even pointing in the same direction anymore as he wobbled back and forth.

I pulled number sixteen to my lips, drinking down the gritty liquid. I felt like there was no room left—my stomach distended and sticking out like I was pregnant. I didn't know what my blood alcohol level was, but it was probably close to lethal.

The world wobbled. I didn't think I was going to make it. Beer splattered on the floor, followed by a thud as the world tilted.

I fucked it up, didn't I?

An ear-splitting roar filled the tavern as I felt hands all around me. Before I knew it was happening, Jackson was helping me back upright, slapping me on the back.

"This's our frontliner right here," he said. "Drank Thragdor right under the table."

That's when I realized I was still technically in the giant chair and Thragdor was splayed all over the floor in a heap of furs and muscle.

Through my drunken stupor, everyone else seemed pretty cool with me, patting me on the back or smiling. I felt like I had passed some test, proving I was a normal bloodthirsty degenerate like the rest of them.

"Oh shit," Jackson said as I tumbled out of his grasp.

The next thing I knew, I was being carried under someone's arm like a rolled-up blanket, my face smooshed against a warm lump.

"I've got a girlfriend," I slurred, trying to wriggle out of the headlock.

"I don't fuck kids," Pepper 's voice responded with a bit of laughter on the edges. My feet were dragging on the floor as she unceremoniously threw me onto the bed. "See you bright and early, you cocky menace. You got a big day tomorrow," Pepper said, closing the door.

I fell asleep before I could even process what she just said.

TWENTY-THREE: WARBLECOCK

Someone pounded on my door as the bell tolled too many times to count.

"Fuck off." I covered my head in my arms, but the pounding insisted. The world swam as I got out of bed and stumbled across the room. "I'm coming. Holy shit, stop pounding so loud."

I opened the door to see Gretchen's icy glare. Great.

"You're late," she said, turning on her heel to leave. She must've lost a bet or something.

Speaking of losing bets, my head pounded.

Irritation flared in the back of my mind. Ae had fallen onto the floor at some point and she wasn't happy about it.

"Sorry," I told her, clutching my head. I picked her up and she practically vibrated. She was feeling more… awake?

I hurried to get around, splashing water on my face, but then I stopped myself. Gretchen could eat my ass. I was going to take my time.

I warmed up my stiff muscles with light stretches, moving into bodyweight squats and pushups, reveling in the light burn of physical exertion. I still hadn't pushed my body to accept the new strength stats from my heart meridian unlocking. A part of me missed all the time I had in the dungeon. It was like I hadn't had a single second to myself since stepping out of that thrice-damned place.

I reached around two hundred, realizing I would need more than body weight to push myself to my new strength, so I gave up. The smell of food called to me.

The tavern was half full as I arrived at the bottom of the stairs. Probably fifty or so people lay around in various stages of undress, clearly as hungover as I felt.

Jackson and company had a table in the middle of the floor rather than a booth. Marie and Rochelle sat on his lap while Gretchen stood off to the side, angrily tapping her foot.

"It's about time," Gretchen said.

"Holy shit, Gretchen, my head is pounding. Can we not do this?" I was already done with the day. Between her and the PDA squad, I was already over this whole party thing.

The quiet archer perked up, pulling herself away from Jackson. "I can heal you," Rochelle offered.

"If you wouldn't mind. It would make me easier to get along with," I said, trying not to look at the catgirl glaring at me. She still had the headband on. I wondered if she had human ears as well or if she could barely hear all the time. If that was the case, her constant pissy attitude made sense.

Rochelle placed her hands on my chest and a scent of lightly roasted pork filled the air. As I felt my hangover disappearing, my mouth watered as I tried to convince myself I wasn't thinking about eating the quiet archer. She was so close. I could—

I shook my head. I needed to squash these evil vampire thoughts and get some food. My inner dialogue got a little dark when I was hungry.

The headache disappeared.

"Shit, that's way better," I said, thanking the archer. "Why is my mouth so dry?" I mostly said it to myself, but Rochelle answered anyway.

"It only heals the damage, not the dehydration." Rochelle smiled. She twisted back and forth, not making eye contact. If she had on a skirt, it would've been swishing. I was starting to get what Jackson saw in her.

"Thanks, I appreciate it," I said. Awkward energy filled the silence, so I walked away.

I didn't see Pepper anywhere, so I decided to find food myself. I didn't want to admit it, but the urge to eat a party member had me a little shaken. Food was a higher priority for me now.

I pushed the door in the kitchen open, glad to be away from the eyes of the tavern floor. Griselda hummed to herself, cooking pans of food. A witch's cauldron of liquid bubbled over the fire. She motioned for me to come and I closed the door behind me. I could hear yelling from in the tavern room. It sounded like Gretchen was giving someone a piece of her mind.

I saw the corner of Griselda's mouth turn up in a knowing smile.

"Are they always like this?" I plopped down in a chair. "Jackson and party," I clarified.

"This is them behaving," the cook said. "I think they want to make a good impression on you."

"Is it normal to have multiple partners around here? Not to judge, but I can barely handle one girl, let alone more."

Griselda laughed. "No, it's not normal out here in the Fringe. Fringe women are a real handful, raised to be independent and strong. City girls tend to be more used to the competition, accepting being in the background." She placed a plate in front of me. "There are stories from the Sundown Sultanate about such things. A harem of women surrounding a strong adventurer, killing dragons by day and sharing a tent by night. I'm sure the whole thing was made up, but poor Jackson might not know that."

I was five bites deep in my food when a thought struck me. "I don't have any money to pay for this," I said.

"Getting that party out of everybody's hair is payment enough. Without a fifth member to fill out their party, they hung out in the tavern and caused problems."

"That bad, huh?"

"Oh, you'll see. Just make sure to keep yourself alive out there. We're close to the Twilight. It's no place for junior adventurers."

"Stone!" I heard someone yell. "Get your half-sized ass out here!"

I shoved the last five bites of my breakfast in my mouth, taking the time to wash my plate. I gave one final thankful nod to Griselda as I bolted out the door.

Gwap and Pepper were talking to the party. The goatman stroked his beard, looking concerned, which didn't bode well.

"Hey guys, what's up?" I said, walking up.

"The Commandant is giving us a quest. He's about to send it to us," Jackson said, indicating I stand in line with the others.

Gwap produced a scroll and handed it to Jackson.

New Quest Assigned to Party:

Trouble in the Pass!

Quest Description: Travelers have been reporting danger near Gully Pass. Inspect or eliminate the threat.

Quest Reward(s): 150 Bronze (identify), 500 Silver (eliminate)

"Well, that's vague," I said. I thought back on what Elder Waza said. Did she somehow give us a blank check to get out of town?

"Gwap, this not a junior-level quest," Pepper said, reading the scroll. "Gully Pass is near the Twilight. Silver-level monsters have been spotted out there."

"Town council decided it time for Thunderbreak to fly or fall," Gwap said. "Out of Gwap's hands."

"Or maybe a certain halfkin is stirring up too much trouble in town," Pepper said, shooting me a side glance. "I'm sure the whole town knows about last night by now."

"Either way," Jackson said. "We need to prepare. If you have nothing else, I would like to begin." Jackson issued a sharp salute.

"Granted." The goatman returned the salute. "Stone, meet Gwap in office," Gwap said, turning and leaving.

"There's an office?" Marie said.

"It's behind the suspicious bookshelf," I said. "How did you miss it?"

"I never go upstairs sober," the girl said, smiling at Jackson.

"Ah, yeah, that will do it." My cringe meter was going crazy around these people.

Jackson caught my shoulder as I followed Gwap. "Here." Jackson placed a small bag in my hand. I peeked inside to see glints of silver. I opened my mouth to protest, but he stopped me.

"A loan," he said. "We will either be on the road for quite

some time or barely at all, so be prepared for the former."

"Thanks." I placed the bag in one of my pouches.

The party filtered out through the door as I ascended the wonky steps.

The bookshelf was ajar, so I let myself in.

"Commandant?" I said, looking around. He was bent over the desk, clearly working on something.

The goatman looked up.

"Hmm, little dragon arrives." Gwap produced a letter, placing it on the desk. "Here, letter from Waza. Stone has weird taste of mate."

The goatman grinned.

I rolled my eyes. "The first of many love letters after my display last night."

"Hmm. Yes, Gwap hear about duel. Little dragon need caution. Many ask questions. Questions dangerous for little dragon." The goatman was back to his work. It was weird to see him so serious. It was making me nervous.

"Ah," I said. "Already?"

"Indeed," Gwap said. "Stop stalling. Open letter. Gwap busy."

I grabbed the letter, curious to see what the goatman was working on. A large puzzle was spread on the old goat's mahogany desk. It was only half done, but it was obviously a painting of Pepper. The artist really captured the size of her personality, barely contained by a string bikini top. The goatman ignored me when I shot him a questioning glance.

"Does she know you have this?" I whispered.

Gwap narrowed his eyes at me. "Little dragon best stay silent, or Gwap say you helped."

I put up my hands up in surrender, taking a step back. "I saw nothing."

I pulled out my knife and slit the letter open. It was a heavy red paper with a golden seal—very Waza.

Stone,

The Church of Solara has already been made aware of your presence and is on their way. I've done my best to give you a quest to cover your absence, but you need to leave by tonight at the *latest. Trust no one. Not even Gwap. I cannot be seen with you, and do not contact me.*

This message will destroy itself.

- Emiline Waza

The letter burst into flames as I read the last word. I dropped it as it disintegrated into a small ash pile on the floor.

Gwap laughed. "Elder Waza loves pranks," the goatman said. "Now out, Gwap busy." He picked up a puzzle piece and eyed me expectantly.

"Good luck with that," I said, giving the goatman a wave on my way out.

"Close shelf," he called after me.

The bookshelf closed with an authoritative snap. I let out a sigh. I was aching to get out there and level up Ae and all this busy work was becoming frustrating.

I found the party waiting for me downstairs. They stood around, looking in different directions.

I knew something was off right away when Jackson gave me an apologetic grin. "It's outside."

"What's outside?" I asked.

"Your mount," Jackson said. I could tell he was struggling to keep a straight face.

"A mount is a mount as long as its size is appropriate," I said, realizing my wager had a lot of room for interpretation. "Oh fuck, what did they bring?" I ran to the door.

I walked out to see Thragdor with the reins of what I could only describe as a giant turkey. It was as tall as I was, if not a bit taller, standing at eye level with me. The turkey fanned an aggressive tail display in irritation, flaunting brown plumage mixed with greens and blues. It struggled against its reins, trying to swipe at Thragdor with wicked velociraptor-like claws.

"**Inspect**," I said, afraid to even read it.

Warblecock (Lvl 3): A moderate-sized variation of the avian family, a warblecock is known for their relative ease of raising for meat and their bad attitudes, often given to unruly children as mounts to train them to appreciate more docile animals.

"It's…" I trailed off, looking over the bird. Everyone hung on my word, looking for a reaction. "Perfect," I said.

Everyone seemed dumbfounded as I snatched the reins out of Thragdor's hands. The warblecock's claws flashed out at me, the new subject of its ire. Its heavy wings spread wide as it flapped.

Thragdor smacked the creature in the back of the head, completely throwing off its attack, and sending it into a pile of Thanksgiving on the ground. "Well, here you go. This here's the meanest warblecock in all of Avila. Pepper, does this satisfy the agreement?"

"It does," Pepper said, leaning up against the side of the tavern. I did my best not to picture the puzzle Gwap was putting together, but the more I tried not to think about it, the more I did.

"It got a name?" I asked, patting the feathers on the back of the still-recovering bird. It had to be seeing stars after Thragdor's hit.

"Cobbler." Thragdor patted the bird before giving me a patronizing wave. "Good luck.

"Cobbler?" I said slowly. The name was either a stroke of genius or the dumbest thing I'd ever heard. One of the girls laughed.

I turned back to see the warblecock inches from my face. It seemed to realize the big man was leaving. We were both on the ground in a flash—a whirlwind of feathers, squawks, and curses.

"Bad Cobbler. Bad," I yelled, throttling the bird with both hands as it tore my pant leg with its claws.

"That's fucking it," I said, my patience running out.

I pulled the sol out of the bird, pure panic in its eyes as it struggled to get away. I cast **Steadfast**, pinning it to the ground as I turned my legs to stone. Cobbler gobbled in panic as I drained its sol to power my spell.

"Oh damn," Jackson called. "You're not called Stone for no reason." The girls laughed.

The warblecock stopped struggling, so I released **Steadfast**, venting the rest of my sol into **Wyvern's Breath**, black flames shooting from my mouth. I heard some polite clapping, people mistaking the display as part of an act. The bird watched in horror, the black flames reflecting in its eyes.

"Well, are you gonna bond it or what?" Marie asked.

"Bond it? Like, I've got to play with it or something?" I said. The bird was tired but still had the energy to snap at me as I tried to pat its head. "I don't think that's gonna work."

"Well, first you check to see if the beast has a center," Marie explained. "If it does, you can use some of your sol to bond it. Eventually, you'll be able to summon it as your relationship grows, but at first, you'll feel a sense of where it is, and it'll be able to sense when you call it."

"Cobbler here would use that information to get farther

away from me," I said.

"Probably," Marie said, shrugging.

I sent out a thread of sol to see if I could bond with the big turkey. It was tired but could sense what I was doing, purposely clogging its mana channels as I tried to enter its center.

"Hold still, you big chicken," I said, but the warblecock fought me even harder as I pushed the sol into his center. Finally, I felt something snap in place.

New Mount Detected!

Race: Warblecock (Lvl 0)

Name: Cobbler

"What the fuck? It says it's level zero now."

Jackson laughed. "Yeah, it resets when you bind it. That's why people do it when they're young and grow up with their mounts. My horse, Blade, is nearly level nine." Jackson summoned a black horse out of thin air to prove his point.

I barked out a laugh. "You named your horse Blade?"

"I was 7. At least my mount isn't a big chicken named after a mediocre dessert."

"Touché," I said.

"Well, we will be off," Jackson said, patting me on the shoulder. "We will meet back here by 19th bell."

The party quickly left, and I thought I heard laughter as soon as they rounded the corner.

Twenty-Four: The Price of Money

I cut across town, my sulking turkey in tow.

Unfortunately, the marketplace was on the other side of town, about a half-hour walk from the tavern. I could hear people chuckling as I walked by. This town was really getting on my last nerve. In the meantime, I leaned into the character, tilting my head back and walking with an air of authority.

The market was bigger than I thought it would be. It was like a strip mall in the shape of a giant horseshoe wrapped around a center area. I was relieved to see it was just busy and not packed like the roads on the way over.

I looked around for something to do with Cobbler, realizing most stores wouldn't like it if I brought in the grumpy dino-bird.

Luckily, the marketplace had a place to tie mounts, so I could tie Cobbler at the row of horses and birds that looked like ostrich-sized cassowaries. It was kind of like back home when someone would park a motorcycle and a car parking spot.

I checked to make sure Cobbler was securely tied, but he had enough room to move around and sit.

"Don't cause trouble. I'll be back," I said, my eyes passing over a saddle on one of the larger birds. "I wonder if they make saddles for warblecocks."

The turkey snapped his gaze to mine, recognition burning in his eyes. He obviously knew the word and I took that as confirmation.

"All right, be good," I told the warblecock.

I looked around the big horseshoe, trying to figure out where the armorer was.

I stopped at a sign that had a big shield on it. "Yeah, that's probably it," I said to myself.

A burst of heat hit me as I pushed open the door. A bell chimed, announcing I had entered the shop.

"Hey, no kids in here," a gruff voice barked.

"Ain't no kid, Grandpa. Besides, I have good silver. You really going to turn me away?" I called back. This was going about as well as I expected it to.

The man looked up from the forge, sweat dripping down his gray beard. "Oh, you're that gremlin everyone's talking about," he said. "Get out."

"Silver still spends the same."

"This is a human smithy. No nonners."

"What? You don't have anything that's like kid size? I need some light armor, something to go over the forearms, maybe something for the shins. I mean, I'm not asking for a fucking plate mail here, man. Do you want my money or not?"

The man hesitated, so I pulled out some silver coins, laying each down with a percussive clunk on the wooden table in the middle of the shop.

"Aye," he said slowly, greed winning over prejudice. "I'll fetch you some gear. It just got traded in so it's got some dents and scrapes. It's a simple chainmail tunic, arm and shin guards, and leather gloves. No helmet. Five silver."

I knew for a fact I was getting fucked in this deal. Well, more accurately, Jackson was getting fucked in this deal. The man looked at me, daring me to say anything. If I tried to haggle this, the equipment would probably disappear, and I'd get thrown out of the shop.

"I ain't got all day, gremlin."

"Fine. Yeah, whatever," I said, scooting the money forward.

The armorer took the time to count each coin in front of me. Going as far as biting one of them to make sure it was authentic. He almost seemed disappointed they were real, sticking them in a pouch before going to the back to grab the gear.

I looked around the shop in his absence. It looked like the guy did good work. I sent up a silent prayer that this gear that I bought wasn't absolute shit.

"Here," the man said, dropping a box that clunked in front of me. "Bond it and get out."

"Pleasure doing business with you," I said, inspecting the gear and pushing sol into it.

New Equipment Bonded!

I opened my equipment screen as soon as I got the notification.

Soulbound Equipment:

Clothes: Linen Tunic, Linen Pants, Leather Boots, Leather Gloves

Armor: Chainmail tunic, Steel Bracers, Steel Shin Guards

Weapons: Chainbreaker

Misc: Adventurer's Belt, Guild Amulet, 4 Silver

"**Equip all**," I said, the armor settling over my clothes. The gear was nicer than I expected, and Ae didn't stand out so much now. The armorer made it sound like it was all beat up, but it only had scratches here and there. Frankly, I preferred it this way. I didn't want to look all shiny and new like Jackson and company. It fit perfectly, too perfect.

"Hey, smithy," I called.

"If you're not about to spend more money, get out." The smith didn't even look up from the forge, hammer strikes filling the spaces between words.

"This gear changed size. Why couldn't I buy a full-scale armor?"

"It doesn't change that much, fool," he snapped. "Gear can't change size more than five percent of its total size. Now, if you're done, get out before you bring down the value of the rest of my gear, and people think we're friends."

"Whatever, man," I said.

Walking back out into the market, I felt a little more deadly, legitimate even. I expected to be bogged down by the weight of the new armor, especially the chainmail, which had to weigh forty pounds in and of itself, but it didn't feel any heavier than a winter coat. Sure, it slowed me down, but it wasn't a big deal. It must have been that new strength I was working on. I would have been struggling underneath this new gear a few levels ago.

Speaking of struggling underneath this new gear, I needed to find some equipment for dear old Cobbler.

I pushed open the little half door to the shop with a saddle on it. It felt like the doors to a saloon in an old western. What would this person be called anyway? I mean, a cobbler is someone who cobbles. Is someone who saddles a saddler? I doubted the owner would appreciate that question, so I'd think of them as saddle people in the meantime.

"We don't serve kids," a female voice called to me as soon as I walked in.

Solara damn it, were we really doing this again?

I decided to cut to the chase. "I have silver, and I'm ready to buy things."

"Now, that's the kind of language I want to hear." A young woman appeared from behind the counter, her twin braids flowing over her shoulders. "A gremlin? What you want?"

"A saddle and potentially saddlebacks for warblecock, if that's something you carry."

"Oh yeah, the kids love those things. Not a lot of ponies in these parts, and horses tend to be too dangerous," the woman said. "What kind of leather do you want?"

"Durable and in my price range," I said, putting two of my remaining four silvers on the counter.

"I got just the thing." The woman pulled a bundle of leather off the wall. "If that's all you need. I'll have to ask you to leave. Don't want people associating us." The woman smiled apologetically.

"For what it's worth, I get it," I said, grabbing the saddle. "I appreciate you being half decent. Everyone else around here treats me like shit."

"I prefer animals over people anyway," she said, smiling at me.

The fuck was that supposed to mean?

"Light of Solara upon you," she called as I reached for the door.

I smiled politely at the woman and left the store. The lady seemed nice enough, but holy shit. I found myself still processing the encounter as I wandered over to Cobbler.

I found Cobbler struggling against his reins, trying to murder a small cat. The cat sat just out of the edge of the bird's range. It had that smug air that only cats have, licking its paw.

"Cobbler, knock it off," I said, patting the bird's back.

Cobbler reared back to peck at me, clearly all worked up.

I breathed in some sol. "**Steadfast**."

The bird's beak bounced off my rock-hard forehead with a loud tink. I could have sworn I saw a chip from the beak fly off. The bird stumbled, rattled from the impact.

"It's nice to see you too, buddy," I said, patting the dazed turkey's head. It wasn't his day. "I got you one of those saddles we were talking about."

The warblecock gobbled pitifully, collapsing to the ground, pretending his legs didn't work.

"Shut up, you big baby. What if I told you we're gonna leave here soon, and you'll get to murder whatever you want."

The warblecock cracked open an eye at me and then kept pretending to be injured.

I laughed.

Getting the saddle and saddle bags on Cobbler was an exercise in patience, but I kept promising the bird he would get to do murder, which seemed to keep him calm. The straps were confusing, but it set in him nicely.

"Time to head to the general store and get some supplies," I told Cobbler. "What do big murderous turkeys eat anyway?"

Cobbler gobbled, looking at me as if that cleared that up.

"Sure thing, bud, I'll do my best." I walked beside him, not wanting to try and ride him yet.

My experience in the general store was radically different from the others. The checkout girl didn't even look at me as she tallied my total, extending a hand for me to pay. It was a painless experience, and I was able to pack Cobbler's saddle bags with provisions and essential goods.

The nineteenth bell chimed as we made our way back across town. I kept feeling like we were being followed but didn't see anything as I returned to the tavern. The whole shopping trip had me on edge, and I didn't want to leave Cobbler alone, so I brought the big turkey into the tavern with me.

The party was waiting for me, eating some stew. Massive packs burgeoning with equipment and gear were stacked next to them. They had to be bigger than I was.

"Y'all pack enough?" I said, placing my pack next to theirs. Most of my belongings were with Cobbler, but I did pick up a light messenger bag to keep on my person.

"There's no point in living uncivilized. I know you are probably used to sleeping under the stars, but we require some privacy," Jackson said. Rochelle and Marie blushed.

Oh Solara, what had I done to deserve this?

Time to change the subject. "That's a lot of gear. Are we expecting a hard trip or something?" I regretted the words immediately. Marie looked like she was going to burst with laughter. "Shut up, you know what I meant."

Jackson was unfazed. "We're heading on the West Road today. So, it should be pretty easy."

I groaned. "Why would you curse us like that? You know that's how that works, right? Like, as soon as you say everything is gonna go well, it immediately goes to shit."

"Stone, you didn't tell me you were superstitious." Jackson laughed.

"Halfkin, why is the warblecock in here?" Pepper said before considering it. "You know what? Never mind." Pepper plopped a plate of food in front of me as I sat down at the table.

Pepper addressed the party. "You are going to want to make yourself scarce. I've been getting questions about our resident halfkin all afternoon."

Jackson nodded. "Thanks for the warning, ma'am. As soon as Stone finishes eating, we'll head out."

I scarfed down my food, and the rest of the party handled their massive packs, pulling them outside.

Cobbler and I walked out of the tavern to see four people and four giant packs, trying to figure out how to fit on two horses.

"Hey, I'm no mathmatologist, but I don't think that's going

to work," I said.

"Are you casting a spell?" Marie said, tilting her head at me. The move made me think of Ae, and it hurt my chest a bit. "Stone, are you alright? Did I say something?"

"Nah, it's just something my grandpa used to say. Don't worry about it," I said. "I'll get Cobbler all set up."

The warblecock perked up at his name.

"It's time, my dude," I told the turkey, patting his back as he pecked at some grass growing between the cobblestones of the road.

Band-aid off. I jumped on his saddle.

Cobbler bucked like a bull at the rodeo. Everything spun as tried to hold on, but there was little to grab onto and Cobbler was way nimbler than a bull.

"Woah, there, buckaroo," I yelled. "Bad Cobbler, bad!"

My back hit the ground, and the warblecock danced in circles, howling like a wolf.

"Fine, you big baby, but we're trying again later," I said, making sure nothing in my messenger bag was broken.

Jackson and crew sorted their shit out and got situated on the two horses, placing the packs in the middle of two riders. Jackson and Gretchen rode Blade, and Marie and Rochelle rode a white and brown mystery horse.

The party departed, the others at a slow trot, Cobbler and me at a light jog. At least I wasn't carrying the gear. Cobbler might be an ass, but at least he was content being a pack mule.

The town was hitting its evening rush. Someone threw a slop bucket out the window as we walked, splashing on the ground. I didn't look too closely but saw chunks fall out of the bucket. Even though we were near a bakery, the smell of baked goods didn't cut through the overwhelming smell of shit.

Gretchen must have seen me wrinkling my nose. "Disapprove of us, gremlin?"

"Bold use of the word us," I said. If Gretchen's eyes could've shot lasers, they would have. I rolled my eyes at her. "Yeah, this place is fucking disgusting." I motioned to the shit-filled gutters in front of an eating establishment. "At least I shit in the woods like a gentleman."

"The city is much the same. Doubt you've ever been in a town before," Gretchen said.

"Gretchen, be nice," Jackson said. "Stone is doing his best. You can't blame someone like him for not appreciating Avila's charms."

I'd about had enough of everyone. "I'll have you guys know I've been in places with millions of people, and I've seen things that you've never seen before. This place here is nothing more than some backwater village. So, forgive me for not being impressed."

"Don't halfkin live in the grassy plains, though?" Rochelle asked.

I let the conversation die, dropping back with Cobbler to follow the horses through the growing crowd.

Silence hung between us as we finished walking through the town, approaching the gates. The guards acknowledged our presence with a nod as we left through the western gate, the sun at our backs. The dark horizon of the Twilight hung in the mountains before us.

We stopped to take a break a couple of hours from town. Even with my increased stats, the constant jog was getting to me. Even Cobbler murdered insects with less enthusiasm than usual.

I rubbed my forehead. The physical exertion was bringing my headache back.

"Still dealing with that hangover?" Marie asked.

"Yeah, I'm still not feeling up for today."

"Yeah, physical healing takes the hangover away but doesn't replace the lack of sleep," Rochelle added.

Jackson laughed. "It was nice to have some energy in the tavern again. The Adventurers Guild has been pretty low here of late."

"Why is that?" I asked.

"Rumors of a war and a subsequent draft have been making rounds." Jackson accepted some food from Rochelle, continuing to talk while he ate. “The Sundown Sultanate has been posturing for war with Solendia, allegedly.”

"But aren't we in the Fringe?" A war was the last thing I needed added to my list of problems.

"Wuxia and the Fringe are vassal states to Solendia. The Sundown Sultanate and the Dusklands are on the other side," Jackson explained.

"The other side of what?" I asked. I was definitely missing something.

"The sun?" Jackson shot me a questioning glance. "The sun hangs over Zenith, the capital of Solendia. The most powerful magic is performed there, sol so thick you can see it in the air."

“So you've been there?” I had more to say but talking while jogging wasn't the easiest thing in the world.

“My father took me a few years ago. He was out on business and I was able to sightsee with my mother. It was nothing but gleaming white towers and magic constructs. There the sol is so thick, they run horseless carriages off it.”

“My brother is obsessed with those,” Marie chimed in. “He got Father to buy one, but the sol in Wuxia wasn't thick enough to run it right. He ended up having to charge a sol gem to run it. He'd sit there for twenty hours to have enough for a single trip into town and back.” Marie shook her head in disapproval.

My imagination sprinted at the prospect of magic power machines. If no one had invented an airplane yet, I was going to blow a lot of people's minds once I got in contact with an open-minded engineer.

The conversation died down as rations got handed out. I had pemmican, jerky, and hardtack, but others had some food folded in fabric that almost looked like fruit cake. At least my hardtack would work as a backup weapon if Ae was out of commission. That's the thing about travel rations, the harder it was to eat, the better it kept. The only one that wasn't eating was Cobbler, who was eyeing all our food with big turkey eyes.

"So, what all can this guy eat?" I asked, pointing to Cobbler. "Besides bugs and seeds."

Marie shrugged. "Seeds, insects, small animals, and stray children," she said, laughing at her own joke.

"What can I give him as a treat? He seems kind of down." I patted the warblecock and was surprised he didn't protest.

"Yeah, I've never seen a warblecock so calm before," Jackson said. "All things considered; he's been behaving extraordinarily well. My dad gave me one as a kid and it chased me around for a whole year before I could even pet it. I don't think anyone ever thought to intimidate a warblecock through a display of magic."

I was confused but remembered no one knew about my **Feast** spell weakening the bird. To their eyes, I'd wrestled the turkey down and spit a jet of flames.

Marie dug into her pack, pulling out some jerky. "Here, he can have some of this."

I grabbed some of the jerky, holding it up for Cobbler. The bird was too smart for his own good, gingerly taking a piece and looking with wonder, not at me, who had given it to him, but Marie, who had produced it from her pack.

"Fine, be that way, you big turkey," I said.

Cobbler whipped his head around, lifting a leg to kick at me.

"Cobbler, no," Marie said. "Bad Cobbler." She fished around in her pack, giving the bird some more jerky.

To my shock, the murder chicken obeyed, Cobbler nuzzling up against her hand.

"I hate all of you," I grumbled, chewing on my pemmican.

Twenty-Five: Tsundere

Turns out big trees cast long shadows.

My ability for observation truly knew no bounds. I pushed my seven intelligence to its very limit as I guided Cobbler down the forested road.

The road didn't strike me as heavily traveled, missing the deep tracks the eastern road had leading into town. However, the presence of the road itself did imply people travelled this way often enough to need one or it was old enough that it existed before the Twilight was as wild.

It could've been because I was so small, but the shadows made the forest feel massive, leaving me feeling like an ant or whatever an ant considers an ant. Completely gone was the peaceful feeling I would get in a forest back home. This was a restaurant for the powerful and halfkin was on the menu.

This world was so foreign feeling. I was still struggling to adapt, barely staving off that mental breakdown I knew I was going to have once everything calmed down.

I sent a mental pulse to Ae, checking in. While I was glad she was responsive at all, I looked forward to leveling her up more.

We only spent a few hours on the road. I could still see the smoke rising from Avila's chimneys as we made camp.

I looked back at the sun cresting over the hills in the distance. My internal clock said it was night, but by all accounts, it still looked like dawn. Was this what living underground felt like? Just a constant stasis of environment?

We camped off the side of the road, setting up in a little clearing around a pit used for a campfire by other travelers. Since it wasn't raining and the cold wasn't all that bad, I didn't set up my cheap tent.

On the other hand, Jackson's tent was ridiculous. A giant complicated thing with way too many poles. If we weren't in a magic fantasy world, I would've called bullshit that that thing even fit in their packs.

Odder still was that Gretchen was building a tent all by herself. It was plain like something a boy scout would make with a tarp. Did they not all sleep together? A piece of me assumed they all dog-piled on each other. Ah, well.

I lit a fire while the others were busy, enjoying the mundane process of pulling together tinder and sparking a fire by hand. I had considered trying to use **Wyvern's Breath**, but I wouldn't trust anything cooked over a fire of those acidic flames. I didn't want to accidentally wipe the party at breakfast.

Even though the cold didn't bother me as much as I expected, it didn't mean the flames didn't feel pleasant on my skin as I dropped into some meditation.

My center used to be a little more than a pinprick, but now it was almost the size of the tip of my little finger. I was on the verge of leveling up, a persistent tightness in my throat that had become my new norm. In fact, if I really tried, I bet I could do it right now, but the thought of being one level away from losing Solara's Mercy filled me with some anxiety. The only reason I wasn't losing my shit right now on the edges of this so-called Twilight, was because I knew I wasn't going to permanently die if I got offed by a giant chicken.

Speaking of giant chickens, Cobbler had settled down next to me at the fire, cooing softly. I was starting to suspect his murderous attitude was all a front, and he actually was a big baby.

I hadn't paid much attention to my bond with the bird, but it worked differently than my one with Ae. Instead of a cord connecting us, it was more like a loose sense. If I closed my eyes and spun around, I could point in the bird's direction. Sometimes, I could swear I felt a hint of emotion, but nothing concrete. Overall, I hoped we would start to get along. I knew the warblecock was intended as a joke, but I bet Cobbler could fight like a cornered raccoon in a donut store if really pressed.

I checked back in with my center, spinning it slowly like Ae had instructed me. I hadn't earned any more wisdom, at least not that I could think of, but I still wanted to keep myself on the edge of what my abilities were capable of. More than once, that little bit of premonition wisdom gave me saved my hide more than once. No wonder humans on the wisdom-focused Path of Light were such a force. They were basically lightning Jedi. Screw that.

I knew the real thing I needed to work on was strength after unlocking my heart meridian, but a piece of me was avoiding it because I was already so physically tired.

What was up with the whole unlocking thing anyway? It had never been explained to me. I knew I had a meridian connected to each stat. Would I get a boost every time I cleared one? If so, that sounded like a good way to get more power without losing the Mercy.

The sound of boots approaching pulled me from my rumination.

"Hey, Stone, you want the first watch?" Jackson asked. "The girls are pretty tired, and I was wondering if you'd be up for it."

"Yeah, sure. I was doing some meditation anyway. Who am I waking up?"

"Well, Gretchen's already asleep, so let's do Gretchen. She should be the most rested by that time."

"Sure thing, boss, I'll stay up as long as I can."

"Outstanding."

I did my best to ignore the giggling coming from the tent as Jackson slipped in with Marie and Rochelle.

To my horror, the giggling continued. This group's lack of popularity was rearing up. Fifth wheel, indeed. Jackson should find another girl to add at this point and roll as a harem pack.

Either way, I looked for stones that were heavy enough to push my strength. I was sore from the day's activities, but my free time was limited, and it seemed like the thing to do. Ae stressed that training was the key to getting everything out of my stats.

I rifled through a series of heavy objects before finding a stone about the size of my head that pushed my strength to its edge. Holding it directly above my head, I dropped into a deep squat. I felt that slight shake and a light burn of my muscles tightening up in a new way. I dropped down again, keeping the repetition slow, holding the stone directly above my head as my arms shook. I felt a little paranoid about the rock dropping on my head, but I figured I could roll out of the way or something.

I was ten repetitions in by the time that the shaking got intense. I had to grit my teeth to push to come back up. I knew I only had one or two more in the tank, trying to get to the point of failure. I dropped down at thirteen and knew I could not come back up. I shifted forward, letting the rock drop into some soft earth, barely making a sound on impact, and falling onto my butt as the weight came out of my hands.

Sweat beaded my forehead. The forest around us seemed normal as I did a lap around the camp, waiting for my body to recover. The long shadows made it hard to make anything out, messing with my depth perception.

It took four laps for my heartbeat to go back down. On the next round of squats, I did eleven repetitions, then seven, and then four. I worked this pattern until finally, I was gritting my teeth to get one repetition.

Wiping the sweat from my forehead, I felt content to stare at the fire. The dull background noise of distant animals and birds continued to churn away. I knew firsthand the type of threats that lurked in these woods, like that dino-sized murder bird, but despite it all, I felt pretty confident we could kick just about anything's ass out here as long as we worked together.

Without the sun moving, I had no idea how long it had been, but I did notice the emergence of a large golden moon in the sky. It became more visible as it drifted away from the sun in the east. It was either way bigger or way closer than Earth's moon, taking up a pretty aggressive chunk in the sky. If I had to guess, it was five or six times the size of Earth's moon. I rubbed my eyes. It looked like there were structures on it, like people had made it there and built things, but it could've been my imagination. I couldn't tell for sure.

The moon drifted across the sky as I waited, looking up and down the road, waiting for trouble to pop out of its own butt, but nothing happened, and my eyes felt heavy.

I knew when I took a second too long to blink that it was time for me to wake up Gretchen, which I was avoiding and half the reason I had stayed up as late as I had.

I stood in front of her tent, ready to get mauled to death.

"Gretchen," I whispered next to the entrance.

Nothing.

"Gretchen," I said, trying to knock on the tent entrance, which was an exceptionally difficult task on loose fabric.

Nothing.

"Fine, you've given me no choice." I undid the button holding the tent flap closed.

I peeled back the flap, afraid of what I would find. Gretchen was curled up into a ball in a pile of blankets, a fluffy black tail wrapped around from her lower section up to her face, the tip twitching slightly.

"Gretchen, it's your turn for watch," I said, gingerly poking her with a stick. I wasn't about to lose an arm over this.

The cat girl murmured, her cat ears flicking out from underneath the arms covering her head. "I don't wanna."

"Not an option, princess," I said, considering poking her again with the stick. "Your daddy told me that you're on watch next, so get your cat ass out here."

"He's not my daddy," the catgirl mumbled, unwrapping herself from the pile of blankets.

I didn't even want to know what she was wearing, and I didn't stay around to look. I felt Ae go cold against my armor and knew it was time to run. I was already getting off easy in the interaction we were having so far and didn't want to fuck it up.

I poked at the fire, wondering if the catgirl had gone back

to sleep, when she plopped down on the other side. She looked like shit, still trying to rub the sleep from her eyes and fiddling with the black choker on her neck. It was a weird choice and didn't go with the frilly clothes she had on. If I didn't know better, I'd say she was going for French maid vibes. It was interesting she had the headband back on, pushing her cat ears down.

Against my better judgement, I decided to say something.

"Don't you need to be able to hear to keep watch?" I said. "I don't want to get mauled to death because you can't hear."

The sleepiness snapped from Gretchen's eyes as she looked at me with a sharpened gaze. She lifted a finger to her lips, shushing me, casting a worried glance over at Jackson's tent.

I was shocked, understanding what she meant. "Oh, you've got to be kidding me," I said, looking at her and at the tent. How could they not know she was a whatever they called catgirls here.

"Stay out of it, gremlin," she said.

Ah, there was that bite.

"At least I'm not embarrassed of who I am." I shrugged. "I don't care who knows."

"Why? So everyone can treat me the way they treat you?" Gretchen said.

"Ouch, man. Put those claws away," I said, feigning injury. Gretchen's increasing anger just made me smile. "Fine, I'll cool it on the cat puns, but you need to quit being so shitty all the time."

"I don't need advice, Stone," she said flatly.

"Uh huh." Mocking her probably wasn't the best call but I couldn't help it.

Gretchen gave me a weird look, clearly wanting to say something. Her mouth opened and closed a couple times before I decided to push it.

"Yes?" I said, fighting against the urge to say 'cat got your tongue?'. "Just spit it out. I can tell you have something to say."

Gretchen sat for a moment, her tail broke free and swished behind her, lost in her own world.

"Why aren't you collared?" Gretchen asked.

That was not the question I was expecting. How would I answer this without giving my abilities away? Charisma urged me to keep it simple. "Collars don't work on me."

"Don't work on you? How?" Gretchen leaned forward, intensity in her eyes. "How do you do it? Tell me."

"Are you going to tell me why your boytoy doesn't know you have cat ears?" I nodded towards Jackson's tent.

"That has nothing to do with this," Gretchen said between clenched teeth.

"Yes, it does. It's a trust thing. I don't hand out secrets for nothing," I said. Silence stretched and I ended up yawning.

“Look, I’m tired.”

“Fine. I don’t need help on watch anyway.” A cold veneer returned to her voice.

I gave her some finger guns, leaning my back up against Cobbler and closing my eyes. I wondered how long it would take to fall asleep, but the next thing I knew, someone was shaking my shoulder.

"Oh shit, I'm awake," I said.

Cobbler must have moved at some point because I was lying on the ground. The big traitor was eating food out of Marie's hand.

"Do what you gotta do. We're about to hit the road," Jackson said, pointing over her shoulder with his thumb.

I wandered to the edge of camp, finding a tree that needed watering. It felt like the longest piss of my life as I daydreamed about coffee and what I would do to get it. I had looked for it in the general store, but they didn't have any, and when I tried to describe it, the checkout girl refused to speak to me.

Not long after, I tried to ride Cobbler again, and for about five seconds, I thought we were getting somewhere, but then he bucked me right back off, doing his little dumb circular dance as he gobbled in victory. I was starting to think the big turkey was fucking with me.

No, actually, he was definitely fucking with me.

Gretchen kept sending me looks, which made me feel like I

had something on my face, so I kept wiping my mouth, thinking that that's what it was, but it felt like every time I looked over, I caught her looking away. Like, damn, should I tell her I have someone I'm interested in already?

Ae was my friend, right? Panic flooded through me. Does being turned into an object and bonded for life count as the beginning of a formal courtship in elf society? Oh Solara, was I married? I'd have to clear it up with the elf once we raised her level. I hated all of this. It was so confusing.

I caught Gretchen looking at me again. Oh God, this was the last fucking thing I needed, an angry tsundere catgirl after my halfkin meat. I mean, there was no way, right?

"How was watch last night, Gretchen?" I ventured, hoping she would be a dick about it.

"Don't speak to me, snake bait," she said, pure ice in her voice.

Immediately, relief washed through me. She was just weird.

"Our little Gretchen here is not a morning person," Jackson said, patting her leg. It was the first time I had seen him be physical with her. My 'something's not right here' vibes started to tick. Jackson didn't strike me as a bad dude, but something about this felt… off.

Speaking of feeling off, I noticed something, or rather a lack of something.

The background noise was gone.

The pervasive silence carried weight. Everyone else seemed

to become aware of it at the same time.

The sound of a sword being drawn filled the sonic void as Jackson drew his weapon. "Contact left!"

Twenty-Six: Contact

Jackson waved a double edged monstrosity of a sword in the air.

As the blade passed out of the shadow and into the sunlight, the runes running down the center glowed for a second. Jackson pointed the blade at one of the creatures. "Halt, creature. State your business," he called, but the creatures ignored him.

"Hobbs," Gretchen said, pulling out matching daggers.

Now, I had no idea what a hobb was, but judging from the context clues I was getting, I assumed they were the dozen or so things pouring out of the left side of the trail. They were bipedal ferrets standing a little taller than me, walking upright and carrying little weapons. They were completely covered with fur and looked a little ridiculous standing on their little legs with their long bodies on top. Their armor was basically trash and scraps, consisting of bits of leather, fur, and rusted chainmail. They would have been adorable if not for the humanoid skulls that topped each of their heads like helmets.

"**Inspect**," I said.

Greater Hobb (lvl 4): The greater hobb is a subset of the Polecat family, being the largest and most intelligent of the family. The greater hobb is known for living in large communes and a familial penchant for thievery, leading to the famous saying, '*If you see a hobb, you've already been robbed.*'

I pulled my messenger bag a little closer as the hobbs chattered at each other, clearly speaking some language as they swarmed the party.

Marie and Rochelle hit the ground hard as the horse bucked them off. Their packs spilling their gratuitous contents and quickly getting scooped up by the hobbs moving through the area.

"They're after the packs!" I called, realizing adorable woodland creatures were robbing us.

"No!" Marie yelled, getting into a game of tug-of-war with one of the hobbs grabbing her things. Spears lashed out, making her retreat.

Rochelle pulled out her bow but couldn't hit any of the fast-moving little creatures. The hobbs' bodies undulated, moving like they didn't have a single bone in them, dodging the arrows with a flick.

Marie's tussle with the hobb over her pack hadn't gone unnoticed, causing them to swarm her.

"**Golem Armor**," she cried. She covered herself in a layer of rock, covering her face with her arms as she huddled on the ground.

Jackson's horse disappeared with a pop as he ran forward, leaving Gretchen behind to defend two packs.

"**Thunderbolt**," Jackson yelled. Lightning shot from Jackson's hand, striking the ground near Marie, sending the hobbs into a brief retreat.

Gretchen was doing well, holding out her small blades and making herself a force to be reckoned with. She twirled through the air, hissing at a few as they approached her, revealing small, pointed teeth. The hobbs backed up, pointing and chattering. A word spread out among them, anger evident in their eyes. The hobbs attacked the party with new vigor.

Everyone but Gretchen.

The hobbs were out for blood this time, ignoring the downed packs entirely. I put my back to Cobbler as the hobbs swarmed us, picking at him with long bone-tipped spears. The warblecock seemed afraid of the weapons, taking me by surprise.

"Cobbler, get back," I yelled, activating **Steadfast** and taking a hit meant for him. I could barely pull any sol out of the air in the shadows of the trees. To my horror, the whole party was fanning out and not regrouping, letting the villainous polecats move about as they pleased.

"Stop fanning out," I called as Jackson threw out another ball of lightning, completely missing one of the slippery ferrets. This whole thing was going to shit. Were we really getting our asses kicked by Zootopia rejects?

My moment of distraction cost me a spear scraping my side. The chainmail took most of the damage, but it still hurt.

Cobbler gobbled out a war cry, charging the hobbs with new anger. The hobbs were careful not to come in reach of Ae or his talons, keeping their distance from us as we charged. The sol was so thin that I couldn't launch any meaningful attacks. I hated to play one of my cards like this, but the party was distracted, and we were in a pinch.

"Cobbler, I need to get ahold of one of them," I told the bird. Cobbler looked unconvinced. "I'm going to light one on fire."

The flames of murder flicked in the warblecock's eyes as he grabbed ahold of one of the spears poking at him with his beak, pulling the hobb off balance. It was all I needed.

I was on the hobb immediately, biting its neck like the pipsqueak vampire I was, and driving Ae into its side. The sol I turned cold as I drank it, Ae sending a chill through the downed ferret. The hobb kicked against my armor, his slashes meaning nothing to my chainmail, but it still felt like I was being punched in the gut.

Ae let me know she had enough and the hobb collapsed. Blood stained her white hilt as she sent out waves of sleepiness.

Wyvern's Breath erupted as a thirty-foot jet of black flame shot over the shocked line of ferrets. Spears, fur, and leather bubbled and popped under the sticky, corrosive flames.

Cobbler fanned his tailfeathers, crowing like a rooster. He

flapped his wings as if to make the fire stronger, further sending the polecats back.

A shrill whistle filled the air as all the hobbs disengaged. The ferrets immediately abandoned the enflamed weapons and armor, fleeing into the trees.

The smoldering remains of the battle lay scattered across the road as we all stood in stunned silence. Cobbler stood next to me, fluffing out his full display, dancing back and forth from one foot to the other.

"Oh, what? Now you're gonna pretend you're the one that's scared them off?" I said.

The bird looked reproachfully at me before wandering off to peck at something.

I turned to the party, the frustration I suppressed during the fight bubbling to the surface. "So, what was that?"

"Hobbs," Gretchen said like I was the dumbest person that ever existed.

"Shut up, Gretchen," I snapped back.

"Don't talk to her like—" Jackson started.

"You didn't work together. What the fuck was that?" I said. “You let them grab our stuff.”

"How dare you talk to us like that," Gretchen said.

Marie and Rochelle had the wherewithal to look at least somewhat embarrassed. Jackson looked about as angry as I'd ever seen him.

I cut them off. "If that was anything threatening, we would have all died as you guys fanned out and fought for yourselves. Why didn't we form up into a defensive formation? Marie is the tank, so why weren't you using her to create distance so Rochelle could get off a shot? I don't think she hit a single thing the whole fight."

"It happened so fast, okay?" Rochelle said, looking embarrassed for being mentioned. "I don't normally shoot while being attacked."

Gretchen pushed the shy girl out of the way. "What exactly were you doing anyway? You waited to use your attack."

"At least I fricken did something," I snapped back.

"Gretchen, be nice. He's just feeling flustered." Rochelle said.

"No, he doesn't get to come in here and boss us around," Gretchen said, pointing a finger in Rochelle's face.

I threw up my hands. "How have you guys survived up to this point?"

Jackson didn't make eye contact. "The Commandant has been sending us with one of the high-level adventurers while we looked for a fifth."

"Oh, you gotta be shitting me," I said, trying not to facepalm. I walked away with my hands on my head. Should I leave them? I hoped they could help me with my quest from Ae, but I didn't want to be part of this trash fire. That bounty almost felt worth not dying with this group of nitwits.

Jackson broke my train of thought. "All right, Stone and Marie up front. Rochelle, you take center behind them. Gretchen and I will take the sides." Jackson looked us all over. He was clearly imitating someone, and his demeanor changed. "We will practice from here on out, with contact, followed by a direction, then drill. So, 'contact left drill' to indicate a simulated contact. Am I clear?"

A chorus of affirmation followed, from Gretchen and I muttering a response to Marie's enthusiastic 'yes.'

Marie pressed her shining assets against Jackson's arm. "Oh babe, I love it when you take charge."

I looked over at Gretchen to see we were making the same look of irritation. It was a weird moment. A silent understanding that what was happening here was uncomfortable.

"What about my missing pack?" Rochelle complained. "I can't stay the night out here without my things."

"And because of our gremlin problem, we can't go back to town," Gretchen added, eyeing me with annoyance.

Jackson waved them off, walking to the edge of the road, looking at where the hobbs had fled. He stood up a little bit taller before clearing his throat. "They left a trail in the snow. We can follow them and get our packs back."

It took every ounce of my power not to sigh. "Aren't we supposed to be on a quest, not going on some harebrained adventure to cover up our fuckups?"

"Marie and Rochelle need their packs back, and I'm going

to get it, whether you come with me or not," Jackson said. The girls cupped their hands in front of their chests, staring at him in admiration.

Jackson and the party took off into the woods, leaving Cobbler and me on the road.

I let out a sigh as Cobbler looked at me, waiting to see if we would follow. "Come on, bud, let's see how far this train takes us."

The hobbs had left a pretty clear trail in the snow as they dragged the bags and their wounded through the woods. Jackson strode forward off the trail, stomping on seemingly every twig along the way.

"Maybe we should try to be quiet," Gretchen suggested, her voice a strained sweetness.

Following the party on the trail was an exercise in extreme patience. They were not only loud but moving slowly.

Jackson was a lost cause, having all the grace of a barbarian. Gretchen and Rochelle moved silently, whereas Marie kept apologizing verbally whenever she stepped on something. I did surprisingly well. It was probably some hidden halfkin power.

For what it was worth, Cobbler was the quietest of us all, moving through the forest with a grace I didn't expect from the bird, exuding the air of an ambush predator.

We walked for hours. The path wove and intersected all over the place. Multiple times, we had to decide which way to go, the path diverging and twisting up the mountainside.

The enthusiasm the party had initially, started to fade as the girls struggled to lug the remaining backpack not carried by Jackson.

Finally, Jackson broke the silence in an arbitrary clearing. "We stop here," Jackson declared. "Rochelle, what time is it?"

"Oh, it's just after twentieth bell," Rochelle said, pulling out something that looked like a big stopwatch.

"What is that?" I said, looking at the object.

"Oh, this is a lunarwatch," Rochelle said. "The mechanism is attracted to the position of the moon. So, when you line the compass up with the gravitational pull of Terra, it tells you what bell it is."

I looked at the timepiece. The markings showed the first bell was when the moon was directly above us and the twelfth was when the moon was directly away.

"That's pretty cool. I've never seen anything like that," I said.

"I doubt a nonner would have one," Gretchen said. "They're expensive."

"Well, on that note," I said. "I'm going to see if I can catch anything in that lake just up the way. I'm tired of dry provisions. Gretchen, are you cool with taking the first watch, and I'll take the second?"

"Fine," the catgirl said. I had expected more of a fight but took my victory.

The others put up their tents as I walked away. I could hear the girls complaining about their lack of personal items. Solara would have to forgive me for not being overly sympathetic.

Cobbler followed me and, to my surprise, was more interested in whatever I was doing than what was happening at the camp.

"Ready to catch some fish?" I asked the big turkey. I wasn't sure if he ate that type of thing, but with his track record, he ate anything he could get his beak around.

The warblecock gobbled, flaring out his wings. I took that as a yes.

It only took a few minutes to reach the small lake we had passed. Little bits of ice floated in the center, matching where the shadows were cast.

I snatched up a straight branch and made a spear with a sleeping Ae as Cobbler waded out in the water, standing on one foot and holding the other in the air, ready to strike.

Cobbler was much better at fishing than I was, catching three small fish in under a half hour. My **inspect** spell indicated they were a species of crappie, a little squat fish with rainbow scales on its back.

Cobbler ate most of his fish as soon as he caught them, only handing any to me after eating six. The bird was a glutton. Still, I had five fish after an hour or so, enough to share a bit. Gretchen seemed like she snapped back to being an ass today, so I wondered if a little peace offering might bring her a bit more to my side. Not to be racist, but my experience with cats back on Earth led me to this conclusion. They only respected anyone who fed them, and even then it was just barely.

Gretchen poked the fire with a stick as we walked back into camp. Cobbler immediately sat down and fell asleep, his neck pulling in and his head resting on his body.

"Want some fish?" I asked the catgirl. I hoped this wasn't racist as shit. Her eyes lit up a little, telling me I was making the right call.

"Are you sure?" Gretchen asked.

I tossed her two of the fish, suspending my three over the fire on my spear.

"Thank you," she said. It was so quiet I almost missed it.

"Yeah, no problem. These trail rations suck ass," I said, pointing to the saddlebags on Cobbler.

Gretchen hesitated, looking at the tent behind her before looking back at me. "Don't judge me."

"I will keep all judging internal," I said. The catgirl narrowed her eyes at my joke, but her heart wasn't as in it as usual.

Gretchen removed her headband, letting her black ears spring up. It was crazy how much they blended in with her hair.

"I'm jealous you can even hide," I said, watching the catgirl shake her tail free under her skirt. "Like, what can I even do? Walk on stilts?"

Gretchen laughed, covering her mouth immediately, looking back at the tent behind her and covering her ears with her arm. The move reminded me of Ae being self-conscious of her elf ears. I was starting to piece together it was a big indication of race.

After a minute or two of silence, it was obvious the rest of the party was asleep.

In a flash of sharp teeth, Gretchen took a bite of the raw fish. I was glad I didn't promise not to judge because I did a little.

"Got a problem?" she challenged, talking around a mouthful of white fish.

"Me?" I said, pointing to myself. "I'm renowned for my open mind and lack of judging. I've eaten raw fish a time or two myself." I gave her a thumbs up.

Gretchen devoured the fish, letting off a low rumble of a purr as she did so. Not a bone or scale was spared her wrath. It made me a little queasy, but I was a fire-breathing vampire hobbit, so who was I to judge?

By the time my fish were done, Gretchen had excused herself to her tent, leaving me to watch. I saw her pause for a second, almost as if she was struggling to say something, but she decided against it, her swishing tail slipping into the tent after her. The whole interaction made me miss Ae's company.

Ae appeared to still be sleeping, her presence quiet in my

mind. I pulled out the knife, laying her on my lap, when I suddenly remembered something I picked up at the general store. They sold these little kits for taking care of weapons. It included a nice little case, a whetstone, a cloth, and oil.

I fetched it, **inspecting** Ae as I sat back down.

Chainbreaker (Lvl 2, Soulbound): This evolving weapon is bound to the soul of Ae'silin DeArdent, the Chainbreaker. This is an evolving weapon and will change with time. Kill beings with sol to upgrade.

"Good job," I told the knife. "We'll get you back up and running in no time."

I held Ae up in the light and confirmed my suspicion. Blood had made its way down in the ornate decoration of her hilt, gumming up the areas between jewels. I had wiped the blade in some vegetation, but it was clear it needed more. I opened the kit, pulling out a soft bristle brush to knock the blood out.

Ae woke up as soon as the bristles touched her cross guard. I could feel her attention on me, it was sharper than before.

"Is that a no?" I asked. This was uncharted territory for me. Why couldn't any of my relationships be normal?

Ae sent out a flash of impatience.

I got back to cleaning the precious stones. She almost hummed as I did so, pulsing contentment. I was glad she liked the attention, but it felt weird.

I ran a finger along the edge of her blade. It felt sharp but didn't cut me. I remembered Ae drawing blood on the Elder immediately and tried again, pressing harder. She still didn't cut me. I shrugged, grabbing the oil and the cloth.

Ae amped up in anticipation as I put some oil on the cloth. If I thought it was awkward before, I was way past that now. I almost didn't do it, but Ae sent me a sharp prod of anger.

I put the cloth on her blade, drawing the oil down its length.

Ae radiated pleasure. Like some white knuckle grabbing the sheets type energy. I almost dropped her, looking around to make sure no one was seeing this.

"Stop it," I said, embarrassed. "Is that really necessary?"

Ae didn’t let up. My cheeks were on fire as I fished oiling the blade. I put her in her sheath as she radiated smug contentment, getting mad when I took my hand off the hilt. I had to take a walk after putting the cleaning kit back to calm down.

I meditated the rest of my watch. Marie left the lunarwatch out, so I could track time. I woke up Jackson next.

I fell asleep against Cobbler the instant I lay down. I didn't even notice the silver ring flashing for an instant as I extended my hand.

TWENTY-SEVEN: ARACHNOIDITIS

I woke up to yelling in the camp.

I grabbed Ae, rolling to my feet to face an attack, but instead, it was Marie and Rochelle yelling at each other while Gretchen and Jackson pretended to be anywhere else.

Marie and Rochelle looked like borderline different people. I hadn't even registered they had been wearing makeup this whole time, but I hadn't been looking all that hard.

"I know you're hiding some," Marie yelled. Black marks ran down the side of her face, telling of smeared eyeliner. It gave her a wild look as she pointed a finger in the shorter girl's face.

"I'm not hiding anything," Rochelle yelled back. Her ordinarily neat braid was a wreck, with loose, wavy strands going everywhere.

Gretchen sat to the side, examining her nails as if nothing was happening. She seemed relatively more put together, but her look had always been plain.

I decided to make myself scarce. Cobbler was already AWOL. Bastard.

Jackson made eye contact with me as I started to slink away, catching me in the act.

"I will help Stone catch some fish for breakfast," he said, walking towards me.

I was already halfway into the woods when he said it, recognizing a powder keg when I saw one. I lived with my uncle and his three daughters at one point. My insane cousins were all the education I needed on the subject.

The girls shot Jackson a glance that could melt steel. Gretchen looked up from doing whatever it was to her nails. I could tell her tail would be swishing with interest if it was out, but her face had no emotion. I suspected most of her emotions were expressed in her tail and ears.

"Come on, Stone," Jackson said. "I'll leave these ladies to freshen up." He practically pulled me into the woods.

"Holy shit, dude," I said, keeping my voice low. "What did you do?"

"Quiet, Rochelle has great hearing." Jackson sped and walked towards the lake. "I saw the remains of your dinner last night." He was talking semi-loudly as if putting on a play. "And thought it would be good to treat everyone to a fresh breakfast."

"God damn, dude, is it really that bad?" I kept my voice down.

"The Fringe is more dangerous than you think," Jackson said, still in his stage voice. "The monsters only get worse as you go further west."

"Are we really doing this?" I said, wiggling out of his grasp on my arm.

"Oh yes, lots of people have tried to tame the Twilight. The Kingdom of Dawn's Edge was the most recent, but it too fell without a human hand to quell the infighting." Jackson was clearly reciting something.

"What happened?" I wondered how much of what Jackson knew would differ from what Elder Waza said. At this point, I didn't trust anything not from Ae's mouth.

"Hmm. No one knows what happened other than one day, they were gone. Without their heavy hitters to protect their settlements, everything crumbled into dust. Allegedly."

"Right." I wasn't sure what we were talking about at this point.

"There's rumors around the Guild," Jackson said. "Rumors of settlements out here. Sometimes, hunters see them. Sometimes adventurers hear something from someone who heard something." Jackson petered off as we arrived at the lake. Cobbler, that traitor, was already at the lake, eating a freshly caught fish.

Jackson let out a breath as if he had been holding it the whole time. "Oh, thank Solara. I had to get away. Rochelle tried to stab me this morning when I rolled onto her hair, yelling something about not having her hair spray."

"Sounds about right," I said. "My cousin once stabbed a girl who stole her favorite chapstick." I threw Jackson a stick as I started to sharpen mine. I knew this whole thing was a cover, but I was hungry.

"We need to get their bags back as soon as possible," he said. "For everyone's safety."

"Sounds like it," I laughed. Jackson didn't. "Hey, but you got your health. You've got three girlfriends. I mean, that's a lot. Gotta keep an eye on what you got going for you."

Jackson laughed, but it didn't reach his eyes. "Truthfully. I can barely handle two of them. Hell, I can barely handle one of them."

"Hard time going multiple rounds?" I asked, trying not to smirk at my joke.

"As if. No, that part's covered," he said. "Instead, they gang up on me."

I raised both my eyebrows immediately.

"Not like that," Jackson clarified. "They have little meetings, make decisions, and then conspire to lead me to those same conclusions. They think they're super clever, and I don't know. It's like they want me to think I came up with the ideas."

"Dude, I think that's just being in a relationship," I said.

"At least normally it's one versus one, but I'm permanently one versus three. I have no chance. If I've got an afternoon free and want to go hunting or something, it's like, no, they've all decided I'm taking them out."

"Couldn't you maybe let one or two go?" I ventured. "Gretchen seems pretty detached."

Jackson examined his finished spear point, looking back over his shoulder. "Don't breathe a word about this because I'll deny it, but Gretchen is my favorite. She doesn't care I go hunting or go out with my friends as long as I want. She just goes along with the others, not to make a fuss. She isn't always hanging off me or making a scene."

"She does seem… aloof," I said, desperately trying not to drop cat puns. "You should tell her that, by the way. She might be afraid of you rejecting her for not being like the others."

Jackson snorted. "As if. The others should be nervous about not being like Gretchen. My father says women calm down as they age, but my mother leads him around by the nose. A level sixty-three adventurer hopping to the call of a middle-aged woman still under the Mercy." Jackson laughed. "Besides, Gretchen would probably leave if I broke up with the others. It's almost like I'm the accessory, and they would prefer to be with each other."

"This sounds like it's got some weird dynamics," I said.

"You have no idea. It's exhausting to track what they want, what they don't like, and what I've promised them. It's a full-time job. I swear I need to hire someone to manage them. I almost failed my last year of the academy because of it." Jackson looked exhausted.

"Blink twice if you need help." I snapped my fingers. "You should designate one of them as the lead girl and have her manage them. Which one did you start dating first?"

Jackson hesitated. "They came to me and asked me out all at once."

The missing pieces of the puzzle started to fall into place. I thought Jackson was some womanizing genius, but now I thought he was a rich boy being taken for a ride. But how did Gretchen fit into this? Were they a bunch of non-humans trying to hide in plain sight?

"I'm starting to believe you've been conned," I said. "But I understand your reluctance to give it up."

Jackson nodded, focusing on the fish we were scaring away with our conversation. "I can't deny the benefits."

We shared a laugh at this, letting the conversation die as we focused on actually catching something.

Despite it all, a bit of me did feel bad for Jackson. It sounded like he was getting handled by a crew of shrewd women.

We returned to camp with over a dozen fish to find the girls chatting around the fire like best friends.

They issued polite greetings like they weren't about to come to blows not even an hour ago. Rochelle was even braiding Marie's long red hair.

Jackson fell into his normal rhythm, complimenting them and showing off his fishing prowess. I watched it all with new eyes, giving Cobbler a side glance as if he was also in on it.

I zoned out as I cooked my fish, but the girls were all over Jackson, praising him and cooking his food for him. Before, I had seen the behavior as weird, but now it was like the boy was caught in the clutches of harpies.

A seed of doubt wormed into the back of my mind. What if Ae did the same thing to me? I clung to the idea of Ae being genuine, but I was her only option. It was very convenient.

I dismissed the idea. For now, I would choose to take Ae at her word. Besides, she'd never given me a reason to doubt her before.

My brain was in a fog as we broke camp, getting back on the trail. Snowflakes drifted in the air as we followed the mountainside, heading towards a valley shared with the neighboring mountain. Bits of some kind of stone structure poked above the trees in the bottom of the valley.

"Gully Pass," Jackson told the party. "Seems we've been taking a shortcut this whole time."

Three or four hours into our hike, motion caught my attention as something darted out of the underbrush.

Lightning leaped from Jackson's hand, leaving the creature little more than a smoldering stain on the trail.

"A dire rabbit," he said, looking around. "Something could've been chasing it. Form up."

The party snapped into formation. The smell of pork wafted through the air as they drew on the ambient sol, as thin as it was. Barely even a sliver of the sun hung on the horizon. I drew Ae who hummed in anticipation, her handle growing cold.

We heard the thing before we saw it, crashing and stomping through the snow-covered bushes crowding between the trees.

"Steady," Jackson said. We all held our breath as it got closer.

The thing burst into the trail, roaring, its mouth opening sideways. Interconnected teeth parted, sending spittle flying. The thing looked like a white gorilla with ram's horns and a fucked-up face. It reared up to beat its chest with heavy fists.

"**Inspect**!" I yelled, taking advantage of the opportunity.

Highland Gorli (Lvl 14): A member of the great apes family, the Highland Gorli is a solitary and violent member. They rarely travel together and are known to be ill-tempered and territorial.

The party hit hard while the creature was in the middle of its display and I was still reading. Lightning arced as an arrow hit its throat, piercing the skin but not going deep. The lightning burnt fur but didn't cause any more than a light burn on the ape's skin. The gorli roared.

Cobbler fanned his feathers in a counter display, crowing at the beast, drawing the beast's ire on us.

Its fist swung down on me.

I knew I had no chance of stopping it, a wild plan forming.

I went with it, not having enough time to veto it before I was sent packing back to the dungeon.

The fist descended as I plunged Ae into the gorli's hand and out the other side, catching her point in my palm. Ae seemed to know not to cut me and I decided now was the time to test it. Worst case, we had someone with a heal spell.

I activated **Steadfast**, letting Ae go wild as I drew sol from the gorli, using its energy to lock me into place.

The world became black as the spell took over my body. All my senses became dull in a complete cast of **Steadfast**. I normally wouldn't use the costly spell on my whole body, but I didn't want to get my eyes exploded by an angry gorilla.

Sol ran through my hands, letting me know my gambit worked, **Steadfast** eating it up as soon as it passed my center.

Long moments passed. I became isolated from the fight. It was the tradeoff of absolute defense.

The sol source cut off, and **Steadfast** immediately failed, all my senses rushing back in an instant.

I threw myself backward, afraid the fight was still going on, but it wasn't necessary. Marie stood over the gorli, viscera dripping from her stone-covered hands, the creature's skull caved in.

"Ewww ewwww ewww," Marie said, letting the rocks fall off her skin as she shook the gore off of her hands. "That's so gross."

"God damn," I said, getting up. The party had done a number on the beast while I locked it down. It looked like it got hit by a bus, ice running up its arm.

"Excellent work, Stone," Jackson said, clapping me on the shoulder. "That technique put the beast at our mercy. A level fourteen, too."

A gasp cut off my reply. "I didn't get any sol," Marie said, panic in her voice.

"Get back," Jackson called. "It might not be dead."

A tense moment passed as everyone formed back up. I was conflicted. Should I tell them me and Ae ate it all?

I was left to struggle with my internal dialogue as the party watched the dead gorli.

"Stay back," Jackson said, moving forward to kick the corpse. "It is certainly dead. No one got anything?"

Everyone shook their heads no.

"Curious." Jackson stroked his chin where a beard would be in a few years. "Something odd is going on at Gully Pass. Something might be siphoning away sol. This might be far more urgent than anyone predicted."

Light glinted in my hand, drawing my eye. It was subtle, but the ring glowed for a second. I checked again but nothing this time. I stayed silent, not wanting to work the party up over nothing.

"Stay in formation," Jackson said, waiting for me to reach

the front. "There might be more."

Hours stretched as we walked. It's difficult to describe the type of fatigue you get from being constantly on edge. The tension had us all jumpy, and the growing silence of the woods making it worse.

Ae slept like a baby, processing her level up. I was excited to see how aware she was when she woke up.

As we walked a strange scent wafted in the air. It was like the centipedes… but not at the same time. I had grown used to the wild smells of the forest; venison, pine, pork, but this was something else.

We didn't even hear the thing before it hit us. It darted out of the woods, barreling over Gretchen before we could react.

Cobbler reacted before Gretchen hit the ground, kicking the creature hard enough to send it airborne. The beast hit a tree with a sick thud.

The thing was like a wolf, emaciated and maybe half the weight it should've been. Its fur was gray and malted, with patches missing. Spider-like legs stuck out from its sides, emerging from seeping wounds. It had an extra set of eyes growing mismatched on the sides of its head.

"It's got arachnoiditis," Jackson yelled as the swish of a sword leaving its sheath cut through the air. "Don't let it bite you!"

"**Golem Armor**!" Marie had her armor on and pinned the beast before it could recover. Its eyes lulled maddeningly as

Jackson's sword severed its spine and its head fell off into the snow.

As Marie turned back to normal, the blood hissed against her skin. I scooped up handfuls of dirt and tried to wipe it off as the others looked over Gretchen, ensuring she hadn't gotten bitten. Luckily, besides having the wind knocked out of her, she seemed fine. They were talking to each other in hushed tones, and I followed suit.

"The fuck was that?" I whispered.

"Arachnoiditis," Jackson said. "It turns you into a spider hybrid. It's always on the edge of spider territory to soften up their prey."

"Did you say spiders? Like, how big are we talking?" I asked, a feeling of dread filling me.

"Bigger than you, that's for sure, if the stories can be believed. I've even heard rumors of ones with the top half of a human and the lower half of a spider." Jackson shuddered. "This is some poor luck."

The silence dragged on as we continued. I felt considerable relief when Rochelle finally stopped us, letting us know it was twentieth bell. I don't think I was the only one ready to stop.

The group set up camp in relative silence. It was a pleasant spot; a snowmelt stream ran next to the little clearing. The water tasted incredible after the long day's walk.

The rest of the members retired to their tents as I took watch.

Jackson lingered to talk to me. "Remember, with the arachnids so close, don't leave the camp for any reason, no matter what you hear."

"Sure thing," I said, giving him a thumbs up.

The rest of the party disappeared into their tents. I sat with my back up against a tree, staring out under the perpetual dawn. The quiet of the woods made sitting there harder, every sound amplified against the backrest of swishing leaves of the gentle breeze as if everything was trying desperately not to be heard.

Out of curiosity, I looked down at my ring, noticing the glow getting stronger in a certain direction.

Right at Gully Pass.

I reviewed the ring's description, hoping I was wrong.

Silver Ring of the Hunt: This enchanted ring glows in the presence of ascended creatures.

Shit. I looked at the tents and the other were already asleep. I would tell them tomorrow. The extra reward wasn't worth getting wiped, but where would I go? I could sneak to the Guild through the little town gate but what then? I concluded those were tomorrow problems.

"Ae," I said to the sleeping knife. "We might be in some shit."

TWENTY-EIGHT: CONCERNING CATGIRLS

Gretchen was already awake when I knocked on her tent.

Knock was a strong word. It was more like gently patting on the flap.

Gretchen opened the flap immediately, stepping out into the cool mountain air. She followed me wordlessly back to the little fire that we had concocted. The silence of the woods felt heavy as the cat girl sat down next to me rather than across as she had the nights before.

Something was off.

The fire popped and sizzled as we sat there. I knew I was technically in the right to go off to sleep, but there was a tension in the air.

Not like a romantic tension or anything like that. It was more like the tension that builds whenever someone pulls back a rubber band and everyone's waiting for it to snap.

"You didn't tell him," Gretchen said. It wasn't a question but a statement. She looked down at the fire, holding the end of her tail in her lap with both hands. "When you were alone, you didn't tell him about me."

"Tell who about what, exactly?" I had a suspicion about what this was, but I needed it to be absolutely clear before addressing it. I had a long history of misreading situations like this. "I don't know what your continuing problem with me is, but I'd rather we get it sorted out. I'm getting really tired of this game of—" I almost said 'cat and mouse,' but caught myself. "… guessing," I finished.

Gretchen's ears twitched and lay down flat. For the first time, I realized she wasn't wearing her headband.

"I hate you," Gretchen said quietly. "You didn't tell Jackson I'm not human, and it's made me hate you more."

"Why?" My brain scrambled. Was this some cultural thing I was completely missing? Were halfkin the mortal enemies of catkind or something?

"I thought I was done when you saw me. I thought you would sell me out immediately. I set up a contingency, preparing to be outed, but no. Instead, you wiggle out of everything. No jail time, no sentence, no collar"

"But you rescinded your statement." Now I was really confused. "The Captain told me himself."

"This is exactly what I'm talking about," Gretchen said. "You get away with everything. I don't know who removed my statement, but it wasn't me. Then, you waltz into the Guild like you own the place, joining a team at the recommendation of the Commandant, of all people. Worse, they accept you. You meet a challenge head-on against someone three times your size and win. Watching the Guild pat you on the back—" Gretchen's voice choked up as she gripped her tail harder.

I didn't know what to say. Was she jealous of me? Why? I wanted to tell her I was lucky, and I've had my hard knocks too, but felt that would make it worse. The silence dragged on, so I stayed quiet, hoping the silence would compel her to continue.

"How dare you say nothing?" Gretchen said so quietly I could barely hear it. "Letting me pour my heart out like a concerned littermate."

"Gretchen," I said gently, praying my charisma would swoop in and save me, but even it was silent. "I don't know what you want from me. I'm not about to go around telling everybody your business. That is what this is about, right? You're afraid I'm gonna ruin your thing with Jackson and the rest?"

Gretchen laughed. It was one of those dark laughs you have when you don't really think something's funny, but there's nothing else you can do. "You don't understand, do you? I'm not here by choice, snake bait. I was bought, trained, and sent here. I worked for years just to be swept up as a glorified babysitter and part-time prostitute."

"Jackson bought you?" My assumptions about the man crumbled. Did he lie to me? He said they came to him. He acted like they trapped him and not the other way around.

A realization hit me. "Holy shit, you're wearing a collar." I pointed to her choker necklace. "That's a slave collar, isn't it?" I felt dumb for not realizing it before.

Gretchen bared her fangs into a smile. She was so careful to keep them hidden, and now they were out. "Unlike you, who's been walking around flaunting you're free, I'm on the end of a leash. Jackson's too sweet to do what needs to be done, and his father knows it. Did you know Jackson is the most promising swordsman of all his brothers? But instead of working feverishly like the others, all he wants to do is go hunting or hang out in the tavern with his little friends at the Academy. The only one to show talent like their father, and he lacks all of the drive."

Another piece of the puzzle fell into place. Jackson *was* being conned, but not by who I thought it was.

Gretchen continued. "I was pulled out of training by Jackson's father, that monster. He commented I had the right look, opting to test my *services* for himself. Do you know what a level four is to a level sixty-three?"

I shook my head, horrified by where this was going. Gretchen looked at me, but her eyes went through me as if she was seeing something else.

"A plaything," Gretchen said through gritted teeth. "I passed, whatever that means. I fought him every step of the way, but he just laughed. I was forced to train up to level nine, dragged naked through the woods, and made to fight to the death, right on the edge of losing the Mercy. He killed me himself the last time. He said I needed to be fresh for his son, with no bruises or scrapes. He collared me like a house pet and sent me to babysit some brat with two highborn ditzes who didn't even realize their fathers were paid for their participation."

"Holy shit," I said. To her credit, Gretchen didn't look like she was going to cry but rather strangle something to death. "Forgive me if this comes off as rude. I just don't understand what this has to do with me."

"I—" The word got stuck in Gretchen's throat. "Jackson's been so nice to me. He treats me like the others, even though I won't sleep with him. I don't gang up on him like the others or throw a fit when he wants to go out. I'm supposed to be his bodyguard and plaything, to protect him, not—" Gretchen's voice broke. She looked away from me, covering her mouth.

"Actually fall in love with him," I finished when it looked like she couldn't. "You thought I would ruin it," I put together. "That's what this is."

"For all the suffering I've gone through to amount to nothing, when some wide-eyed halfkin appears in the middle of the woods and spots me without my headband. The thought of Jackson finding out I wasn't some little farmgirl but a disgusting nonner. I would have been beaten, abandoned, and probably dropped off with the nearest whorehouse until the Mercy wore off, and finally, someone ended it."

"No," I said immediately. "You're wrong."

Gretchen opened her mouth to argue, but I cut her off.

"Now, shut up for a second. I heard you out. Now, you'll

hear me out. Jackson adores you and would release you from whatever contract you're under in a heartbeat if he could."

Gretchen looked unconvinced, her ears lying down flat.

"You know, of the three of you, you're his favorite. He told me that yesterday. You're the one he would want to run off with. All the things you listed are all the things he likes about you."

Gretchen was stunned. "But..." She looked at Jackson's tent. "But the others do the things I... can't."

"Gretchen, I don't think you're a bad person, but I think you're just in a tough spot, so, against my better judgment, I'll offer my services."

"What do you mean?" Her eyes were locked on me now.

"I'll ask you this once, and if you say no, I'll never bring it up again, okay."

"Okay," Gretchen said slowly.

"Do you want me to take your collar off?"

"It's keyed to Jackson's father. No one else can take it off." Gretchen's demeanor shifted to anger. "Are you toying with me? I open up, and you mock me?"

"I don't need a key, Gretchen," I said evenly. "Do you want your collar off?"

Gretchen squeezed her tail between her hands so tight I thought she'd break it, crimping the end at an odd angle.

"But then how would I—. How would that work? Would I have to run away?"

"Look, I don't have the answers to that. All I'm saying is, if you want the collar off, I can try. I've done it before, but no promises, all right?" I paused, considering something. "I do have one condition if you agree."

Gretchen looked at me, the threat in her eyes mixed with bafflement. "What's your condition?"

I folded my arms. "Don't ask me how I do it. That's my line. I don't care if you know I can do it, just leave it a mystery."

"Deal. Do it." Her response was immediate.

"Just like that?" I was taken aback by how fast she agreed.

"Do it before I tell you no."

"All right. I have to touch the collar. Don't stab me or anything, alright?" Why did this feel so familiar?

Ae pulsed at my belt. She was awake and already sending me irritated emotions as I neared the catgirl.

"Only touch the collar and nowhere else. I might be collared, but I still have claws." Gretchen's nails extended, sending me an unnecessary warning.

"Solara save me, Gretchen. I'm not interested in your little kitty tail. Calm down," I said, partially for Ae's benefit as well.

I placed a hand on the choker, right on the black jewel in the center. Gretchen extended her chin, almost like she was trying to escape my hands.

The collar thrummed with power. Not as much as the chains that held Ae, but it would give them a run for their money. The thing was a work of absolute artistic mastery, the channels and lines being hidden in wires underneath the fabric of the choker necklace, the jewel on the front cleverly worked in with the rest of it.

With a little jolt of panic, I realized draining the collar would probably make me level up.

Doubt crept through my mind, and I looked at Gretchen. The tip of her tail swished between her clenched hands, white knuckles betraying her calm image. Was I going to deny her this because I wanted to be covered by the Mercy a little longer? And what would that say about me as a person? Could I live with that kind of choice? She would believe me if I told her I couldn't release her from the collar.

No. I would do it.

I spun out my center, trying to pull the sol through my hand.

Nothing. I felt it flex but nothing came out.

I repositioned. It was skin tight with no obvious latch, so I had to press my hands on either side, standing directly in front of the seated catgirl.

"Problem?" Gretchen asked.

"Working on it," I said, trying to focus.

I felt the sol flex, and Gretchen made a little sound, almost like a hint of pain. I spun my core harder, trying to pull the sol through my hands, but it just wouldn't pop.

"If you can't do it, I understand," Gretchen said. "The fact you can even manipulate it like this is a testament to whatever abilities you have."

A dark temptation to let her stop me floated through my head. "No, I've got one last trick up my sleeve, but it's going to be weird."

"Whatever it takes," she said.

"I'm gonna hold you to that because I have to bite your necklace."

"Bite?" Gretchen's eyes snapped open. "Why would you have to bite it?"

"No questions. Remember, this is part of the agreement. I free you. You don't ask me how."

"It's just the implications," Gretchen said. "Creatures who drink sol—"

I interrupted her. "Shut up. Don't think about it. You either let me do it or not."

"Solara save me. I've made a deal with an actual demon," Gretchen said, claws extending from her fingertips.

“Hey, it’s your choice. Are we done here?" I asked.

Gretchen surprised me and shook her head no. "Just do it, please."

The cat girl moved her shoulder-length hair to the side, extending her neck for me to bite.

Ae went nuts, a wave of cold stinging me.

"One second please," I said, whirling around and pulling out Ae. "I'm not seducing the catgirl. Keep your shirt on."

Ae protested.

"Yeah, yeah I know. Just don't kill her alright?"

"Are you talking to someone?" Gretchen asked.

"No questions," I said over my shoulder.

My voice dropped to a whisper as I held Ae close. "Are we good?"

Ae was clearly unhappy but the cold receded back. I shook the frost off my hand, putting her in her sheath.

Gretchen was holding back a lot of questions.

"We all have secrets," I said. "You ready?"

"Yes," she said, extending her neck again.

I put a hand on Ae's hilt, feeling her ramp up again. I sent a wave of assurance her way. I could see how being trapped in an object might fuel some insecurity, so I was giving her a big pass on this one.

Biting the flat necklace was easier said than done. All the objects I had bitten before were things like chains and large round objects, which were easy to get my mouth around, but this one was flat. Like magically flat.

I gnawed at the collar for an embarrassing amount of time, unable to get purchase.

"What's wrong?" Gretchen asked.

"I can't get under it to bite it," I said. “I might have to bite into your neck a bit.”

"Do it. I've gone this far, what is a little more."

I had to drag my teeth along her neck to get underneath the choker. It was super awkward, and her breathing getting heavier wasn't helping. Ae was getting madder by the second, her limited patience running out quickly. I had to get this over with.

I tasted a little bit of blood mixed in as I finally got around the collar, slipping a canine tooth underneath. The resistance popped, and the sol flowed into my center. Gretchen gasped as I pulled, making me think I was probably pulling from her as well. The taste was sweet, like a donut, but there was a weird mix of something else, almost like fried chicken, which was probably the bit of sol from Gretchen.

"Sorry," I muttered around the collar.

I tried to pull the collar away from her skin, only drawing from it. Gretchen picked up what I was doing and pushed away, arching her back in the process. I placed a hand on her chest, pushing her back to get more leverage.

Gretchen groaned under the tension, her breath coming in

gasps under the pull on her neck.

Frost ran across my belt, biting into my skin. Ae practically vibrated, trying to get out of her sheath.

Sol swelled into my center, draining it in a torrent. I rated this collar at maybe half of what each of Ae's chains were. The need to level pressed against me in force as I choked down the last bit of sol. The collar was just about empty.

The sound of a sword being drawn cut the silence.

Twenty-Nine: The Other Guy

"Gretchen, what is this?"

The last bit of sol from the collar drained right as the words left Jackson's mouth, my neck entirely swollen to the point I couldn't speak.

Gretchen screamed, reflexively covering her ears. The drained choker necklace tore under the sudden movement, sending me tumbling back. My back hit the ground hard, the necklace hanging from my mouth like a scrap of fur from a fresh kill.

The pressure in my neck was too much. I clamped down on my center. The level was coming slowly but it needed to be done right now. My body was giving me no choice. I frantically spun my center, clamping down on the pressure.

Chaos erupted around me.

"I loved you! How dare you," Jackson roared. "You're both dead!"

"Jackson, it's not—" Gretchen said, stepping back.

"**Thunderbolt**," Jackson yelled.

Lightning arced from the end of Jackson's hand, a loud crack following a split second later.

Gretchen twisted over the lightning bolt with inhuman grace, landing on all fours. Dual blades appeared in her hands, crossing to meet Jackson's wild strike. The cat girl hissed, crumpling back under the force of the hit.

Jackson raised his sword to strike the fallen catgirl.

Congratulations! Ascended to Level 9. +1 Cha, +1 Con

Wyvern's Breath leaped between them, drawing a line across the camp. Frustration billowed into my chest. I couldn't say anything. My mouth tried to form words as my center pressed my windpipe closed. Rochelle and Marie stumbled out of the tent in various states of undress, gasping at the fully revealed Gretchen lying in the dirt across from Jackson.

"Jackson, stop," Gretchen pleaded. She looked exhausted, probably from the sol I accidentally drained.

Jackson was beyond words, leaping across the flames and hacking at her without a bit of skill behind it. Gretchen barely staved off his strikes with her knives.

Marie and Rochelle scrambled forward, but I was faster, croaking out **Steadfast** just before colliding with the enraged swordsman.

I never felt the impact, the world going black as I bared into Jackson, my spell taking hold.

I counted to three, waiting for my sol to reach a comfortable level.

I came out of Steadfast to see the tail end of Gretchen flying into the woods, the girls holding Jackson back.

"I'll kill her," he said, struggling against Marie's golem form.

Jackson's eyes snapped to me. "You." He was so fixated on Gretchen's apparent betrayal that he'd forgotten I was even there.

"Jackson, it's not what you think," I got out, my voice raw.

He snarled at me, breaking free of the girls holding him back.

My knife met his sword as he swung down on me. Tendrils of electricity ran down my arm, but it wasn't enough to break my grip. I slipped his strike, punching him in the side, his armor tanking the blow. We separated, circling each other.

"I should have known not to trust you," Jackson said. "They warned me."

"I freed her, you idiot," I said. I looked over to the girls, who looked a mix of confused and horrified. "Your father bought her."

"Lies!" Jackson tried to overpower me, swinging down on top of me for a second time.

I realized words weren't going to work, and I was going to have to slip in there and make him stop. I switched gears, going from trying to defend myself to trying to incapacitate.

I barely deflected his blade with my knife, striking his chest with my open palm, "**Feast**," I yelled, sucking out a glob of sol.

The move startled him, making him stumble for a second, but I didn't let up. I used the heel of my knife to smack him in the side of the knee, trying to take advantage of his stumble, but he saw the move coming, moving out of the way and jumping backward.

"**Thunderbolt**," he yelled.

I twisted, feeling the heat of it sizzle past my face as Jackson went for the kill.

Luckily, the girls hadn't gotten involved yet. Hell, I was barely holding against Jackson alone.

Jackson twirled his blade, taking a stance I hadn't seen before. I recognized he was now getting serious.

Jackson charged. Everything about him was locked in and smooth. His blade was almost unpredictable, striking forward like a snake.

"**Steadfast**," I yelled, barely deflecting a blow with a heavy arm. If I hadn't activated the spell at the last second, he would have pierced through my chest.

Luckily, activating my ability threw off his groove, and he was off balance for a second. I got within his guard, locking my ankle behind his and sending him to the ground in a tumble.

I was more skilled with ground fighting than he was, but he was nearly a third more of my height and double my weight. He was able to body me, grabbing me with both hands.

Suddenly, I was airborne, sailing towards a large tree.

"**Thunderbolt**," he yelled again. I had just connected with the tree and was too stunned to move, sliding to the ground. I knew this was probably going to be respawn for me.

I heard the ability proc. The lightning struck and hit something, but it wasn't me.

I opened my eyes to see Marie in her golem form standing in front of me. Immediately, the rock armor fell away as Marie collapsed to the ground. Cobbler had Jackson pinned to the ground by the throat, a single talon an inch from his eye.

"Cobbler, down," I called, rolling to my feet.

The turkey shot me a questioning glance.

"Yeah, I know. He's confused. Once he calms down, let him up."

"**Recover**," Rochelle said, placing her hands on Marie's chest. I saw the flash of the healing spell go off as I peeled myself off the ground. My back had made an impact on the tree.

Cobbler let Jackson up, and, to his credit, he ran to the fallen redhead.

"Marie, I—" Jackson started, but Marie pushed something

into his chest.

It was Gretchen's collar.

"It's a restriction collar," Marie said. "It's true."

Jackson reeled back. "My father—" His head whipped over to me. "How is this empty?"

"I let her go," I said.

Jackson didn't hesitate, picking up his sword and bolting into the woods after Gretchen, calling her name.

I thanked the goddess herself. For a moment, I thought I'd vouched for an asshole. Through the party link, I could vaguely tell Gretchen was fleeing back towards town. Impressively fast, too.

I let out a breath, gearing up to follow after them.

Lightning cracked in the distance, making my stomach drop. What was Jackson fighting?

My wisdom saved me, screaming at me to throw myself backward, almost landing in the fire in the process.

A spider thudded down, its long fangs piercing the snow where my boots had just been. A wash of seafood scent slammed into me, solving the mystery of what I had been smelling.

The dog-sized spider was every bit as horrifying as the centipedes. It was covered in varying shades of gray hair, almost blending in perfectly with the shadows cast by the trees. It reminded me a lot of a wolf spider with its eight large saucer-like eyes staring at me with a level of intelligence that disturbed me to the very core. It tilted its body in a way that almost expressed confusion.

Rochelle fired an arrow, connecting with the spider as it leaped to tackle me. The impact sent it rolling.

"**Inspect**," I said, throwing a half-burnt log at the spider. Cinders arced through the air as I read the description.

Twilight Moon Spider (Lvl 2): These spiders are members of the arachnid family and are renowned for camouflage and intelligence. Rarely hunting alone, these spiders often overcome their lack of strength and speed with numbers, paralytic venom, and cunning trap-making. If you've seen one of these, there are ten you haven't.

With every sentence of the description, my hackles rose. Ae practically leapt into my hands, as I scrambled to fight.

The moon spider hissed as the flaming log connected with its bulbous body. The spider squealed, rolling in the cool snow to put the embers out. Cobbler went into full murder mode, tearing the distracted spider with his claws. The thing died with a flash of sol.

Marie went to say something, but I held up a hand to stop her. Dead silence covered the camp as I looked up at the trees. The hair rose up on the back of my neck as I felt eyes on us. Maybe it had just been one spider, and I was paranoid, but I swore I could smell more spiders every time the wind blew.

I saw movement in the canopy and knew I was right. "Run!"

My wisdom went ballistic as the trees exploded with motion. Chittering filled the silence as spiders ranging from the size of a Dachshund to a Great Dane either dropped down or burst out of the underbrush.

It appeared what was harassing Gully Pass had found us after all.

We were being corralled deeper into the pass, and I fucking knew it. With the path after Jackson and Gretchen completely cut off to us, we scrambled towards the little river on the edge of camp. I scooped up a half-burnt stick from the fire, the spiders slinking back from the flames as I swung it in an arc.

I grabbed Rochelle, who had fallen during the encounter, pulling her up by the collar towards the stream. Marie was frozen, her eyes wide as saucers at the unfolding nightmare fuel.

"We gotta go," I yelled, knocking Marie out of her stupor. Even Cobbler was on board with a retreat, already tearing downriver like a bat out of hell.

We hit the river at full speed, our boots splashing in the flowing water. It was about a dozen feet wide, and I was surprised to find how fast the current was.

The girls outpaced me as I cursed my stupid short legs. I had to take two steps for every one of the girls. Taking up the rear also meant I was target number one. All I could think about was that saying about escaping bears my grandpa always prattled on about. 'You don't have to run faster than the bear to get away. You just have to run faster than the guy next to you.'

I was that guy, apparently.

The spiders ran along the water's edge, not venturing deeper, hissing and spitting globs of purple fluid at us. The water boiled where the venom hit, not encouraging me to tank a hit for someone.

A roar grew in the distance, the stream's flow growing to the point it swept me off my feet.

"Waterfall," Rochelle yelled, the roar swallowing some of her words as it also swept her down.

I struggled to stay above the water. "I'll take death by waterfall over spider," I struggled to get out, taking in some water with the words.

"I don't think we have a choice," Marie yelled, losing her balance. Cobbler had his wings tucked in like a duck swimming alongside us, seemingly unbothered by the turn of events.

The urgency of the spiders increased, some of the smaller ones jumping in the water with us, just to be swept away as well in the rolling current.

Other rivers had joined the one we were in and transformed it into a full-blown rapid. We all screamed as we saw the edge approaching, unable to do anything but keep our heads above water and watch.

The waterfall flung us all airborne.

To say we enjoyed the experience to varying degrees was an understatement.

Marie took it the hardest, covering her eyes and screaming at a pitch I didn't know was humanly possible. Rochelle laughed wildly, extending her arms like a deranged eagle. I took the fall with cold apathy, looking over the winter valley below us and spotting a crumbling stone fortress looming in the distance.

But Cobbler. Cobbler was in heaven.

Cobbler spread his wings, launched by the speed of the river, gliding as we fell like bricks. I could only see the warblecock from below as he broke free of gravity and soared for the first time.

Good for him.

I hit the water like brick on concrete, driving all the air from my lungs on impact.

I plunged into the depths, my boots mercifully hitting the bottom. I pushed off, trying to distance myself from the fall, immediately being swept away by the increased current.

The familiar darkness of suffocation came for my vision as I tried to get more than a brief gasp of air above the surface. The current was too much.

My head hit something hard, and everything went black.

THIRTY: THE DIVE

I woke up to being dragged.

Someone was pulling me by the collar, my waterlogged boots dragging in the loose rock of the riverside. Everything swam as healing energy chased my headache away. What happened?

A hand covered my mouth.

"They're close," Rochelle whispered in my ear. The girl looked haggard, a long bloody scrape across her cheek.

I nodded, and Rochelle uncovered my mouth. We were on the bank of the river, the waterfall roaring in the distance.

A blanket of silence hung over the forest as Rochelle pointed out a hollowed-out stump the size of a small building. A crack ran up the side, just big enough for one of us to slip through.

The archer was putting on a brave face, but I agreed. We needed to hunker down.

I kept my head on a swivel as we dashed to the stump. Every slight noise sounded like an explosion to my waiting ears. I poked my head through the crack. After a moment of indecision, I judged it would be a tight fit, but we could make it work.

I slipped in.

Covered in darkness, I **unequipped** and **re-equipped** my clothes, leaving off my armor. The dry clothes settled against me as Rochelle ducked in.

I checked myself over. I hurt everywhere, so there was a lot to examine. My hands confirmed all my limbs were in the right places, although I felt like I'd been hit in the face of the baseball bat.

Rochelle pulled up a piece of bark to close off the entrance. The stump went pitch black, and if it weren't for my ring glowing, I wouldn't have been able to see anything.

Worry flashed through me, and I pulled Ae out of her sheath. Cobbler had all of my stuff, and I lost my messenger bag sometime during the fall, so I didn't have anything to wipe her off besides my clothes. To my relief, she was fine, although she seemed worried. About what exactly, I wasn't sure. There was a lot of that going around.

Rochelle had a blank expression on her face. She looked somewhere between shell shocked and determined, too in the zone to be cracking now. We both took a second to catch our breath, listening to see if we were compromised.

I was about to talk when something scurried across the

stump. It started as a few here and there but grew to a torrent as the spiders ran over our hiding spot. I covered my glowing ring, eyes fixed on the entrance.

Slowly, the sounds faded, and all I could hear was the roar of the river.

"All right," I whispered. "How fucked are we?"

"This is all my fault," Rochelle said. I could see her bravado slipping.

"How about we sort out the blame later," I said. "What happened while I was out? Where is Marie?"

"They took her," Rochelle said. "The spiders took Marie. Everyone's heading for the center of the valley." Her calm visage was back, but her hand shook as she held her bow, which barely fit in the space we were in.

I felt out through my bond with the party. Sure enough, what Rochelle said was true. "Why would they be heading for the fortress?" I asked. "Gretchen and Jackson should've been smart enough to run."

"Stone," Rochelle said. "I don't think Gretchen and Jackson had a choice."

I paused, thinking over our options.

"Alright, I know this will sound cold, but we're all covered by the Mercy here." I felt like a dick leaving them to their fate, but that was the point of the Mercy after all. Some lessons had to be learned the hard way, and we all were about to learn to stay the fuck out of spider territory.

Even in the dim light, I could see that Rochelle paling. Why would she be taking this this hard? Hell, I'd heard them talk about being wiped before.

“Rochelle," I said slowly. "Everyone is covered by the Mercy, right?"

I knew instantly we had a problem by the look on her face.

"Marie leveled up after the fight with the wolf," the archer explained. "She didn't want anyone to worry."

My stomach dropped. This was just about the worst-case scenario. I knew what we would have to do, and I hated it. To make it all worse, Gretchen told me she was close to leveling up, too, so we had to assume she might not be covered, either.

A dark part of me considered cutting and running, but my list of allies was thin and was deadly close to growing thinner. My only job was to keep Jackson alive, and I'd be left alone by the Guild. What would happen to the struggling swordsman if most of his harem got permanently flatlined?

"Well, we know where the party's going, so that's good," I said. "The only thing I can think of is we sneak in. We grab them and run."

Rochelle nodded once, a look of acceptance locking in. We both knew our chances were slim, and a grim fate awaited us. To her credit, the noble-born girl didn't back down.

"We can't leave these things out here," Rochelle said. "We have to kill them. What if they capture someone else?"

I wanted to agree. I really did, but the glow of my ring left me uncertain it was even possible. Plus, our primary objective should be the safety of the party. It might have been calloused, but it was every party for themselves out here right now.

"Rochelle, do you know what this ring is?" I held the ring up for her to look at.

"No?" The archer was confused by the change in conversation.

"Inspect it." I watched her reaction, hoping I was overreacting.

Rochelle muttered the word. Even said so low, I could hear it shimmer in the quiet.

Rochelle gasped. "Solara save us. We have to tell someone about this. Ascended creatures are dangerous, even for the Twilight."

"What exactly is an ascended creature?" I asked. "I know they're powerful, but not the specifics."

"The academy only touched on them a little. Basically, it's a creature that's leveled up to the point it can form a core. They normally have a human level of intelligence and all their monster instincts," Rochelle explained. "It's a death sentence for any party under silver rank. Stone, we're not even bronze!"

"Life sometimes leaves no options," I said. "Once the spiders move on, we will have to go out there. I won't leave them to their fate. I don't know if you've ever died by insect before, but it's rough."

"I deserve it," Rochelle said. "I knew about Gretch. This wouldn't have happened if I'd told Jackson."

"You knew?" Apparently, Gretchen wasn't half as sneaky as she thought she was.

"I saw her changing but didn't say anything," Rochelle said. Her hands twisted around the bow. "I figured Jackson had exotic tastes and thought nothing of it."

"Let's get everybody out of this, and we can sort it out as a party later. All of us," I said. I knew I had terrible bedside manner, but I was trying. "We're going to have to get all these secrets out if we're going to work together."

"What about you? What about your secrets?" Rochelle asked, looking at me.

"Not all of my secrets are mine to share, but since we're about ready to do this, it's best you understand what I can and can't do."

Rochelle nodded, waiting for me to go on.

"I have an ability called **Feast**," I said. "I can drink sol from magical objects and living things. The downside is I have difficulty pulling ambient sol from the air like you guys. This means I don't have a constant flow, but I can take it in a large amount at once if I latch onto something powerful."

Rochelle pulled away from me, her eyes wide in the low light. "Sol eater." It was an accusation, not a question.

I waved away her concerns. "Yes, yes, yes, I know that's what it's called, and no, I'm not going to eat you guys." I decided to leave out the part about everyone smelling delicious when they used magic. They didn't need to know that.

"So that's what was happening with Gretchen," Rochelle pieced together. "You ate her collar."

"Yeah, she was pressing me about why I wasn't collared, and I let it slip I could take them off," I said. "If anything, if I'd kept my mouth shut, we might have been able to slip out of this."

"No, you did the right thing," Rochelle said. "That ability is insanely powerful."

"Yeah, but it means I have to get close," I said. "Like, really close. The problem is that due to my race if I don't end a fight in the first thirty seconds, I'm done. Since you're an archer, you can cover me from the back, but we'll have to strike fast and hard, being extra careful about what fights we engage in."

Rochelle nodded her head. "It feels wrong, but I'm choosing to trust you. My mother used to tell me sol eaters would come for me when I was bad. They are usually assumed to be myth but there's always rumors of sol eater rings in the city, preying on those who wander alone."

Rochelle's explanation confirmed my suspicions that sol eaters were vampires. Now, I felt lame.

I checked on the party. It appeared they had been pulled the rest of the way to the fortress while we were having our chat.

On a whim, I checked on Cobbler and noted he was in the opposite direction, back up where the waterfall was. I sent a ping out along my connection to him, requesting help, but I got nothing in response.

"Typical," I said. "That damn bird is running in the opposite direction."

"Can you blame him?" Rochelle asked. "Besides, it takes even a mild-mannered mount a year to answer their owner's call."

I would have to count him out of the fight. It was probably for the best, anyway. I didn't know if he'd come back if he died.

"Yeah, we get what we get," I said, looking down at the ring on my finger.

"I'd put that away if I were you," Rochelle said, checking her gear. "If we're trying to be stealthy, we don't want a beacon on your hand."

"Right, right." I slipped the ring off into a pouch on my belt.

Rochelle moved the bark out of the way, and little bits of dawn light slipped into the stump. She wiggled out, keeping low. I followed suit.

I looked upstream at the falls. We were probably a mile downstream from the waterfall, about halfway to the fortress, judging by my glance earlier. The river looked like it ran directly to it, but I was only able to see bits of the fortress over the treetops and the remains of the wall bisecting the valley. My guess was this fortress used to be a barrier between the Twilight and the Fringe, but now, with its crumbled walls, it wasn't keeping anything out.

My head hit bark as Rochelle pulled me back into the stump. At first, I had no idea what the problem was. Everything looked clear, but the archer pointed into the trees, her sharp eyes catching something I missed.

The light of the dawn sun pierced through the tall trees above us, a single beam ruining the perfect camouflage of a spider perched overhead. It was dead still, waiting for something to walk along the river bank.

This wasn't going to work.

Rochelle shoved something into my hand—a reed from the side of the river. She must have snatched one up while I was busy sightseeing. She mimed, putting it in her mouth and looking up. I had no idea what on Terra she was on about until she blew the contents of the reed out, forming a tube.

I looked at the frigid river and then back up at the trees. The last thing I wanted to do was get back in the river, but we didn't have a choice. We were lucky to see this one spider. Just how many were we missing?

I blew into the reed, its guts spilling out as Rochelle filled the pockets of her tight-fitting leather with rocks. I caught on and equipped my armor. We didn't want to float or be swept away.

Rochelle held up her hand, solely counting down with her

fingers.

Three.

Two.

One.

We sprinted out of the stump. Rochelle dashed ahead with her long legs, but I stumbled, my boots making a sucking sound in the mud, tripping me up. I rolled into the water as five spiders stopped at the edge, rearing back and showing their mandibles. The weight of my armor took me under immediately as I scrambled to get oriented.

The water was somehow more frigid than before. Usually, the winter cold in the Fringe didn't bother me, but now that I was soaked, I was freezing. Hypothermia might kill us if the spiders didn't manage it first.

I waded into the water until I was standing, and the reed was the only thing breaking the surface.

A hand tapped my shoulder as the archer got my attention. Rochelle was a good foot taller than I was, forcing her to wade deeper.

I pointed forward, getting a thumbs-up from Rochelle, who was checking to see if I was okay.

Moving felt like running in space—slow, leaping steps down the river. The current was still flowing strong, putting constant pressure on my back. I'd been so focused on the trees above I'd failed to recognize this river was similar to the one near Avila, its bottom also covered in black and white pebbles. There must have been some rock formation around here resulting in the odd rock coloring. Familiar crocodilian fish swam in the water, eyeing us as they passed but leaving us be.

The cold soaked me to the bone as we continued. The aquatic animals were content to leave us alone, but I noticed we were gaining many followers as time passed. More and more crocodilian fish ganged up behind us like a school. Rochelle saw it too, urging me to go faster, her long legs pushing her out ahead of me.

The fish kept inching closer. Why this change in behavior? They left me alone in the river outside of Avila. I looked myself over, trying to figure out was different.

A streak of blood stretched from a tear in my pants. I'd cut myself when I tripped on the riverside.

One of the fish nipped at the back of my pants, grabbing onto it. Ae was already in my hand, piercing downwards. Ae bit, cutting a gash along its gill. Little tendrils of ice crystals floated in the water around the strike as the fish leaked ribbons of red blood.

The other fish swarmed it, sensing the blood in the water. Blood splashed out everywhere like a red dye, splattering against my clothes.

The fish descended on me, ripping at my clothes and bouncing off my arms.

I tucked the reed in my belt, needing both hands free to fight. One of the crocodilian fish lashed onto my leg, drawing more blood, which only added to the frenzy. I ripped it off, took a bite and drank its sol in a gulp.

On a gamble, I cast **Wyvern's Breath**, wondering if it would work underwater. I desperately needed another attack spell, but this spell was all I had for offence. The purple flames petered out immediately but left behind a stream of slime mixed in with the bloom of blood. Water fizzed as the acid ate at the fish it contacted. The fish went crazy as the spell drew out even more blood, distracting them from me, who was now leaping away, my lungs on fire.

An arrow gingerly floated by as I realized Rochelle had tried to assist me, only to discover bows did not work underwater. She grabbed onto my wrist, pulling me further away from the mass of blood that was happening behind us.

I grabbed a broad leaf from one of the native plants, wrapping it around the cut on my leg, stifling the blood. Rochelle saw what I was doing and touched me, pushing out her healing powers. My lungs screamed for air. I put the reed back into my mouth, poking the top over the surface and blowing out water as I was dragged.

I frantically gulped air through the reed, afraid I would have to surface. I tried to catch my breath through the small hole, my vision distorted. I was not getting enough air.

We hit something hard as I recovered, almost knocking the reed from my grasp. I breathed in a spray of water as my hands grabbed an iron grate, the river's flow pressing us into it.

A massive stone wall crossed the river, a single underwater

grate allowing water through. It seemed we had encountered a problem.

THIRTY-ONE: THE GUARDIAN

Even through the underwater grate, I could see the webs on the other side of the wall.

The water distorted my view, but it was clear the fortress would have been grand in its heyday, with towering battlements and imposing walls, but now it was a pile of rubble, cracks running through its once-formidable structures.

Web strung everywhere—houses, walls, stables, pillars. Webs decorated with little white bundles choked up any empty space, up high, low to the ground, it didn't matter.

What I didn't see, though, were spiders, and that made me more nervous than anything else. The whole place screamed, 'Hey, this is a trap. Good luck.'

My lungs were nearing their limit. The current was stronger here, pinning us in place as we gazed to the other side of the ten-foot-wide iron grate.

Rochelle tugged on my sleeve. We surfaced, our backs against the wall, our heads just poking over the top of the water. We were in some heavy shade of the trees that had encroached upon the wall, but Rochelle still pulled a lily-pad over to cover our heads so we could talk.

"They're definitely in there," Rochelle said. "They're dead ahead in that main building. The one with the spire."

"Yeah, I think so." Everything felt wrong about this, but what choice did we have? Time was ticking down.

"All right, you're the one with the bag of tricks. How are we getting in there?" Rochelle asked.

"I could try to melt the bars," I said. "I don't know how long that would take. There's barely any sol in the air around here, especially in the shade."

"If you had a source, could you do it? Something to drink?"

"I mean, yeah, probably. My **Wyvern's Breath** is corrosive, so we could try to knock some of those bars out and slip right in. The river would let us cut right through, underneath all those webs."

Whatever Rochelle was about to say stayed in place as we heard chittering sounds on the wall.

Ducking back into the water, we watched in horror as hundreds of spiders flooded over the wall next to the river and into the woods. It looked like a torrent of legs and gray.

"We could follow them," Rochelle whispered. "They're clearly after something."

Flames sprayed in the distance, lighting up the forest.

"Fuck no," I said, another bout of flames shooting in the distance. My eyes fell on the tree shading us. The tree was at least thirty paces across and tall enough that I could barely see the top, its green leaves glinting in the sun. Surely it had some sol to spare. "I might be able to pull sol from that." I pointed.

"You're going to kill a Guardian?" Rochelle looked scandalized.

"A what now? I thought it was just a big tree." I was surprised by her reaction.

"Yeah, it's a Guardian of the Forest," Rochelle said. "It's against the law to cut one down."

"Well, I won't tell anyone if you won't." I shrugged. "Besides, you want to go over there?"

More flames leaped up in the distance, further away this time.

Rochelle looked conflicted, clearly morally objecting to this plan. Maybe I was teetering too close to evil vampire for the archer's taste.

I crept out of the river, keeping my back to the stone-gray wall as I slipped towards the Guardian. Luckily, a large, exposed root was on shore, threading into the river.

I took Ae and cut a line into the thick root, getting down to the heart of the wood like butter.

The backlash was immediate, Ae making it clear she didn't like that. Startled, I wiped the sap stuck to her blade off on my pants, which just further upset her.

"Just go with it, please," I whispered to the angry knife. Her response was unpleasant, to say the least, with ice forming on her grip. I sighed. "I'll do that thing with the oil later."

I wasn't aware knives could blush.

I shaved the bark down with a now compliant Ae, sticking my face into the wedge I'd made.

The sol came out slowly. It was almost sticky. Usually, drinking sol was kind of like drinking water through a straw. This was like trying to drink a milkshake. It tasted like Earl Grey tea with a mix of something wild and twiggy in there.

But it was potent, my center filling up quickly. It was going smooth. Too smooth. I grew increasingly on edge as the seconds passed.

I was almost halfway to full when a deep thrum echoed through the forest, sending birds to the sky in a cloud of wings.

A loud groaning followed after the bellow as the Guardian towering over us began to sway. I threw myself into the water as the roots moved, sending out ripples in the river.

Rochelle grabbed me by the collar, throwing me into the water near the grate. All pretense of sneaking was gone as I splashed down, the tree shaking itself into a frenzy. A branch swung around and hit the nearby wall, crumbling a large section into rubble.

I spit **Wyvern's Breath** onto the metal grate. The acid

fizzed away at the iron bars, streams of bubbles climbing to the surface.

Rochelle tapped on me frantically, urging me to hurry. The Guardian's roots pushed further into the water, searching for whatever had injured it. I noticed some of its leaves had turned brown instead of a bright green.

I felt bad for stealing from the Guardian, but at the same time, I had no choice. If I could, I'd make it up to the angry tree, but now wasn't the time.

It appeared the tree wanted its sol back.

I grabbed a gulp of air and plunged underwater, spitting more **of Wyvern's Breath** in a big circle. I braced myself against the top of the grate as I stamped onto the center of the circle I had made with both feet. It didn't even budge.

Nearly all my sol was gone, and I knew we wouldn't make it in time. The roots continued to swarm forward faster than the acid could cut through the iron.

Out of nowhere, spiders swarmed the tree, spitting acid at it. This angered the tree further, sending it into a pure rage, thrashing and tossing spiders from its branches.

Bubbles formed around Rochelle's face as she screamed underwater, a root hitting her and sending her into a spin.

I reeled myself back, pulling back my legs and swinging them forward as hard as possible. I only had one shot at this, my sol running low. If I timed this wrong, my legs would crumple into the grate.

"**Steadfast,**" I said, bubbles simmering with the incantation. I dumped all of my remaining sol into my legs, which were moving through the water quickly.

I activated the spell at the last second, my stone legs colliding with the center of the grate. My legs hit with a thud that sent a shockwave through the water. My heart dropped, but then I felt the grate give, sucking me through. I reached back and grabbed my partner, who was fighting a root with a small knife. Unfortunately for Rochelle, the part of her I was able to grab was her long ponytail, dragging her along with me through the grate as the river whipped us into the fortress.

The current didn't let up, sweeping us under the tangle of webs and into a manmade channel. I tried to hold on to Rochelle but lost my grip as we bounced off debris in the water. More than once, I swallowed water, trying to get air.

With a final lurch, we hit something solid. Our backs hit hard. The current pressed us against a new grate, this one half above the waterline, another wall towering over us.

I unequipped my armor, pulling myself to the side like climbing a ladder. I pulled a semi-conscious Rochelle behind me, up and into the vegetation dominating this section of the fortress.

Vines ran up the sides of buildings through cracks and walls. Bushes, shrubs, and grasses sprouted out between cracks in the concrete and grey paving stones.

A massive cathedral loomed over everything. The remains of stained-glass windows pockmarked its side, leaving jagged bits of color sticking out. Even though they were broken, I could piece out by the remaining bits that the windows had held images of a sun. If I had to, I'd bet I was looking at a temple to Solara.

And that temple was precisely where the signatures were for the rest of the party.

I slunk back down in the bush, pulling out my ring and putting it on.

I hoped my worst fears weren't true and the ascended creature would be elsewhere. I slipped the ring on, and it glowed brightly, almost like a flashlight, pointing right at the cathedral.

Rochelle saw it, too, cursing under her breath.

I slipped the ring away.

"You good?" I asked the archer.

"My ankle," Rochelle said, **unequipping** a knee-high boot. Her ankle was blooming with purple spots. She sent a pulse of healing into her leg but still winced when she wiggled her foot.

"I say we poke through one of those windows and see what we're up against. I can't make any plan unless I know what it is," I said.

"It's a queen," Rochelle said. "That's the only way this makes sense. These many spiders don't work together unless they're under the control of something."

"All right," I said, looking over the injured Rochelle. "I'm gonna go and see what's going on in there, and you stay here and rest, alright?"

"No, I'm coming with you." Rochelle tried to hide the wince, but I saw it, pushing her back to a seated position.

"For the fight, yes, but I'm smaller and quieter than you, and I'm not currently fighting an injury," I said. "If I'm not back within fifteen minutes or so, use your knife to activate the Mercy, and we'll meet up later."

Rochelle's eyes went wide at the implication.

"Look, insects killed me before, and it's a better way." I tapped Ae on my belt.

Rochelle nodded, clutching the little knife she kept in her boot.

I gave her a nod before slipping out.

The stench of arachnids hung in the air as I slipped out of the underbrush and into a dilapidated building next to the wall. The area between the wall in the cathedral was only about fifty feet, but it was mostly open, the remains of a pleasant courtyard alongside the building.

I scanned the inside of my hiding spot. Two bodies slumped up against the wall. They were hobbs, still clutching their weapons. What were those things doing here?

I pushed those questions to the back of my mind. Looking back out to the area between the wall and the cathedral, I could still hear the tree fighting the spiders in the distance.

I decided to go for it, sprinting across the courtyard as fast and quietly as possible, keeping low and in the shadows.

The cathedral was even more intimidating up close, making me feel every inch of my stunted height. I almost felt woozy just looking at the spire reaching towards the sky, a golden tip shining in the sun's light.

I pressed myself against its bone-white walls, lining up underneath a broken window. I jumped, pulling myself up to look in.

THIRTY-TWO: REAPER

Sunlight filtered in from holes in the roof, dust flitting in the vertical beams.

A feminine statue dominated the back of the chamber, looming at least fifty feet high. Covered in moss and vines, a crown of stars nearly touched the arched ceiling. At her feet was a pool of water circling her like a moat, now stained green. Rows of pews stretched out in front of her, filling the rest of the chamber not occupied by the dried hunks of bodies that lay discarded over the floor. Most looked like hobbs, but a few humanoids were spread among them.

My eyes swept over the ruin, following my party bond up to the rafters. Strands of web hung from the beams with little bundles on the end. Hundreds of victims hung from the ceiling, but only three held our party members.

Whatever lived here had been highly successful at hunting.

I scanned the room, but nothing moved. Not a sound was made. I didn't like it, but I wasn't going to look a gift horse in the mouth.

The courtyard was still empty as I rendezvoused with Rochelle, slipping into the bush.

It was all too easy, my discomfort rising by the second. I wasn't this lucky. I'd never been this lucky. If there was one constant in my life, it was ill luck. At best, the universe treated me with indifference.

"They're hanging from the ceiling," I whispered, pointing to the cathedral. "There's no one in there. If you shoot them down, we can grab them and run."

Rochelle frowned. "This feels like some kind of trap. It's too quiet."

"Do we have a choice?" I countered. "Marie's only chance of making it out of this alive is if we risk it."

Rochelle looked unconvinced. "I feel like we're missing something."

"Definitely, but we're not going to be handed an opportunity on a platter," I said. "I say we go ahead and jump on it. Every second longer we take, there's more of a chance this goes sideways and something worse comes up."

I helped Rochelle to her feet. She put on a brave face, but I could tell she was struggling with her injury. I figured **Recover** couldn't heal bones and she had broken something.

I poked my head out. The coast was clear, and I hated it. The feeling I got in the mushroom forest resurfaced. I felt like I was being hunted.

We slunk back to the window, the spiders still fighting the Guardian in the distance. I made a mental note to leave Guardians alone from now on.

I boosted Rochelle up, and she slipped through the tall window. I climbed up after her, landing softly on the cathedral floor. My boots sent up two puffs of dust, revealing streaked marble underneath.

The scent of seafood hung in the air so strongly it was disorienting. I'd fallen into the habit of relying on my sense of smell to tell me when something was coming up on me, but now that it was everywhere, the sense was useless. It was like being in a room too bright to see.

It was dead silent in the room as Rochelle pulled out her bow and strung it up in a quick motion. In a flash, she fired off three arrows, using the bond to know the right bundles. I was already moving to go collect our friends.

On the way, I cursed my lack of hindsight. I wished I had destroyed the grate so we could jump into the river and make a quick getaway. It would've taken us out to the Twilight, but still.

I watched the arrows arc, cursing under my breath. We had no good options and every step represented tough choices.

Rochelle's arrows flew perfectly, slicing through the three strands and dropping the party. The bad part about this was that they were at least thirty feet up, and that fall was going to hurt.

I winced as three slaps echoed through the quiet cathedral,

sending up puffs of dust on impact.

I waved through the cloud, grabbing two of them and dragging them to the window, weaving between pews.

I considered pausing and looking around, but the jig was up. It was all speed now. We needed to grab them and escape as fast as possible. I piled the third one against the wall, pulling out Ae and using the deadly sharp knife to slit open the waxy web.

Gretchen looked at me with wide eyes, her mouth trying to move to tell me something. She looked alarmingly conscious but unable to control her body, her breaths coming in rhythmic gasps. She looked desperate, but I had to move on.

I freed the other two in quick succession. They also were weirdly conscious. Their eyes darted all around and looked at me with frantic energy.

It didn't matter. The plan was to toss them to the other side and make a break for it.

"Alright, Rochelle," I whispered, looking around.

Where was Rochelle? I ran back to the chapel floor, looking for the archer. I made eye contact with Gretchen. Her eyes kept glancing upward.

My head snapped up, and not even five feet from me was a face staring down at me, serrated teeth behind a sharp feminine grin.

"Greetings, morsel," a sickly-sweet voice said.

Eight legs hit the ground with not even a sound or speck of dust disturbed. She stood up to her full height of at least fifteen feet, every ounce the spider queen I assumed she was.

My ring practically vibrated in my belt pouch.

The queen looked me over as I did the same. Her lower half was that of a spider, and everything from the hips up was a human woman, not a thread of clothes on her milk-white skin. Her human parts were thin and fragile, looking like a sickly young woman or a starving model. In contrast, her spider body was bulky and lined with thick black chitin.

Ae sent me pulses of excitement. She was hungry. I got the sense from her that she wanted nothing more than for me to plunge her into the heart of this being. She was practically begging me in the back of my mind.

Charisma kicked into high gear. I gave a short bow to the queen. "Greetings to you as well. Might I know the name of your ladyship?"

"A silver-tongued halfkin. How delicious," the queen said, her predatory grin widening. "You may call me Valencia."

Valencia moved like a snake, with her human body leading. She slithered down to eye level with me, leaning so low that her breasts nearly touched the floor. Her head was at least twice the size of mine, and a heady scent of seafood and perfumed flowers slammed into my nose.

"Explain to me then, silver-tongued thief. Why are you stealing from the mouths of my children?" Valencia's mouth widened, showing teeth dripping with venom. The black of her eyes swelled to encompass the entirety of her eye sockets, creating two black voids looking at me.

"An accident," I said with a casualness I didn't feel. "I mistakenly chased my prey into your territory, and I'm simply retrieving what is mine."

"What is yours?" the queen said, cocking her head to the side, her long black hair pooling on the floor like a pile of silk.

"You see, I am a sol eater. I joined this party intending to consume them myself, yet they somehow bumbled right into your clutches. Maybe we can split them as recompense. If you give me the redhead and the catgirl, I'll leave you the rest."

The spider queen laughed. "Delicious. Dark. Bold. You sol eaters truly are a different breed." Valencia stood back to her full height, her face returning to something more human, moving soundlessly over to where I had stacked the party. She picked up Marie and Gretchen like they were nothing, tossing them to me. The girls tumbled and rolled to my feet like ragdolls.

The risk I'd taken was calculated. I knew that Rochelle and Jackson were definitely under level ten and would be covered. If I could get Marie out of here and double-check Gretchen's level, even though half the party would be wiped, it'd be no harm, no foul, and we'd live to fight another day.

"Go on," the spider queen said, gesturing to Marie at my

feet.

Marie's eyes looked at me wide and in horror. I realized they weren't in on my lie and that I was looking every inch of what they were afraid I was.

I needed to lean into it.

I picked Marie and Gretchen up by their hair, dragging them behind me. "Well then, I'll be taking my leave."

A rush of air. The queen was in front of me once again, leaning down towards the floor at eye level.

"The agreement was never that you could leave but that we could split them." Valencia tilted her head, smiling at me. "It has been a long time since I've eaten a sol eater, and I'd rather you be plump and near to bursting when I do so. So hurry up and eat your snacks so I may have mine."

I laughed, playing it off. Charisma told me I needed to keep the queen feeling in control, or she would stop playing and wipe us like smears on the floor. "Alas, so I have been outsmarted. Your cleverness was truly not overstated. I thank you for allowing me to enjoy these last meals. Although, you must forgive me for taking my time."

The spider queen looked pleased, backing away. To my horror, she all but disappeared. Every ounce of her changed color to blend in with the wall. If it weren't for the white of her eyes still shining out, I wouldn't have even been able to see her.

I looked down at Marie and Gretchen. I had no idea if this plan would work, but at this point, I was straight ad-libbing before I plunged a knife into my heart to try my chances back in that dumb dungeon.

I kneeled next to Marie, her body still limp, tears collecting on the sides of her wild eyes.

I was afraid even to speak my plan out loud. I had no idea how well the spider queen could hear, but I'd be willing to bet it was better than any of us.

I made eye contact with Marie, desperately trying to make her understand that I wasn't going to eat her. We made a long eye contact as I lifted her hand, biting into the meat of her thumb.

Marie squeezed her eyes shut, pushing the gathering tears out, but made no effort to pull away.

The sol immediately tried to dump down my throat, but I didn't activate **Feast**. Instead, I breathed sol out of the air, trying to push it in the opposite direction. I cast **Cleanse**, trying to force the spell into her body instead of mine.

Marie writhed, screaming, her limbs thrashing as the slow poison ripped through her body. Black oozed from up underneath her nose as her breaths came in ragged heaves before she collapsed into an unmoving heap.

Relief washed through me. Marie had played it up.

Polite clapping filled the cathedral.

"Sadistic," the queen called. "Truly sadistic." The queen rushed out of hiding, coming forward and looming behind me.

"I've never seen a spell like this." the queen said, laying a hand down on Marie's neck. "You infected her with corruption? Interesting."

I grabbed Gretchen's hand, knowing my time limit had just fallen to zero. Gretchen looked at me with interest as I bit her hand, a glimmer of hope still left.

The queen watched me with interest as the spell rolled through Gretchen. "Oh, you clever little morsel."

For the first time, I noticed the queen's hands ended in little sharp black points, the flesh becoming hard like the ends of her spider legs. She thrust her hand down towards Marie's chest, not breaking eye contact with me as **Cleanse** rolled through Gretchen.

An arrow exploded through the spider queen’s shoulder, sending a splatter of black blood onto the floor.

Many things happened at once. The queen's hand impacted Marie, but her fingers sparked along granite armor instead of finding soft flesh. Gretchen, who had been playing the victim's part, now had two daggers in her hands and was lunging forward, and I threw Ae at the spider queen as hard as possible.

Immense power flooded the cathedral, threatening to push me to my knees, the arrow in the queen’s shoulder melting like ice in the sun.

Valencia intercepted Gretchen, catching her knives with her bare hands, pushing the catgirl into a rotted pew, which collapsed on impact. The queen looked up into the rafters to see a still injured Rochelle posted up in the corner. Two more arrows were already airborne by the time anyone noticed her.

"Die," the queen commanded as she smacked the arrow out of the air with the back of her hand, drawing another spattering of blood.

I looked around for Ae, but she was nowhere to be found. Through the bond, I heard laughs and spotted her silver hilt sticking out of the back end of the spider's body. She was feasting as fast as she could, drawing in the queen's energy in the form of a stream of blood soaking into the gems of her cross guard.

I felt hope bloom. We just needed to keep the queen busy and wear her down.

A ten-foot scythe appeared in the spider queen's hands, slicing an arrow out of the air.

The plan had just gotten a lot harder.

"We need to get Jackson and run," Gretchen yelled, grabbing my arm.

"None of you are going anywhere," the queen said, still unaware she was being siphoned by a sentient knife. Ae pulsed in the back of my mind, begging for time.

"**Inspect**," I said, jumping out of the range of the massive scythe.

Valencia, Queen Twilight Moon Spider (Lvl 17, Ascended): Queen of the Gully Pass Twilight Moon

Spiders. This being is ascended, taking on a class and forming a core. Valencia has taken the **Reaper** class, specializing in high-speed and sweeping hits. Weak to fire.

The queen laughed, maniacally swinging her scythe in a playful slowness that pushed Gretchen to her limits. The nimble catgirl was barely able to jump over the strike as it shaved the hair off her long black tail.

I locked eyes with Jackson, who was desperately trying to get up but failing because of the poison in his system. Veins popped out in his forehead from the effort, his sword just out of reach.

I sprinted across the room towards the downed spellsword, only for my wisdom to go crazy. I threw myself on the ground, a whoosh of a scythe passing directly over me.

"Oh, no, no, no," Valencia said, kicking me with one of her spider legs back towards the other members of my party. "Remember our deal? That one is mine."

Marie yanked me to my feet, putting me beside her. She wore her stone golem armor, with Gretchen on the other side.

"Let's do this," Marie said, her voice cold and sure.

We surged forward. Light gleamed from airborne arrows as we confronted the queen head-on.

Arrows glanced off the queen, leaving bloody lines along pale skin. The queen laughed, sweeping out with her scythe.

“**Rend**,” the queen yelled, the word thrumming with power.

The weapon practically glowed, the air vibrating around the weapon distorting the air like hot asphalt in the summer.

I knew instantly this strike was going to be a problem, already throwing myself to the floor. All the playfulness of the queen's earlier attacks were gone. We were seeing the real thing.

Marie was the first in line and took the hit on her heavily armored shoulder, sending the blade upwards at an angle, a shower of sparks in its wake.

Hot pieces of rock burned my skin as the deflected strike went well above me, who had already been ducking downwards. My stomach twisted as the blade continued on, gathering speed as the strike continued.

It's hard to make the right call in a split second. A battle was often decided by a single mistake. Marie had tanked the hit, I ducked below it, but Gretchen had jumped, airborne with nothing to push off of.

The cat girl twisted in the air, using her tail to reorient herself sideways as the blade continued.

Valencia redirected the scythe, arcing it up at the last second, sending the blade towards the ceiling.

The scythe passed directly through the catgirl's stomach, splitting her in half above the hips.

THIRTY-THREE: LIGHT

Both halves of Gretchen spun in opposite directions, her blood spattering on me as I finished sliding across the floor.

At this moment, I found out it's one thing to die a horrible death yourself, but it's an entirely different experience to watch it happen to someone else.

I wasn't the only one discovering this. Jackson writhed from where he was sitting, foaming at the mouth as he struggled to move.

The queen almost looked as surprised as we were. "Oops," she said with a girlish giggle, flicking the blood from the monstrous scythe. "I suppose I owe you a felid."

Gretchen was dead before both halves hit the floor, her eyes already glazed over. She either bled out instantly or had her center sheared in half. I slapped Marie's leg. She was frozen, staring at the two halves of Gretchen lying on the ground.

The queen was already coming around for another attack, twirling the scythe above her head in an unnecessary flourish.

The queen spun with unnatural grace, slicing an arrow out of the air with her weapon. Another arrow bounced off the queen's hard chitin.

"That's enough," Valencia said. "**Web Snare**." The word thrummed as the queen extended a hand, a ball of white web shooting from it, spreading in the air like a net.

The injured archer couldn't move in time, getting tied up and knocked clean from the rafters. The fighting paused as we watched her writhe like a cat in a bag as she fell fifty feet to the floor, landing with a sickening crunch on a stone altar and sliding limply to the floor.

"Now, where were we?" the spider queen said, sweeping her scythe wide as she returned attention to us.

Marie roared, charging at the spider. The queen struck downward, but Marie intercepted it with her golem armor, crossing her arms above her head. The cathedral's marble floor cracked from the impact of the strike, dust flying up in a shockwave. Marie buckled but held.

It was good enough for me.

I used the opportunity to dive at the queen's legs. A scrambling kick knocked into me, sending me into a spin, but my heavy chainmail kept my momentum forward. My hand barely caught one of the spider's back legs.

I locked my arm around the limb on impact, biting as hard as possible. The sol rushed into my center, but I was already casting another spell. I dropped into **Steadfast**, using the queen's sol to power the thirsty spell, hoping that between me and Ae, the spider queen would flag.

I gagged as the darkness snapped into place, blocking me out of the fight. The sol tasted horrific, like gunpowder in scrambled eggs. Sour with a spicy undertone of gravel.

The taste. I recognized it. It was exactly like that damn corrupted centipede. Remembering the pain of removing the corruption from my channels, I released myself from **Steadfast** to find the landscape around me had drastically changed. I hadn't been under the spell for more than a few seconds.

We were outside in the courtyard. Broken glass and pieces of stone lay all around as I fell off the spider queen's leg.

The queen looked haggard. Somehow more pale than before and breathing heavily. I followed her gaze back to the cathedral, and the pieces fell into place.

In a new hole in the wall stood Jackson. He looked like he was about to drop, smoke rising from the tips of his outstretched hand. An unarmored Marie lay unmoving at his side, but the party bond told me she still lived, if barely. He needed help, and I was going to deliver.

I unleashed **Wyvern's Breath**, dumping the corrupted sol and coating the queen in acidic flames. The spray was magnificent, stretching nearly forty feet and spraying like a firehose. My lips singed as the acidity splashed. Black tinges of corruption mingled with the purple flames, the nasty substance sticking in my channels.

The queen barely spared me a glance, wiping the flames off

with a bare hand. The acid dripped down her white skin and onto the ground, leaving her completely unscathed.

"**Smite**," Jackson yelled, his voice hoarse. He looked like he was at his limit, in danger of falling at any moment.

White lightning arced from his fingertips, converging into a wild beam. The queen lifted her scythe, intercepting the arc of electricity as it crackled along her white skin, little wisps of smoke rising from it as she screamed.

Despite the successful attack, I knew we were going to fail. Jackson had fallen to one knee, completely exhausting himself of what energy he had. Marie was down. Gretchen and Rochelle were dead. Ae had failed to weaken the spider, and my only offensive attack was ineffective. On top of it all, Cobbler had abandoned us. I cursed the turkey through our bond, calling him a coward.

The spider queen shook off the blow, moving with unnerving grace to the downed spellsword. She was haggard, just as tired as the rest of us, but still too strong for our low levels. We just couldn't bridge the gap. I urged Ae to drain the queen faster and got an oddly coherent snap back from the knife that she was doing her best, and it wasn't her fault we sucked.

Valencia smacked the rune-covered sword out of Jackson's shaking hands as I ran to do… something.

Valencia towered over a downed Jackson. "You will regret that," the queen said, her voice dripping with honey. The queen raised her scythe high for a strike, not on him but the unconscious Marie next to him.

I wasn't going to make it. I surged forward, cursing my small legs. If only—

Something red bolted out of the sky, impacting the queen's face with an audible crack. The momentum twisted the monster's human half, pinning it to the ground as spider legs went skyward. The grey cobblestone of the courtyard cracked as red flames splashed out in a ball of light. I was absolutely baffled, shielding my face from the heat. Who cast this? My confusion only amplified as a cloud of arrows entered the flames from the wall behind me.

Hobbs appeared along the walls, continuously firing arrows at the downed queen as the flames died. The queen breached the flames, an arrow sticking out of her charred skin as she threw herself into the waterway.

As the flames receded, a lone warblecock fanned the dying fire with his wings.

"Inspect," I said in complete bafflement.

Warblecock (Lvl 12): A moderate-sized variation of the avian family, a warblecock is known for their relative ease of raising for meat and their bad attitudes, often given to unruly children as mounts to train them to appreciate more docile animals.

"Cobbler, you fucking bastard," I yelled, a hint of a grin spreading across my face. "Have you been out grinding while we did all the hard work?"

The velociraptor-sized bird shot me the cockiest look I'd ever seen as hobbs cheered from the walls. In Cobbler's uplifted talon was an oversized eye, its stem hanging to the ground.

I looked back at the water, still feeling tension in the air. There was no way the queen was dead. I'd seen her take Jackson's thunderbolt to the face and shake it off.

Cheering died as water exploded from the channel. Valencia crawled back onto the bank, covered in red burns pockmarked with seeping blisters and bits of black char. She threw her head back and let out a piercing wail that echoed along the valley, blood running from her empty eye socket.

Spiders flooded the walls, ignoring the hobbs and running to their queen, covering her like a blanket. She mewled like a cat, wailing and cradling her burnt skin. The spiders turned to dust at her feet, the burns on her skin fading with each death as a thousand of her children ran to her aid.

Ae sent me a message over the bond. We needed to strike now before the queen absorbed all the spiders. Only she needed to survive to restart the colony.

I ran forward just as the hobbs sounded the call to retreat. "Get Marie and run," I shouted at Cobbler.

The warblecock needed no prodding, taking off towards the downed terra mage.

With a shrill whistle, the hobbs sounded the retreat, taking this development as their cue to leave. In their defense, fair enough. I didn’t want to be here either.

The leader wore a bag that looked suspiciously like the saddle bags I'd bought for Cobbler, which I’d just registered he wasn't wearing. Did that shithead buy the loyalty of a tribe of ferrets with *my* saddle bag?

I laughed at the thought, getting back to business. I sent a silent prayer to the goddess. I would get them out of here. My death would mean something.

The queen ignored me as I ran, Ae becoming more frantic that time was running out. I didn't need to win. I just needed to buy some time. I could tell through the bond that Cobbler was over the wall and tearing through the woods like a bat out of hell.

Valencia had her scythe pointed skyward, visibly pulling sol out of the air, a cloud of darkness blooming around her in a twisting display of magic. This being was evil and needed to die. Not just for the party but for everyone in the valley.

A message flashed in the corner of my vision. I barely saw it.

Solara's Hand Activated!

The queen's eyes snapped to me as I stepped off one of her children, leaping to her. I felt a familiar presence in my mind. It was weak, but I felt all its focus on me.

I had already spent everything else. I looked to the air to meet the swinging blade coming down towards me with nothing but my bare hands. I repeated my payer, hoping it would be enough. I willed what I wanted, seeing the process in my mind.

A voice answered.

'Thus, the Goddess Solara crushed the fabric of the nothing, and the Sun burst forth, making ***light****.'*

The world turned white and for split second as I saw the spider queen unmade.

You Died!

Solara's Mercy Activated!

Sent to respawn point...

THIRTY-FOUR: THE BIG QUESTION

I woke in a familiar pool, the pressure on my neck so intense I was barely even able to gasp.

Water splashed as I sat up, grasping my neck. I corkscrewed down on my center, pushing down the feeling. My breathing barely made it past the swell of my center as I twisted and compressed ad nauseam. I hated it had come to this, but I knew I had no choice. I focused on speed. I needed every ounce I could get.

The feeling popped into place, a wave of relief washing over me as the level-up locked in.

Quest cleared: Trouble in the Pass! (Identify)

Reward: 150 Bronze Coins (30ea)

Ascended Being Slain!

Congratulations, Chainbreaker has ascended!

Quest cleared: Trouble in the Pass! (Eliminate)

Reward: 500 Silver Coins (100ea)

Congratulations! Ascended to Level 10. +1 Cha, +1 Dex

Warning: Solara's Mercy deactivated. Death is now permanent.

Money clattered around me as my mood soured. I knew level ten would come eventually, but I hated it was happening now, back in the stupid dungeon. A red light flared as the koi investigated the coins settling to the bottom of the pool.

I reread the division of the loot. It implied that there were five members to give loot to. I checked my party link, hoping to confirm my suspicions.

I felt four distinct links. Where I couldn't tell, but they were out there. The dungeon was probably interfering, but they felt distant, like a thin thread to a distant star. I even felt Cobbler, the cunning bastard. He was probably twice my level now and the leader of a ragtag group of rebels or something ridiculous.

Good for him.

The weapon evolution notification got my attention. Ae was strangely quiet.

"Oh shit, she's in storage! **Equip all**," I said, equipping all my belongings as I jumped from the money pool.

I landed with barely a sound, attempting to grab Ae out of her sheath, but my hand grabbed air.

I looked at my empty hand. The sheath was there all right, but no blade.

Something tackled me just as I pulled up our bond, knocking me onto the floor.

Arms wrapped around my head as my face was smothered.

"Ae," I said, pushing her away so I could breathe. "How?"

"Inspect me," Ae said smugly, tucking silver strands behind both pointed ears. Gone was her golden armor, and in its place was a knitted sweater top and white leather pants. Her black knee-high boots boosted her already intimidating height.

"Inspect."

Chainbreaker (Lvl 14, Soulbound, Ascended Weapon): This evolving weapon is bound to the soul of Ae'silin DeArdent, the Chainbreaker. This weapon has bound the element of **Ice** and is an evolving weapon. Kill beings with sol to upgrade.

"I took a little shortcut," Ae said, bopping me on the nose with her pointer finger. "I can only do this for a few minutes a day, and didn't want to waste it."

"This is amazing news!" I picked the elf up by the waist, spinning her around. She had to lift her feet so they wouldn't drag on the ground, but I pretended not to notice. "You can finally guide me in this weird world of yours. I've been a walking disaster, stumbling from one fuckup to the next."

Ae gave me a weird look. "I will do my best," she said, nodding uncertainly.

I kept my face neutral. Ae was usually a bastion of confidence, possessing a hard edge about her. The Ae before me seemed… soft. Something was off, but I smooshed those concerns down, enjoying the moment for what it was.

"I can't wait for you to meet the others," I said.

Ae sneered. "I don't like the hissgirl. She gets too close."

I could feel an intense protectiveness through the bond. Why would she be this possessive?

Ae stared at me with intensity, and a single question rose above all the others. Something that had been bothering me since the day I stepped out of the dungeon.

"Ae, there's something I have to know." I stared into her silver eyes. I'd been afraid of this moment and wanted to clear the air.

Ae reacted immediately to my change in tone, becoming serious and putting a hand to her chest. "My wielder, what is it?"

Her face was inches from mine, flooding me with a scent of mint and steel. She blushed as my gaze intensified, a bloom of red filling pale cheeks and extending to her pointed ears.

"We're just friends, right?"

Ae smacked me.

EPILOGUE: REBORN

Grond frowned as he looked over the map in front of him.

The orc leaned over a wide table, his bulging muscles wreathed in gold bands. The only clothing on his red skin was an ornate fur loin cloth and a fearsome axe across his back. Surrounded by a grand tent, orc women slept in a pile of furs, their scant armor still piled where Grond had thrown it the previous night.

Grond looked every inch a successful warrior.

But he was not a warrior. Not anymore at least. The Grand Vizier hadn't fought physical battles in a long time, finding his place behind a desk more potent than his axe had ever been.

Grond's thoughts were interrupted, an orc in golden battledress entering the tent, bowing to the vizier.

"You called?" the orc asked. In the privacy of the tent, some formalities could be waved.

"Yes, Visna." Grond welcomed the newcomer. "Any word

from Solendia concerning the Fringe expedition?"

"None, sir," Visna replied with a fist across his chest.

"Send another messenger," Grond said. "Use my personal funds, bribe whoever needs bribing."

"Was the vision so dire?" Visna asked.

"It is, Visna. It is critical if we want to survive what's coming," Grond replied. "The old gods are waking. This is known."

"This is known," Visna repeated. "It will be done. I trust your judgment. We all trust your judgment." He bowed before leaving.

Grond looked back over the map. There was so much distance between where they were and where he needed to go.

Grond pulled up his blessing, as he did whenever he doubted himself.

Ephret's Hand: The mortal representative of Ephret, God of battle and childbirth. Hands become closer to their patron god by upholding their tenets. The Pact restricts gods from directly interacting with the world and their Hands carry out their will.

"It has to be true. The rest were." Grond stroked his black beard. Visions from Ephret were fickle, requiring copious of amounts of blood and… indulgence.

Grond's eyes flocked to the pile of sleeping orc women. He

had hoped for a new vision but the God was silent last night.

Grond looked at the circled spot on the map, a small town out in the middle of the fringe called Avila. According to his last vision, he needed to get there as fast as possible.

Solara had finally regained enough power to summon a Hand. Glimpses of a previous life flashed in the orc's mind as the halfkin introduced himself as Stone. He didn't know why, but his gut told him this was someone he once knew.

None of this was what worried Grond. It was who the Hand was talking to.

One of the most notorious killers of the last age—Ae, The Dawn Serpent.

The story continues in Sol Anchor Book Two

LETTER FROM THE AUTHOR

THANKS FOR READING MY BOOK!

"Sol Anchor" was a long time in the making. I took my first creative writing class in college back in ye olden days of 2014 while I was still in the military. Many terrible books have been written and summarily thrown in the trash since.

Yet, here we are. You made it to the end, and I think that's super neat. Go leave a review on Amazon.com or send me a strongly worded email about my proclivity for cursing and innuendo to benjamin.darr.author@gmail.com. Frankly, I blame the military for that.

I'd like to thank my beta readers for all the new and inventive ways you humbled me, my parents for homeschooling me in the middle of nowhere so I had nothing to do but read, and my wife for putting up with me asking her to read something I wrote at all hours of the day.

See y'all next time!

- Benjamin Darr

Ending Stats

Name: Stone McGracen

Race: Halfkin

Path: Hunger

Level: 10

Unlocked Meridians: Throat, Gate, Heart

Spells: Inspect, Feast, Wyvern's Breath, Cleanse, Steadfast

Blessings: Solara's Hand

Stats:

Int: 7

Wis: 6

Cha: 19 (+2)

Str: 9

Dex: 8 (+1)

Con: 3 (+0.6)

Spirit: 22.4

Soulbound Equipment:

Clothes: Linen Tunic, Linen Pants, Leather Boots, Leather Gloves

Armor: Chainmail tunic, Steel Bracers, Steel Shin Guards

Weapons: Chainbreaker

Misc: Adventurer's Belt, Guild Amulet, 100 Silver, 30 Bronze

Made in United States
Orlando, FL
10 December 2024